Praise for *The Last Enchantments*

"Irresistible ... The novel bursts with intelligence and wit as Charles Finch brilliantly examines our most secret longings and desires. In the tradition of *Brideshead Revisited* and *The Line of Beauty, The Last Enchantments* casts an enduring spell."

—Amber Dermont, author of *The Starboard Sea*

"*The Last Enchantments* is a witty, wonderful book about that tender age between college and true adulthood. Charles Finch's sensitive, lyrical, and heartfelt writing charms to the very last page."

—Cristina Alger, author of *The Darlings*

"In prose that glides effortlessly from scene to scene, Finch captures the fleeting time in people's lives when their every decision, from career to lover, seems freighted with eternal consequence. . . . A vividly evocative love letter to his alma mater . . . Highly recommended."

—*Library Journal* (starred review)

"The strength of Finch's novel is its vivid portrayal of Oxford University in all its history, along with the school's ancient and quirky traditions, and colorful student body and faculty."

—*Publishers Weekly*

"Finch captures the American perspective on aristocratic Oxford ... As in Evelyn Waugh's *Brideshead Revisited* (1945), Oxford sets a regal and stunning backdrop to *The Last Enchantments,* giving it a timeless and rich ambience that is, well, enchanting."

—*Booklist*

"Will grapples with the consequences of his upbringing and begins, painfully, to arrive at the truth about himself . . . Will's story is about the space that perpetually separates the interim pleasures of college and the vagaries of adult life—and it is within that space that he must ultimately find some semblance of peace."

—*Shelf Awareness*

"Intense, fast-paced, psychologically intriguing, and wonderfully written."

—Susan Richards Shreve, author of *You Are the Love of My Life*

"Charles Finch has perfectly captured the heady pleasure of young people falling in—with each other and with the kind of big ideas that can swallow a person whole. . . . The novel's enchantment lies in the atmosphere he evokes, and a reader will close the book almost feeling he himself has been to Oxford for a year to study, drink, dream, and find himself."

—Lydia Netzer, author of *Shine Shine Shine*,
a *New York Times* Notable Book

"Brings to mind *Brideshead Revisited* or *The Great Gatsby* . . . likely to resonate with teens, especially intellectual, emotional ones, coming into their own sense of an ending as they go on to their next life stages."

—*School Library Journal* (starred review)

The LAST ENCHANTMENTS

CHARLES FINCH

 ST. MARTIN'S GRIFFIN ❧ NEW YORK

THE LAST ENCHANTMENTS. Copyright © 2014 by Charles Finch. All rights reserved. Printed in the United States of America. For information, address St. Martin's Press, 175 Fifth Avenue, New York, N.Y. 10010.

Excerpts from "The Trees" and "Maiden Name" from *The Complete Poems of Philip Larkin* by Philip Larkin, edited by Archie Burnett. Copyright © 2012 by The Estate of Philip Larkin. Reprinted by permission of Farrar, Straus and Giroux, LLC.

Excerpts from "The Trees" and "Maiden Name" from *The Complete Poems* by Philip Larkin. Reprinted by permission of Faber and Faber, Ltd.

www.stmartins.com

Designed by Steven Seighman

The Library of Congress has cataloged the hardcover edition as follows:

Finch, Charles (Charles B.)
    The last enchantments / Charles Finch.—First U.S. Edition.
      p. cm.
    ISBN 978-1-250-01871-7 (hardcover)
    ISBN 978-1-250-01870-0 (e-book)
    I. Title.
    PS3606.I526L37 2014
    813'.6—dc23

2013031731

ISBN 978-1-250-06325-0 (trade paperback)

St. Martin's Griffin books may be purchased for educational, business, or promotional use. For information on bulk purchases, please contact the Macmillan Corporate and Premium Sales Department at 1-800-221-7945, extension 5442, or write to specialmarkets@macmillan.com.

First St. Martin's Griffin Edition: March 2015

10 9 8 7 6 5 4 3 2 1

For these very dear

FRIENDS

Katie Beck

Emily Braid

Becca Chodroff

Chris Compton

Dan Compton

Alice Cresswell

Rob Crowe

Megan Edwards

Megan Ingraham

Kelly Jones

Andrew Joseph

Tom Jenkins

James Kelly

Jenny Kishan

Kristin Knox

Will Lawrence

Julia Mason

Hannah Mays

Holly Morse

Sean O'Reilly

Emily Popp

Laurence Publicover

Natalie Sanderson

Julia Shanks

Sarah Tate

Sophie Tiezel

Nuala Trainor

Laurel Wheeler

Jameson Workman

I wanted to incorporate everything, understand
everything, because time is cruel and nothing
stays the same.

—Norman Rush

CHAPTER ONE

When I was a self-serious child of ten or eleven I believed that novels were largely about the weather. In a fit of ambition I would start *The Rainbow* or *Lord Jim*, books I carried around school in the hopes that someone might ask me what I was reading, and which perhaps I thought would inaugurate my career as, what, a grown-up? A thinker? I'm not sure. Every one of them opened with the same thwarting descent of description: It was an unusually hot March evening in upper Cornwall; the rain in Burma had been going for days; the clouds lowered over the moor. The first eighty pages of *A Passage to India* are a description of some caves. I'm pulling that number from memory, so it may be inexact, if anything too low, but the point stands.

I suspected that in the end humans would walk into this weather—I remember feeling a spark of excitement when a "cart" threatened to provide me with some in *Return of the Native*—but I attached no special primacy to them. I rarely made it further than six or seven paragraphs into any of those books, which left my illusions about their nature intact. Finally when I was twelve some intelligent adult—likely my mother—got it over with and gave me *The Catcher in the Rye,* and I found the same banal and vibrant sanities everyone does in that book.

Really, those novels were right, however: There are times in life when the weather and the landscape seem suddenly as if they're for you alone, and for a moment there's a novelistic pressure, an interiority, to gazing out through a window at the snow, or the sun.

I'm thinking of the late August afternoon when I was supposed to leave New York for England. It was uncommonly cold for the month, and there was a heavy rain, the kind of day that reminds you, oh, of course, the other seasons are coming soon.

"Are you hungry?" Alison asked.

I shook my head. "Not especially."

"Come on, we're forgetting something. You had pizza last night, we got soup from Veselka. What else are you going to miss?"

"Well, you." My tone had it both ways, mocking this kind of straightforward tenderness and taking credit for it, too.

She rolled her eyes. "My hero."

We were in the living room of our apartment on Horatio Street. Its estranging collocation of familiar objects—its picture frames, its hanging garden of pots, its chromatically organized bookshelves— seemed so much like a vision of life to me, now that I was leaving.

"I should go soon anyway. I have to check all these bags."

"Okay." She stood up, her long brown hair falling down her shoulders. There was a tangle of silver necklaces spilling in and out of the top of her shirt, and her sweet, intelligent face—prone to worry—was drawn inward with concentration. "Last check, then. You have the bag of medicines I packed for you."

"Yes."

"And you have a sweater handy in case it's cold when you get in."

I pointed toward the largest suitcase. "Yep."

"And do you have a book?"

"*The Captive Mind,* it's sitting right in the outer pocket of the blue bag. With my headphones. And the sweater."

"And that bag of pretzels I got you for a snack?"

"And that bag of pretzels you got me for a snack."

"And your passport."

I felt my eyes widen. "Oh, no."

She smiled to acknowledge the joke, and then when my face didn't change her expression grew uncertain. "Wait, are you kidding?"

I stood up, my ears hot, my face tingling. "I didn't even think about it."

"Where did you leave it after you got your visa?"

"Seriously, I don't know."

We spent the next fifteen minutes rifling through our uncluttered apartment like thieves. I inspected every pile of paper I could find, old bills, Christmas cards, making no effort to reassemble them before I moved on. How long did it take to get a passport? Or could Alison's dad get me a temporary one, good for a week or two until she could find mine and overnight it to England?

I was in the bedroom, sifting through our drawers of clothes, mine empty now, when I heard her call out. "I found it."

"Oh God, thank fuck." I ran to the living room, where she held the passport up in triumph. "Is that definitely it?"

"Yeah, it was next to mine. From Montreal in July."

I took it and flipped to my picture to make sure. "Jesus. Thank you."

I looked around. "The apartment is a disaster. I should clean."

She looked at her watch. "No, no, you don't have time. I'll tidy it up when you're gone."

"Thanks, babe." I put the passport in my pocket, a stiff, awkward panel of hide. "Should we go downstairs?"

"Just come lie with me for a minute first, would you?"

"In bed?"

"Yeah."

We went into the bedroom. She kicked off her shoes and slipped herself into the sheets, and as I followed her in she pulled me close, her encircling arms a loose, too loose, fortification, the walls of a city anybody could get into or out of. "A whole year," she murmured after a minute.

"It's not even that long."

I loved her more than I had in months, months. Our breath began to even out, the silence of the battering rain. I looked at the bedroom, gray in the unlit afternoon, at the cheerful battalion of photographs of us along her dresser, and next to them at her perfume bottles, clustered in their leather tray. The quiet disloyalty of objects. How serious it is to be young!

It seemed impossible that the next morning I wouldn't blunder sleepily out of that bed, that it would be elsewhere, in different time.

Alison and I had first lain together this way four years before, during college. We had been on a few dates already, but there was still a formal element to our conversations, even our kisses. One Saturday my friends Geoff, Ben, and I spent a few hours throwing a football to each other on Old Campus. We stopped as it began to get dark, and even though I was hot and dusty I decided to drop by her room; I hadn't been there yet. She lived in Connecticut Hall, a building made of that salmon-white brick common to all of the remaining colonial houses in New England, on the third floor.

She answered the door in a hoodie and navy shorts, with YALE written in white along the hem on her left thigh. "Hey," she said and looked past me up and down the hallway, as if I might be part of a group. "Is everything okay?"

"Yeah, yeah, I just wanted to say hi."

She looked puzzled for another instant, but then her face opened with comprehension. "Oh, good, sure. Come in. I was watching TV."

We sat on her bed to watch together. I fell asleep right away. I remember briefly waking, feeling cold and shifting my weight into her body. Her hand was stroking my head, and her neck, where my face was buried, was warm and fragrant and sleepy, like a hayfield at the end of summer.

Now, essentially for the first time since then, our two bodies would be apart, we would be apart. She looked at me. "Are you sure I can't come to the airport?" she said.

"No, no, go to the fund-raiser."

"Okay." She looked at her watch. "You should leave, you'll never be able to get a cab in this weather."

In fact I got a cab immediately, my day's travel misfortune already allotted to the passport scare, and we loaded my bags into the trunk and the backseat.

"Look out for some treats," she said. "They might be squashed, I guess."

I smiled. Whenever I went on trips alone I would find things that she had tucked into my luggage, magazines, Snickers bars. "Thanks."

She gave me a kiss. "I'll see you soon."

"In a month. It's practically tomorrow."

"Ha."

I got into the cab. She was standing with her arms folded, watching me, from the dry of the awning. I got out and gave her a last kiss on the cheek, and she smiled and squeezed my hand. Then I left.

Right then I wanted what we all want: both things; to leave and to stay at the same time. I looked through the window at the wet-blurred taillights of the cabs around me, their brightness an increasing proportion of everything visible out in the world. I remembered that day in college, how after we woke up Alison and I had spent half an hour making a poster to welcome Bill Clinton to a meeting. We both belonged to the lower reaches of the upper reaches of the byzantine bureaucracy that ran the Yale Democrats. That was how we'd met.

"What should I put?" she asked, sitting cross-legged, marker in hand, hair back in a ponytail.

"I would avoid mentioning blow jobs."

"What about kneepads? Or impeachment? Or Ken Starr? Or Whitewater?"

"Maybe impeachment if you have a good joke."

"No, come on, what should I put?"

"Hm. Maybe something about Bulldogs? Go Bulldogs? Bulldogs for Bill?"

"I think I'm going to draw some bunting and write just 'Welcome Home,' in big letters," she said. "I think he'll appreciate that."

"It'll definitely come in handy the next time you go to a rally in Arkansas."

"He went to school here. That's like a home."

As the cab moved north toward the Midtown Tunnel, I opened the outer pocket of my suitcase to fetch my book and came across a bag of Twizzlers, which had been on Alison's list of the foods they didn't have in England. I opened it and ate one and thought of that phrase, *That's like a home.* I had reached the age by then, twenty-five, when I had finally stopped believing, in some illogical and hopeful chamber of my heart, that one day we might all gather up our things, reassemble, my friends and I, Alison, and go back to school again together. Yet here I was, returning in a way. Without them, fine; but without her, that seemed unkind.

———

My first exchange with an English person was at Immigration.

"Coming from?"

"New York."

"Didn't bring anything dangerous or alive, did you now?"

I laughed. "I don't think so."

He gave me a sharp look. "What's that?"

"I didn't."

He looked down at my immigration card. "Says here you're going up to uni, then? English literature?"

He said these last two words as if they were individually irreproachable but hilariously stupid side by side. "Yes, sir."

He stamped my passport. "Well, you're not so clever yet."

Not much later I was on the train to Oxford. It was a bright day, and from the window I gazed at the distant concavities of the landscape, the green swales that dipped away from the tracks and then rose in steep hills to meet the afternoon light. Intermittently I dozed, with the heavy wakefulness of the overnight traveler. Finally in the last half hour of the trip I got some real rest, and woke only when an old woman pushing a cart came through the train. I bought a cup of coffee from her.

When we arrived I took a cab to my new college, Fleet; at Oxford every student belongs both to the university and to one of its forty constituent colleges, each its own dominion upon a few acres, with its own library, its own bar, its own chapel. From the cobblestone lane outside the college I looked up and saw its high white spires, and through the tall, black-iron gates a stretch of green grass. I would wait to look around, I thought.

Instead I fetched my room key from the porters, a group of men in bowler hats and gray wool suits. The porters' lodge lay just inside the gates. ("Cheek," said one of them lazily when he had to leave his tea to help me.) From there I turned right down a lane just near the gates and found myself at the Cottages, a row of twelve brick houses, haphazardly rife with ivy, where Fleet's graduate students lived. It was also the corridor that connected the college to the center of the city.

My house was the third to last, with a flagstone courtyard before it and a long, slender garden full of fading trees behind. At the door I staggered to a standstill under my bags, panting slightly, then with a last great crash went inside and let everything drop off my shoulders in the entryway. Above me, halfway up the stairs, was another student.

"You look as if you've been on a death march," he said.

"I overpacked."

He smiled, and we met on the second step to shake hands. "I'm Tom Raleigh. If you're William Baker you're room four, next to me. Anyway I don't imagine you're Anil Gupta, in room two, or Margo Peabody, room one. Let me take some of those bags."

Tom was English, tall, thin, and pale, with freckles and bright red lips. Looking at him for the first time I saw a trace of privately educated cruelty in his heavy-eyed expression, of wishes met, small worlds conquered. He picked up three of my bags, and I hauled the rest up the stairs behind him. On the second floor were two doors, and through his I could see half-unpacked boxes and a squat refrigerator. "My sister dropped me off this morning," he said. We stopped in front of the heavy oak door just next to his, which was mine. My name was printed on it in gold leaf.

He put down my things. "Get settled, then knock on my door for a beer if you like. My sister also filled my fridge before she left."

"Thanks, I will."

He hesitated and then grinned. "Americans everywhere," he said. "That's Oxford now, I suppose."

I closed the door behind me and called my mother. "Hey, it's me. I made it."

"Oh, my God!"

"I'm in my room, just got here."

"I can't believe you live in another country! What is it like? What can you see?"

"It's not bad." I looked around. "There's a fireplace, but it has a radiator in it. I have a couple of windows, so I can see the yard. Wait, if I lean out—I'm leaning out, and I can see the back lawns of Fleet. Just like that picture I showed you online, only they look bigger."

"I can't believe you're there! Is it beautiful?"

"I haven't seen much."

"Can you get the *Times*?"

"Mom."

"What?"

"It's England, not North Korea."

"Do you want me to send it to you?"

"Please don't be ridiculous."

"I can't believe you're in England! What did Alison say?"

"I'm about to call her."

After we hung up I lumped down into one of the armchairs by the window—I couldn't face unpacking—and looked out.

I had a strange, displaced feeling, heightened by fatigue. It was a mystery to me how I had come to be here. Not practically—after my last job ended I had sent in an application, a late one, but I was so settled in New York that it had never seemed likely to come to anything. A number of events in the year that preceded my arrival in Oxford had pushed me toward a change, but I might as easily have gone to Shanghai or Bermuda.

It was true that I had never felt more at home anywhere than college, and that I missed it. Oxford, specifically, was linked in my mind with a peculiar blended sense of peace and grandeur. I had a weakness for that. This was my first time in England, but it was

a country, dangerously, that I had loved for much of my life, especially during the unhappy and turbulent days of my childhood, when
I devised a kind of imaginative home there without ever having
been, based on the books to which I exiled myself: Sherlock
Holmes, Kenneth Grahame, C. S. Lewis. Why had they once made
me so happy, I wondered? The calm, the civility, the safety, I
suppose—lengthening shadows on the cricket pitch, tea at five—
all of it foolish. There's no lasting safety to life. The only thing that
will become of anyone is death. Yet: I felt an exhaling happiness to
gaze out at the English sunlight, the English trees. Soon enough I
fell asleep again.

There was a knock on the door thirty or forty minutes later. It was
Tom. He took the other armchair, and for a while we talked, feet
up on the windowsill. He asked if I had looked through college yet.

"No, have you?"

He shook his head. "Not in years. My sister was at Fleet. My
father was at Magdalen, and I remember that better."

"Where did you go?"

"LSE. I haven't been in Oxford for ages. Shall we go see it, do
you think? It's fucking hideous, I bet, but I'm sure the porters will
show us around."

Three porters were sitting in the lodge. They looked at us so
dourly, as if we, the students, were the only blemish on their otherwise perfect happiness—which may well have been true—that I
suspected the sign posted by the window that read ASK US FOR A
TOUR! to be insincere.

"We were thinking about a tour of the college."

"JERRY!" they roared in unison.

"Bloody hell," said Tom.

The head porter pointed to a door at the far end of the lodge. "Jerry'll show you about. He likes 'em, the tours. I can't be asked personally."

Expectantly we looked at the door, and after a moment an immensely dignified figure, not above five foot three, stepped through it. He had dark gray hair, a paunch under his college-crested blue sweater and college-crested blue button-down, and glasses that made him look like an owl.

"Tour?" he asked in a voice full of hope.

"These lads want to see the college," said one of the porters.

"This way, this way, this way," said Jerry, walking through the door to Fleet's high front gate. "Tour begins now. Only two of you? Good, excellent, I like a smaller group."

These were the only complete thoughts that Jerry spoke. The rest of the tour he conducted in a single chattering run-on sentence, unpunctuated and unceasing, stylistically similar to *Finnegans Wake* but without that book's charm of comprehensibility.

Still, it was very beautiful—that half hour of a late Oxford afternoon when the harsh white light of midday and the melancholy pink of evening merge and everything turns gold, soft and dim, generous, coloring the city's high towers at a slant.

Fleet is a modestly venerable place. The first Oxford colleges came into existence when the university did, just before 1300, and Fleet was four hundred years younger than they were, respectably old but not ancient. (This is within the hierarchy of the colleges, among whom to have been established after the United States achieved independence from Great Britain is considered gravely humiliating.) Like most colleges it was divided into irregular quads, circumscribed by high buildings. First Quad, or "Firsts," as Jerry denominated it, was directly through the high archway that led into college from the street, a rectangle of shaved grass looped with a slender stone path. Opposite was a bell tower. Like all of the other buildings in college it was made of the same honey-colored stone as Parliament, with the same intricate filigreed stonework, and like Parliament, indeed like all the buildings of the college, the bell tower seemed to bear in its beauty and mass a strange immunity to life, to time.

"...oldest gargoyles and grotesques in Oxford, dating to the foundation of Fleet and the construction of the tower, now if you'll follow me here you'll see on either side of the First Quadrangle two three-story dormitories, same quarrystone as the chapel and the dining hall, keep up, keep up, Fleet's first master was a gentleman named Merryweather, known abuser of opium—thought he saw unicorns flying over the Radcliffe Camera—quite inappropriate—wholly inappropriate—entirely impossible, of course—a brilliant linguist, however—portrait in the hall—"

Continuing to speak the whole while, Jerry trotted us briskly through Firsts, into the dorms and the bell tower, up to the top, and back down again. ("Bells, bells, wonderful bells," was his full gloss when we reached the pinnacle of the tower. Though he did tell us as we descended that several people had jumped from the tower and died over the years. "Fantastic," said Tom.) Then he took us through a narrow corridor at the back of Firsts, paneled with the names of the war dead and lit with old black hanging lanterns, into the Second Quad—Anna's.

It was a hexagonal stone courtyard, not very large, without any grass. Ringed around the hexagon was a row of medieval houses, overgrown with rose bushes, that Fleet had bought with its first endowment and turned into the library. Over their roofs we could see all the dreaming spires of Oxford, ranged together for a quarter mile. There was a dusky hush in that small courtyard, a silence through which even Jerry's voice couldn't break, really.

It seemed deeply romantic to me. What fools Americans can be for England.

"... named for Queen Anne, as no doubt you know, this way to Third Quad, mustn't linger, Queen Anne founded the college in 1702, portrait of her you'll see in dining hall, now Fleet has graduated four Nobel laureates, try not to let the side down, lads, ha, ha, four Nobel laureates, two in physics, one in medicine, one in literature, this way, through the gate, should have had at least one in peace if you ask me, several of the young gentlemen I've seen have done quite a lot more than their bit for peace, but you have to ask the fellows in Stockholm about it—now—this way—through the gate, as I said—come along."

"What do you think we should do tonight?" Tom whispered. Jerry had put ten feet between us with his short-striding canter. "We could try to scare up one or two other people from the Cottages"—the other arriving graduate students—"and then drag them over to the Turtle."

"What's that?"

He looked at me wide-eyed. "Shocking cultural ignorance."

"What is it?"

"The big nightclub down in the city. Horribly dodgy. I bet Anil Gupta knows all about it."

"... Third Quad, our newest addition here at Fleet, contains the preponderance of our dormitories—sleeping halls—halls of residence—"

Third was unspectacular, but it had one great virtue: the Fleet Tavern. Because the drinking age in England is eighteen, not twenty-one, every college at Oxford had its own bar. The consequences of having regular access to a bar in my dorm at Yale would have been catastrophic, but then drinking is different for American students, who are always on a desperate hunt for extralegal means of getting drunk and when they find alcohol drink it as quickly as possible, so it can't be taken away from them.

"Will the bar be open?" I asked Tom in a low voice, seeing the sign.

"I shouldn't think so. The undergrads don't come till next week. They're meant to be the best bops in Oxford, Fleet's. After St. John's maybe."

"Bops" were what Oxford called dance parties. "Is the bar just for the undergrads?"

"No, no, but it's mostly undergrads that go there. A lot of graduate students here never come out of their rooms."

As it happened, though, the bar was open. Jerry showed us inside. Through the wide doors that covered one wall of the room I glimpsed the lawns behind the college. It was these for which Fleet was most famous; most colleges had just such long, manicured stretches of grass, but Fleet's, lying against the river, were the largest and best-situated. We didn't go out, that evening, and I wouldn't see the lawns, or Sophie, for another two days.

"... and that, I think you'll agree, gentlemen, was a thorough tour of Fleet College. Welcome. I'll leave you here for your pint of beer."

Other than the bartender, who was smoking a cigarette by the jukebox, flipping through it with a look of moralizing distaste on his face, the bar was empty. He was a big guy with black hair down to his shoulders, glasses, and a soft, affable countenance. His name was Jem, we would find out later. We bought two pints of Carlsberg from him and took them to the other end of the room to play a strange version of pool with wooden dowels sticking out of the table, which Tom told me was called bar billiards.

I found it easy to talk to him, perhaps especially after the shared comic formality of the tour, and as night fell outside we had a long unforced conversation. At first it was about neutral subjects, sports and travel especially. (He had spent the year since his graduation from LSE traveling through Asia. "Mostly sex tourism," he said and laughed at his own joke.) He had an ambling way of walking around the pool table, a boyishness left intact by going away to school—I recognized it. Gradually we began to ask each other more personal questions. I told him about Alison. He'd had a girlfriend until recently, too, Daisy.

"What happened?" I asked.

"She dumped me. She wanted me to stay in London."

"That sucks."

"Oh, I don't know. Perhaps it's for the best."

"We're only an hour from London by train."

He laughed. "She isn't very bright."

His course at Oxford—that was the term for any degree program—was the Bachelor of Civil Law. He had studied law as an undergraduate and had a job waiting for him at Freshfields at the end of the year, one of the Magic Circle firms, which made his course ornamental, a distinguished but inessential garland. Really it was a tactic to delay the start of his career for another year.

I perceived at some point in those first few hours of our acquaintance—later in the year, when I was better attuned to British mores, it wouldn't have taken me as long—that he belonged to the upper classes. His accent should have alerted me immediately, with its long vowels and back-of-the-throat intonation, but really it was his reference to Ascot ("Daisy and I got hammered at Ascot last year, it was lovely, we snogged in one of the private boxes all afternoon and shook hands with Prince Philip, the old racist") that signaled it first.

Tom grew up in South Kensington. His father was a banker who belonged to a landless cadet branch of a ducal family, and his mother was first cousin to a Sussex title. She did administrative work for this cousin's land-mine charity two days a week. They were both formal people, Tories, with clear ideas of their responsibilities. They sent Tom to Westminster when he was eight; his older sister, Katie, to Roedean. Their small assertions of class—his father's membership in a Northumberland hunt, his mother's activities at the National Portrait Gallery, their Vizslas—were conscious, I think, rather than reflexive. To nearly everyone they seemed an exalted family; to those whose opinion genuinely mattered to them, however, merely a decent one.

Tom, too, was a terrible snob. As a carbuncular he had been to the Ritz and the Savoy for coming-out balls, served as a page at one or two demi-royal functions, and rowed for his school. There is nobody as hopelessly vulgar as a British aristocrat, and he bore their customary equipment, the signet ring, the diamond tie pin, the colorful handkerchiefs, the Toryism, the rah. He openly looked down on me for being American—"News from the colonies?" he asked when I got mail—but that was nothing to his scorn for the people of his own country whom he believed to be fraudulently claiming a connection to his class. These were the rugby-obsessed MPSIAers—*Minor public school, I'm afraid*—and Brookes frauds, pretending they were entitled to *their* signet rings, the Sloane Rangers, the affected Barbour "northerners" who implied a great deal of land somewhere the other side of Yorkshire. Like all authentic snobbery—backed by public affirmation, by heritage—it was disagreeable and also cunningly pleasant, an occasional remoteness that made his friendship seem more valuable. It also made it all the stranger when he picked the person he did to fall in love with.

This account of his life—his account, Westminster, LSE, Thailand, Oxford, the City—makes it sound perfectly ordered. Indeed until five years earlier it had been that way. Then it had changed.

The house he grew up in was at the center of a long row of identical alabaster town houses, divided by hedges. There were two family dogs, Charger and Sandy, and one day he arrived home from school to find them out on the sidewalk, sniffing at a hedge.

He called them, and they ran to heel—well-trained animals—and went up the steps to his house, number seventeen, with him. It was then that he noticed the door was open and began to feel a sense of panic. He called out to see if anybody was home—his father's car wasn't in its spot, but that was usual enough—and his sister came to the door, flanked by two police officers. There were tears on her face. "What happened?" he asked. (They had always been close—one of the first things he told me as we played pool was that they talked every day still, though she was in Syria, working for the government, and I remembered that she was the one who had dropped him here at Fleet.) One of the officers put a hand on his shoulder and told him then that his parents had been in a crash with a food delivery truck on the M4. His father had died immediately. His mother had lasted fifty minutes.

For all the time we spent living side by side—and soon we were good friends, even best friends—I wouldn't know any of this if it weren't for two conversations. The second happened later in the year, when he was drunk and told me the story from start to finish. The first was that first day, when he told me the following.

After the funeral he and Katie had written thank-you notes to all the relatives who had been there. They had a great-uncle in an assisted-living home in Devon, who was unable to come to London, but who had written them an e-mail. It said, "Your father was a fine chap, so sorry he's died, LOL, Uncle Arthur." They responded without acknowledging the strange sign-off, and after that begin to get a series of similar terse, lunatic messages, laughing at the horrors of the world: "Doris in the next room died, LOL, Uncle Arthur." "Kidney bad again, may need surgery, LOL, Uncle Arthur." "Still missing your father, LOL, Uncle Arthur."

Tom was smiling as he told me this—and in retrospect it's amazing that he told me it at all, so soon after we met, unless he was trying to get it out of the way that he was, as he jokingly said, an orphan, like Oliver Twist—but I didn't understand.

"What the hell did he mean?"

"Some idiot at the home, the person who taught him how to use the computer, told him it meant 'lots of love.'"

"Oh Jesus."

"I know."

Tom wanted to go out, but I was too tired—tomorrow, I said. We walked back through Fleet together, but as I turned out of college toward our house he pulled his phone from his pocket and looked up, restless, and said good-bye, that he thought he'd walk around a bit. I went up to my room and started to make my bed.

When that was done, I called Alison. "Hey, it's me."

"Hey."

I could picture her in underwear and a tank top, cross-legged at the center of our bed, biting her bottom lip, her eyes bright and brown and expressive. Then I realized that no, of course she would be at work. The time difference.

It's hard to describe someone you know as well as I know her. She grew up in New Canaan, new money, and had a tendency to be cliquish, bossy, and unreflective, traits that four years in politics had only sharpened but that vanished when you knew her well enough. I thought primarily of her consideration, her love, and that we felt matched.

"I made it," I said.

"Your mom called me, yeah."

She sounded mad. "I tried you before, right when I got here."

That was a lie. "Are you sure?" she asked. "I don't have a missed call from you."

"Maybe check again?"

"No, it doesn't matter. How is it?"

"Okay. I'm really tired. I met a guy in my dorm and we got some beers, but I think it was a mistake to drink."

"Can you get *The New York Times*?"

"Why does everyone keep asking me that?"

"You get moody if you don't read it in the mornings."

"I miss you."

"I miss you, too. It sucks."

Then—it's a fault of mine, an eagerness to conciliate, to please—I said, "Maybe this is a mistake. Maybe I should just come back."

To my surprise, she was the one who said, this time, "It's only a year."

"You're right. One year."

"By the way, did you see the Gallup they just released?"

"You know I can't get the *Times* here."

She laughed. "Asshole. No, it was like forty minutes ago."

"What are the numbers?"

"They're good. Look them up. My dad is saying he could get us both on McCormack, if you came back. Back to Ohio."

I ignored that. "You're ready to leave the congressman already?"

"You know me. I like the trail best. Anyway, a moron could write up these press releases on school outreach."

"But you get to deal with the reporters. You like that."

"That's true."

After John Kerry lost the election—and we both lost our jobs—she had decided to stay in politics. She was tougher than I was about it. She wanted to keep on fighting, the next campaign, the next candidate, fuck the world. In any campaign they say that you need your volunteers to drink the Kool-Aid, so they'll still knock on doors when it's ten below or lend their spare bedroom to a junior pollster who can't find a hotel room—but that's the volunteers. I was on the senior staff and I was still drinking the Kool-Aid, which was a mistake. Alison believed in the *cause,* in the big picture, and she hated George Bush. It's different to fight against something than to fight for something, though. I believed in our guy, Kerry. Worse than that, I really, sincerely believed he was going to win. I was certain. Right until the last people in Ohio voted.

We talked for an hour. She had been crying almost every day before I left, but now she seemed okay. When we hung up I thought of the evening before, the sky that heartbreaking lavender of late twilight in the summer in New York, when even as I had waved good-bye to her for the last time, stepping into my taxi, my other hand had been reaching into my pocket to check that my passport was still there.

Then, though, I thought I was safe, for some reason I couldn't discern the conversation took on a sullen edge. When I asked what was wrong she said nothing was wrong. I pressed her.

Finally she answered. "I just don't understand why you left."

"Jesus, this again."

"Yep, this again."

"What's changed since the start of this conversation, Al?"

I knew the answer—she could be lulled into forgetting that anything was amiss, but when she remembered she was angrier than before. "It would be one thing if you had invited me to come with you."

"What would you have done over here?"

"Whatever I wanted if I had time to plan for it."

"So you would have given up your job?"

"Of course! Are you insane?"

"You're lucky you have that job, Alison, my dad isn't even—"

"Oh, here we go. Boo-hoo. The world revolves around Will."

"Don't be a jerk."

She laughed. "Me? Is that right? Because the way I seem to remember it is that *you* left without giving me any warning, and *you* totally fucked up my life and barely said sorry and now you're acting, acting aggrieved, because I'm upset about it, as if I did something wrong by not liking that you—"

"It's time to get over it." After that there was a long pause, tense with fury, and I knew I had made a mistake—but I didn't care.

She started to shout, and slowly it became all of the arguments we'd already fought out, the old injustices brought forth like a peddler's goods, the trip I'd once cancelled at the last minute, the high school boyfriend with whom she exchanged birthday phone calls. Finally she hung up on me, but I called her back over and over until she answered, with a hiss, "My secretary can see you're calling, we'll talk tomorrow."

"Do you think I give a shit about your secretary?"

She hung up again. I called her, angry, again and again. Soon both of her lines went straight to voice mail.

I sat still for a minute, phone in hand. Then I dragged myself upright to unpack my clothes and find a T-shirt to sleep in. I wrote an e-mail to a list of friends, telling them I had arrived. When all that was done I went over to the window and sat down again, feeling unrepentant. Because I had heard that staying up late was the key to getting over jet lag, I forced myself to stay awake. It's a kind of madness. Soon enough loneliness crept in; I began to picture our apartment, warm and well lit, but who cares, I didn't care, I was here. In the end I fell asleep in one of the armchairs, the windows cracked open, the night air still warm even as it drizzled, and the small boats clicking against each other in the river: one of those times when the uneven, discarded sounds of the world outside remind you that the world doesn't care, and the comfort of that feeling.

When I woke up late the next morning, I felt better for sleeping, and remorseful. It was too early in the States now to call, but I sent Alison an e-mail apologizing—not just for the argument but for leaving.

After that I went through the nonsense necessities of entering any institution: enrolled officially, claimed my student ID, confirmed my arrival with the English Department. Then I had to register my passport at the office of the provost and promise not to blow up anything in England, and between that and the immigration desk at Heathrow I was half convinced myself that I had designed complex plans to level the British Museum and only failed to carry them out through sheer forgetfulness.

Still, the charm of being somewhere new lived on. It had been too long since I experienced the self-distancing happiness of a new city. For lunch I found a pub, which I never visited once afterward but seemed to me then perfect. While I ate I read through the newspapers I'd bought that morning—*The Sun, The Guardian, The Independent, The Times*—and tried to puzzle out who David Blunkett was, or why people hated the Chelsea Football Club. After I had eaten I left and took a wandering walk through the city.

It was what I had hoped it would be. Savvier Americans than me have a costume-drama dream of England, and now here I was, turning each corner to find myself in an alley barely wider than my body, and it would be called Logic Lane or Magpie Lane and look as if it hadn't changed since Disraeli was prime minister and we still had Burma. Nearly every building was made of the same golden-white stone as Fleet, reaching high into the air above the low, shingled roofs of the shops. There was Tom Tower as I walked down Cornmarket Street, and the deer park near Magdalen Bridge. I stood in the tranquil, muting stone courtyard of the Bodleian, with its carved walls flying up high around me. Americans go to Oxford and Cambridge—but especially Oxford, I think—with an idea of it. I did, anyway. It didn't fail my expectations.

As the sun was falling I returned to my room, happy. I went to my computer to check whether Alison had written back. She hadn't. I wrote again, more plaintively, faintly angry.

When I had been back for a few minutes I heard Tom's voice on the stairs. I looked out of my room and saw him with what looked like an Indian teenager, short, smooth-faced, covered in gold rings and chains. He wore rimless glasses.

Tom introduced us. "Hey, Will, this is Anil Gupta. Anil, this is Will Baker, our housemate, the one I was telling you about."

"Good to meet you," I said.

"What's up," said Anil, giving me a wide smile and a multistep handshake in which I attempted to participate. "How goes, how goes," he said when it was done.

Even though Anil dressed and spoke like Jay-Z, his accent was perfect BBC, educated India. He never turned his "er" into an "a"—it was always "player" or "gangster" exactly. I think it took away from his credibility as a member of the underground hip-hop community. So probably did the fact that he was studying applied economics.

"Welcome," I said.

"Is it true you're from New York?" he asked.

"I am. What about you?"

"The very elites of Mumbai." Neither Tom nor I knew how to respond to this. Anil rode the pause before saying, "So, do you gents like rap music?"

"Some of it," I answered.

"Hate it," Tom said cheerfully. "Will, listen. We're going out tonight, and our new housemate wants to come along. What do you think, is he in?"

"For sure," I said.

So at eight o'clock we went to the Fleet Tavern. This time there were two people there. One was Jem, the bartender, wearing a Stiff Little Fingers T-shirt, smoking and staring at the jukebox again. He greeted us and went around the bar to pour pints.

The other person there was new: an Asian girl with pink and black hair, a half-visible tattoo sneaking below the sleeve of her T-shirt. She had huge breasts. Her iPod headphones were in, and she was reading a textbook.

"Hey!" Anil called out immediately and walked toward her.

"Oh no," said Tom.

"What are you reading?" asked Anil.

She removed one of her earbuds, and we could hear what sounded like electronica to me. "What?"

"What are you reading?"

"An essay about pluripotent stem cells."

"Doesn't sound very interesting," Anil said doubtfully.

"Well, I finished Harry Potter."

"Do you want a drink?" Anil asked, but she said she was okay. She started to read again.

"Are you a new grad student?" I asked.

"Yes," she said, eyes still on her book.

We waited for a minute. Behind the bar, Jem was grinning at us. He gave an exaggerated thumbs-up. "Well, hope to see you around," I said.

No answer. "Is it too soon to tell her that I want to spend the rest of our lives together?" asked Tom as we left the table.

We played bar billiards and spent several rounds of drinks— orange juice for Anil—glancing constantly and covertly in her direction. She never looked up from her textbook.

Surprisingly early Jem called out for last orders. I went up with my empty glass. "Last call at nine thirty-seven?" I asked.

"Fleet time," he said, shrugging.

"What's that?"

He looked at me with new interest. "Oh, are you a new student, then? I figured you were just one of the graduate students I never saw during term. I'm Jem." We shook hands. He had a thick midlands accent. "I'm a third year. Undergrad."

"Cool."

"Yeah, the bar doesn't usually close till midnight, but before term we only keep it open from five to ten for you lot. I'm the manager, actually. It's good fun. There are about ten of us who bartend."

"Any grads?"

"No, all undergrads."

"You should think about hiring a graduate student. It might get more people to come here."

He laughed. "You asking for a job?"

I hadn't been really, but suddenly it seemed like it could be fun, and I said, "Sure, if you have one open."

"I'll let you know." He lit a cigarette and took a sip of his own pint. "What are you here to study?"

"English. You?"

"Oh, classics. I work on Sallust these days."

"Are you going to be a classicist?"

"Lord no."

"Then what?"

"Fuck all, hopefully. I wouldn't mind traveling. Probably a banker."

"You?"

He grinned. "Me."

"So what is Fleet time?"

"It's a college joke. You'll start hearing it if you pay attention. Fleet's pretty relaxed, you'll find, compared to Merton or somewhere swotty like that, and if you're a bit late or early you just say, 'Well, Fleet time,' and it's a big laugh. You can even say it at a tutorial once or twice a year. I use it as an excuse to close early." He smiled, cigarette hanging loose in the corner of his mouth, his glasses slipping down. "Nice to meet you, though."

I went back and played a last game of pool with Anil and Tom while Jem closed up. When I had finished my beer Tom said, with a look of resignation, "To bed for you?"

I said no, that I felt energized and awake, and immediately he brightened. "The Turtle?"

"Why not," I said. "Anil?"

"This is a nightclub?"

"Yeah."

"Then I am coming. We must invite our new friend, too," he said and went straight up to the girl with her textbook. To Anil's genuine surprise she declined his invitation. Tom gave her a hesitant, unacknowledged wave good-bye, and we left.

As we passed the Cottages I asked them if we could stop so that I could send an e-mail. Really I wanted to check, though. There was still no word from Alison. *Fuck her, then,* I thought, and ran back outside to meet up with my housemates.

The Turtle didn't look like much from the outside: a stairwell leading down to a basement; a few loud girls troubling the alley upstairs, smoking and arguing. There were two mountainous bouncers checking ID under a dim yellow streetlight. As far as I could tell they wore nothing but leather. They squeaked when they moved.

Tom was enthusiastic. "I haven't been here since I was fifteen, but I loved it. Ungodly hot, of course, because it's underground. They play great music, lots of eighties songs."

"And hip-hop," said Anil.

"I don't think so."

"None?" Tom shook his head, and Anil said, "That does not meet my definition of clubbing, friends."

Tom laughed. "A thousand pardons."

"They let you in when you were fifteen?" I asked.

"My sister found me a driving license."

We made it past the leather twins and downstairs. At the front bar there were seven girls in short skirts, with a line of twenty-one shots in front of them. Tom went and took the menu from the end of the bar and said something to one of the girls.

"Orielgasms," he reported when he returned. "Vodka and Midori."

It turned out there was a shot named after every college, not just Oriel; Fleet's was called the Golden Fleets, a rare literary allusion on that list, and it was made of Goldschläger and apple vodka. (*The nectar of Hades!* reported the menu excitedly.) We ordered three of them right away, of course. I drank two, because Anil didn't want his.

Even sober Anil was confident about his appeal to women. Several times when I was speaking he would hold up a single finger, turn to a passing girl, and stare at her intensely. "Sowing seeds," he would say after the girl had gone. Then there was his catchphrase, dashed liberally into his lectures about hip-hop and the elites of Mumbai: "Haters gonna hate." It wasn't clear that he perceived with any great depth of comprehension what the phrase actually meant, since he said it with a complete lack of contextual discrimination—he got it right occasionally, more often not. There was joy ("Have you ever been to London? I love that place! Haters gonna hate!"), there was disappointment ("I can't believe that girl wouldn't give me her number. Haters gonna hate."), and there was occasionally even philosophy. ("We all get old some day, you know? Haters gonna hate.")

The more we talked with Anil the more Tom and I seemed like

old friends. He and I drank more than I usually would have, shots first, then a round of Vodka Red Bulls, then some more shots (house vodka only cost a quid, probably because it was literally toxic), then a round of Snakebites, then another round of shots, and pretty soon the world was blurry, and I kept ordering drinks, with a feeling of obscure revenge against Alison, and Anil seemed like the funniest man alive.

The Turtle was made up of seven or eight rooms that together formed a long, narrow, zigzagging corridor. ("No truth to the rumor that this was actually Hitler's bunker," said Tom at one point, with the air of someone repeating a joke they had once found incredibly funny.) Each room was different than the last, one all neon, one crowded with couches that smelled like pot. We moved from room to room, stopping to get drinks in each one.

By the time we reached the dance room, a long narrow cave toward the very back of the club, it was past one o'clock. We were shouting because of the noise, except Anil, who hadn't had anything to drink and mistakenly thought that we could still hear his stories.

"DO YOU DANCE?" I yelled to him and Tom, interrupting a long description of the Gupta family's rivalry with the Mauryans.

"YES!" Tom shouted, and Anil said, with becoming scorn, "OF COURSE I DO."

"LET'S GO OUT THERE!"

"I DON'T WANT TO LEAVE!" said Anil, and I said, "NO, LET'S GO DANCE WITH SOME GIRLS!"

Once in a while dancing is immaculate, a perfection; you understand why raves exist: When you've timed the drinks correctly and they lift your mood and your energy, the songs are ones you all know, and you look around at the girls, their happy lost faces, their long earrings, something limbic, their skin just damp with sweat to the touch, the whole thing. That night I almost couldn't take the joy of it. Tom and even Anil, too, looked gleeful. With Anil as our leader we moved among a few amorphous groups of girls, some of them interested, some not, until in one of them I came across Jess.

She was blond, not too tall, and very pretty, with an angled face; she was flushed with the exercise of dancing, her hair fixed back and high with a clip. We danced with her and her friends for a song, and then I started to dance just with her, though cautiously at the start, so that it never seemed exactly as if it was just the two of us; we remained part of the group, only on a longer and longer tether from them. She was a great dancer. Finally when a Daft Punk song came on her face lit up and she grabbed my hand, as if she couldn't believe it, and after that just the two of us danced, the pretense of the group forgotten. Then at some point our faces brushed and we kissed.

How did it happen? I can't remember. We didn't stop and kiss exactly. We went on dancing, and even returned to our friends now and then. Then near three o'clock the songs slowed down, and she led me by the hand over to a wall, where we kissed—more deeply. Tom kept looking at us, but I ignored him. I remember thinking that I didn't care, it wasn't me, it was something else, and soon the sovereignty of my impulses grew confused and I started to think about Alison and Jess as the same person. We did a shot off of a tray from a roving waitress, and then Jess went to the bathroom and I was alone. I started to think about my father, how I had the same boring undistinguished decisive traumas as everyone else, and the delight of the people on the dance floor looked muted and far away. Then Jess came back with more drinks and kissed me, and the dark moment passed, the exhilaration returned. We went back out to dance. She was with four friends, all British like her. They had nothing to do with Oxford. Tom had his hand on one girl's hip; I couldn't say where Anil was. They greeted us with catcalls, and I smiled modestly, as if to convey that my conquest spoke for itself. Then Jess told them we were leaving and led me back through each of the rooms of the club and outside, where we hailed a cab.

Have I lost your sympathy? I lost my own, of course; almost immediately, but not in the cab on the way back to her apartment, not yet, I was still thinking about those e-mails. Then, too, it was the first time I had cheated on Alison, and simply to have a new body under my hands, new breasts, new skin, was overpowering. I don't know. I don't know what I was doing.

"Is this called pashing?" I asked her in the cab

She laughed into my neck. "You Americans. What are you, a student?"

Styudent. "I am. What about you?"

Again she laughed. I found her lightheartedness irresistible, after all the sheer emotion of the past few weeks with Alison. So little was at stake for once. "No, I'm not."

She had a crowded flat that she shared with two other girls. "It's ever so messy," she said, "but then they're still at the Turtle, so it'll be quiet. Here, come on, this is my room."

We fell onto the bed. It was cluttered with clothes and magazines and makeup, the usual magic of a girl's room. She pushed them to the floor. There was the scent of her perfume in her hair as we kissed, and her breasts, which I could see the tops of in her scooped T-shirt, full and pinkish, looked beautiful. I put a hand to them.

"Mm," she said and unloosed her bra.

I hadn't realized how much I missed first hookups: when the awkwardness is pooled between you, something to laugh about together, that high school feeling of excitement and apprehension before routine and comfort set in. She pulled off my shirt and then hers and we kissed like that, both still in jeans and shoes, our naked chests together, giving each other goosebumps, nipples hardening as they brushed skin, all of it warm, all of it soft.

"Did you roofie me?" I asked after a while.

She laughed and pushed me onto the bed. "You're cheeky." Then she straddled me, kissing my neck and my lips, her back arched so she was pressed into my hard-on. She started to undo the buttons of my jeans. "Let me have it," she said.

I stopped her hand and said, "I have a girlfriend."

"In the States?"

"Yeah. Is that a problem?"

She covered her breasts with her arm. "It's a pity."

"I'm sorry I didn't tell you before."

She was silent for a moment, then lay down beside me, one arm over my chest. "It's all right. I had fun."

"Me, too."

"Maybe find me on Facebook, in case things change. I like you."

"What's Facebook?" I said. It was 2005.

She laughed. "Look it up and find me. It's Jessica Marten."

I took my shirt from the floor, and we kissed again for a time, standing up. She let her arm drop and pressed up against me.

"Oh, well," she said, her breasts softening into my ribs. "This is nice, at least." Soon, though, there were voices in the hall, her roommates returning, and she gave me a last kiss and pushed me out through a side door, saying good-bye.

So I left. I hadn't noticed it as we came in, but in the courtyard of her building there had been a party. Half-deflated balloons had blown into piles; there were overflowing garbage cans. There were also six or seven abandoned beers, standing on a ledge, chilled by the night air. I took two. I put one in my pocket and opened the other. I held on to the last moments that I could ignore what I had done.

Out on the street it felt suddenly not cool but cold, and the first violet paleness of dawn was emerging imperceptibly from the black of the middle night. It must have been four.

Suddenly, after just a few steps, I had a terrible sense of what I would find at home—that there would be e-mails from Alison, apologizing that she hadn't been able to write back sooner, she had been away from her computer, the congressman had been in Staten Island all day and she had been with him, she was sorry, too, the fight was stupid and ridiculous, we were fine, it was only one year. What had I done? Two days away from America, and this had happened. It seemed so shamefully short a time. It told its own story. I thought of Motherwell, when asked how long it took him to paint one of the *Elegies,* saying, "Thirty seconds and a lifetime."

As I walked down Jess's street I saw a pretty blue mailbox that said MARK AND JUNE LENOX on it, the names curlicued with small white painted lilies, faded now, a woman's touch, ten years old, from when they had moved in, and I felt a foreshadowing of the violent regret I knew was coming. I felt triumph, too, and physical pleasure, and horror with myself. It was a muddle. It's rare to surprise yourself. The dim streetlamps still shone at intervals before me, and by their light I could see the austere and enduring spires of Oxford, rising in the middle distance, untroubled by human grief.

When I came to the end of the street I knew roughly where I was in relation to Fleet and started back toward home. As I went I pulled on the T-shirt I was carrying and realized that it was the wrong one. I turned it inside out and saw that it was pink and bore an inscription, in Union Jack–colored glitter: BRITISH GIRL.

I laughed. Then I took a sip of the beer and within a few seconds of swallowing it I lurched toward a potted plant beside another blue mailbox and threw up into it. When I was finished I wiped my mouth, swished it out with beer, then stood, looking up at Oxford, feeling that I was finally there, and drank the rest of it.

I had only just started walking again when the peal of the different colleges' bells startled me out of my still reverie, each with its own melody, all out of kilter with one another. So it was five in the morning. The walk was another fifteen minutes, and as I drew closer to the Cottages and Fleet I kept thinking to myself, *Shit, shit,* but also, somewhere else, *early days, early days.*

CHAPTER TWO

I come from that vague northeastern gentry inside which families dip and rise, but from which perhaps they never depart entirely. My first paternal ancestor in America was a man named Abraham Backer—described as "surly and ill-tempered" by John Winthrop, who was so surly and ill-tempered himself that the description has an inflection of admiration in my reading of it. Abraham's great claim to glory in life, other than venturing across the ocean to the Massachusetts Bay Colony in 1623, was the inadvertent submission of his family to wholesale slaughter by a group of Pequot Indians, who, again in the words of Winthrop, "burned them in their wigwams." Great.

All families are equally old, whether or not there are records of their age, but Abraham is mine, and I feel a half-serious pride in him. Nobody in history is more real to me. He left seven books to his son William—who survived the Pequots—in a time of almost unexceptioned illiteracy. Before his death he was a magistrate in the colony. These cinders from the fire of life, those seven books: I feel his human presence down the years. I can imagine that he breathed as I do, stretched his stomach too full with food, loved his dog, annoyed his wife.

My mother's family has its own tales of *Mayflower* glory, and on both sides there are the leavings of long centuries, the painted sea chest that traveled from Boston Harbor to China aboard my great-great-great-grandfather's clipper ship, the set of silver hairbrushes descended from *Age of Innocence* New York. There is the large, privately printed, grammatically dubious family genealogy, assembled in the fifties and annotated in its margins with ferocious corrective irritation by my grandfather. There's the *Social Register*, the anecdote of Colonel Simon Baker and George Washington sharing a carriage from Boston to Virginia. The *Cherry Orchard* tales of lost houses and subdivided lands that could have been ours, ought to have been ours. I went to the same boarding school that my father and his father and his father did. The same college, too.

Then there were the manners. To say *"beverage,"* or *"pardon,"* or *"patio,"* or any of a few dozen other words was within my family to commit a grave solecism. Cheerfulness in social situations was considered perhaps the greatest virtue a human being could possess, and its cousin, stoicism during adversity, was second. To have a complete matching set of silver flatware—no, hopeless, your silver had to have gotten mixed up over the generations.

Indeed, anything that matched at all was considered to be in poor taste. "They have matching sofas and chairs," my mother reported to her sister when we visited Alison's parents for lunch in the city once, not thinking that I could overhear her from the next room. Years before that she had told the same sister that a friend from college had left his knife and fork akimbo on his plate, and that another had seemed to brag (imagine!) about going to Southampton.

In this way I grew up conflating stylistic and moral choices. *Drapes, home, gift. Purchase.* Anything that savored of upsell. The code was self-effacement—my people were Yankees, and when I see the popular representations of WASPs I cringe at the vulgarity, the Greenwich and Nantucket imprint in the public consciousness, lobster reds, sneering ski-slope kids. My male relatives wore unbranded khakis, windbreakers, and digital watches. They carried combs. Their shoes were as cheap as possible and ordered in bulk from catalogs printed in black-and-white; the only articles of clothing upon which it was acceptable to spend a great deal of money were a suit, a shirt, and possibly a hat. My grandparents, all four of them, would rather have walked through Times Square naked than utter the word *"summering."* Society has shifted toward money now, and money is what makes you a socialite. There was an older way.

In one way this was a small part of my life, and in another all of it. It had the poverty of imagination that wraps like an involucre around any dead world—meeting on the platform at New Haven, all those Fitzgerald second-order signifiers—but it would have taken a greater strength of character than I had to reject their accretion of meaning as false.

This has something to do with Oxford. Not long before I moved to England I turned twenty-five, and like everyone I slipped into adulthood like a delinquent through the back door, never quite sure I hadn't been seen. The future was decided: Alison and I were settled together; we would work in politics; we would live in New York.

It was not an unhappy thought to me, but there was a titration of loss in those certainties, and perhaps for that reason, Oxford in those first days seemed to me like the last of something in my life. Once more I could look out upon the coming years, as I had for so long, and see a future full of nothing, full of everything, before all the choices I made started to become irreversible. It was only a year—and I very probably wouldn't even have taken that year if it hadn't been for the terrible and disorienting things that happened around the time I put in my application.

I don't know. I do remember that on the afternoon in my second week at Fleet when Tom and I first went out and visited the lawns, I felt a difference in myself. Space could induce what I had once imagined only time could: forgetting. I thought, *Oh, so this is why people leave places. This is what a new start feels like.*

As I said before, Fleet's lawns were considered unusually fine. The college had a lot of land, and from the stone terrace outside of the bar, just behind Third Quad, the long stretch of grass looked almost limitless because you still couldn't quite see the natural boundary of the river. The lawns were divided in two by a slim stone path, and just at the river there were loose groups of interchangeable teak chairs and tables, one of them usually overturned, none of them very tidily arranged.

Tom and I went out there at the end of the afternoon. He had a rugby ball and tossed it underhand to me. I caught it—"See, you'll have it in no time"—and we started jogging farther and farther apart, so that we had to give the ball long heaves.

After ten or fifteen minutes an older man with a tennis racket started walking toward us from the courts nearby, waving. "Hello," he called when he was still twenty feet off, looking at Tom and not me. "I'm Gobbs, statistics. Have you played before?"

We stood up and shook hands. "He hasn't," said Tom, and they shared a cutting little laugh. "I played in school. Not at uni. I'm a graduate student. We both are, in fact."

"I reckoned you might be. Listen, how would you feel about trying out for Fleet? We have a good deal of fun. Last year we came in seventh, which isn't shabby considering that there are forty teams. If you want we could have a throw now, I could tell you about it."

Tom nodded, looking curious. "D'you mind?" he asked me.

"No, no. I want to check out the boathouse anyway."

The two of them started walking away down the lawns, talking and hurling the ball at each other with the teeth-baring aggression that passes for friendliness among upper-class Brits.

The river was glossy, narrow, and quick, a beautiful green color, with the white and maroon striped college punts strung along the near bank. (The punts are riverboats, low flat things you pole along the river in, notionally with champagne and strawberries, in real life more often with beer and crisps.) The sun, westering, heavy, and hazy, was in those great final throes of energy before the sky whitens and clears, and evening comes. I stood and watched it. That immense body, dying trillions of feet away from me, still warming my face with its steady insensate chemistries.

Sometimes we're available to change. The grass was high by the river, and when I was five or six feet from the water, half-stumbling in it, I saw Sophie for the first time. She was tall and thin, with long auburn hair down her back, wreathed in the gold light of a late summer five o'clock. I thought I had never seen anyone so beautiful in all my life.

I felt a terrible longing for Alison.

In the ten days since the Turtle, my guilt had become constant. There was no residual joy—or very little—in thinking of Jess, except occasionally when I remembered what her body felt like. Certainly if I could have erased what I had done I would have.

It had also made me clingy, and when Alison and I spoke on the phone I spent the time reassuring myself that she still loved me. Of course, for her nothing had changed, and so I could never elicit quite the tone I wanted.

"I wish I could see you," I would say as soon as we started talking on the phone.

"You, too!" she would answer, too lightly for my taste. "So much has been going on at work, Martinez, you know, in the fifth—"

Then, feeling actually close to tears, "I would seriously pay a hundred bucks to just lie down with you for ten minutes." (Oh God, the cringing when I think of this.)

"You're so sweet."

"I mean it."

"And a little bit of a girl."

"Ha."

She laughed. "Don't sound so miserable, I'm only teasing."

I'm sure it gratified her to know that we had reversed roles—that I was handling the change badly, not her. "I don't know if I can wait a month to see you. When's the last time we spent that long apart, the summer after college?"

"I'm doing okay with it, I really am."

"Thanks."

"I just meant that I can live with it. It's only a year."

"I was wrong, a year is fucking forever."

"Oh, shit. That's my dad on the other line. He might have some good news about the governor's bullshit seaport thing for me. I'll call you back in like four minutes."

"I'm supposed to go to the pub, but I can wait if—"

"No, go, make friends, we'll talk tomorrow—I love you—bye—shit, there it is again—bye—"

I would picture her familiar face, her slender hands, and feel a wave of anguish. What was I doing here? That was my frame of mind in Oxford, that afternoon.

I was walking along when I saw Sophie, but I had accidentally come too close not to say hello. "Hey," I called out.

She turned with her arms still crossed. "Oh, hi," she said. She had been looking down the river and turned back to it, leaning over the water and staring. "You can't see a scull coming up toward us, can you? You're taller than I am."

I looked. "No, nothing. Are you waiting for someone?"

She turned back to me. My first impression of her was that she was distracted and faintly bad-tempered, as pretty girls can be if they are not emptily sweet, but then I realized something else was going on. There were tears in her eyes. "Yeah."

I had been walking toward her but stopped now, leaving a tithe of space between us. "Is everything okay?"

"Oh, I'm fine," she said, tucking a dejected strand of hair behind her ear. Almost immediately she was crying. She wiped her tears away more quickly than they came with the heel of her hand.

"Is there anything I can do?"

"I'm sorry, I'm not ever like this—"

"No, don't apologize. Do you want to sit?"

She sniffled. "Why not."

When we were on the chairs I was silent for a minute or two. She had been throwing bread to a family of black birds with red bills, and she started again, smiling weakly when they took it. Finally I asked, "So are you in Fleet? Are you in the Cottages?"

"Yeah, I just got here. Number five. What about you?"

She had a lovely, lilting accent, posh but with sweetness at its edges and a faint heaviness in its vowels that I learned later was from Yorkshire. Even in her vulnerable state there was something imperious to her.

"I'm in three."

"You must think I'm nuts."

"No. Everyone gets this way sometimes."

"But not me." She studied me for a second. "I'm breaking up with my boyfriend today."

I smiled and said, mildly, "On a boat?"

"He was supposed to pick me up." She sighed with her whole body. "But he's always fucking late, or he ditches me, even for things like this. God, I hate him."

"Then congratulations. Right?"

"Listen to me." She gave her head a quick, sharp shake, took a deep breath, and smiled a smile set with the determination not to be foolish. "So what do you study? What's your name? I'm Sophie."

We shook hands. "I'm Will. I do English. What about you?"

"French."

"A master's, too?"

She shook her head ruefully. "Probably for the long haul, actually, the DPhil. Are you American?"

"Yeah, I'm from New York."

Unlike most people, she didn't rush to prove that she knew the city. "Oh, lovely," she said and looked down the river again.

"Have you met anyone yet?"

She looked back at me. "Not a soul. I only just got here on Tuesday."

"I think a bunch of fun people are going out tonight, if you want to drown your sorrows." I was referring to myself, Tom, and Anil, so "a bunch of fun people" might have been misleading, but who cared. "To the Royal Oak."

"I wish I could, but my department has these introductory seminars every evening this week. Refreshers, they're supposed to be, vousvoyering. It's an insult, but they're mandatory."

"What about next week? There's the opening Formal Hall in First Week." There were three terms at Oxford, Michaelmas, Hilary, and Trinity, each with nine numbered weeks. Just then we were in Noughth Week, as it was called, when the students arrived and settled in. First Week would be the formal commencement of the fall term, Michaelmas.

"Oh, I'd love to go to that," she said and looked genuinely pleased.

In a formal tone, I said, "If you come you may tutoyer me."

She laughed. "Seems hasty."

"I feel as if I'd known you for decades. I've known you in a relationship and single, and I have to say I prefer—"

She laughed and was about to speak when from not far off a voice barked out her name. "Soph."

It was her boyfriend, I guessed; he was sitting in the stern of a scull for two, handsome and very tan, shaggy-haired, an instinctive smirk in his expression. After he had called for her he set about the work of turning the boat, so we had a moment before she went to him.

She stuck out her hand again. "It was nice to meet you," she said. Then, in a lower voice, she added, "Wish me luck."

"Good luck."

She went. "Who was that?" I heard her boyfriend ask her.

I didn't watch them go, turning back toward Fleet and finding Tom after a short while. He said good-bye to Gobbs and apologized for running off, and we started to walk back to the college, again tossing the ball back and forth. It was an hour full of meetings; I told him about Sophie, and on the way back to the bar we met a girl who would be one of our closest friends at Fleet, Anneliese.

Then again, in those young hours of the school year there were always chances to meet new people. There were movie nights, cocktails with the Master on the lawns, unskilled games of croquet that devolved into a kind of loose, horseless polo. All of these activities originated with the MCR, or Middle Common Room, which was the graduate students' chief social center. It was located in three rooms on the ground floor of First Quad, with a view of the gates and porters' lodge, and had couches, a kitchen, and a television. At a cheese-tasting there in Noughth Week Anil became friends with Tim, or Timmo, as we all eventually called him, a short, silent, very strong personage—not overburdened with charisma—who Anil assured us belonged to the very elites of Liverpool.

Timmo's chief ambition in life was to participate in any reality TV show, ideally *Big Brother*, which was culturally definitive in England as it never was in America. (Aside from the normal half-hour show every night, one channel on British TV had a twenty-four-hour feed of the *Big Brother* house, in obeisance to the insane demand of the public, apparently.) It was never totally clear, though, *why* he wanted to be on the show.

"Do you want to be famous?" I asked him one day.

"No way," he said with a snort, as if I knew nothing at all about the nature of television.

"Or rich?"

"He is rich," said Anil quickly.

"Why do you want to do it, then?"

"It looks like a laugh." (Loff, as the Brits pronounce it.) "And there's some lovely girls on there."

Whenever he got drunk he would practice his confession-booth monologues, which he had planned out in arresting detail. Example: "I *know* I shouldn't have had sex with Keeley, but Ricky can fuck off. She had her choice." We would nod appreciatively at his slurred and heartfelt speech, our faith in humanity, and Oxford, too, shaken. Keeley's identity is one of the world's ageless mysteries.

These early MCR events were in the next weeks; for that afternoon, we found Anneliese. She was kneeling by a tree, holding a seventies-era Nikon—she came from a family of amateur photographers, we learned—and staring down at something on the ground with great concentration. She was an earnestly pretty person, round-faced with gray eyes and curly brown hair.

We went over to see what she was looking at. It was a flat grave marker with weeds growing over it. "Can you read this?" she asked, pointing to the old, faint cursive.

I couldn't, but Tom could. "Francis Cholmondley-Chapman. Looks like he died in the Crimean War, 'that freedom might not perish from the earth.' It also says 'and who fought that fighting might end.' Sorry, chaps, missed that one."

"Ah," she said, with a radiant smile on her face. "That makes me happy for the first time in days. A true English experience."

"Have you not been happy?" asked Tom.

Her face turned serious. "No, not at all," she said in her German accent. "I'm homesick, you see. It's very bad. I haven't made any friends yet, either."

This was so like her. She was incapable of dishonesty. It meant that to know her for a few minutes was almost to begin to love her.

"You have two now," Tom said with embarrassed gallantry, and she beamed at him.

"Oh, good."

We invited her to the bar terrace, where we had beers and watched the sun finally vanish. She had done an undergraduate degree in physics at the University of Göttingen, she said, but her parents had pushed her into that, both being scientists themselves, and she had decided upon graduation that she wanted to try history instead. That was why she had come to Oxford. She was from Berlin originally.

Everything about the Crusades, her subject, was deeply shocking to her, as if it were still happening somewhere not far away. "They roasted the Saracens alive over brushfires and ate them, the cannibals," she told us. "I think it was awful of them. And they had scurvy and bled out of their eyeballs, too."

Here is a story to tell you about Anneliese.

At Fleet there was a new graduate student named Steffen, from France, who became famous immediately throughout the college for his rudeness. If you spoke to him he mumbled and walked away, and he actually cursed at one of the most complacent porters, Laurence, to the delight of the undergrads who witnessed it.

One day later in the year, that winter, I saw him on the steps of the Sackler Library, all the way across town, speaking with tremendous and unwonted animation. I could hear what it was about—the food in Fleet's dining hall, whose quality he seemed to interpret as a personal insult to him as a Frenchman—but I hadn't even known he could speak in full sentences, and it was only after twenty or thirty seconds of eavesdropping that I realized the person with him was Anneliese. She told me later that they had lunch every week. Thinking of her, I might put it this way: Most people think they're the same with everybody, when in fact it's one of the rarest qualities I know. She was.

In any event, Anneliese filled out our small, sectile, but durable group. There were Tom, Anneliese, Anil, Timmo, and me, with Sophie and a few others drifting in and out of our daily lives. What ratified our friendship was the first Formal Hall of Michaelmas term, and everything good and bad that followed it.

On the first day of First Week I got a note in my pigeonhole from an old professor at Fleet, St. John Jarvis. My mother had told me to expect to hear from him. In the sixties he had taught at Columbia on an exchange and become friends with my great-uncle, who was in the philosophy department there. The note offered me a cup of coffee the following afternoon. There was a sketchy map drawn on the envelope. It said to cross the river beyond the lawns by a footbridge, then take a dirt path a half mile to his house.

"Have you heard of someone named St. John Jarvis?" I asked Tom.

"Sinjun, not Saint John."

"Excuse me?"

He stopped reading his e-mail and looked at me. "When it's a proper name in England it's pronounced Sinjun."

"Well, have you hard of Sinjun Jarvis?"

"No, why?"

"He's a don. He pidged me an invitation to coffee."

"Don't fuck up his name."

"I'm not going to say, 'Hey, Sinjun!' Tom."

I arrived the next day, two minutes late. I could still hear the last of the city's tower bells ringing four o'clock, but otherwise his huddled brown Middle Earth house seemed like the only one for miles. It was at the edge of a growth of apple trees, with green fields beyond them.

Sinjun himself answered the door. He was an enormous, barrel-chested man, who, though he was seventy-seven, looked as if he were in the prime of late middle age. I had expected must and stink, a polite half hour, but there was none of that. His hair was still dark, and his great florid face grinned at me.

"Come in, come in," he said. "You're three minutes late, but we'll spare you the firing squad. You look just like your uncle George, you know. Same nose."

"Thanks."

"I don't know that it's such a wonderful compliment. Sit right there on that couch. Larissa, the coffee! I hope you don't like tea? Never touch the stuff myself, I think it tastes of ashes. I spent four years with your uncle, the Amiables, we called the Americans. I never met a man who liked women more than George—that is, I've met many men who liked women more than they liked George, but none that liked women more than George liked women."

He laughed, and a black woman came in with a chased silver pot of coffee and nodded at me. There were two cups on a square marble table, and a plate of cakes and sandwiches between them. The room was high-beamed, with a wall of windows looking out over his gardens and a sleek, modern, vacant feel. On the wall there was a Hodgkin print, and on the mantel a Henry Moore nude, a room reduced to simplicity by money.

"I'm glad you came—look, have a cake. I was fond of your uncle, very fond. I was chuffed when his wife wrote to tell me you were coming to Fleet. He died when, was it—"

"In 1999."

"Just so. It's a terrible pity he never lived to see the millennium. They say, you know, that nobody dies in the last month of the year. Everyone wants to get to New Year's. Wait and see what happens. Then they drop like flies in January, poor buggers."

"It could just be the cold."

"Maybe. Now, drink some of this delicious coffee—I take it strong, I have to warn you—and eat a finger sandwich. There's a ham set and a cucumber set. I can't recommend the ham, sadly. She's never gotten the knack of it." I thanked him, and he settled back in his chair, leonine. "Can I assume that since you've come here to study English, the last thing you want to do is become an English professor?"

I smiled. "Why do you say that?"

"It's harder to get jobs in America with a degree from Oxford, for one thing, because a DPhil only takes four years to earn here, as opposed to seven there. Seems less serious to them. My friend Wimsatt got terribly annoyed with their condescension over the length of the doctoral programs when he visited America. For another, you Ivy League Yanks like to treat Oxbridge as a finishing school. Don't think I haven't noticed. I don't resent it, mind you. It's what I would've done in your shoes, oh, in a heartbeat, but I doubt that you want to have a career like, say, Professor Norbrook's, or my friend Greenblatt's."

"No, not really."

"If you saw Greenblatt's wife you wouldn't mind. Makes the MLA worth enduring. Leave that aside, though, what *do* you want? You were in politics? I bet you liked that—a chance to prove you're clever."

"All the good professions are that way, aren't they?"

"Yes, though for some reason politics especially. You get the provers in there."

I considered this. "I guess that was me. I did like the power." I smiled. "It's probably healthier to be here, less chaotic."

Even as I said that I realized it was only partly true. The energy of the campaign, the long hours, the cold pizza, the conference calls, the competitive banter, the jokes, the urgency—I missed all of it.

"So, if you don't go back to politics?"

"I think probably I will. My girlfriend still does it, in New York."

"Ah, long distance. She's still in?"

"She wants both of us to do it, like a team." I paused then. Something about his tone invited confidence, made secrecy seem slack. "Her father is the head of the congressional fundraising committee in New York. He may run for office himself soon enough."

He whistled. "Money?"

"Yeah. He was in real estate when he was younger." Then, with a feeling of guilt, I added, "He bought his way into politics, actually. No talent of his own for it, but money, and strong convictions."

"You should get married. It'll be good for you. Then you should cheat." He took a gulp of coffee. "I had a girl at Columbia—Kitty, a student, which means I shouldn't tell you, but there it is. If I had ever married it would have been her."

"Do you have any children?"

"I hope not. Just nephews that I know of, three," he said. "Big boys. They play cricket, like I did."

"How did you decide what to do?" I asked. "To go into academia."

"How did I decide? Well, I was passionate about it." He shrugged. "Couldn't imagine anything else."

"I don't think I feel that way. About Orwell."

He nodded and then gave me an odd look, half fond, half shrewd. There was a sheaf of papers on the table between us, and he picked it up. "I'm glad. If you seemed right I was going to suggest—I'm the chair of the committee for a fellowship Balliol disburses."

I realized I had been tricked. Or that was too ungenerous a word—appraised. I think I blushed. "What fellowship?"

"Doesn't matter. Take the papers, if you like, there's a chance you'll want to stay here for another four years, but don't, don't do it for a fellowship or out of lassitude. Stay here for a year, see Europe, get an honorable second. God, but I envy you."

I took the papers. It was funny; I envied him. I had looked at his CV online, nine books, two of which were still widely taught, and he wrote now for *The Observer* and *The Times Literary Supplement*. He had been a visiting professor in New York, Tokyo, Stockholm, and Cape Town. He had obviously fucked about ten thousand women. His achievements were behind him. When you're young, people keep telling you how lucky you are to have all of your choices in front of you. I don't doubt I'll feel that way one day, too, but it's an old person's dream.

In truth, I arrived at Oxford feeling half like a failure. It was 2005 already. I had been out of college for more than three years, and time seemed to be running out the way it only can when you're twenty-five, and armed to the teeth with it. I woke up in the middle of the night with a hollow feeling in my chest, panicked about what I would become. I had a friend making three million dollars a year at a hedge fund and another friend who had just been elected to the Rhode Island Senate. All I had was the Kerry campaign—and Alison, I would tell myself in the middle of the night, at least I had Alison.

There were times when I wished I could be done with all of what I was good at, books, reading, writing, speaking, thinking. Too much analysis, too quick a brain. Too many words. It was a kind of fever. Sometimes I thought I had the temperament of a scientist, just not the intelligence. I wanted to be a scientist in the age when good birth, a knack for organization, and a pleasure in careful labeling were enough—when you could simply record the time of the sunset and the sunrise, measure how long it took different types of flowers to bud, dig up bones, and make wildly inadequate conjectures about their origin: the whole time of civilization when the imponderables of life were broader and softer, before polymers, before relativity. It's the wish of a stupid mind.

Jarvis and I talked about all of this. I stayed for three hours, two hours longer than I should have, two and a half longer than I intended. I kept thinking about the fellowship.

"We'll have to do this again," he said when at last I was going. "I mean it."

"Thank you for inviting me. It's easy enough to feel lost here."

He shook his head. "No, within a week you'll be at home. When does Fleet have its first bop?"

"Third Week, I think."

"I went to one, you know. Anything but clothes was the theme, meaning you had to dress up in anything but clothes. There was a young woman in a tinfoil bikini, and there were a great deal of poorly fastened socks. About ten years ago, this would have been."

I laughed. "Did you have fun?"

He thought for a moment. "At my age the beauty of these young people, the women, is a personal affront. They're so very lovely, and too stupid to know it." He smiled and opened the door. "Have fun. Come see me again in a month or two."

As I walked back across the fields toward college, I called Alison.

"Hey, it's me."

"Will! Hey! I'm running out of the door, though, I can't talk."

"To where?"

"To work."

"Oh, of course." I could hear the click of her high heels on the hardwood floors of our apartment.

"What's up?"

"What do you think I should do after this year?"

"I don't know. Get a job?"

"Thanks, problem solved."

She laughed. "It's tough here right now. Kerry people are having a shitty time."

"What about your dad?"

I heard her turn the sink on. "He could probably help you, but more with a staff position like I got, or maybe with the DNC or the DCCC. None of the House campaigns are hiring, but who knows how it will be in a year."

"That guy I told you about last night, Jarvis, is in charge of this thing called the Swift Prize."

"Okay."

"Not that I would ever apply, it's just crazy. It comes with five years of room and board, and the annual stipend is twenty thousand pounds. There's no teaching, no . . . but only four people get it a year."

"So?"

"Nothing, really."

"Do you want to keep doing English? We talked about that. You can always come back and do your doctorate at Columbia."

"This professor—"

The sink turned off. "Will, you have to tell me you're not staying in fucking Oxford for five years."

"No! I'm telling you about this guy."

"I would love to see you do English, but I don't care about some prize that keeps you over there for a hundred years. As long as we're together, right?"

This was a talismanic phrase of ours. "As long as we're together."

"Shit, there's the doorman calling, my car is here. I've got to go, really I do. Bye, sweetheart. Call me later. Don't do this, please, don't make me worry. I love you."

I walked home, unconsoled, through a misting and irresolute rain.

That Saturday's Formal Hall was my first. It had been a busy week—classes had started, a few hours a day with a bright group, all of whom were consumed by Virginia Woolf or James Joyce, one or the other, nearly without exception. I was settling into the city. I could find all the main streets by now. I had forgotten about Jess, the whirl of life making that night seem very distant. When you start to feel as if you belong to Oxford, its walls rise around you. She was outside of them.

Tom, Anil, and I walked into Formal Hall together. We ate most of our meals in the same room, but it had been transformed, pushed backward in time. You can picture it, I'm sure, the sparkling candlelight cast upon half-full glasses of red wine, the byzantine ceremonies, the head porter in his tails, the young men and women in robes, the witty chatter building to a white noise. Along the walls were portraits of the Tudors; the food was inedible, the wine excellent; there was a series of ancient rituals to observe at each mealtime. All for the sake of twenty-year-olds on their way to dance to Usher songs at a place called Filth.

The first tradition we learned about, from the older students at the table around us, was grace. Before each meal the master said grace in Latin, and there was a bitter, centuries-old dispute between Fleet and Merton as to whose grace was longer. In recent years things had escalated. Fleet added a word to their grace to make it twenty-six words, Merton added two to make theirs twenty-seven, Fleet bumped over top of them again with twenty-eight. Then Merton made *theirs* twenty-eight, too, as a conciliatory gesture, but all the dons at Fleet put their heads together and added a word anyway. The term before I arrived, Merton, in the equivalent for Oxford graces of a nuclear attack, rewrote theirs to make it thirty-five words long. Fellows at Fleet felt the shame of this keenly. For months while I was there the dean walked around in a state of unconstrained grief.

The second tradition was pennying. If you could bounce a penny off of the table and into anyone else's glass while they weren't touching the glass, that person had, was absolutely required, to drink it down to the bottom. This was theoretically to save the queen, because the queen's picture is on the penny. ("These little bastards, ruining the best of Fleet's cellar by tossing copper into the wine," I once overheard the same dean say when he thought nobody was listening except the master.)

We arrived at Hall in high spirits. Tom and I, ready early at the Cottages, had spent half an hour watching Anil put on a fashion show. After several changes he emerged from his room in a black velvet jacket with gold epaulets, wearing a tie of scorching neon yellow.

"That tie is a little bright," I said.

"Haters gonna hate," said Anil, and he had a point.

At Hall we sat with Timmo and Anneliese, and then vigilantly watched the entrance of the undergraduate girls. They had arrived a few days before with trains of duffel bags and weepy mothers.

"At LSE the grad students got the pick of the undergrads," Tom whispered to me.

"At Yale the grad students were like lepers."

"Americans do everything backward. Even your toilets go backward."

"That's Australia."

We sat, poured out a glass of wine each, and were immediately pennied. As for Anil, he was pennied dozens of times but refused, imperiously, to drink, which alienated him from the undergrads around us. It also made him a celebrity. At the end of the night there were thirty or forty pennies in his untouched glass of wine, and the captain of the undergraduate rugby team had come over from high table to see the apostasy for himself, a look of deep consternation on his face. "Aren't you going to drink it?"

Anil, arms crossed, said, "Absolutely not."

"Blimey," said the captain.

That was later. Before they had served any food, Tom grabbed my arm. "Look," he said in an urgent whisper.

It was the Asian girl from the bar, with the pink and black hair and the tattoos. She was wearing a not-much-of-a dress. "Maybe she'll sit with us."

As if she had heard—though she couldn't have—she turned in our direction and caught us staring dead at her. She rolled her eyes and sat down in the first open seat she could find. In a way it made me glad Sophie hadn't come.

Except that then, ten minutes after our twenty-nine word grace, as we were eating soup, she appeared at the door, in a long gold and white dress, hair up, a glittering black clutch held in her two hands, almost as if she were nervous. She was alone. I wondered if she knew her housemates yet, and waved at her tentatively, as she scanned the room. When she saw me she smiled and came toward us. My heart fluttered. I made Anil move down.

I introduced them to her. She and Tom had friends in common, and places, too, which they discovered quickly enough. Then she spent some time querying Anil about his course and his origins. When the soup was gone and there was a moment when Anil and Tom were talking to each other, she turned to me, and we talked.

"I can't believe you saw me cry. You're in select company."

I laughed. "How did the breakup go?"

"It had to be done."

I nodded and raised my glass. "Congratulations."

"And you, do you have a girlfriend?"

"I do."

"What's she called?"

"Alison."

"She's here?"

"No, in New York."

In an idle tone, she said, "I wonder if it'll last."

For the rest of the meal she and I talked exclusively to each other, without any break. It was unusually easy, and as they brought dessert, a gelatinous cylinder of something, mousse, panna cotta, who knew, I realized that it was making me miss Alison, the presence of a woman near me—and that it was making me miss having sex, too. Sophie looked more ethereal than Alison did, as if she held more back, and also as if she lacked Alison's sturdy intelligence, but she traded it in for something more evasive, more alluring. She had very high cheekbones; light hazel eyes; slight, reddish lips; and a body that was slender but curved, long-limbed. She smiled more to herself than to me. I found her enthralling.

Though she was never very autobiographical, that night and in the next weeks I did discover a little bit about her. Neither of her parents worked. She grew up in a stone parsonage in Yorkshire, though they spent a month each spring in London and a month each fall in the French countryside, where she had learned to speak the language. Her father kept horses and pigs, and her best memories of childhood were of their matutinal visitations to the barn, each with a mug of tea. At the age of eight her parents had sent her—"I was sent," she said, using the passive voice, which seemed indistinctly sad, as if nobody were quite responsible—to boarding school. There she was unhappy, though she never elaborated on how, or indeed even said outright that it was the case. I could simply tell.

She did tell me one story about it. As a child she had asked for a dog every birthday, and on her sixth birthday she had woken up to find a springer spaniel puppy outside her door. Before an hour was out they were inseparable, and within a year I think she was closer to Chessie—as she called the dog—than to any human. She had no brothers or sisters. When the dog had thrush at a year old, Sophie didn't sleep for forty hours.

Two years later, with the car loaded to take her to boarding school for the first time, Sophie had gotten into the backseat of her parents' Land Rover—rather bravely, from the sound of it—with her dog.

"Why d'you have Chessie in the car?" her father had asked.

"She's coming with me, of course."

Her father laughed, a laugh that no doubt seemed innocent of meaning to him but to her, as a child, felt like a Roman emperor's whimsical malice—parents forget how long a single word can bore into a child, forever—and said, "No, no, she has to stay here. None of the girls will have a dog. Imagine!"

That was the worst moment of her life—and you could judge

her for that, for of course many people have many worse moments every day, but only if you don't remember what it's like to be little, and how it seems as if nobody could ever understand you.

"Is she still alive?" I asked.

"Just about. But she's old. Every time my mother calls I'm sure it's to tell me she's dead."

During high school she had spent a year away in France. She went to university at Durham—which is a kind of mimic Oxbridge, a consolation for the unlucky—and studied French literature. She was somewhat scornful of England, but she was loyal to her class, in favor of the monarchy, supportive without much interest of England's rugby and cricket teams, unable to imagine residing anywhere else permanently, even France. Still, she had imprinted on her character the restlessness, the half-hidden strangeness, of the traveler. I went to boarding school much later, at fourteen, but I think it helped me understand her.

She was telling me about Durham when Anil interrupted us.

"Sophie," he said, "would you like to hear how we cook soup in Mumbai?"

"Of course," she said politely, though it was evident that Anil had allowed for no other possibility in his mind.

As he rambled on I got pennied again. My hand had slipped from my cup as I stared at her in some indirect way; and I drank deeply again, and started to forget.

After Hall finished and the professors had processed away to wherever they drank port, we went to the lawns. There was a traditional handbell concert in Anna's Court at ten, but none of us were in a rush to see it except Anneliese, who ran down every English tradition she could find, corgis, clotted cream, faded gravestones. She must have seen the Ceremony of the Keys six times.

I was drunk. Tom and I lay on our backs, our ties loosened, gazing up at the stars. I've never been able to tell the constellations, though I don't mind. To know them would organize away what amazes me about stars, their random density, their numerousness.

They were all curious about America. It was Timmo who said, "Is it true everyone in America's fat, then?"

"Yes," I said.

His potato face expanded with pleasure. "Really!"

"Not the movie stars. Or the president. Or me."

"But mostly?" said Anneliese.

"No, no. I do remember thinking midwesterners were fat when I lived there."

"Where?"

"The middle part of the country."

"The Great Plains, they call it," said Tom knowledgeably.

"Some of it," I said.

"Where'd you go?" Anneliese asked.

"I was in Ohio. Iowa, actually, then Ohio."

"How fat were they?" Timmo asked, eyes gleaming. I've always thought there was something humorless about people in peak fitness. "Very fat?"

"I'm not sure how to say ..."

"Well, how many stone were they?"

"How much is a stone?"

"Fourteen pounds," said Sophie.

I thought for a second. "Maybe the fat men are twenty stone, or something. Really it's the fat kids, though. You would see a family of four, each eating like two hamburgers and a large fries, with a large Coke, and then maybe a McFlurry after that."

All of them looked gratified, especially Anil, at this intelligence. "Oh, dear," he said.

"I can't say I haven't done the same," I admitted.

"Why were you in Ohio?" asked Sophie.

"I was working for John Kerry."

"Mate, bad luck!" said Timmo, looking genuinely moved.

It was a sign that even someone as civically diffident as Timmo would commiserate with me, and there was a chorus of agreement. This was during the middle of the war in Iraq, two years after "Mission Accomplished," and Bush's reputation in England—which had never been high—was as a martial coward and an enemy of the poor.

"Was it fun at least?" asked Sophie. "The campaign?"

"It was amazing." The bottle of wine came to me. "Everyone's working really hard, and you're all tired but you're in it together, too, if you know what I mean, and there are constant little romances, and once every few days your candidate will come in and give a big rousing speech, and then you're always putting out fires."

"But losing must have been just awful," Anneliese said.

"It was."

It still felt fresh. I had been disappointed, for Kerry and for myself. I had been relieved to go home. I had been tired, definitely really tired.

Above all, I had been angry. I became interested in politics during high school, probably because it was considered a mark of intelligence, and when I reached college, and Clinton was president, the field had possessed a glamour for me—in its plain ambition, its competitive cleverness. I was a traditional liberal, for reasons that seemed self-evident, and which I probably acquired naively. Of course poor people ought to have better schools; of course the death penalty was wrong.

That glamour soured and my opinions intensified and clarified in the early 2000s. By the time I was in Oxford—partly because of the personal ignominy of losing the campaign—those feelings were too deep, ranting, almost embarrassing. I could see people retreat to politeness when I began to express myself, even like-minded people. I hated the president and his privileged, plausible, errant allies. What angered me almost to madness was that their rich and luxurious lives were, *like mine*, predicated on inherited privilege, and yet I felt—one always feels—that I was different. The inequality of circumstance for which I had felt guilty my entire life was to the president something to enshrine in the law. I would rather have shot myself than direct some minimum wage worker to pull himself up by the bootstraps. I looked at his face and could see a deformed version of my own—the British dream, inherited money and status, not the American dream, which seemed to me an outright falsehood by that stage. We went to the same high school and same college, Bush and I. I think I hated him even more than I hated the suicide bombers, young idiot kids, with who knew what mythology of early death and sorrow behind them, with who knew what loss traced into their rage.

I admit that even greater than my public anger was my own selfish anger. I had been born into a generation doomed politically by its stupid, credulous, narcissistic parents. These baby boomers! They were the reason Europeans grew wary now at my accent. They had squandered my good name, and the planet, too; they had squandered their own parents' legacy of stoicism in their welter of sexual and narcotic self-indulgence; in a few years they would squander into their maws the whole economy of the world and become the only American generation better off than both the parents and their children; and for all that they believed they had the moral high ground! They talked about Selma, Birmingham, and Vietnam, while my friends and I, brighter I think, certainly more responsible, at ease with the endowments of sex and drugs, smart, ambitious—we got to walk in pointless, well-meaning marches against Iraq, global warming, whatever. I had to live guiltily in the half-shadow of those my age who died at war, while all I could do was run off to Oxford, from the real world into a dream world, a coward with his self-righteousness and his anger, doing nothing about it now that the campaign was over. A hider.

Anger and anger and anger—and behind it disappointment, in the world and myself. That was what I felt when I thought about the campaign now.

There was no point in saying it just then.

"Aren't we supposed to go back to the lawns for the bell ringing?" asked Anneliese. "It's starting soon, too!"

"Fleet time," I said, yawning.

"I need to stretch my legs," said Sophie. "I'll be right back."

It was colder and my head had cleared. I watched her go, her long, lean body falling into the shadows. After a decent interval, I said, "I'll see what happened to Soph," and Tom winked at me. I frowned at him.

She was on the phone when I found her, and I noticed, with some surprise, that she was smoking.

She hung up just as I was reaching her. "You've caught me," she said repentantly. "But I'm glad it's you."

"Can I have one?"

"If you promise not to tell."

"Promise." I lit the cigarette she gave me, cupping my hand around the match to keep it out of the wind. "Aren't you glad you came out to Hall tonight?"

"I am glad, I am. I spent too long worrying about Jack for my own good."

"That's your ex?"

"Mm." After that answer she went silent, looking into my eyes for a period that grew less and less excusable. I found her so beautiful, painfully beautiful, her hazel eyes, her long and thick hair, with a thousand rich shades of copper, brown, auburn, and blond in it, falling around her bare throat, flying up around her face in the cold night, the faint scent of it creating some previously absent intimacy between us.

Why is it that a person can seem just right to you, once in a while? Perhaps it wasn't Sophie herself but everything about my life just then, being in Oxford, the heightened sense of chance, the distancing away from myself. As we stared at each other I felt sharpened by this newness into love. The stars and trees and wind, all of it.

As I had known she would when she handed me the cigarette, she leaned in and kissed me.

"Sorry," she said after a moment. I started to say something halting, and she laughed and turned her head away. "I'm sorry. Really, that was stupid. I drank too much."

"I like you. I barely know you, but I—"

"I like you too."

Oh fuck, I thought.

Here's a story.

Alison and I went to work for John Kerry at the same time, during the weeks before the Iowa caucuses. We were in Des Moines, operating from the state headquarters. At that point it looked certain that Howard Dean was going to win both the caucuses and the candidacy itself. Inside our campaign there was the disheartening sensation that we stood in opposition to a great popular tide of liberalism—but we believed that Kerry could beat Bush, and that Howard Dean, though many of us secretly preferred his politics, couldn't.

Alison was in the press shop, where she wrote the campaign's press releases for local news outlets, many of them to do with farming, the manufacture of farm equipment, and food processing, which were the three most significant industries in the state. She also occasionally appeared on camera, usually either for insignificant outlets (the Davenport, Iowa, CBS affiliate) or when they needed a young face (she was once on MTV). I was on the senior staff, meanwhile, consulting on the statewide vote strategy and, especially toward the thin end of the campaign, trying to organize endorsements. We had narrowly missed out on Al Gore, who had come out for Dean a week or two before, and we needed someone big. That night my job and Alison's dovetailed, because we were both trying to get Mike Polsky on the phone.

Polsky was a writer at the *Des Moines Star-Herald,* where he ran the editorial page. He was a bratwurst-and-beer guy with a thick mustache and big glasses, very intelligent but in his outlook essentially provincial. For forty-five out of every forty-eight months he wrote about ethanol subsidies, highway bills, that kind of thing. When he wrote about national subjects during those forty-five months nobody but Iowans listened or cared.

For three months out of every four years, however, around the time of the caucuses, he became more important, to those who really know about these things, than any national media member. His endorsement meant everything in central Iowa. About a week before the caucuses we had turned down Tom Brokaw because our guy, Kerry, only had twenty minutes between campaign stops, and Polsky wanted to talk to him. That was how significant the *Star-Herald* endorsement could be. Even Polsky's Christmas party, which for three years before the caucuses was probably more like a polka convention than anything you could find in D.C., turned into a K Street and Capitol Hill reunion.

That's the guy we were trying to get on the phone. He always published the morning of the caucuses, and before he filed we wanted to get a last word in—he loved Alison, liked me—or even, if he wanted, get him on the phone with Kerry one last time.

For hours now he hadn't picked up his phone.

"He's going with Dean," said Alison.

"It can't be Edwards, right?"

She snorted. "Come on."

We were in a closet with two phones and a desk, which because of the scarcity of space in any campaign headquarters was a grand fiefdom. Some junior organizer peeked around the door. "The Davenport turf is—"

"Get the fuck out of here and bother someone else," I said, in a tone that I can't imagine I ever used at Oxford but was second nature to me during the campaign.

The organizer apologized and left. Alison sighed and tore a chunk of crust off of a piece of cooling pizza. "What the hell are we going to do?"

Just then someone altogether more respectable, Rix, came in. He was the candidate's point person in Iowa, erratic but politically a savant. "Polsky?" he asked.

"Nothing yet."

"Jesus Christ, get your thumbs out of your pussies."

"We're on it," said Alison.

When Rix was gone, I said, "We're on it," in an eager voice.

She laughed and threw the crust at me. "What are we going to do?"

Around the campaign office we were a kind of golden couple. The candidate himself knew us by name and joked with us about our relationship. We were certain our first kid's godfather would be a president. Embarrassing to admit it.

"Maybe we should just go find him. We know he's not at the *Star-Herald* offices, right? I've bugged Myers about it like six times, Jennifer Fabianski, too. Neither of them has seen him over there."

Those were Polsky's bosses. "So he's at home. We can't go see him at home."

I smiled. "Why not? That's what Carville and Stephenopolus would have done." *The War Room* was our favorite movie. "Those guys didn't wait for things to come to them."

She sighed. "But if we rub him the wrong way—"

"Do you honestly think he'll endorse John fucking Edwards because two Kerry staffers bothered him at home?"

"I think that's exactly the kind of thing he would do, yeah."

I grabbed her hand. "Come on, Al. Let's do it."

So we walked out through the bullpen, where droves of volunteers were making calls, and through the staffroom, where Rix was screaming on the phone, and got in our rental car to drive out to the Des Moines suburbs.

It was, and had been, about five degrees outside. With the wind chill, five below. Even within the heat of the car nobody ever felt quite warm.

When we got to Polsky's house the lights were off. "Shit," said Alison.

"Polsky, you asshole, where are you?" I said.

Suddenly Alison gasped. "Jesus, is that him?"

I followed her eyes and saw a brown lump in the snow on his lawn. "No way."

We both got out of the car and into the freezing air—it was so cold that after thirty seconds you couldn't feel your face, the kind of cold that doesn't feel cold as much as painful, like an Indian burn— and ran to the brown lump.

"Polsky?" she said.

The lump groaned.

"Mr. Polsky?" I said.

"Help me, for fuck's sake," he said. His voice was sluggish.

We lifted him onto our shoulders. "What happened?"

He didn't answer. His knee was at a weird angle to the rest of his body, and I think he had been passed out. "We've got to get you to the hospital," I said, which is a sentence that sounds like a hospital-TV-show joke until you have to say it.

That roused him. "Gotta file."

"It can wait," said Alison.

We wedged him into the car and took him to the hospital. Once we got him there the nurses put him on a stretcher, and he disappeared for two hours, while we sat and waited.

"We should stay here, right?" I asked.

"Obviously."

"Rix has called me twice."

"Ignore it. Or text him."

Finally the nurse came out to find us. "You can see your friend."

"C'mon," I said.

"No, wait," said Alison, "let's get him something hot."

The soup we got him, honestly, I think, won John Kerry the caucuses in Iowa. Actually that's absurd—he likely would have won anyhow—but it seems to me now there's at least a chance that the last few thousand votes we needed to get to a plurality came out of that odd and fortuitous night.

Polsky was in a hospital bed in a curtained-off area, his face crimson red. As we knew him he was so solid, unusually midwestern, but he now looked different, ebbed down into nothing. "Frostbite," he said, "and a fucking broken leg. It just gave way right underneath me. I passed out."

"Here you go," said Alison and gave him the soup and a cup of hot tea we had bought him, too.

To our surprise, he started to cry. "You have no idea," he said.

"No idea about what?"

"You have no idea" was all he would say. I wondered if he had a wife.

"Is there anything else we can do?"

"Anything *else?*" he asked. "Besides saving my life?"

"Someone would have found you," I said.

"Maybe not," Alison said. She was more ruthless than I was. "Anyway, it was lucky."

Polsky shook his head. "Lucky. I was going home to file, I was gonna go play the big guy at O'Leary's, tease people about the pick, have everyone buy me drinks, not tell shit to anyone." O'Leary's was the bar where the staffers and the press met up every night and drank, a clearinghouse of sorts. He started to cry again. "I mean, Christ in a fucking Chevy, right?"

"Who'd you pick?"

He looked at us. "I hadn't decided. Kerry or Dean, one of 'em. I was still up in the air. Probably Dean."

"Well, shit," I said.

"It doesn't matter," said Alison. "As long as you're safe, obviously."

"Do you think Dean can beat Bush?" he asked.

"No," we said simultaneously.

"Do you have a laptop?" he asked. "I can get my Kerry piece off my e-mail. I write up all the endorsements, see how they feel."

"You don't have to change—"

"I'm endorsing John Kerry," he said, shortly.

I texted Rix. *Al and I got him. Long story. Back late.*

Nobody at the headquarters slept that night, we were so elated. A bunch of us, the senior staff, sat around on the couches, talking about the campaign, about who would get what job in the White House when we won. We played Scrabble and got through huge urns of coffee and refreshed the news Web sites to see what was getting play.

Polsky's endorsement loaded onto the *Star-Herald*'s Web site at seven in the morning, and twelve hours after that we won.

The ecstasy of it was overpowering. Everyone thought we'd come in third, maybe second. It was certainly the end of Dean, and effectively the end of Edwards.

It also marked a turn in my relationship with Alison. Throughout the party that night we kept grinning at each other, and right after Kerry spoke—stopping on his way to the podium to say, "Nice work on Polsky, lovebirds"—we went to an empty conference room and fucked. When O'Leary's closed at four in the morning we picked up burgers at the all-night diner, in a group of ten or so, all of us full of the future, since when you win it seems impossible that you'll ever lose, and then she and I went back to our little studio apartment, the one the campaign rented for us.

Before that night our relationship had been loving, but we had never promised each other too much, in all those years. Now it was something else. "I hope we're always together," she said as we fell asleep.

"We will be," I told her. "This is just the beginning."

Of all the hours I've spent on earth, rising and falling away like waves, I think that I was happiest during that one.

I thought of that night when Sophie kissed me, nearly eighteen months after Iowa; I thought about Alison and realized where we had come from that night, realized that I was in trouble. It was too much of a change, too fast. Jess I could ascribe to madness or unsettledness, but now twice in two weeks I had kissed other people—and Sophie was a different kind of trespass. Or maybe I was just spiraling, or at rock bottom, whatever language of crisis people use—and I understood then why that language exists, it's a comfort to have it there, as if elsewhere, in other places, it's happening to them, too, so often that they need phrases to describe it, it's not just you.

"Do it one more time," I said to Sophie.

She laughed and turned away, and I thought she was going to leave, but she only flicked her cigarette onto the wet cobblestones, then came back to me and put her mouth against mine, cool and soft—tasting faintly of cigarettes and red wine—tasting of silence.

CHAPTER THREE

Idon't know what I thought would happen the day after that. Certainly something dramatic. I woke up—the guilt fainter, perhaps because I was growing accustomed to a sense of such terrible transgression—and half-expected Alison and Sophie to walk through the door together. It shows, the world is always less about you than you think it is.

In fact, it played out differently. When the group went to hear the bell ringers, Sophie had slipped away, and when I saw her two days later she was merely friendly, not unlike Anneliese or Tom. I wondered if she had chalked it up in her mind to free wine and start-of-the-year mischief, or to the end of her relationship, or perhaps even forgotten it.

So it went for that whole first month at Fleet, seeing each other here and there, friendly, unromantic. In those weeks I began to talk to Alison as often as I could, and at the same time I thought about Sophie obsessively. Whenever I went to Hall for a meal I scanned the room for her, and when I passed the laundry room I would hope to see her big blue bag lying on the dryer, because if it was there it meant she would be killing time in the MCR, watching TV or reading. Coming home from class I always looked to see if her white Vauxhall was on the street—she called it "Little Car," and loved it—because twice I had been in the right spot and she had picked me up to drive around on errands, killing the afternoon together. For the first time since high school I experienced that thrilling boredom beneath an unspoken crush, which makes going to McDonald's for fries a stomach-fluttering experience. I remembered for days afterward every accidental physical touch between us, some of them sneaky—letting my leg fall in next to hers as we slouched down on the couch, collapsing into her with laughter when Anil freestyled for us in the MCR one day. Of course, that was all inside of me and nowhere else.

Besides, there was a whole new life to get used to. The first days passed gradually away, and before I realized it I had already been in Oxford for five weeks. The city's wide, intimidating thoroughfares became intimate to us, as we moved outward from Fleet to the bars and the bookshops. During the week after the first Hall, we started our studies in earnest—or rather, with varying degrees of earnestness. Tom did next to nothing, for example, while on the other hand Anneliese began to work long shifts in the history library on Holywell Street.

I have always had the habit of solitude, and I spent a great deal of time on my own, at lunch counters each afternoon, and two or three times a week at the Ashmolean, where I liked to sit by the *Night Hunt* and read. I used to escape at Andover the same way, a respite from the fetor and dirty imaginations and long-running jokes of the dorm, which we loved and loathed at once. It had probably been then that I last spent so many aimless hours with new friends.

These weeks were happy and full, passing in soundless avalanches of contentment. My classes I found deeply absorbing. I had friends—Tom and Anneliese especially—and seeing Sophie gave life a gloss of excitement, without, in the end, changing anything. By the Thursday of Fourth Week, in fact, when Alison came to visit for three nights, I was myself again, removed from the recklessness of those first days. I had only needed time to settle.

Her visit was unremarkable, which was the best thing I could have wished for. Tom and Anil both happened to be out of town that weekend, and so she didn't meet any of my Oxford friends, which seemed strange but apposite. We spent a lot of time in my room, did a little bit of sightseeing. There was a twinge of unreality about having her there. When I dropped her at Heathrow she shed a few quiet tears and walked her solitary way, looking back once or twice, past security, but there was nothing histrionic in it. We had developed a routine by now—a quick call when she woke up at six o'clock, eleven in the morning for me, a longer one when I was done for the day and she was in the doldrums of the afternoon, eight o'clock in England, three at home, cards and letters when we thought of it, and e-mails buzzing back and forth between us all the time— and I knew that would be enough to see us through to the safe harbor of Christmas vacation.

The longer I stayed in Oxford the more confounding the university came to seem. It was very beautiful, home to first-rate researchers and teachers; it was also a scam.

One day I walked into the Fleet MCR and found a group of nine Chinese students, arguing furiously. I knew one of them, Fu-Han, and when he came to the kitchen for a glass of water—I was making coffee—I asked him what it was about.

He waved a frustrated hand at me. "Google."

"What?"

"Our government, it doesn't want us to use this Web site, Google," he said.

I told him I'd heard of it. Fu-Han was a statistician, but he was also more distinctive than the other Chinese students, who tended to be well dressed, polite, and superficially unexceptional. He wore a silver necklace, for example, and he played guitar (appallingly). He sighed and said in rudimentary English—all he spoke—"Most of us, first day we get here, we look up, right, on Internet, Tiananmen Square, Mao Zedong, Hundred Flowers Movement. Like, we can read the truth? But still some of us don't want to know, good behavior, yeah?"

"What is the Hundred Flowers Movement?"

He couldn't be bothered to explain. "Communist event, yeah? So, but now, our government doesn't want us to use it, Google. But we need it, right, for work! For translation! And some of us want to but some of us want to do greater obedience?"

"Okay."

"So, we argue." He shrugged. "Stupid."

"What did you think of Mao, on Google?"

"Ha. Real asshole."

I laughed.

These Chinese students were emblematic of Oxford's flaws. Compared to the great American universities, Oxford is poor, and these students were admitted for financial reasons, nothing else. I liked them, and to make it to Oxford from China meant they were very likely enterprising or brilliant or both—but of the group, six or seven spoke no English whatsoever when they arrived in England. Every college had a similar-sized contingent. They stuck together, working at one table in the library, sitting in the same corner of Hall. To pass their courses they would translate all of their work through Google into Chinese, then translate it back through Google into English. They would pass, just barely, through hard work, and primarily because they studied math or statistics, subjects that didn't demand language skills.

It affected the university. At its core it was still ridden with luxury—each college had a wine cellar worth millions of pounds—but on the peripheries it was a miserly and mean-spirited little place.

Nobody remembered you; in the lesser departments files were lost, the copiers were from the 1980s, the public computers were laughable—like the KGB after the money ran out. Everything was badly run, especially in comparison to Yale, which seemed to me, in retrospect, like one of those exquisitely managed golden-age ocean liners.

Still, I never really think about all that now.

George Orwell once wrote, "There is a widespread idea that nostalgic feelings about the past are inherently vicious. One ought, apparently, to live in a continuous present, a minute-to-minute cancellation of memory." When I think of that fall, and settling in at Oxford, I feel stirred somewhere within to remember how happy I was. Is that the same as sentimentality? If so, is it vicious? I don't know. I'm in the unhappy position of thinking sentimentality is insidious, but of feeling it at the same time so strongly, so deeply. I don't think I idealize Oxford. That's where memory can go wrong, it's true, when you use it as a weapon against the future, or when you bind it up too tightly with regret. I don't regret that I'm not at Oxford. I did love it there, though.

For me remembrance is mostly taken up with acknowledgment of death. When my life fulfills its only precondition—its own ending—my memory will vanish. Nothing is being recorded, nobody is keeping score. Your childhood bedroom, your first kiss. They go with you. Better to think of memory as like food, or sex, or books: a reason to believe in the perishable days. A way to manage being alive.

In the fourth week of term Tom's sister, Katie, came up from London to take us to lunch. She was back from the Middle East for ten days on vacation.

I heard her before I saw her. As I was bouncing up the stairs of our house after a morning at the Bodleian, I could hear a woman's voice singing "On the Street Where You Live" on our floor. I reached the top step and saw Katie, standing in our bathroom with the door open, putting makeup on. She had a quiet, pretty, unstrained voice.

It was surprising after hearing her voice to see that she was ugly, with horsey teeth and intelligent green eyes couched in big, red, laughing cheeks, no makeup. A silver cross on a necklace was the only flair she had of individual style. She looked sunburned a dozen times over.

"You caught me singing," she said when I came back out of my room. "You must be Anil, right?"

"No—I—"

She smiled. "I'm only joking. You're Will."

I laughed. "I'm Will."

"My brother is in his room. I'm Katie." We shook hands, and she called out to Tom, then turned back to me. "Will you come out and eat with us? My treat."

"I'd love to."

"I'm afraid it's only going to be Pizza Hut. It's been Tom's favorite since he was four."

"It was my favorite, too."

"Our parents never took us, either. Not that they were especially against it, just it wouldn't have occurred to them, I don't think, and when Tom asked they didn't seem to really believe he wanted to go there. Except we went there for one of his birthdays. Lord, he was happy. Anyway, that's what big sisters are for, Pizza Hut."

Tom's door opened behind us and he came out. "Katie, shut up!"

Katie laughed. "Such a curmudgeon, such a grown-up."

Half an hour later we had a large pizza, half pepperoni and half mushrooms and onions, and three sodas. There are few things as distressing to anyone who pretends to the title of world traveler than to be seated in an American chain restaurant abroad, but I was happy; in fact, the primary softening of the attitude of my English friends toward my homeland came when we were discussing Kentucky Fried Chicken or Jerry Springer or the show *Alias*. Another proof of soft power in the decade hard power failed.

Tom was less acerbic than I had seen him before, and it was easy to picture him and his sister as childhood companions: explorations together, pillow forts, arguments and tears on small red faces. What was strange was that Katie had none of his aggressive class fealty, and around her, Tom didn't either. I wondered if it had calcified at the death of their parents, since he was still at school, while she, because she was a few years older, had been less in need of armature.

"Will," she said, "I have to compliment you for being much more congenial than the last friend of Tom's I took out. Do you remember, Tom? Daisy?"

"Oh, Christ."

"Daisy was Tom's girlfriend at LSE. She was a very beautiful girl, too—the idea of her in a Pizza Hut is impossible—and Tom called beforehand and begged me to take us to, where was it? Brown's? No, it was the Wolseley? Somewhere with all sorts of Sloanies and Americans—excuse the example, because I love Americans—snap pictures of each other with the waiters. Maybe I should have said Germans. Tourists, at any rate. I had just been posted to Syria—"

"No," said Tom, "you were leaving for Syria in a week. It was close."

"That's right, that's right. Anyway, I was telling Daisy about the Druze, this minority religion in Syria—fascinating, really, they're Muslim but subscribe to some really ancient Gnostic beliefs. And as I spoke she nodded, politely, and then at some point, still nodding, she pulled out a clothes catalog and started to flip through it."

I burst out laughing. Tom was shaking his head sheepishly. "It was a copy of *Vogue*."

"*Vogue*! That's right!" Katie grinned. It made me miss my family. "He feels the need to date these mean, posh girls, but I've always told him that what he needs is someone *nice*. That's the girl I hope he marries, the first nice one he meets, and for my part I hope she's a milkmaid, or works at a makeup counter, or... or I don't know what."

Tom rolled his eyes. "Let's move on."

"I do want to hear about Syria," I said. "Tom told me you worked there."

"I'm a liaison between the British Embassy in Damascus and all the other embassies there, so the American Embassy, we deal with them a lot, and then of course the embassies of the other Middle Eastern states."

"How'd you start doing that?"

"When we were little our parents took us to Egypt, and ever since then it's what I've been interested in. I studied Arabic at university and took the diplomatic test, and now..." She shrugged.

"You must hate Bush."

"No, she takes after our parents," said Tom. "They liked him. Will worked for John Kerry, Kates."

"I don't like him, Tom! I think he's terrible. But then I think Blair's terrible, too."

"You're a Tory?" I asked.

"You've gone pale," she said.

"He's just surprised that you're nice," said Tom.

"I didn't mean to be rude," I said.

"No, don't mention it. I don't think we should be waging a holy war against Islam, or anything like that. In fact, I love it there, the Middle East. I was desperate to get posted there. Your first assignment's always in the sand, they say, and for most people it's a curse, but I was so pleased. Certainly I'm to the left of your president. I wouldn't mind seeing Cameron go in, but that's as far as I'll push it."

"Not his president," said Tom and grinned.

"Do you hate Bush, then?" she asked.

"I do."

She laughed and looked at her watch. "Our train's at two thirty, Tom." They had their bags; she was taking him down to London and they were going to stay at their childhood home over the weekend. It was Katie who had decided to keep it. "After lunch with Daisy, Will, I asked Tom how it was going with her. I was scrupulously fair to her—didn't bring up *Vogue*—and I remember Tom saying, 'You'd better brace Mum and Dad, because that's the girl I'm going to marry.'"

"*Katie!*"

"I'm sorry! I think it's sweet—you were so sweet. You still are."

"I'm not sweet, I'm a scourge," he said.

She took his hand. "You *are* sweet. Will, take good care of my brother while he's up here, okay?"

It was the next day that Alison called me with news.

"Hey, babe, it's me, guess what," she said.

I was walking through Trinity College's front quad, to meet my adviser. It was a wet afternoon, and I knew he would have a fire and tea, so I wanted to get inside, but I stopped. "What's up?"

"My dad might have heard about a job for you."

"Seriously?"

"It's nothing concrete yet, but he's on the case."

"Starting in the summer?"

"No, it would have to be right away."

I didn't say anything for a minute. "I don't think I could take that kind of job."

"You haven't even heard what it is."

"But I just got here—it's not as if I can leave after a month and a half."

"Okay." Then she paused for a while. "I thought you missed me so much."

"I miss you like crazy, but what would going out on a campaign do about that?"

"At least you'd be in America."

"Yeah."

"Why don't I find out whether the job is available," she said.

"No, really, don't worry about it." I looked up at the clock tower—I was a minute late already. "I don't know—what is it?"

"No, don't worry about it," she said. "You were right. You have to go through with it, now that you've started." There was another pause, then she added, "You're not applying for the Swift, are you?"

"Alison. Come on."

"No, I know, we've talked about it."

She didn't point out—this time—that I hadn't told her I was applying to Oxford. "Should I e-mail your dad?"

"Yeah, maybe, just to say thanks."

"I do miss you. It was so nice having you here."

"I know, baby. I miss you, too. I love you."

"Talk at the usual time?"

"Of course."

The MCR officers were constantly organizing: day trips to London, soccer brunches, pub walks to track the Inklings. One Monday night, in Fifth Week, they sent out an e-mail offering a limited number of spots at Merton evensong. Merton was the oldest and among the most beautiful of the colleges, on the last full cobblestone street in Oxford. Its library was the oldest in continuous use in Europe. Its chapel, whose acoustics were famous, was used to record choral music. They would be recording the evensong.

I asked Tom to go with me.

"It'll be all Americans and Japs," he said.

"I'm not sure 'Japs' is the preferred term."

"It sounds like tourist bullshit."

"If you don't go with me, I'll tell Anil your nickname."

He looked at me with narrowed eyes. "What did my sister tell you?"

"Tommy Bear?"

So he came along, and as we entered the hush of the chapel we saw, at the same time, someone we knew: the hot Asian girl from the bar at Fleet. We still hadn't met her. She was standing in the antechapel.

"Now aren't you glad you came?" I asked in a low voice.

She had a new streak in her hair, besides the pink and black. It was silvery. She was wearing a demure, unshredded oxford, unusual for her, but you could just see a sliver of flat stomach between it and her skirt.

"Hey!" said Tom.

She turned. "Oh. Hey."

"Is anyone else coming from Fleet?" I asked.

She looked at her phone. "My friend Virginia was supposed to, but she canceled."

"I know we've met, but I'm Tom. Law."

"And I'm Will," I said. "English."

She rolled her eyes. "I'm Ella. Ravenclaw."

We laughed, but her face remained impassive. When people began to filter into the pews, she waited to see where we led and took the other side.

"What's wrong with her?" I asked.

"No idea. I find us irresistible."

Merton was beautiful. Of course, like most of the old chapels it was what you would design if you wanted people to believe in God, light slanting in paler and weakened from the very high windows, the voices, the stone, a serious house on a serious earth. I don't especially pay attention to the words in church anymore. Instead I let my thoughts sift into each other at random, a meditation: like falling asleep. Sometimes I fall asleep, too.

The evensong began, and in fact the music was as beautiful as I had hoped. I tracked what was happening in the program. Did I have some vague Easter recollection of the Magnificat? Or was it from a CD cover? My grandfather was a deacon at St. James's, too, on Seventy-first and Madison. It's a shame, perhaps. Orwell always said that in a different age he would happily have been a country vicar.

In the eyeline from our pew was the doorway of the church, swung out open—it was still warm—and as the Nunc Dimittis began something terrible happened: An older man, wearing a Merton tie, was walking along when his foot caught the lip of a flagstone. He looked as if he had been hurrying to make it into the chapel.

I immediately started to stand up, but then I saw that two young men were just behind him, his children, probably, along with an older woman, all of them having previously been obscured by the door, and I sat down. "Look," I said to Tom.

"Should we help?"

"They're okay, I think."

As the service went on we watched and whispered as he was treated and then, finally, borne away in a wheelchair.

It was painful to watch it, an interesting small moment, but I mention it only because of what happened at the end of the service. Ella, who sat at a diagonal from us, oblivious to the old man's fall, practically burst out of her seat and toward us, furious. "Have some respect, dickheads," she hissed.

"What?" I asked, confused.

"You can't tell each other jokes during fucking *church*."

Tom, genuinely surprised, said, "We weren't."

"Right, you're both big Christians."

"I am, actually."

I hadn't known Tom was. I shook my head, with what I hoped was a gentle smile. "Not practicing. But I'm sorry about the whispering. We weren't making jokes."

I explained to her then in detail what had happened, and her face changed as I did, from anger to appraisal. After a beat, she said, "Oh. Sorry. I shouldn't have assumed."

What's funny is that Ella, though she had been raised by stridently Christian parents, wasn't herself religious any longer—in fact, she was there solely for the music. Mollified, she walked out with us and then, to our surprise, agreed to have a drink at the Merton bar. It was thus, improbably, that we became friends.

She was from a small town an hour outside of Seattle and had gone to Stanford on a scholarship. Her parents were immigrants and now owned three nail salons—but were not rich, because both were terrible spenders, always in and out of debt, never finding more than seventy cents in a dollar. She had come to Oxford because her adviser was the best biochemist on earth, she thought. Here, too, she was on a scholarship. "I can barely afford this pint," she said, that first night, and laughed. We had already talked about our initial encounter in the bar at Fleet, several weeks before, and she said, "You were just what I thought Oxford would be. Arrogant rich kids."

"Us?" asked Tom.

She shook her head. "Everything here is expensive. Everyone always wants to go out to dinner, or to get drinks, or wants to go into London. My stipend, besides my tuition, covers books and food. That's it."

"Could you get a job?"

"I could, but I just want to get my degree as fast as I can, get the fuck out of here, and start making some money."

It seemed a funny ambition, because she was so different, her hair, her clothes, her tattoo. In the next few weeks, as we grew surprisingly close to her, we began to understand: Both parts of her, angry and ambitious, were characterized by drive, but like so many people of that nature she was, if you were in her heart, exceedingly gentle.

Tom paid for the next round; it was obvious to me that halfway through it, unbeknownst to Ella herself, he was infatuated with her. I never heard him say the word "Japs" again, anyway.

On the Saturday of Sixth Week there was going to be a bop, the first big one of the year at Fleet's bar. The theme was Moulin Rouge. Because it had been my hardest week of work so far I was looking forward to it especially; most of the last four nights I had stayed up finishing an essay on *Enemies of Promise*. My usual haunts at Fleet—the bar, the Hall, the Cottages—I had abandoned in that time for a solitary carrel and a thermos full of coffee.

On the Saturday of the bop I got a text from Sophie.

Are you going tonight? If so dressing up?

Of course.

What about now? Am at loose ends.

With Tom, we're bored. Punting?

Perfect.

It was my first time. We went into the boathouse and fetched the pillows that went in the middle of the punt and the long pole that you used to push yourself along.

"I'll go first, shall I?" asked Tom.

"I don't see why you should. I want to have a go," said Sophie.

"I'll just start us off. I did it once with my sister."

So Sophie and I sat facing each other in the middle of the boat, or really came closer to lying down, our hips about even and our legs crossed and propped on opposite sides of the punt. She was wearing a hooded sweatshirt and jeans, the hood pulled up against the wind and stray wisps of auburn hair flying across her face.

It was beautiful. The swift river was no wider than an alley in some parts, and there was a breeze, scattering red and yellow leaves onto the water. High above us the towering trees on either bank met and twined in the warm sky.

We had two half-bottles of wine rolling around the bottom of the punt, outriders for the great troop to follow that evening, and we had ice, gin, a bottle of tonic, and three glasses stolen from Hall. It took one gin and tonic to get Sophie tipsy.

We were a ways down the river when she said, hiccupping, "Let's play I Never."

"Is that the same as Never Have I Ever?" I asked

Tom looked uncertain, but Sophie said, "It is, it is. Jack played when he visited the States."

"You go, Will," said Tom.

"Why me?"

"You're the American, you're supposed to be an extrovert. Sophie and I've got British restraint."

Just as he said that Sophie hiccupped. "Extremely genteel," I said.

She laughed, and then someone, maybe even her, started the game. By the time we got to the pub, we had passed through several rounds:

Tom: *Never have I ever had sex in the Bod.* Nobody drank. "We all have to do it at some point," said Tom. "It's an Oxford rite of passage."

Will: *Never have I ever hooked up with a British person.* Tom and Sophie drank.

Sophie: *Never have I ever hooked up with an American.* Tom and I drank.

Tom: *Never have I ever worn a T-shirt that misidentified both my nationality and gender.* I drank.

Will: *Never have I ever fallen into the Cherwell.* Nobody drank, but I tried to push Tom in as retaliation.

Sophie: *Never have I ever had a threesome.* Nobody drank. "Sophie's raising the stakes," I said.

"STORY!" bellowed Tom, giving the punt a hard shove forward.

"No!" she said. She was laughing. "I've never done it. I thought all boys wanted to. I think it's disgusting." She had the giggles, which made us laugh, in lessening waves, until there was a long moment of silence. She dragged her fingertips along the water, looking up at the warm autumn sun, and said, "I love this. I want to stay forever."

"In Oxford?"

"It already feels like home," she said. "Better than real home." It was a strange thing to say: Of the people I knew at Oxford, the three in that boat were those most inclined to self-concealment, and she more than either Tom or me, I think. I don't mean that she was a cipher—indeed sometimes her feelings were too plain, her coloring making it easy for her to flush, her sensitivity real and acute and deeper than most people's. Nevertheless there was always a final expressionless retention of privacy to her, even at moments of great intimacy. I thought it was the same as for me: early pain, and then the impassive years, retreat, outward blankness, panic. Tom, whose parents had died so recently, was less cool, more erratic, more available.

"Five years of French, though," I said.

"I like French."

"Have you heard of the Swift?" I asked.

She laughed. "Of course. Who would I have to sleep with?"

"Maybe you should apply."

"I wouldn't get it. French isn't very academic, unless you do theory or literature. I'd like to be a historian somewhere pretty, who gets to visit Paris twice a year."

This, too, was odd about her: Her friends from Cheltenham and

Durham were in the usual garrulous professions, marketing, fashion, the BBC. Another sign of interiority, perhaps. Or ascesis. Or liability even.

Soon we reached the pub. It was the usual docking station, but we didn't have time to go in because the punts were due back an hour later. Tom said he would run inside to get us beers for the trip back downriver.

The wind gusted up after he left, loud and blustery. Each of us looked away. Ammons said it—how strange we humans are here, raw, new, how ephemeral our lives and cultures, how unrelated to the honing out of caves and canyons. We looked up at the trees and down at the river, the difficult majesty of the world. We were silent.

Her hand found mine then and took it, until our fingers were twined like those high branches over the river. She had been looking over her shoulder at the fields across from the pub, scattered with cows and hedges, incidents of life, but she turned back to me and in her gaze acknowledged for the first time in five weeks, since that first Hall, that there was more than friendship between us. I felt my heart quicken.

"You know I like you," she said quietly.

"What do you mean?"

She sat up and crossed her legs Indian-style, so that our faces were close together. "What do you think?"

"Like that?"

"Like that. But you have a girlfriend."

We were still for a moment, staring into each other's eyes. Then I kissed her. It was only a touch of lips, but I felt dizzy with happiness; I could smell her hair, feel the cold of her cheeks, I could feel her body moving closer into mine; it seemed all imminence, all future. Our hands were still together.

"Mm," she said, eyes closed, a sound of satisfaction, the sound she made sometimes when she smiled.

I saw Tom opening the door with an armful of beers. "He's coming," I told her.

"Don't say anything."

"No, of course not."

I don't remember punting home. When I got back to my room I was hollow with nerves. I called Alison.

"Hey," she said.

"Hey. What's up?"

"I was asleep." I heard her moan, shifting under the covers. "Shit, it's late. I went out last night with Christian and Margaret, down to a new place on Jane Street. I can't remember what it was called, but there were tons of people you know there, for one that asshole Patrick—"

"Alison, I have to say something."

Her guard went up right away. "What is it?"

Are there are any words you can say, during a conversation like that, that don't sound as if they came from television? In a way, as well, she was the one person I most wanted to tell about Sophie, the person who knew me best, who could have comforted me. She would have understood the faint anguish of wondering for every minute of the last six weeks what Sophie was doing. There was nobody who understood more than Alison, and as I considered this I loved her especially.

"I can't believe I'm doing this on the phone, but I think we need to take a break."

There was a long silence. "You're joking, right?"

"I'm so sorry."

"Oh my God, Will. Oh my God, don't say that, you can't—"

You know what she said, all of the usual things, specific to us this time around but part of every conversation two people have who have loved each other and are breaking up. I searched for relief in her voice, or anything that would pardon me, registration, even ambivalence. None of it was there. Only disbelief and anger.

After we had been speaking for more than an hour, she asked, sniffling, "Do you love me?"

"I love you as much as anything."

"Then what the fuck, Will."

"I'm not ready. It could be that in a couple of years I'll be ready."

"I wish you knew how shitty that sounded."

"I do."

She laughed somberly. "No, you don't. What's funny is that I knew the second you applied that this shit was going to happen. Do you remember me telling you that? On the stoop that day? You're so fucking restless all the time. Listen to me: You're going to hate this. You're going to be so unhappy. Because now I'll be what you don't have."

"I know it's true."

"But still?" When I didn't say anything she started to cry again. "Oh my God, you asshole."

I was hurting someone I loved, and as the words came out of me I think I almost would have taken them back. Her voice made me want to cry, too. She had experienced none of the emotions I had since I had come to Oxford, neither the sense of alienation nor the subsequent fear of that feeling, the clinging love it induced.

"Is there someone else?" she asked.

"Of course not. I can't imagine loving someone other than you, or wanting to be with someone more than I want to be with you. And maybe we will end up together! But right now—"

"Just don't do this till Christmas, Will. Wait until then and we can actually *see* each other and touch each other and—"

"I'm sorry."

"What about my dad? What about—"

"What?"

"What about our stocks?"

"What, that Apple stock?" Her father had given this to us once, as an early wedding present, he said—we had laughed that off but had both, I believe, felt bound by it, just as perhaps he had intended. "I don't know. That's not a reason ... I don't know."

"So you just want to split it?"

"I don't care about it, no, or I mean—listen to me, it's not that I can't see us still having a life together, Alison, but right now I feel like I'm twenty-five and I ..."

There was another pause. "What? You feel like what?"

"I'm sorry."

She was silent for a while. "I was just thinking, yesterday, I was thinking about that night senior year? At Miya's. Your surprise birthday."

When she said that my eyes started to sting, and a lump came into my throat. "Al."

"Do you remember how happy we were? I was thinking about it because I saw Patrick, he was there, and I can still picture exactly where everyone was sitting, and how much we all loved each other."

"Maybe down the road—"

"This is the road, stupid." She started to cry again.

"I'm sorry," I said.

"You're not, you're not," she said helplessly.

"I do love you."

"Will you call me tomorrow?" she asked. "Just call me, so this isn't it. This specific conversation can't be it, this conversation."

"Of course I'll call you tomorrow. Tomorrow morning."

"We had Christmas at your house last year."

"I know."

"I don't know what I'm going to do."

"Don't do anything. Just give it a day."

She blew her nose. Her crying had subsided. "Okay."

"Alison, I never want to hurt you."

"It's fine, it's fine," she said at last, her voice distant now, as if she were calling from a faraway world, where people kept their promises. "I'll let you go."

She didn't, though; we were on the phone another forty minutes, until at last we hung up. I didn't feel any of the sense of liberation I had expected. I tried to remember Sophie, but it didn't give me any joy, away from the spell of the trees and the water, not just at that minute, and I went over to my desk and looked at the picture of Alison and me that I had there, from Halloween, her dressed up as a cowgirl, me as a cowboy, and I was still buzzed but in an unhappy way now, and it all felt like too much, I felt alone, and I wanted to take it all back, I wanted none of it to be true.

Tom was in town, picking up his costume for the bop, and I couldn't get Anneliese on the phone, so I called Ella.

"Hey, it's Will," I said.

We had hung out nearly every day, meeting up to watch movies or have lunch, in the three weeks since evensong at Merton. "How was punting?"

"Can I come hang out?"

"Your voice sounds funny."

When she said that I decided not to tell her. I cleared my throat. "Better?"

"Yeah. Come over! I'm getting ready for the bop. Can you bring drinks?"

"I have wine."

"Perfect. If I'm in the shower, just let yourself in."

Before I left I put on my costume for the bop—a bunch of us

were going as the Rat Pack—and took a shot from a bottle of Patrón that Timmo had left in my room. I fucking hate tequila, and the bile of the taste, my theatrical shuddering, improved my mood.

Ella lived two doors down from us in the Cottages, in the kind of room that anyone who has been to college has seen a hundred times, with a corkboard full of photos of her and her friends, scarves dimming the lamps, a prettily made bed, and a live, un-placeable scent, a girl's room, candles and laundry, drifting in the air. If you met her you would never have guessed she had that kind of room. Except for the posters. They were all for bands I didn't know.

She only listened to two kinds of music: punk and (the one that had taken her to Merton that day) classical. Her parents had made her practice the clarinet for hours every afternoon as a child, and instead of making her hate the music it had made her love it. She listened to it constantly, and after she put a CD on she had the vex-ing habit of asking, "Do you know what this is?" when she knew nobody had any idea.

"What do you think this is, William?" she asked. She had come to the door to hug me, and now she was rifling through her clothes.

It was some symphony. I looked very serious, narrowed my eyes as if I were thinking hard, and said, "This is *Cats,* right?"

She looked back at me disbelievingly, a blue top in one hand, and said, "No, you idiot, it's *Finlandia.*"

"No, no, this is from *Cats.* I saw it on Broadway with my grand-mother."

"It's not fucking *Cats!*" She grinned and shook her head. "I'm getting in the shower."

I drank more than half of the wine from the bottle I had brought while she was showering, and e-mailed some friends about Alison. I felt shivery, manic. It had been a long time since the future was a secret. I turned off *Finlandia* and put on loud music.

When she came back she called out over the noise, "Turn it down! Let's talk!"

She was in a white towel, smooth-skinned, still damp. For half a second I thought about trying to kiss her.

"I have vodka," she said, walking over to her desk. "Let's do a shot."

"To what?" I asked.

"To evensongs. Prost."

I took a shot glass from her. "To evensong."

We drank that one, then another. "Can I tell you a secret?" she asked a few minutes later, as she put her makeup on in the mirror.

"What?"

She turned and grinned at me. "I might let Tom kiss me tonight. If he's lucky."

"What!"

"I feel frisky. Dressing up. Drinking. You know."

"You punk rock chicks."

She laughed. "We love to kiss dudes, it's true."

"How about second base?"

She gave her boobs a heft over her towel. "He should be so lucky."

The drinks hit me all at once, or something else did, and I said. "Let me see."

She looked at me, in the mirror. There was a soft smile on her face. "My tits?"

"Yeah."

"You're drunk."

"Before you're Tom's."

"Are you crazy?"

"You don't have to. I was joking."

She squinted at me in the mirror, smiling but suspicious. Then, after a beat, she turned and let her towel drop, and I felt a huge pulse somewhere down in the root of my body. Her nipples were hard, small, and pink; a strand of wet hair stuck to her left breast.

"Wow."

She giggled and lifted up her towel. "That's the only time that will ever happen."

You would think it might be awkward after that, but it wasn't; the drinks had done their work. I felt ready to see Sophie; ready to start the whole folly, love and fucking and fighting, over again. I texted Alison something comforting and indeterminate then turned my phone off for the night.

Jem had been working all day with a committee of five first-year girls to turn the college bar into the Moulin Rouge. The night before he had sent out a Facebook message inviting two dozen people to come early, including Ella, Tom, and me, nightly stalwarts of the bar. We stopped by my house and shouted up the stairs for Tom, but he wasn't there.

Anil answered instead. "Hey, gangsters!"

"Anil, come down!" Ella said.

"It takes a great deal of time to become the brown Frank Sinatra!" he shouted.

"Well, fucking hurry!"

"I'll be there in good time, my friends!" he shouted back at us. "Go without me!"

At the bar Jem's exhausted harem was putting the final touches to the decorations, then staggering upstairs to put on their sluttiest dresses. (The reward for their labor was free drinking till eleven, by which time they wouldn't need any more.) Jem waved us to the bar, where a line of undergrads stood. He addressed us.

"All right," he said. "This is a lockdown situation. The bop starts in twenty minutes and before then nobody will get into this room, and I mean not the fucking Master himself. Not the fucking chancellor of Oxford." Everyone nodded, awed. "Let's do some shots."

With some ceremony he depressed a button on the jukebox, and a whoop went up at the opening chords of the college anthem, "Back for Good," by Take That. When it came on everyone in the bar would wait until the chorus and then sing along: *Whatever I did, whatever I said, I didn't mean it: I just want you back for good.*

Jem poured fifteen shots of lime vodka and at the chorus we downed them and then sang in unison as he poured another round. On the second chorus he had two shots ready. Fifteen minutes later we were already drunk. Jem opened the doors.

The first people in were Anil, wearing a fedora and a pinstriped suit, with a cigarette holder between two fingers—I felt a wave of affection for him—and Tom, who, true to his public school breeding, had dressed up as a woman: Shirley MacLaine.

"You look ludicrous," I said.

"I feel marvelous."

The bop started at nine o'clock, and by nine fifteen it was a melee. At nine thirty Jem, looking harassed, beckoned me up to the bar and shouted over the dance music, "You wanted a job, right? Come work for forty-five minutes, just while the first rush is on, and it's yours."

"I should warn you I'm drunk."

"That's ideal."

So I poured drinks for the dense press of people, sweating in my suit, mixing up orders, accepting five-pound notes from high-spirited girls whose outfits would have shamed their teachers at Marlborough, until at last there was a break in the crowd—just in time for me to see Sophie come in.

I waved at her. "Come get a drink!" I called.

She looked beautiful. Do I say it too much? Certainly I thought it all the time. She wore a white, summery dress that just showed the push of her breasts, and a white headband pulled her hair back. She leaned in and kissed me on the cheek, then instead of retreating held her face close to mine so that we could understand each other.

"Who are you supposed to be?" I asked over the noise, still having to shout.

"Lauren Bacall! You know she named the Rat Pack, right?"

"Shit, I should've been Bogie. He went to my high school."

"What are you doing back there?"

"Bartending."

"Are you going to work all night?"

"Only until ten o'clock."

"Come have a cigarette with me when you're done."

I smiled. "Okay. Do you want a drink? On me."

"D'you know, I still feel tipsy from that gin in the punt."

"One more won't hurt."

She smiled at me, her cheeks dimpling, and in her mellifluous English accent said, "Just a Red Bull and vodka, then."

I made it and handed it to her, promising I'd be outside at ten.

As it happened I couldn't get away from the bar until ten thirty—I texted her to change the time to then—and when I waded out among the revelers Ella caught up with me from behind, wasted.

"Are you off to kiss her?" she shouted, hips swaying, the red straw in her glass crimped under her finger as she took a sip.

"Who?" I asked.

She grinned at me. "Just do it. Don't even think about it."

"Okay," I said.

"Where the hell is Tom?" she asked.

"Are you off to kiss him?"

"Fuck you, Baker," she said and laughed.

By then the feverish dancing was at its crest, and when I went outside to the flagstone terrace it was mostly empty. Sophie was on the phone, the ice cubes in her empty drink crowding each other as she tipped her cup up to get one last sip from it. When she saw me I got an apologetic eye roll, and she mouthed, "Just a second," and walked away.

I sat down on a bench, cooling off in the night air.

"Sorry," she said when she was done.

"It's fine. Cigarette?"

She looked behind her toward the bar, where we could see Anneliese and Timmo. "Yeah, but let's hide from Anneliese. She'll get cross with me."

"Shall we go out by the river?"

"Oh, let's," she said and smiled.

I couldn't tell what I thought about her, as she walked a half step ahead of my pace. Was it love? No, I was too cynical to agree to that, and too jarred.

She intimidated me. I had reached the point in life when the ignominies of middle school were long gone, but still as I watched her walking that night, her cool, pale shoulder blades jutting above the back of her dress, the gazes of pimpled undergraduates following her, I understood that like all beautiful women she reflected back to me a simultaneously heightened and attenuated sense of what I was worth.

The black night was crisp, full of stars and moonlight, and as we crossed the wide lawns the trees by the river listed in the wind. We went and leaned up against the boathouse. I took a pack of Dunhills out of my jacket pocket and gave her one, which I lit.

"Cheers," she said.

"Are you cold?"

"It's warm enough."

Probably it sounds as if we were alone, but in fact it was quietly chaotic by the river. There was a newly minted couple discreetly making out against a tree, and two drunk freshmen who were shouting at them from a safe distance, and someone trying to unlock the punts to steal them, and someone else trying to climb into the tennis court, which was surrounded by a high fence.

Our hands found each other, and she looked over at me quickly, smiling.

"Can I kiss you again?" I asked.

She put her arms around my neck. "I wish you would."

We stood there for twenty minutes then, our hands underneath each other's clothes and in each other's hair, our breath quick, our skin a strange mixture of hot and cold. I felt overwhelmed by a longing for her body—not a sexual one exactly, but as I kissed her I wished I were kissing her, as I touched her breasts I wished that I were touching her breasts. My desire overran reality. I couldn't understand it.

Finally we stopped, only because the undergrads had at last loosed one of the punts from its chains and were making down the river in it without a pole or paddles, laughing wildly, drinking from bottles of beer, unsure of what they were doing.

"Tossers," she said affectionately. We watched them until they were around a bend in the river; then she turned to me and took the lapels of my jacket in her hands, pulling me close and grinning. "Alison's a lucky girl."

The one thing I knew I wasn't going to do was tell her that Alison and I had broken up. It was too soon. I didn't even know my own mind yet—and though I wouldn't have admitted it, there was also part of my brain that was worried about losing Alison's father. I kept thinking about that job.

I looked at Sophie and my mind changed.

"I broke up with Alison tonight," I said. "After we went punting."

She let go of my jacket and looked at me. "You did?"

"Yeah."

"Shit, Will."

"It doesn't mean anything about us—not at all. It was just the right thing to do, regardless of . . . of whatever."

"Shit," she said again.

"What?"

"There's something you should know. You remember my boyfriend, right?"

"Your ex?"

She never talked about him, though once she'd mentioned that he had just left Sandhurst. She looked up at me without speaking, and after a second I understood it.

"Oh," I said.

"That day—"

"Right, right." I paused. "You said you liked me."

"I do."

"But . . ."

"No." She took her arms away and turned toward the river. "I made a mistake. I thought you had a girlfriend."

Faintly I could hear the noise of the bop. I felt sick with unhappiness; I could still taste her mouth on my lips, but it already seemed to have happened, our kissing and touching, a long time ago, somewhere else.

"Maybe you should break up with him," I said.

"I can't do that."

"Why?"

She stepped back. "I've been wrong," she said. "I'm sorry, Will. Really I am, I swear."

As I was going to say something, a cry came up from the lawns, a hundred feet away, and we both turned to look. It was Anil, tearing toward us and laughing helplessly. On his heels was Tom, his dress drenched, shouting, "Anil, you fucker, get back here!"

Anil flew by us with a huge, winning grin, and then Tom, now laughing, too, smacked my arm as he careened by, and as I turned to watch them go Sophie squeezed my hand and said, "You stay here," and took off back for the large bright din of Fleet.

CHAPTER FOUR

Michaelmas ended not much later, twelve days. There was a weeklong break; very few people from the Cottages planned to remain in Oxford for it. Anil had flaunted his first-class ticket to Mumbai, Tom was going to meet Katie in Dubai for four nights, and even Ella, chronically short of money, was traveling to Budapest with the Fleet Chamber Orchestra. My original intention had been to return to New York. When I knew that I didn't have to see Alison, however, I called Delta and pushed my flight to Christmas.

The fallout at home from our breakup was severe but distant from me, the way a thunderstorm sounds when you're swimming in the ocean and dive down. Friends called me to express their disbelief; my mother cried; in Oxford, of course, no one had met her, though Tom, Ella, and Anneliese were all sympathetic. Really the only part of it that affected me at all was Alison's voice—for we still spoke nearly every day. Our conversations were mild, unimportant. I think we were trying to make our separation gentle. There's that horrible moment after a breakup where you realize you've gone from knowing everything about a person to knowing nothing about them, when you go from getting worried if they're twenty minutes late to dinner to learning months after the fact that they went who knows where, on safari, to Antarctica, to the moon...

"You could still come back," she said when I told her I was going to be alone for a week.

"I should work," I said.

I wouldn't be alone, either: The other person who stayed behind was Anneliese, and we spent the week together.

Everyone departed on a Friday, and she and I had a bleak night at the Turtle, emptied now of all but its hardiest patrons. Even half of them seemed to be asleep. The leather twins, scowling, simply waved us by without checking our IDs.

As we left, one drink later, we vowed not to repeat that dejected experience, and by Sunday we had developed a routine. Each morning we went to get coffee and eggs at a restaurant in town called Porter's, and then we would retreat to the warmth of the MCR to spend the rest of the morning watching a movie. After that we separated for a couple of hours to work at our libraries, and then at five o'clock we would bike into town—I had acquired a clumsy black single-speed bike by then, a necessity in Oxford—and find somewhere to hang out.

I remember one day in particular, either Tuesday or Wednesday of that week, when we stopped into Blackwell's, a bookstore on Broad Street, opposite the Bodleian. We spent hours reading in two armchairs, with big stacks of books between us, occasionally talking. At seven we wandered down to the Turf for our evening beer.

The Turf was a low-ceilinged place, blackened by time and smoke, and had one of its original menus posted over the bar: a wood panel that read DUCK OR GROUSE. In the summer they opened a stone terrace in front, but in the cold the best seat was a plush curvetted bank in the bow window of the front bar, with pint glasses hanging above you in a brass rack. She drank cider (much cloudier in England), and I had a Guinness.

One of the last books she had been reading at Blackwell's was about youth culture and Germany, and jokingly I said, "So, did that neo-Nazi book convert you? Are you a Nazi now?"

Very seriously, she answered, "You can't say such things to a German, Will."

"No?" I asked, surprised. "I'm sorry, Liese. You're the only German person I know."

"Then you only know half of one anyhow, because I only grew up there a little," she said.

"I thought you were from Berlin."

"I am." She had a curious German music to her voice, one of those rare German voices, always female, that sound beautiful. "Or my family is now, you see. I grew up in Japan until I was nine, then in Cologne, and just before I went to university my parents and my little sister returned to Berlin. They live there now."

"Japan!" I said.

She nodded and laughed. "In Tokyo."

"Do you speak Japanese?"

"Badly. I went to the American school there."

"That's crazy."

She laughed. "Crazy. That's the only word you and Tom ever say. I don't think I even learned it in English class—that way, I mean."

"You probably didn't learn any slang."

"We did, too!"

"Like what?"

"We would say 'cool' or that something 'rocked.'"

"Yeah," I said, trying not to laugh, because Anneliese was famous at Fleet for misusing colloquialisms—saying she didn't give any shits about something, using the word "jester" instead of "clown." ("You are honestly being two jesters!")

"Anyway, what German slang do you know?" she asked irritably. She knew why I was grinning.

"You have me there."

"Then I came here, and you all say different things, like 'crazy' or 'peace out' or calling somebody a gangster."

"That's just Anil."

She furrowed her brow. "Hm."

I took a sip of Guinness. "So did you feel like you weren't at home in either place? Like, German in Japan and Japanese in Germany?"

She nodded. "Mm—yes. Like that third-culture book."

"What's that?"

She looked at me with surprise. "I suppose it might have been more popular in Germany than here? It describes children who grow up abroad, how their families have one culture, their environment has another, and out of confusion they become, what's the word, hybrid. A third culture."

"A feathered fish." She smiled. "I think everyone feels like that, not just people who grew up in Germany and Japan."

"No, no. You have the same framework of references as the people who were born in America in 1981, you know. I don't. My references are all mixed up. In fact, they've proven that someone like me would be more compatible with a person from … with a Swedish-Mexican, say, than with Hans."

She giggled. Hans was an angry Bavarian who studied linear geometry at Fleet. "Poor Hans."

"Oh, Hans isn't so bad. But yes."

"Well, then I'm glad to be a third-culture kid."

"What do you mean?"

"I grew up in America and now I'm here."

She laughed, that inimitable pitchy laugh anyone who knows her would recognize even on the end of a transatlantic phone line, or across a crowded room, and said, "That must be why we're friends!" She held up her beer. "Cheer to that."

I raised my glass. "Cheer."

We walked back to Fleet, Oxford's ramparts and battlements white and cool to the touch, never gold any longer as they had been in the long evening hours of our first arrival, when it was still just summer. Our destination was the bar, which amid all the dimmed windows of the college was bright and at least a little lively, since—I should have said—Jem was there over the break, too. He had stayed because his parents didn't know he smoked, and he couldn't face a week of sneaking cigarettes and spraying himself with Febreze.

He kept the bar open for a few haphazard hours every night, and gradually the three of us got into the habit of meeting up to play the video quiz machine. Jem could answer questions about science and British sports, I did movies, books, and art, and Anneliese knew everything about history and music.

We won eight pounds each, and at a little after ten o'clock Anneliese and I said good-bye to Jem and left. We thought we would watch a movie in the MCR. As we left she seemed quiet. I wondered what was on her mind. Soon we were passing through Anna's, and she put a hand on my forearm, stopping me.

"You mustn't think about it all the time," she said softly, looking into my eyes. Her own eyes were gray and beautiful, comprehending. "Truly."

"Okay," I said.

"We can speak if you like."

"No, no." She was probably Sophie's closest friend in Fleet. "Maybe later. I've been talking about it with you too much."

"I know. I worry because you stopped."

There was a huge blue couch in the MCR's TV room, and we gathered up all the blankets and put on one of the Harry Potter movies. Both of us fell asleep during the movie and slept through straight till daybreak, when the sun woke us up. Then we made coffee and finished the last half hour of the movie, laughing together, before we separated to go work at our departments' libraries. Again before we parted she gave my forearm a squeeze, and as I cycled toward Manor Road, I remember thinking: *friendship. The highest pleasure.*

In the two weeks before this, between the bop and the term break, I had gradually fallen into a terrible agitated state of anguish, the kind I had forgotten existed, in which I could think of nothing but Sophie. It hadn't been quite so bad at the start of that period of time, when I assumed I would continue to see her in the MCR or at Hall—but she stopped coming. When I realized her absence I felt first glad that I could have a clean break from her, but then slowly it began to make me uneasy, and at last, after four or five days, I became obsessed. I would wake in the morning and immediately wonder what she was doing, and though in those first moments of consciousness I would tell myself that today would be different, that for instance I wouldn't check outside of her house to see if her car was there, after a few minutes I would find myself walking outside to the street to check nevertheless. Certainly I wouldn't text her; but then every morning I texted her, something innocuous, asking if she meant to be at lunch for instance, and it would be agony until my phone pinged, which usually it didn't, but if it did I would feel such delight—except that it was always Tom or Anil, someone, until I hated the sight of all names but hers. Other than classes I spent my days on my bed, watching TV shows on my computer, trying to distract myself. There was no way I could concentrate enough to read. I began to push for an earlier and earlier start to our evenings in the Fleet bar, until eventually I began to go over alone at six o'clock and wait for everyone. On the way I would check the MCR to see if she was there, and then the laundry room. Then I would check the Junior Common Room's laundry, which was out of the way, to see if she was using it instead to avoid me, since I had once seen her blue laundry bag there, though I couldn't be sure it wasn't just an identical bag, and anyhow she was never there. If nobody had come to the bar by seven I would walk back to the Cottages to see if her car was still on the street. If it was gone I would sit on the brick wall outside of my house, looking at my phone intently, as if I were contemplating a very important message, and then usually I would text Anneliese and ask if she knew where Sophie had gone. She sometimes did. At moments it seemed possible to me that I literally wouldn't be able to live any longer. Even physically: There was a kind of persistent low-grade nausea and a pain in the nerve endings of my skin, which made it horrible when my clothes shifted or I was lightly touched. Throughout the day I looked at the pictures on my phone—my fixation, like a wood fire, nourished by ravaging itself—because three or four of them were of us, until I reached the point when even the pictures on either side, of Anil or Timmo or whoever, had become familiar to the point of abstraction.

I saw Sophie in person twice during those twelve days. The first time was by accident, and in fact when I least expected it. I had a meeting at the English Department, and for once my mind was away from her. As I left the building I saw her striding down St. Cross with a tall dark-haired guy in a blazer and checkered pants, and worst of all a Blues tie. I watched them until they disappeared, and then stood there a while longer. It hadn't been Jack.

The next time I saw her was outside of the Cottages. It was the Thursday before vacation, a day before most people were planning to leave. She was loading her car. I was in love, I thought when I saw her. I thought of Alison. "Sophie!" I called, heartsick. She had taken up so much of my mental life that I had partially forgotten she was real.

She turned. "Oh, hey, Will."

"Where are you going?"

"I'm off home. Well, I'm going to see Jack for two or three days, then home for break."

Her bags were stacked on the curb. "Here, let me help."

She was wearing a down vest, puffy enough to make her look small and fragile. "Thanks."

"How've you been?" I asked.

She was going through her things in the car, avoiding my eyes. "Really busy."

"Hey, did you hear about those kids?"

"What kids?"

"The ones who stole the punt?"

She looked up. "What happened?"

"They got rusticated."

"What, *expelled*? For what?"

I shrugged. "For stealing a college punt. I think they get to come back in Trinity term maybe, but they won't graduate with their matriculation."

"That's crazy."

"I know."

She glanced at her watch. "I do have to go," she said and opened the car door. "I'm already running late. Have a good vake?"

"You, too. Give Chessie a hug for me."

For the first time she looked at me with warmth and, leaning toward me on one foot, gave me a fast hug. "I will. Bye."

That was the worst afternoon. At first I thought I had handled the whole thing well, but then I wasn't sure. There was a great deal I could have said. It was colder by then and grayer, and when the sun appeared it was sharp and white, not soft and yellow. For a few days the geese had passed southward overhead. *Two or three days*, I kept thinking, and though I imagined them having sex, the image that had more force to make me unhappy was of them walking hand in hand. For some reason as I envisioned it she was looking up at him and smiling, her face full of unwonted animation, and he was looking off into the distance—she was working for his affection—and the setting, though I had no idea where he lived, was a country lane, except it looked almost like the bird sanctuary at my high school. *Two or three days.* That night I got horribly drunk and fell asleep early, and when I woke just after midnight I was drenched in sweat, with a metallic taste in my mouth, as if I needed salt. I turned on all my lights and ate something. Then for a long time I stood at the window and stared out at our backyard, at the river. She had seemed so final by the car, somehow. At last I went back to sleep. When I woke up the next morning, the hour-to-hour pain of missing her had diminished, but the feeling of loss was stronger. Perhaps it was because she was gone. Everyone left that day, and then in the next week Anneliese's company taught me to turn my mind away from the whole thing.

Most of these days I spoke to Alison. There were any number of times when I nearly asked her to forget it all and get back together. I didn't, though.

One day during the term break her father called me from New York. "Will, it's Jim Sawyer."

"Hi, Jim."

"Alison gave me your number." I could picture him in his mid-town office, a regatta pennant and a fraternity picture from Dartmouth over either shoulder on the wall behind him, his epaulets. Squash at the Racquet Club with a former governor that afternoon, a room at the Four Seasons later where he could peacefully paw at his mistress. "What is all this she tells me?"

I wanted his good opinion still. "As much as I love Alison, at this stage—"

"We welcomed you into our family."

"I'm grateful for that."

"Right, right. Well, this is a courtesy call to let you know you're not going to get near Democratic Party politics again. What do you say to that, wise guy?"

I almost laughed. Wise guy! He didn't have that power; but then, I thought with a disconcerted premonition of future anxiety, what power did he have? To what degree could he make his threat true? Halfway?

"If you ask Alison, I don't think that's what she would want," I said.

His voice got cheerful. "You fucked up. Bye, Will."

Alison laughed when I told her about the conversation but didn't contradict what her father had said. I started to wonder about that job she had mentioned, a week or two before we broke up, and for a while then I would get a panicked feeling, about her, about work, about Sophie, when I woke up at the three in the morning and stumbled into the bathroom to piss: What was next? Why had I come here? What would become of me?

After vacation everyone had returned with stories of fun, but they left it behind them at home; cold, dreary, unweathered days, early December. I knew from Anneliese that Sophie had come back, but I only caught glimpses of her. I tried not to look for her. Most of my time I spent at the library, working.

Finally I did hear from her, though, in the second week of the new term. She sent out a group text, which read: *Hey everyone—will you come out on Friday? My BF is in town and wants to meet you! Will be at the Turtle from 8:00, first round on me!* Then I got a personal text, in which, though I parsed it like a scholar of the Torah, I couldn't discern much meaning: *Really hope you can make it.*

I decided to go, though I knew it would be painful. Tom, Anil, and Ella, who had separately offered in light voices to do something else, seemed relieved, and the four of us went together, waiting patiently in line outside to receive the benediction of the two bouncers before we went again down the murky stairwell.

Sophie was at a table with four guys, and the one nearest to her had an arm around her shoulder, though he was turned back toward his friends. That was Jack, I knew. I had seen him on the river a couple of months before.

In time I came to know him. His full name was Jack Lyme-Taylor, but usually his friends, and even she, called him the Jackal, or just Jackal. He was tall and handsome, with a particular type of reckless charisma that I knew by then was bred into upper-class boys by their public schools. He was broad-chested, with short hair and ruthless blue eyes. His face had an expression free of self-doubt, and I think that despite his love of house music and ecstasy he was a vestigial creature, belonging to an age when a man might live eighty years without being contradicted by any person other than his father.

He was capable: He could score a try, tip a bellman, ride a horse, sit the stroke of an eight, dance a waltz, and slaughter whatever country estate animals the time of the year demanded. Then there was his name. It was Timmo who explained that a hyphenated last name—a "double-barrel"—was considered aristocratic in England, presumably because it meant one of his great-grandfathers had married a woman of such high birth that he had agreed to append her name to his own. His father was a half-famous man called Captain Waldo Lyme-Taylor, often in the glossies as the squire to a royal at some hunt ball. He'd had Jack very old, at fifty, and now lived most of the year in Africa. He always looked badly sunburned in his *Tatler* pictures, wizened up, preserved in the salt of his name.

"Jack, these are my friends from Fleet!" said Sophie when she saw us, nudging him in the ribs, and rose to kiss us all on the cheeks.

"Pleased to meet you," he said, not quite looking at us, and turned back to the person he'd been talking to.

"Jack!" she said in an outraged voice.

"What?"

"Come meet them!"

He looked at us stonily, sighed, stood and shook hands, and said that he was Jack, in a tone that suggested the fact was currently more of a burden than a pleasure to him. He muttered his friends' names.

"What up, gangsters?" asked Anil.

Oh Jesus, I thought. "Yeah, what's up," said Jack.

"We haven't seen much of you this fall," I said. They had made room, and we sat down at the table.

"Been training," he said.

"Training?"

He looked at me as if I were stupid. "The army. At Sandhurst."

"Oh," I said.

"You a Yank?"

"Yep."

He nodded, as if really that said it all. A song ended, and the silence of our conversation merged uncomfortably with the silence of the club. At the opening notes of the new song Anil perked up, and said, "Oh, I love this! It's Big Pun!" Jackal's interest in Big Pun was so slight that he merely offered a phatic grunt and, as if conceding our failure to us, turned back to his friends.

"I'll get the next round," I said, and exactly as I had hoped she would, Sophie said, "Shall I come, too?"

Waiting our turn at the bar, she said, "I'm sorry if this is shitty for you, Will. I hope you don't want any drama."

In my mind I had grown so close to her, had made her such a part of my life, that this surprised me, because it showed that on some level she didn't understand me at all, how highly and antiquely I value reticence. "Of course not," I said.

"I am sorry, really."

"It's fine. I mean, I do like you, of course, but," I said, trying to sound calm.

"The thing is I'm in love with Jack."

"You mean with Jackal?" I asked.

She looked at me beseechingly. I noticed that she had on a gold and ruby pendant, which I thought was new. I couldn't be sure, but I had mostly memorized her. "Will, please, just pretend nothing ever happened between us."

Even as she said that, she took my hand in hers under the bar. "Okay," I said.

"I have to go. I'll tell them I have to go to the bathroom. Please, Will."

Ella came up thirty seconds later, pink and black hair tucked back behind one ear and falling loose over the other, and I was relieved to see her, a friend—and she was a girl. Anneliese was away that weekend.

"Sophie had to go to the bathroom?" asked Ella.

"I guess."

"I came up here to help you."

"Thanks."

She smiled. "They like Tom at least," she said. "He's ignoring us now, too." She looked at me intently. "Maybe you and I should get two extra Orielgasms, just for us."

"Okay."

"Don't be sad, please." She studied me. "You like her, I guess?"

"Yep."

There was a pause. "You know, I like Tom," she said.

I was taken aback. "Really? Not just at bops?"

"He's ignoring me. It doesn't help that one of Jack's friends keeps trying to feel my boobs with his elbow and make it seem like an accident, either."

I laughed. "I don't think he's ignoring you," I said. "He likes you."

She looked up at me with hope. "You think so?"

It was one of those moments when you see that the depths of other people's insecurity is the same as your own, that if only we could admit it, we'd see we're all in the same bind—but we can't. "I think so. If anything he's probably given up. He had a crush on you."

"Why the hell didn't you tell me that?" she asked.

"You couldn't tell?"

"At first when we all started hanging out I could, I thought I could, but then, I don't know . . . maybe I got in my own head." She looked guilty. "I wondered if maybe he didn't like Asian girls. He's so racist."

In the next couple of hours Jack got very drunk, like military drunk, and sometime later when we were all dancing he heaved an anchoring arm around my shoulder. "Hey!" he shouted over the music and, it felt like, the lights. "You're Will, right?"

"Yeah," I said, thinking that he knew perfectly well that was my name.

"Just wanted to say, no hard feelings, mate."

"Sorry?"

"With you asking her out. It's no big deal. I wish everyone could have a girl as good as Soph. It's a battle out there, love, you've got to fight hard, you've got to . . . but didn't you know she had a boyfriend?"

"That was before I knew her very well."

"No hard feelings, like I said."

About ten minutes later, dancing near Sophie but not too near her, trying to be a friend—being pathetic, in other words—I spotted, out of the corner of my eye, my townie, Jess, in the same spot on the same dance floor where we first met. My face lit up, and we moved toward each other.

"It's you!" she said.

"No, it's you!"

I was drunk, and I tried to kiss her. She pulled away. "No, no, no. You're the one with the girlfriend."

"Not anymore!" I shouted back.

"Really?"

"Yep!"

"Are you lying?"

"I swear!"

She looked at me suspiciously, then sort of smiled and kissed me back. I wondered as we started to make out whether Sophie was watching.

It's hard to be miserable when you're having sex, though I tried, for form's sake.

We were back at her apartment again. She put on a CD—the Yeah Yeah Yeahs—when we got to her room, and lit a row of tea candles along the windowsill. I loved looking at her body, her hard nipples, the bridge her panties made over her hipbones before she slid them off. I buried my face in her neck, in her dirty blond hair.

I had introduced her to everyone at the club, and Jack had, not very subtly, started to make fun of her accent. Finally they had fallen out.

"Where do you work?" he asked.

"In a teashop near Blenheim Palace."

"And where did you prep?" Jack asked.

There was an explosion of laughter, but Jess, phlegmatic, rolled her eyes, less bothered than I would have been in her position. "Some of us have parents who don't want to send their kids away to get bummed by prefects," she said. "They love us."

Jack's smallish eyes went hard. "No, really, Jess, let's hear it, where did you go to school? St. Paul's? Maybe it was Marlborough?"

She stood up. "You're a schoolboy Bullingdon fuckwit," she said. "And just so someone tells you, you're about twenty percent as good-looking as you think you are. Your forehead is huge, for one. Come on, Will, buy me a drink."

Jackal's face was surprised and then scornful. I shrugged and stood up with her, and Sophie, whose eyes had widened, almost smiled at me. Ella followed us loyally to the bar, not Tom.

"These Brits are such idiots," Ella murmured to me as Jess ordered drinks, and I smiled and nodded in agreement. "It's like imagine if we took country clubs seriously."

Jess and I had our shots (woo-woos, God help me) and decided to leave. "Sorry about that guy," I said as we got in the cab. "I barely know him."

She ignored me and called up to the front seat, "Have you got the radio? Louder, please." Then she said, "Let's make out until we get home," and put herself in my lap.

I didn't sleep afterward, though she did. I lay there for a while, content. Finally I decided to go. "I have to get ready for a breakfast at college," I whispered to her, gathering up my things.

"Liar," she murmured in her sleep. "Find me on Facebook already, would you?"

"I will, I promise."

As I was walking home in the pale purple light that fills the sky before the sun—it was the same path home I had taken on that first night Jess and I met—I called Alison.

I could hear the noise of a bar in the background. "What are you doing? Isn't it like five in the morning there? It's midnight here."

"We had a night out."

"Are you drunk?"

"Stone cold sober. I had my last drink like two or three hours ago. We've just been watching a movie. Listen, Alison—"

"What movie?" she asked.

"*L'Avventura.*"

"And that didn't put you to sleep at three in the morning?"

"Listen, Alison, I need you to promise me you won't hook up with anyone for a while. Don't make out with anyone at the bar tonight, okay? Where are you, R Bar? Or one of those places on Rivington? Hop Devil?"

"Excuse me?" she said with an edge of anger in her voice. The noise of the bar got fainter, which must have meant she had left to hear better, and she was out on the sidewalk. I could picture New York around her so clearly, my home.

"I know, I know, but imagining you with someone else makes me unhappy. Can't we say neither of us will hook up for, I don't know, six weeks, or something? Just until then."

"Do you know how weird that is to say to me?"

"Have you hooked up with someone already?"

"No. Have you?" she asked. "Did you tonight?"

"Jesus! No, of course I didn't. It's been on my—"

"Because you call me at five in the morning, telling me you don't want me to hook up with anyone, and from where I'm sitting—"

"Alison, no. You're misreading me. Please, I'm just asking that we have a grace period thing, where neither of us hooks up. For each other's feelings."

She was silent. "Okay," she said at last. "If you promise you won't."

"I promise," I said immediately.

I think of the great poem: *The self, what a brute it is. It wants, wants.*

I can't make any excuse for myself, beyond describing the almost existential sense of relief, of possessiveness, that I felt when she gave me her word. It was so much more powerful than the guilt. All of the white lies and the black lies I told Alison that year, I don't know, I'm not sure. They're even less defensible because I was so sensitive to pain myself. I was young. Still, I knew it was wrong even then. It doesn't mean I didn't do it.

For several days I didn't see Ella. I texted her and she didn't reply. Finally on a bright Thursday morning I went to her room and knocked on the door.

"Who is it?" she called out.

"Will."

"One second."

"I can come back," I called out.

"No, you're good, one second."

She answered the door in her pajamas. Her hair was a snarl, her eyes puffy. "Hey," she said.

"Are you okay? You've been missing."

She frowned. "Not really."

"You have, since the Turtle. For a second when you didn't answer I wondered if Tom was going to be here."

"God knows where he is."

"Did anything happen?"

"Not really, no. I tried to kiss him."

I wasn't fooled by the dispassion of her voice. "He didn't kiss you back?"

"He was acting weird. And then I realized that while I had been talking with Sophie, after you left and everything, that he had been with some girl, dancing. I think he went home with her. He knew her from somewhere. Jack did, too. You wouldn't believe how they were acting, talking about all this stuff I don't know about, posh stuff."

"Shit."

"I shouldn't have tried. I feel like a fool."

"Why haven't you been around? Or answered my texts?"

She shrugged. "You two are best friends."

"So? That doesn't matter." She didn't answer, and I understood. I touched her arm. "Let's go get coffee."

"I have no money," she said.

"That's okay."

"No, I really have no money."

I saw her face: grim, as it had been the first times we saw her, and now perhaps close to dissolving. It was one of those times when the world feels against you. "My treat," I said. "I just got a check from home."

"Well, hooray for you."

"When you have a hundred patents and I'm an English professor you'll have to fly me to Davos, or wherever. Just consider it an investment."

She settled down—she was never very volatile, a still person—and we walked into Blackwell's and got coffee and sandwiches. When I asked Tom about the night later that day he answered cagily, not mentioning Ella at all, and we never talked about it afterward.

Though there was a forlorn and lovelorn spirit to those early winter weeks, mostly full of studying, there was one bright spot: Timmo's audition tape for *Big Brother*. He decided to make it once and for all, not long after we met Jack and I saw Jess again, and he asked for help from me and Anneliese. It took a couple of days.

The footage they had already shot consisted for the most part of Timmo working out. Evidently Anil had scored it, because the soundtrack was mostly Nas deep cuts. Once in a while Anil himself slipped into the footage to change the CD player in the corner of the room, offering a thumbs-up or a giddy wave to the camera before he left the frame.

I told Timmo it wasn't what *Big Brother* wanted, unless possibly they needed an education in the recent work of Talib Kweli.

"But that's me, that's Timmo," he said. "England will love that."

"Only if they get to see it," said Anneliese. "Then they will, of course. But will a workout tape on its own get you onto the show?"

"There's a gym in the *Big Brother* house," he said.

Anneliese, always inclined toward generosity, said, "Perhaps you're right."

"He's not," I said. "Anyway, are you sure you really *want* to go on a reality TV show where there's a camera in the bathroom, Timmo?"

"Of course," he said stoically, like Sydney Carton.

"Of course," Anil echoed.

I sighed. "Well, the first thing we need is a shot of the two of you."

"Why?"

"Anil is hilarious."

"Thanks, Will!" said Anil.

"No problem."

"I don't know if he should be featured when it's Timmo who wants to be on the show," said Anneliese.

"Haters gonna hate," Anil said with unshakable conviction.

I told Timmo his best chance to be on the show came from being an Oxford student, and suggested we film him around town.

He looked doubtful. "I like the video of the workout."

"We'll just get a little extra footage, then."

"Okay."

Someday, when anthropologists or Martians study our age, I

hope they come across Timmo's audition tape for *Big Brother.* I imagine them puzzling over it as if it were the *Book of Kells,* dismayed by its incomprehensibility, intrigued by its polysemous meanings. In the reshoots we took Timmo all over town, and he refused to do anything but mumble the word "Oxford" over and over—because, we later figured out in our review of the footage, he was devoting so much energy to flexing his muscles. Then there was Anil. Now that it was in his head that he should be in the video he tried to sneak into every shot "accidentally," which rendered nearly all of our footage useless.

"I don't think I understand their friendship," Anneliese whispered to me, looking troubled.

"It's simple, they're both insane." Timmo was doing push-ups in the center of Radcliffe Square. "I don't know why he's wearing a tank top, either. I wish we had a wardrobe consultant."

"He has more muscles than you."

"He has more muscles than a seafood restaurant."

This was the kind of joke that went straight to Anneliese's heart, and she burst out laughing.

Anneliese, Anil, and I spent hours cutting the footage together on her Mac. She had shot it all excellently—had grown up with a camera in her hand—and we edited it into quick and enjoyable moments: Timmo singing "Total Eclipse of the Heart" in falsetto when he thought nobody was listening, Anil crooning the mistaken lyric "Turn around, bright guys" moments later, Timmo flexing on the top of Fleet bell tower, Timmo and Anil in suits getting pennied at Hall.

Anil was ecstatic, and once we put in enough workout shots even Timmo was satisfied. "Thanks," he said. "I'll mention your names on the show."

"I'm holding you to that," I said.

I still have a copy of the tape. I watch it when I'm feeling blue.

"You won't believe it when I show you," I said to Ella afterward, drinking at the Fleet bar. "What an abortion."

"Don't say that around a Catholic, Will," she answered and hit me on the arm.

By early December I think we were finally unsurprised to be at Oxford. In the first two weeks of the month, Jack was in and out of town, annoyingly visible, and I couldn't catch a glimpse of Sophie. The restlessness I felt at this started to spend itself toward Jess. I first texted her on Thanksgiving—unregarded in England, except for a few jokes about red Indians, but Fleet had thrown a small celebration for us—and invited her to come to the bar in college.

She responded to my text with a call. "Do you always sleep with girls and then ignore them?" she asked.

"Always. I run through two or three hundred a year."

"Hilarious."

"I'm sorry."

There was a moment of silence. "I'm just going to come to your flat," she said.

"It's just a room, it's not much of a flat."

"You've seen mine. How different could it be?"

She arrived in an imperious mood, determined, unpacking four cans of Carling, lifting the window, and saying, "We need music. Let's have some cheese."

"Cheese?"

She looked over her shoulder at me from my computer, where she was already scrolling through my iTunes. Her face was aghast. "Do you not know *cheese*, Will Baker?"

"What is it?"

Now she turned the chair to face me and began to list songs. "It's 'Wonderwall,' by Oasis."

"Well, I know that."

"No, it's more—it's when everyone knows all the words, like 'Angels' or 'Love Is All Around' by Wet Wet Wet."

"The Wets."

She rolled her eyes. "It's all those Verve songs, 'Bitter Sweet Symphony' and 'The Drugs Don't Work,' it's 'Common People' by Pulp, it's 'Alright' by Supergrass, it's 'Back for Good' by Take That—"

"I know that one."

"Then we'll start there," she said.

She put on the song and dimmed the lights in the room and came over and straddled me, searching in my eyes. "If we sleep together will you call me this time?"

"Okay."

She looked beautiful in the half-light, with the opening chords of a terrible, wonderful song, a song that affected me, playing along to her smile. When the sex was over, though, my unspoken—unthought—logic, that even if I couldn't have Alison or Sophie at least I could have something, collapsed: Lying in bed while she went to the bathroom and showered, I thought of all of them at once and separately, over and over.

Yet there can be a greater intimacy to lying in bed with someone you don't care about than there is with someone you do, because the lying in bed is the sum of your relationship, and because the conversation there, the little jokes and games, is flooded with meaninglessness and therefore with meaning. There has to be loss in life—lost connections, people you barely remember, nights that fade into matterlessness. Whatever Facebook thinks about it.

When I woke up in the morning, groggy, she was awake already and looking at me. Her face was sad.

"Hey," I said.

"Hey."

"What is it?"

In a singsongy voice, she said, "Oh, nothing. I wish I didn't like you."

"It's hard when I'm so irresistible."

"Ha, right."

We hooked up again and she showered again, emerging just in time to see Ella and Tom—Tom was abashed at Jess's appearance in a towel, which annoyed Ella—and then she dressed in my room.

"You don't want anything serious, I guess?" she asked as she sorted through her purse.

"I don't know if I'm ready right now for—"

She smiled. "No, I get it. Some girl who goes to," and she put on a posh voice, "Oxford."

"It's not like that, not at all," though that's uncannily what it was like.

She stood up. "Okay. I've got to go to work."

In the empty spaces of the next months I saw her when I felt like it. She didn't raise the idea of anything serious again—it was only dancing at the Turtle and movies in my room, and sex.

That first morning I went and hugged her before she left. "Do you need money for a cab?"

"No," she said lightly, then let me go and raised a hand to wave good-bye without looking back.

A beat passed before I realized I couldn't withdraw the offer, that anyway her footsteps were going down the stairs already, and that she had taken it exactly as she should have. I think it was the worst thing I did all year.

None of this matters, I realize that. Not who loved who, not people's disappointments, not Timmo's audition tape. Directly before Christmas there was a severe corrective to our autumn self-indulgence. I'm tempted just to say what it was, not to try to make it a surprise.

Maybe I'll just tell it as it happened, beginning with the night before.

All the students were packing to go home again for Christmas, the school year almost halfway gone. I had been working a lot at the Fleet Tavern by then, but one weekend Tom and I decided to take off to London. I had gone into the city alone twice that fall and had a look at the museums, but he and I had never gone together. Besides, he said, it was criminal that I hadn't seen Gordon's, his favorite bar. Also a fourth-year undergraduate named Lula, who had 477 friends on Facebook—that was a vast number in 2005—was going to have a party at her house. We didn't know where we would stay, since neither of us was close with Lula, but figured that if worse came to worst one of Tom's friends would put us up. He had invited them all to the party. (*Invite everyone xxx :) see you there you darling lovelies!* Lula had written.) The trip would mean cutting a class for me, but it was with a professor I didn't like much, Dr. Drayton, who was obsessed with Faulkner and usually spent the last twenty minutes of every class, whatever subject it was meant to be on, from Marcuse to Aira, talking about *The Bear.*

We got off the train and went to Notting Hill. Lula's family lived on one of those mansion-lined squares there with a private garden behind it, to which only residents had the keys. The house that they inhabited, except Lula's brother, who was away in Tanzania on his gap year, was a modern one, cantilevered up onto stilts and with ribbonlike horizontal windows. They must have gotten permission to knock down something old to build it, because the rest of the houses on the block were cream-colored Georgian ones. It was striking, but only because of the old houses on either side of it—the way the Guggenheim needs the plain brick town houses on Eighty-ninth Street to shock you.

At the entrance were Lula and half a dozen giggling friends from Oriel. They had a computer, and to enter the party we had to prove we were friends with Lula on Facebook, or if we weren't we had to add her. If someone wasn't on Facebook at all, they had to drink a shot of vile tequila that Lula had acquired on her own gap year, with a worm on the bottom, but when we arrived the bottle was still full. "It's all such a joke," she said as we proved our friendship. "I'm really through with Facebook, it's getting so tacky. I thought it deserved a send-off, though, don't you? And secretly I adore it, of course. How do we know each other, by the way? You look familiar. Do you spend a lot of time at the Turtle? I stopped going in second year but now I'm back in love!!"

It was a balkanized party, populated by small self-segregating groups. There were a bewildering number of staircases. One bedroom was full of pot, and potheads; another as full of coke, and cokeheads. We dropped our coats and backpacks in a closet along the front hall and went into a long dining room, then got two Coronas and headed up a random staircase to see what we would find.

I won't describe the long hours of the party much: seeing everyone Tom had ever met in public school or after; meeting up with his friends, who all treated me roughly as the Jackal's friends had, despite Tom's imprimatur (a Yank, eh?); the blurry hours of drinking and dancing with random undergraduate girls whose names we wrote on our palms so we could add them on Facebook the next day; everyone finally, drunk or high enough, beginning to pool in the main room downstairs just shy of midnight; Lula's extended and smashed speech upon receiving a cake at one in the morning, followed by foam falling into the backyard and everyone rushing out to dance in it.

It was at just after two o'clock, many hours into the party, that my line of vision cleared, and Sophie stepped into it.

"Soph!" I shouted.

"Oh my God, Wills!" she said, and with a surge of adrenaline I saw that she was delighted to find me there—that for the first time since the bop at Fleet, a month and a half before, she had no diffidence in her manner. "Is anyone else here?"

"Just Tom!"

We hugged and gave each other a kiss on the cheek, a kiss that brushed close to our mouths. She pulled farther back than she needed to, almost by way of recompense. "Let him stay there!" She shouted above the din.

"Did you prove your friendship with Lula at the door?"

She laughed. "I've known her for ages. We went to the same school. Half the people I ever knew are here, all of them bankers. It's hideous."

I was drunk and energetic, and it felt so good to be together that without any hesitation I took her hand. "Is he here?" I asked.

She looked down at the floor shyly and shook her head. "No."

"Come on."

I led her by the hand through the dancing swarms. It was impossibly loud. At last, walking away from the noise, we found an alcove along a hallway to the kitchen. In the dim light its daytime objects seemed touchingly foreign, as if they came from a world that had nothing to do with DJs or dancing—the phone with a long cord, the cheerful pink notepad next to it—and after being at the party it seemed also especially still. I sat back against a table scattered with bills and mail. She leaned in and kissed me.

"I've missed you," I said.

"You, too."

"It doesn't have to be weird."

"Don't start that. Give me another kiss."

For ten minutes we stayed there, then another ten. She smiled as she pulled away from me at last and suggested we go outside and have a cigarette together. Lula's station at the front door was abandoned, and the air was brisk, the streetlights shining a sallow gold over the massive row of white houses. They looked comfortable and immovable, those houses, built and kept with men's money, with men's salaries. Large, red, hale men with capacious laughs who voted Tory and drank decent wine and wore expensive watches. Members of Parliament, men from hedge funds. Sophie and I held hands and I pictured us, middle-aged, living here.

"I have to go," she said when we had stubbed our cigarettes out.

"What?"

"I'm late."

"Didn't you just get here?"

She shook her head. "I was up in Peregrine's room, Lula's brother, with all the girls. For ages."

"Are you going to see Jack?"

She leaned into me and left her head on my shoulder. "Yes."

We stood like that for a few minutes, sometimes tilting our faces to kiss again. Then Lula stumbled out of the front door with a cigarette.

"SOPHIE!" she screamed when she saw us. "My God, Billy Lownes has gotten tedious. I used to think he hung the moon. And those boys from Albion Hall are absolutely disgusting. How the scales fall from your eyes. Oh, Soph, I'm so glad you came!"

Sophie grinned. "Lu, do you know Will Baker? He's my favorite friend from Fleet."

"Hullo, Will."

"Would you two entertain each other while I find my coat?" Sophie said, and skipped back up the front steps of the house.

"Are we friends, Will?" asked Lula when Sophie had gone.

"We are. Before tonight, even."

"Oh, hurrah," she said, putting her arm around my back and facing me, "then would you give me a birthday kiss? You look lovely under the streetlamp."

"What about Sophie?"

"I won't tell, darling."

I could have said no, maybe, but I knew Sophie would be a minute or two and so with one eye on the door I gave her a long kiss. We disentangled just in time to see the girl I loved come out of the house again. The betrayal felt warm under my skin. At last I knew something she didn't.

The two girls hugged each other and said good-bye, and then Lula, her cigarette long cold by now, went back inside to find another wind.

"Good-bye, Will," said Sophie. She had a pink scarf wrapped tightly around her throat, her long hair tumbling over it, and that scarf pushed the two of us outside of the refuge of the party, placing her back in the real world.

"Isn't there anything I can say that would make you like me, Soph?"

Again she softened; that dance. "You know I do."

"Can we meet?"

"No," she said and turned to the street.

"No?"

She was hailing a cab, which slowed for her, as everything did. Turning back, and relenting one last time under my gaze, she came back and kissed me on the cheek before running to the cab. "Oh, Will," she said quietly. Then, through the window of the cab, as it rolled off, "I suppose you could text me. That would be nice."

As the sun rose the last of us, a few dozen people, were draped over couches; there were little squadrons of boys and girls engaged in intense coked-up conversations, a group of guys trying to pool their resources to fill one last bong, a few individual dancers. Lula was asleep on a chaise. Her friends had written in Sharpie on her arms and legs.

"What do you say, Bake?" Tom asked me. We were smoking amid the wreckage of the back terrace, which had small vanishing islands of foam left in it.

"I can barely think."

He smiled. "I lost you for an hour or two there. And Sophie."

I sighed and looked up at the pale sun, its pink vale of light above that fine, pure white of morning. "I know," I said.

He looked at me. "It was fun."

"Really fun."

"Still, if we went back, we could make it to St. John's bop tonight."

I laughed. "I was thinking the same thing."

"Back to Oggsford?"

We kissed the slumbering Lula on the cheek and said good-bye to the one or two people we knew who remained at the party. We went to catch the bus at Hyde Park (the train didn't run so early) and ended up falling asleep on the grass, waiting for it to come, until the driver honked at us. Cold, bruised, hungry, and at least half happy, we returned to our city; we stopped to pick up coffee and a packet of sandwiches and ate them on a bench in Anna's Court, shivering. I talked about Sophie and Lula, and he talked about the memories of his schooldays that the night had conjured up. At eight we stood to leave, and he said, as he did so often in Anna's, "Look at this castle we live in."

We walked back to the Cottages and up the stairs to our rooms side by side; and though I didn't say it to him, as I dozed off it occurred to me that because we lived in these castles, all of us felt like kings.

I woke to a panicked knocking at my door. "Yeah?" I called into my pillow.

Ella came in. "You guys are back from London?"

"What time is it?"

She opened my curtains. "Noon. Will, get up."

"What is it?"

"Have you seen the news?"

"Not since yesterday."

She went over to my clock radio and turned it on to the BBC. The report was about a stabbing in East London. "Is it that?"

"No, no, wait."

I sat up and put on the T-shirt that was on the floor next to my bed. I turned the radio off. "Ella, tell me what the hell is going on."

She sat down on my bed and turned the radio on again. "Just wait, it will come back on. It's every other story right now."

She was right, it was next. In a BBC voice, a woman said, *Authorities have begun their investigation of the bombing that took place in Syria late last night at the British Embassy. According to Sir Denis Busby, the men who raided the compound are unconnected—*

Suddenly I understood. "Not Katie."

Ella turned down the radio. "Someone came in with explosives padlocked to his chest. They tried to clear the room, but at least eight people are dead. Six of them were Syrians, waitstaff, and there was a French couple. But they can't find two people, and one of them is her. Her face is all over the TV."

"Oh my God."

"Do you think anyone's called him?"

"He keeps his phone on silent when he sleeps," I said. I went over to my computer and started to look at the news. "Holy shit."

"What do we do?" she asked.

I turned in my desk chair and looked at her. "Do we tell him? Or wait? Do we let him sleep?"

"I don't know." We were silent for a moment. "I would want to know the second it happened."

"Me, too."

"Okay then."

Birds took off from a tree outside my window, a gust of life, wobbly at first but then steadying themselves with air, only air. "Jesus," I said and felt some hugely complex series of emotions, which I don't think I can even begin to dissect; they were about Tom, they were about Katie, they were about politics. Since in any situation any person is capable of sociopathic selfishness they were about Sophie and Alison, too; they flashed through my head. They were about me.

We went into Tom's room. He was sleeping with one arm off the bed, his face untroubled by his dreams. Ella put a hand on his shoulder, gently, and said, "Tom, Tom," and we woke him up and ruined his life.

CHAPTER FIVE

The writer I primarily studied in my course at Oxford was George Orwell. I believed him to be not merely a great writer but one of the very greatest, in particular his nonfiction—*Homage to Catalonia*, *The Road to Wigan Pier*, his long ruminations about England, Dickens, language, and writing. These seemed to me to have the authenticity and lucidity of the best essays and the humanity of the best fiction. He was a genius, of course, it's impossible to write so simply without being one. Perhaps more importantly, I loved him as a person. "Decency," that word seems to recur so often in his work, that humans should behave as decently as possibly toward one another, a Christian ethic to carry forward beyond the end of Christianity's days. He lived in darker times than my own and never turned his face from what he saw. Certainly I've never known a more honest writer. Ironic, considering the doubtful accuracy of some of his work, but what I felt nevertheless. That was why I chose to study him.

As I read more into Orwell's essays, his letters, and his journals, he became the Greek chorus of my days. One evening in the Fleet library I was glancing at *The New York Times* online and saw an editorial about waterboarding, then turned to a book review Orwell wrote as the year 1939 began and came across this sentiment, "We have now sunk to a depth at which the restatement of the obvious is the first duty of intelligent men." Another time I saw an exhortatory speech given before a few hundred soldiers on an air force base by George Bush (who spent his war in Texas) and Dick Cheney (whose statement that he had other priorities during Vietnam was making the rounds), and thought of the passage in which Orwell wrote, "All the war-propaganda, all the screaming and lies and hatred, comes invariably from people who are not fighting."

I think I only disagreed with him once. The day after Katie Raleigh went missing, I sat in the MCR with Ella and watched the BBC interview Tom's uncle. I thought of the last line in Orwell's diaries, "At 50, every man has the face he deserves." This had seemed so true to me, how smiling or anxiety works its way into the face over time, how it shows character, but here was this virtual father to Tom and Katie—brother to their own father—who looked so haunted and lost, his face deformed by tragedy.

The tabloids found a picture that made Katie look what she was not: beautiful. There were journalists at Tom's door in London, we saw on television. They reported that he had tried to go to Syria himself but been denied a visa. Eventually it emerged that the suicide bomber had been part of a group of Saudi Arabians with ties to a terrorist camp in Khartoum, Sudan. He had entered Syria illegally through northern Iraq. There had been other bombings down the years, of course, Kenya, Tanzania, Yemen, but this one was different—to England anyhow—because of Katie.

On the second day after the bombing there was a report that a young white woman had been seen traveling by car through Damascus, but that lead evaporated and no other emerged. The only certainties were that her remains were not at the embassy and that the terrorist had been driving a blue Mercedes truck. That was all.

Slowly, without fresh news, it became the second story on the news, then the third, then the fourth. Was she dead? We decided that it was likely—in fact, hoped that it was likely, because by then we knew about the hostage videos on the Internet. I never had the stomach to watch them.

That morning we had woken Tom up, and without even looking at us, after he took in the information, he had turned on his phone, seen what was waiting for him on it, and bolted from the room, without a bag, for the taxi stand, his fastest way of making it into London. We hadn't seen him since, nor had he replied to any of our anemic caring e-mails, and I kept recalling how he had seemed to cease to exist when he found out, how his face too had changed. What seemed so unfair was the absence of his parents. He had no margin for this loss.

Even as the national news turned away there was a great stir about Katie around Oxford, and specifically in college. She had been an undergraduate there only a few years before, and many of the staff and dons remembered her, and of course there was Tom. After a few days they remembered that he had friends and sent for us.

The dean of Fleet then was a man named Sir George Ballantine, and like Sir Walter Elliot of Kellynch Hall, the beginning and end of him was vanity.

He was tall, with stiff white hair and a long pink face, a handsome man, and by all accounts an exceptional astronomer. The queen had knighted him "for services to the field of astronomical science" before he was fifty. Yet in his capacity as dean, no minor ignominy was beneath his wonderful brain. If Trinity beat us in rowing, he looked stern at Hall; if Worcester beat us, pale and harried. If we raised less money than Lincoln, he fretted euphemistically about it in unscheduled speeches during chapel. When Merton added those four words to their Latin grace, none of the returning students would bar the possibility of Ballantine jumping off the Magdalen Bridge.

It was Sir George who called for eight of us to come to his private office, two days after Tom had left: Anil, Ella, Jem, Anneliese, Timmo, an undergraduate girl named Allie whom Tom had hooked up with twice, Sophie, and me. I don't know how he found out about Allie. Ella was displeased to see her there.

It was a hexagonal room, with books and portraits of past deans of Fleet lining the walls, big comfortable armchairs and couches around a fireplace at one end of the room, and an immaculate desk at the other. The window was ajar even in the cold, and what must have been a powerful amateur telescope stood on a tripod near it.

He welcomed us in by saying, "Yes, yes, yes, yes, please sit, please sit." He offered coffee, which we all declined because it was nine thirty at night. Afterward Jem said he was famous for offering whatever he knew people wouldn't want because he liked to use his entire personal catering budget on champagne, which he drank throughout the day. I don't know if that was true. Hopefully.

"Ah," he said and heaved a gargantuan sigh. "I knew her, Katherine Raleigh. I'm sorry to say I think her dead."

Anneliese said, "Perhaps they can find her."

"Indeed," he said with what we were meant to see was a sage nod. "Well." Another long pause, then, "This Tom. I never met him. Good chap?"

We assented.

"He'll be all right, in time. The great healer." After this ex cathedra proclamation he offered us another sigh. "You all are coping, too?" Nobody said a word. "Hm. Good. If you need anything I'm always here."

Then he stood, and we were ushered out by the crimson martinet who served as junior dean. In an anteroom to the master's office he asked if any of us had any questions for him. We all shook our heads except Allie, who asked, "When will Tom get back?" The junior dean didn't know. So ended our brush with greatness.

"I'm not sure about you," Jem said, as we walked out into Anna's (where Ballantine's office was), "but I feel loads better." Everyone chuckled except Allie, who was brushing tears out of her eyes. Jem put his arm around her. "Come on, you lot. I'll open the bar early. First round is mine."

So it was in mingled disbelief and banality that the days after Katie Raleigh's disappearance passed. I still thought about her constantly, catching myself staring into space for long stretches at my carrel in Bodley. Someone once told me that if you were careful, your understanding of the people you know who had died would deepen and evolve even after they were gone, like characters in a novel whose reasons for acting you piece together days and weeks past when you've finished reading it. The opposite is true, too: Think of someone who is gone too casually and you lose their capacity to surprise you. Then you find a letter they wrote, or a video, and see how effortlessly your brain has diminished them into a few characteristics. I tried to think about her.

I read in one interview, with a group of Katie's friends from Fleet, that none of them had known her to have a boyfriend. It was a throwaway line, but it was what stuck with me, and combined with the memory of her ugliness this fact swelled in me every so often. I could still hear her as she had been singing when I came into the Cottages the day I met her, "On the Street Where You Live," and that song, light-spirited, lovely and slight, persuaded of itself, seemed to represent in its contours what her life had been missing. She had been so decent (an Orwell word) herself, had seemed so eager for other people's happiness; that made it worse, that apparently she felt no bitterness or envy, and was perhaps stoic in the face of her obscure inner disappointments, which, if she felt unloved, may have been greater than the average person's. Her parents' death, raising Tom, her possible loneliness—how cruel it seemed. I wondered what her world looked like from the inside. I found myself hoping that she had believed in the cross on her neck.

Then, just when it seemed that everything had gone quiet, we had news.

Turn on the TV—good about Katie? Timmo texted me.

With a surge of hope I ran to the common room. So she was alive. When I opened the door I heard the TV going and saw that Ella was watching it alone.

Her back was to me. "Ella!"

She turned, and her face was wet, her black eye makeup smudging down her cheeks. "Oh," she said.

"What happened?'

"She's dead."

"But Timmo said—"

She looked at me curiously and then understood. "Oh. No video. No rape. Just dead. They found her."

Just dead. "How?"

"Shot in the head."

I almost never cry. I do whatever the opposite is, some involution. I sat down. "In Damascus."

"Thirty miles outside of the city, close to the highway. A rainstorm uncovered the body. I guess they just scraped some dirt over her, not much." She gestured toward the TV, as if it were responsible, not her. Then she came and slouched down heavily into the couch, leaning her head against my shoulder and quietly crying. We sat there for a while and watched the BBC. "Should we call him?" she asked eventually.

"You know he hasn't been picking up."

"We should go to the funeral at least. They said on the news that it would be at St. Luke's in Chelsea. There are already bouquets outside and notes—handwritten notes, like posters." She sobbed. "Poor Tom."

"I'm not sure we should go. We should ask him if he wants us there."

"Okay."

I realized I had believed she was still alive. No matter how many people die I still, somehow, live in a deathless world; and then death comes back again and I remember, oh, right, that's what happens; that's where we're going; that's what it all means. At the same time I felt tremendous relief. When a woman is involved there is a restless, should-we-think-it-or-not taint of sexuality, an added fear. This worst fate precluded even worse ones.

We got no answer when we called Tom. We left a message, asking if we could come to the funeral, and started to plan our trip down, all of us—including Allie—but the next day we got back a text that said *No thanks*. Despite this we debated going, before concluding that it would be better to respect his refusal. There would have been something forced about going, I think, our friendship still new, forced into florescence by the hothouse of school. Instead we watched it on television. Like everything else. The clip the news shows had of Tom from the funeral showed him flashing a quick smile at someone he saw, one of those wordless messages of thanks you see go across the room at such events. In isolation it looked strange, though: like one taillight still glowing on a wrecked car.

I liked that they chose the regular old hymns, "All people that on earth do dwell," "Ten thousand times ten thousand," "Guide me, O thou great redeemer." (That last one: I wondered if they chose it because of Syria, "Pilgrim in a barren land...") There was an atavistic pleasure in seeing the family—the three of them who were left—leave the church for the burial ground with the casket between them. They had the body back.

A couple of days after the funeral Ella and I chanced another e-mail to Tom. We told him about watching the service and said we were sorry. Then we asked if he was coming back soon.

His only answer was *Thanks. Probably not for a while. TR.*

"How long do you think till he comes back?" Ella asked me. We were hanging out in my room. "Maybe never, right?"

"Do you really think so?"

"He doesn't need the degree."

She looked disconcerted. "It never occurred to me he would stay away for good."

I shrugged. "Wouldn't it feel wrong to go to a bop after your sister died?"

"You can't not have fun for the rest of your life."

I frowned. "Look around you, though, the parties, Oxford is—"

"Maybe yours is," she said. "I'm here to work. Why don't you work harder at your course?"

"That seems self-indulgent to me, too." My face started to get warm. "Leaving Alison, no job, just for... what... to go punting and worry about Sophie?"

"You can't think about things like that."

"I don't see why not."

Life resumes, of course; that scarcely needs to be said. The week you die magazines and newspapers will go on appearing, all with the same urgency as usual, only on behalf of the living now, and not even in infinitesimal part for you any longer. A new song will come out, something you would have loved and listened to on repeat. There will go on being news: earthquakes, the deposition of dictators, museum shows. They'll keep giving out the Oscars and electing presidents, whose names you won't know. There will be new geniuses. I think of it sometimes and feel sad to contemplate how it will be, this place I love so much, finished with me before I'm finished with it.

Nevertheless, for then, as it will be until I die, it was I who kept going on.

There were ten days until Christmas, and I threw myself into work. Despite what I'd told Ella, I liked being a student again. I looked forward to the evenings I spent in the Fleet library, reading and taking breaks to drink tea with friends. Taking a break between college and Oxford, predictably, had made me appreciate it all.

(I wonder about this: In the future, when we've grown more intelligent, will education change? I think it might, unless we're living in bombed-out shelters, collecting rainwater and avoiding zombies. The long dwindle of learning from five to twenty-one seems pointless for most people. I bet in the future we'll go to college for a year or two after high school, then do life things, marriage, kids, jobs, before returning at forty, like travelers circling home, for another year or two of education. That's when you need it: before it's too late, after you've realized it can get too late. A chance to rejigger. How grateful most forty-year-olds would be to spend two years reading *The Spirit of the Laws* and retraining themselves, I imagine. Then again I also have a theory, widely mocked by my friends, that in a hundred years our clothes will be superstrong exoskeletons, and that people in that time will look back and marvel at us and pity our weakness, our broken arms and skinned knees. Probably I'm wrong about all of it.)

One day in a class I was taking called "Memory and the Spanish Civil War," a kid I didn't know very well, named Sullivan, raised his hand and said, "Isn't *Homage to Catalonia* more important now than anything that ever happened during the Spanish Civil War? Why do we even bother with these different militias and the history of it?"

The teacher, an amused, unhurried woman in her fifties, thin, lucid, effective, who had recently published a book called *Bloomsbury's War* and always had a thermos of black coffee with her, responded, "Well, isn't the logical extension of that question that Günter Grass's books are more important than the Holocaust? What about Iraq?"

"The Holocaust is too provocative as an analogy," I said. "And as for Iraq, we don't know what kind of books will come out of it yet."

"Why should the Holocaust be exempt from comparison?" asked the professor.

"It's freighted with too much meaning."

"Why is that our concern?"

"Once you take any historicity into your reading you have to take all of it," I said.

"There I'm not sure we agree."

Sullivan broke in. "But Grass isn't Orwell," he said. "Orwell's better."

"Victor Klemperer, Elie Wiesel, Primo Levi, whomever you please. *If This Is a Man* can stand against anything. Can we place the work they did above the event that motivated it?"

"No," said Sullivan, "it's—"

A girl from Bath named Helena, pretty but insufferable, interrupted. "And what about Iraq? You could argue that as a war it's commensurate with the Spanish Civil War." Her voice rose a pitch, and she said, "And all these sons and brothers that families lose are still important to them. That won't change because somebody writes a book."

Nobody in that class was in favor of the war, except perhaps an Old Etonian and (we suspected) Conservative named Larry, who treated the reading with a kind of hauteur that precluded him from most conversations. Still, the rest of us rolled our eyes at Helena: cheap points. She was right, but the dynamic of a class like that one always settles a certain way, and ours had settled against her.

Sullivan said, "What I'm saying is that to pretend we're interested in all the little political details and the acronyms of the Spanish Civil War—I don't know, we have this living, vibrant memoir. Why do we place the facts and Orwell's interpretation on the same level, when one is so much higher?"

"But the book wouldn't exist without them," said an excellent student called Ben.

"Of course, of course," said Sullivan impatiently. "That's a given. I'm trying to express something broader."

"There's also the point that Franco was in charge up until not long ago," said Helena.

"But I think I agree with you," Ben told Sullivan. "If your argument is that the facts of the war are less interesting than the facts as Orwell saw them."

"Yes," he said, "but as *Orwell* saw them, not Arthur Koestler, not Martha Gellhorn."

"They're two different disciplines. It's ridiculous to assess them qualitatively against each other," said Helena.

Again she was correct, I thought. The professor stepped in. "One needs the other, clearly. Do any of you know Lyotard?"

I raised my hand tentatively, but she called on Ben, who had nodded vigorously. "I presume you're referring to grand narratives and small narratives—that trying to assemble the limited perspectives of any event into a larger univocal perspective is dangerous."

"Precisely," she said. "Foucault had a similar idea when he talked about genealogy. That a series of fractured narratives makes up what we view in retrospect as unfractured history. Orwell's subjective narrative is probably 'righter' than many historical texts, in the sense that it tells us about small privations in the trenches, bureaucratic stupidity, so on and so forth. But when we search a text for determinate meaning we immediately open it to indeterminacy. Was Orwell being honest? What were his politics? Can we corroborate any of his facts? And most importantly, are we even reading it correctly?

"That's all the time we have. But thank you, Sullivan, I liked your question. That's the way we should be thinking. You, too, Will, Helena. Larry, walk with me to my office?"

It hadn't been that unusual a class, but on the street outside the English building Sullivan caught up with me and said, "Hey, you're Orwell, right?"

(That wasn't an uncommon brand of greeting. "Hey, aren't you Coetzee?" "You're Fulke Greville, someone said?")

"Hey. I am, yeah."

"Fucking amazing, *Homage*," he said. "I didn't think much of *Animal Farm* and *1984*."

"Try *Such, Such Were the Joys,* or any of his essays. In fact, even some of the other novels are more interesting than *Animal Farm,* to me. *Coming Up for Air.* What about you, Joyce?"

"Like everyone else." He nodded. "Although I'm a Joyce Futurist."

"What is that?"

"We try to piece together how Joyce will be read when Ireland is gone and English is a dead language. Essentially it's an anthropological project. We're also interested in how mechanization will alter academic readings of Joyce."

"Can the subaltern speak if he's a robot."

He laughed. "Something like that. Say, what are you doing? Do you fancy a pint?"

It was just past five. "Sure."

There was a cold, thin rain falling, and we walked under twinned black umbrellas.

"So what do you think of that crowd?" he asked.

"The class? I don't know."

We weren't that close as a group, the eleven of us. In the fall we had all gone out for a drink or two, and there was one definite, inseparable friendship, between Helena and a poky girl in glasses called Sam, but that was it.

There were four graduate master's programs in English: Medieval, Renaissance, Victorian, and Modern. I never once met anyone from the Medieval group, but the assumption was that they were abstruse, intelligent, geeky. Interested in Elvish and Aquinas. The Renaissance students were good-looking and romantic, the theater majors of the English Department, full of Sidney and "Whoso list to hunt" and "Sigh no more, ladies, sigh no more, men were deceivers ever." The Victorian group, by contrast, was composed almost entirely of nice girls, either plump or with glasses, all of whom had read *Jane Eyre* and *Wuthering Heights* a dozen times before they were fifteen. As for the modernists, as everyone called us, we fell into two groups: edgy, coffee-driven purists who studied Beckett or Joyce, and the rest of us. There was no gap in intelligence in these two groups, but there was a gap in seriousness. All of the coffee crowd would make it in academia. The rest of us: journalism, writing, advertising agencies, the whole depressing welter of selling words that come out of your brain.

There was some mingling between the disciplines in the fall, and a lot in the spring. By February we would form a group who hung out together and talked about books, with about seven people from across the three later eras (Renaissance, Victorian, Modern) who became friends. On that icy day, though, with *Homage* and a notebook in my hand, I had no true friends among the modernists, and after that day really Sull became the only one.

He was tall and very thin. His background was midlands, middle class, and state school—I think he had been the brightest person in every classroom he had ever sat in. His three subjects were Joyce, the Who, and Bob Dylan. (His favorites, respectively: *Finnegan*, "Baba O'Riley," "Girl from the North Country.") We started to get drinks together pretty regularly from that day forward, and in a vague way it was like being with a friend from home, because it meant not worrying, for a while, about Tom or Sophie.

"You could text me," Sophie had said at Lula's party. For a while I forgot, but then, nearing Christmas break, I wrote to her. I was shopping at Sainsbury's. (We had a kitchen in our house, which was kept spotless.) *What the hell is Yrkshre Tea? That or PG Tips?*

Hopeless ignorance, she wrote back. *Of course get Yorkshire Tea. Thank God I'm here. xxSoph.*

When I returned home I made the tea and went to my desk, where I wrote her an e-mail that consisted of a long pull quote, which contained, I always thought, almost everything you could ever want to know about England:

> Tenthly, one should pour tea into the cup first. This is one of the most controversial points of all; indeed in every family in Britain there are probably two schools of thought on the subject. The milk-first school can bring forward some fairly strong arguments, but I maintain that my own argument is unanswerable. This is that, by putting the tea in first and stirring as one pours, one can exactly regulate the amount of milk whereas one is liable to put in too much milk if one does it the other way round.

There was so much to love in this—"tenthly," to begin with, and then "the milk-first school." The author was Orwell.

What is this? she asked. *Dying laughing, sent it to Lula.*

I forward her the essay. *Following this religiously, although I don't agree that "one can swallow tea-leaves in considerable quantities without ill effect." Last time I tried, Tom called it "swill" and Anil dumped half a bag of sugar in it "for taste," convinced I can do better this time.*

That day inaugurated our new correspondence, and soon enough I learned to love the tinny ping that signaled I had a text message. I learned to rush home and open my e-mail first thing in case she had written. She would write to complain about studying, or remind me about some part of English life I shouldn't miss, or text things like *Hmm. I need egg whites twice as heavy as sugar for something I'm baking. How can I do that without a kitchen weight?* I would think that of course she could look it up as easily as I could, which must have meant that she wanted to be in touch—which must have meant—and so on.

At last, then, we saw each other again. It was a midweek day, the light falling, just past four o'clock. December had given up three weeks of its time, and there were Christmas decorations in the MCR; in another day or two people would clutch home for the holidays. I myself was leaving the next afternoon, the twenty-third of December.

She was doing her laundry in the MCR laundry room, which as far as I knew she hadn't for a long time. (The thing that meant the most to me of anything she ever said was at Lula's party. I said to her, "Wasn't it great, when we were hanging out so much this fall? You never come to the MCR or Hall anymore." She looked at me, a rare lack of evasion in her light brown eyes, and said, "Why do you think I was there so much?")

There was a large window looking into the MCR from First Quad, and through it I could see her back to me, her hair over one shoulder, her head down as she looked at her phone. There were no lights on, and in the gray she looked a figure from Hammershøi, motionless, paused.

"Soph?" I said, coming through the door.

She turned. "Will!"

"What are you up to?"

"Laundry," she said sorrowfully. "You wouldn't believe the

T-shirts I get through. It's appalling. I was just thinking I would make some coffee."

"I was coming to do the same. Should we have a pot?"

In the kitchen she put the ground beans into the filter and then poured cold water from the pitcher in the fridge into the percolator. It only took a second for the smell to fill the whole MCR—that amicable scent, when you had just come in from the cold.

As the coffee brewed I was saying something, about class I think, when she interrupted me to say, "Oh, wait!"

"What?"

"Never mind. Just pour the coffee. I'm going to dash to the Cottages. I have a surprise for you."

"You're coming back, right?"

"Of course. Just wait, okay?"

I poured out two mugs of coffee and put milk in both, then one sugar in hers. Just as I was carrying them over to the couches she came back in, red-cheeked from the cold. I could smell the familiar, understated scent that lingered in her long hair, a layer above the coffee, barely there.

"What's the surprise?" I asked. "Here's your coffee."

She had her hands behind her back, and she brought out a roll of cookies with a flourish. "It's Hobnobs."

My eyes widened. "Holy shit."

"I know."

After I had texted her from the grocery store about the tea, I had texted again and asked what kind of cookies to get. She wrote back simply "*HOBNOBS!*" in all capital letters like that.

Uh . . . que? I texted her.

Hobnobs, Will! The most delicious cookies of all!

Just checked. They're out.

After that, Hobnobs became a running joke in our text messages.

If either of us got overexcited about something, the other would write back, *HOBNOBS!*

"What if I don't like them?" I asked.

We were sitting on the couch now, our legs side by side, touching. She shook her head. "I'm not even remotely worried. You're going to adore them. Just have one."

In fact, they were terrific, these crunchy oatmeal cookies, and as we sat and talked, sipping our coffee, we ate the entire packet. When the coffee was gone too, she said, "We haven't had a secret cigarette in a while, have we?"

"Can you brave the cold?"

"I think so," she said.

We went and stood underneath an elm tree that grew alongside the MCR. "Do you think we'll have snow soon?" she asked, looking up at the sky.

The question felt intimate. "I hope so. Maybe not. I'll be gone."

"You know, Jack is back at Sandhurst, training. I haven't been seeing much of anyone these past two weeks. I've written to Tom, of course."

"We should all hang out after Christmas," I said. "With Anneliese and Anil and everyone."

She smiled. "That would be nice. Is there anything coming up? There's the James Bond bop, right?"

"Not for three weeks or so."

"I have an essay to turn in the Friday before it, though, it's in my calendar. It will give me something to look forward to. I've been longing for fancy dress. I won't be out much till then anyhow."

I wondered if that meant Jackal would be in Oxford. "It's a date."

She looked at me without any wariness. "It's a date. We'll match up our costumes and go together, you and I." There was a beat. "In a group, of course, as friends."

"Perfect."

"But you and I will go over together."

"I'll bring you some Hobnobs instead of flowers."

She laughed. "Okay. Let's do it."

My heart fluttered; they're guiltless lies, the ones told when you're in love. "Great."

We went inside, and I kept her company as she folded her laundry. I didn't try to kiss her when she left, but before she went she leaned into me and rested her head on my shoulder and left it there for a minute, longer, before pulling herself away.

I went home. It had been a long stretch in England, September, October, November, most of December now. I slept throughout the afternoon on Christmas. After that I sat with my mother by the fireplace and we played double solitaire, listening to the Drifters' version of "White Christmas," football on in the next room. It reminded me of going home from boarding school, which had always seemed to make a child of me again. I don't think I picked up a book the whole week I was in Boston. I did manage to send Alison a silver bracelet I had bought her on a day trip to Hampton Court, and received, in her typically sloppy wrapping, a blue gingham shirt from Brooks Brothers and a bottle of Scotch, not to my taste. We spoke on the phone on Christmas morning.

"Hey, it's me," I said.

"Will, Merry Christmas."

I wondered how much longer I could get away with *it's me*. A few months? Forever? Could I always say it: deep calling to deep? "How's the tree? Did you guys all get in the truck and go chop it down yet?"

"Yep, twenty-fourth time around for me. This one's bullshit, though. It's still sticky, and Jenny and I are the ones who have to reach in and decorate it."

That was her sister. "Is your dad drunk yet?"

"It's only eleven o'clock."

"Just tipsy, then?"

"No, he's drunk."

I laughed. I used to love Christmas at her house; everything felt well ordered there, with the particular grace that money, whether we wish it did or not, will give a house, a person, a day. "Thanks for the shirt."

"Oh, will you wear it? You're impossible to shop for, you—"

"No, it's amazing! Just my style."

"Oh, good, when I saw it I thought—"

It felt strangely as if we were still together to me, and because of that I interrupted her and said, "Have you hooked up with anyone?"

"Will."

"Have you?" There was a lingering caesura. "Hello?"

"I haven't. It's none of your business."

"I miss you."

She didn't talk for a second. "Don't fuck with my head."

"You're right."

"I mean it, I—"

"I said you're right! I think it's just the holidays, my dad, whatever, I felt like I missed you. I promise it was only for a second."

She laughed. "You know the way to a girl's heart, Bake."

"We'll talk soon?"

"Yeah, we'll talk soon. I love you."

"I love you, too."

I spent New Year's Eve with a huge group of friends and got blackout, and the next night took the overnight plane to Heathrow, slumbering through every movie and meal they tried to press on me, the sky outside pure black, as if I were traveling between worlds.

When I got back to Oxford, Tom was there.

I could see as the cab pulled up to the Cottages that his room was bright with lights, and I could hear music, just the bass line and the drums.

"Dude!" I called out when I reached the steps.

As he had that first day he met me halfway and took some of my bags. He was grinning. "Surprised?"

"Yes! Welcome back. It's fantastic to see you."

"I'm just having a beer if you fancy one."

"Sure."

We tossed my bags onto my bed and took our seats in the two armchairs by his window. The slender branches of a leafless chestnut tree clicked and swished outside, a shifting black craze against the pitiless blue-gray of the sky. For a time neither of us spoke.

"Are you okay?" I asked finally. "Do you want to talk about it?"

"About what about it?"

"It seems like you're doing okay."

He laughed. "No, I'm doing horrible."

"Maybe you're not ready to be back."

"I can't sit around the house doing nothing. They won't let me go to Syria. I'm too much of a coward to join the stupid army."

"You could take some time off and travel. Going away might help."

"I have to stick close to my family, my grandfather and my uncle. Except I can't be in the house with them for longer than three hours without wanting to put a gun to my head. Life's funny that way, eh?"

"Yeah."

He looked at me. "I'm glad you met her."

"She was great."

"I know it." He sat back and looked out the window, before finally saying, "I promised Ella I'd go out tomorrow night. She knows I'm back."

I knew that the window for discussing Katie was over. So I asked, "Yeah, did anything ever happen there?"

"What do you mean?"

I hesitated, then said, "I think she liked you."

He waved a hand. "No, I already blew that. Anyway I can't get into anything serious. Though I wouldn't mind getting laid."

"It's Thursday tomorrow. We could go to Filth." This was the sketchiest of all the Oxford clubs, every bathroom stall and booth occupied by couples hooking up.

"Sounds good to me." He looked at his watch. "Do you feel like getting food?"

"Sure," I said and started to stand up.

"Wait, though, let's just stay here for a bit first," he said, and it was the closest he ever came to asking me for anything after his sister died.

"Of course."

"What's that you and Jem say? Fleet time, or something?"

"Yeah."

"Fleet time," he said, and leaned his head back on the chair, and closed his eyes.

In the long, cold winter, its mornings and evenings dim, its middays obstinately chilled against the sun, we were lucky to have the MCR. Once or twice at loose ends I spent an entire day there instead of going to the library, watching TV, doing homework, drinking coffee, playing an unhealthy amount of table football. Certainly I stopped in during all the lost pockets of the day—between classes, after I was done at the Bod, before Hall, at midmorning.

There were two rooms and a kitchen in our MCR, and somehow they had managed to fit half a dozen couches along various walls, so there were places to spread out. There was a big TV and a library of DVDs. A couple of soccer balls lingered in the corner, ready for an indoor kick-around. Before Hall the wine committee put out wine, and afterward port. If you wanted to have a party, they would give you cash for drinks and food. Along with the bar and the Bod, it was the indispensable comfort of Oxford for me.

Unfortunately, it was presided over by an oligarchy of morons.

The president of the MCR, an honorific upon which he insisted during meetings, was a small, fierce Italian named Giorgio, with black hair and a pair of eyebrows threatening to merge. His greatest ambition in life was to acquire a new MCR coffeemaker (we had a serviceable drip machine, but his heart was set on an Italian one he had discovered online, which could grind beans, steam milk, and make espresso). His deputy was a Frenchman named Richard, *Ree-shard*, who was dashing to look at but immovably stupid. He adored Giorgio with the peculiar political mania of a cherished lieutenant, and together the two of them knew all the bylaws of the Fleet Middle Common Room Constitution—they always referred to it by this completest denomination—and deployed them without discrimination or mercy against those who opposed their plans.

Their chief opponent was a friend of mine named Peter, a sweet-natured redhead who had been at Fleet as an undergraduate and was now doing a DPhil in classical archaeology. He acted as secretary of the MCR committee and consistently offered his superiors sage and understated advice, which they ignored. We hadn't known him during Michaelmas, but one day near Christmas he and I had found ourselves in the MCR and decided to play chess. After that we played regularly. He was quiet, with a sly, deadpan sense of humor; he didn't like to go out much, but he was good daytime company. Despite his British reserve, his language when the subject of Giorgio and Richard came up would become (for him) violent.

"It does seem ridiculous for us to hold all of the special meetings we have about the coffee machine," he said to me once.

I looked at him wonderingly. "I don't know where your rage is. I would murder them."

"It is a bit much, isn't it?"

"The Espresso Wizard. Please."

He chuckled in a sidelong way intended to show that he agreed but disapproved and said, "Well, yes. Oh, and—is it—any chance that's mate?" He pointed to his queen-side knight.

I looked at the board. "Fuck. Again. Triple or nothing?"

Anneliese went to the weekly MCR meetings out of a sense of duty, and Anil, too, because he adored Giorgio and Richard, but the rest of us had learned long before to skip them, though it meant enduring their snide comments about our lack of Fleet patriotism. Tom in particular hated them. In meetings he never made it longer than fifteen minutes before he either got up and left or offered a strong opposition to Giorgio and Richard's stance on some issue he cared nothing about—whether to buy a copy of the dictionary for the MCR, say, or if the MCR computer should have solitaire and pinball installed on its hard drive even though it might distract people from work and potentially make the computer's wait time longer. Giorgio's positions on these two issues were, respectively, no and of course not. Tom won both times simply by virtue of his doggedness and Giorgio's unpopularity, and once Peter drafted him into a meeting he really cared about for the same reason—Peter thought, and Giorgio and Richard did not, that the MCR should continue to provide small sums of money for graduate students' books. Giorgio said the fund was only erratically in use and that the money we spent could upgrade a potential coffee machine to include a fresh cinnamon production feature. (I'm really not making that up. It sounds like I am, but I'm not; those were his words, "fresh cinnamon production feature.") Tom and Peter won. Anil wouldn't speak to either of them for a week. He told Ella that he had a particular fondness for cinnamon.

Aside from these politics providing a carnival sideshow for us, I mention them because on the day I returned to Oxford, Tom and I decided to wander over to the MCR in the early evening and accidentally walked straight into a general meeting. I was surprised that he wanted to go, because there was a chance that people might speak to him about Katie—but perhaps it was shrewd to see as many people as possible at one fell swoop, and thereby forestall any attempted expressions of pity. In the event it was a night that showed something of Tom's state of mind and also changed our group of friends for good.

What happened was this.

One of Giorgio and Richard's favorite tricks was to pretend to take two sides of a debate and then gradually talk each other into agreement. It was agonizingly transparent, but it worked simply because they were willing to grind the meeting and its arcana of constitutional law out for long enough to manufacture a weary consent.

This was what they were doing when Tom and I came in. We waved to Anneliese and Peter, sitting side by side, she patient and he martyred; she raised her eyebrows with surprised happiness to see Tom and stood to give him a hug.

The issue that day was the MCR clock, which in fairness did need to be replaced. It was from the 1970s, and its hands hadn't moved since I came to Fleet. Still, everyone had either a watch or a phone.

Giorgio and Richard wanted the MCR to acquire an object called the Eternal Clock. Its merits, if you listened to Richard, were endless: It kept Greenwich Mean Time to within a quarter of a second; it only needed a new battery once every nine years; it was a classic work of design. (He was one of those people who have the Eames chair, the Barcelona couch, the Noguchi table, and the Nelson cabinet gathered in one room, taste pushed in so uniform a direction as to declare its absence.)

"How much does it cost?" Peter asked.

"What is the cost of perfection?" answered Giorgio grandly.

"Generally pretty high," said Tom.

"Mr. Raleigh, would you like to be registered as an attendant of this meeting?" asked Richard.

"No, definitely not."

"How expensive is the clock?" asked Anneliese.

"My mum has one," said an anonymous third-year graduate student, who never came to Hall or the bar. His name was Bert. "It cost six hundred quid."

That caused a sensation.

"Six hundred fucking quid!" Tom said.

"Far too much, far too much," said Peter, moved beyond caution.

Anneliese, ever polite, said, "Mine cost five pounds at Dixon's. It works beautifully."

"Is it really six hundred pounds?" I asked.

Richard, with the exhausted sigh of a visionary constrained by the small-mindedness of his subordinates, said, "The fall Eternal costs just about seven hundred pounds."

Everyone started to speak at once. Peter, in what for him amounted to a breakout of Tourette's, said, "Surely this is coming it a bit high, surely, isn't it?"

"Let's buy Liese's clock for a tenner," said Tom, "and she'll make a profit. It sounds like it works beautifully!"

"It works beautifully," Anneliese confirmed, nodding, "and I would be happy to give it to the MCR for free. I love the MCR."

Richard took umbrage at that, in his heavy French accent. "Let us be clear here that we all love the MCR."

Bert said, "It's just so much money!"

"Ask your mum for hers," said Hans.

"We need that money if we plan to continue subsidizing curry nights," said Peter. "Some of the scholarship students wouldn't go out otherwise, because of the cost." Then he added, rather bravely, "I wouldn't, for instance."

Giorgio shifted his eyes away from us and said, "Well, that motion has expired, so," and then, when Peter tried to speak, pushed on, "but the clock, the clock! Really I must demand that you all consult section four in your constitutions just now—"

So our protests came to nothing. Invoking an obscure clause that permitted the president to arrogate 5 percent of the MCR's annual budget for whatever use he chose, Richard said, the MCR would receive this bounty whether there was a vote in its favor or not.

"Generally that's been used if there are unexpected expenses for an event at the last minute," Peter interjected. "Small sums, forty quid, ninety quid. Giorgio, you must remember when the blue midfield line of the table football broke and Jaime appropriated twenty-two pounds to fix it?"

"The president exercises his own discretion in matters pertaining to these funds," said Richard.

"You won't take a vote?"

Giorgio and Richard shook their heads, and among the twenty-odd people crammed along the walls, drinking drip coffee, there was a long silence.

"Then this is fucking ridiculous," said Tom at last.

"Tom?" said Richard. "Civility is one of the principles—"

"You, you are a fucking muppet. As for you, Giorgio, if you really mean to spend our college fees on a fucking seven-hundred-quid clock, you've lost your fucking mind. Peter, is there anything in the constitution about the president acting like Mao? A contingency plan? An assassination provision or something?"

"Is that a threat of personal assault?" Giorgio asked gravely.

Peter said, voice pained, "Um, I don't think—really I don't think so."

Tom threw his hands up in the air, and suddenly it was his volatility, not the clock, that had the room's attention. I thought, *Oh no.* "We just have to let these fucking prats steal our money? It's total fucking bullshit. Do you understand that?"

There was a long silence in the MCR.

One of the Chinese students, confused, broke it. "Who acts like Mao?"

"Nobody," said Richard.

"It's not the end of the world," said Anneliese, standing up and coming over to stand next to Tom.

He must have realized then that the room's silence had shifted its focus from Giorgio and Richard to him.

"You're right," he said. "I've just had a couple of beers."

Then he walked out. I watched him jog away through the window to the front gate of First Quad, back toward the Cottages.

"We need a clock," Giorgio said.

"I don't think anybody is acting like Mao," said the Chinese student, lips pursed with concern.

I stayed at the meeting to lend my support to Peter. It lasted another thirty or forty minutes. Afterward I went back to the Cottages expecting to find Tom, but he wasn't there, and as far as I could tell he hadn't been home.

This worried me. The MCR was a short walk from the Cottages, not quite three minutes, and so to attend the meeting he had only worn a T-shirt, jeans, and sneakers. There was a freezing rain on my window now, and I knew if he were out in that for more than a couple of minutes he would get dangerously cold.

I called him, but his phone was off. So, uneasy but unsure of what to do, I left my door ajar and spent an hour watching some random college football game online.

Then I started to get really worried. I called again, and his phone was still off. It was darker by now; I showered and talked to Ella and Anneliese, but neither of them had seen him. I thought about going out to find him, but where would I have started?

After a while Ella, who hadn't been at the meeting, came over to my room. She was dressed up as a Catholic schoolgirl, with her pink, silver, black hair in pigtails, a white button-down shirt, knee-high socks, and a green checked skirt.

"Why do you look like that?" I asked.

"Hi to you, too. How was the meeting?"

"Bad."

"I'm supposed to go to a fancy dress birthday party for a girl in my lab. He's still not back?"

"No. You didn't have to come over, though, thanks."

"How long has it been?"

I looked at my watch. "Two hours. Hopefully he just went to the pub, because if he's outside—"

"Maybe I'll go tell the porters he's gone, see what they think."

Just then, though, the door downstairs opened and there were footsteps on the stairs. We both went to my door and saw Tom; his lips were blue, and the hems of his jeans were sodden.

"What the hell happened to you?" I asked.

"I went on a walk. Should have brought a coat."

"Do you think so, Doctor?"

"I'll be fine. Hey, Ella."

She looked upset. "You must have pneumonia."

He laughed. "Don't be so serious, Ella, or either of you. Hey, by the way. I haven't seen you in ages."

"Yeah, welcome back."

There was a pregnant moment then. He looked unusually boyish; that lingers if you went to boarding school, I've always thought, a faint lineament of having been abandoned. Suddenly Ella went over and put her arms around his waist and gave him a kiss. When that was done she led him into his room, never looking at me.

Soon enough they were having sex, pretty plainly. I turned up the volume on my computer and immediately texted Anneliese, liveblogging their progress for her. Half an hour later I heard footsteps, and then the shower we shared at the end of the hallway turned on. When Tom was dried and dressed they knocked on my door together, unsheepish, both glowing, and said they were going over to Ella's, she had some wine.

That was how they first slept together. Tom carried a low temperature for a few days after that, nothing serious.

They were inseparable then. I remember one morning as I was leaving for class seeing him lurch home, like a bear newly awoken out of hibernation, from her room. He grinned privately at me. The smile meant nothing; all the merriness was still emptied from his face. He looked like a bare tree in winter: disconsolate, cold-minded, but somewhere within it still the sun abiding.

CHAPTER SIX

At unexpected moments, not very often, I glance up from whatever I'm doing and realize that I have a longing to be inside an airport, on my way somewhere else.

When I returned to Oxford it was about the second of January, and there were still six days until school started again. Not everyone was back. The people who *were* back didn't have much time, it seemed; Sophie was working hard on her long essay, and I was trying not to stake too much hope to our date for the James Bond bop, Anil was still in Mumbai, Anneliese and her family were visiting the Azores, and after that MCR meeting Ella and Tom were in and out of each other's rooms at all hours. I had assumed the three of us would spend our time together, but Tom, with a fervor unusual for him, seemed to want only Ella's company. It didn't bother me. The first two or three weeks are always that way.

So I slipped away like a Bedouin one morning and boarded the early train to Paris. I had a friend there, a girl named Kristen Johnson, and I had e-mailed her the night before, asking if I could still visit.

"I'm dying of boredom, you have to come," she wrote, and it was she who came to meet me in the open air of the Gare du Nord, which was windy and cold, a few snowflakes hanging in the gray air. I hadn't been there since I spent three months interning at the *International Herald Tribune* one summer during college.

"Will Baker," she said, a big smile on her face. She gave me a hug. "I haven't seen you in forever."

We knew each other from the brief, endless, intense final month of the campaign. She had been my best friend there other than Alison. "Since Ohio, right?"

"Jesus, that was shitty, wasn't it?"

"It still sucks."

"And you don't even remember that terrible Gore campaign."

"Aren't you younger than I am?"

"Right, but I took a semester off of college to work for him. You remember the election—come on, this way—but I mean being inside that campaign when the recount was going on, watching him concede to Bush. It was fucked up."

"Did you see about—"

"Lieberman?"

"Yeah, Lieberman. What a dickhead. Murtha, that wasn't bad, though."

"Fucking Murtha." She sighed. "No, it's a big deal. I'm just a pessimist these days."

Kristen was blond and slight, with light freckles around her nose and quick cheekbones; a live, thin, endearing person, full of energy, with a hoarse laugh. She would make an endlessly entertaining wife and mother to some suburban family one day. That's not to say she was destined to be a housewife—in Paris she was a consultant, having grown up bilingual because her mother was from the St. Lawrence River Valley, near Montreal—only that she had the sort of open, good nature upon which a whole family can come to rely without entirely realizing it.

We were out in the seedy area around the train station, with a big McDonald's and a bunch of cheap hotels opposite, the gray and white buildings ridged with black wrought-iron balconies that for all the soot and cell phone shops made them still beautiful, in the way that Paris alone is capable of permitting every area of life, whatever its wealth, the dignity of aesthetic faultlessness.

"You must want a coffee, right?" she asked. "Or do you just want to go back to my apartment and hang out? I'm on call, but realistically I probably don't have to do anything until the start of the week. Everyone takes about six months for Christmas here."

"How far is it?"

"Pretty far. I live in the seventh."

"What, by the Musée d'Orsay?"

"Yeah, how did you know that? Rue de Verneuil, my street is called. Number fifty. In case you get lost."

"Let's get coffee. I was up early to get the train into London."

We went into one of the cafés and ordered two coffees, standing at the brass-railed bar because they would be cheaper there than if we sat a table. It was a policy I loved. People think of cafés in Paris as romantic, but I appreciated them more for their comity, the loud workmen in neon vests downing *noisettes* over *Le Parisien,* friends to everyone, shoulder-edged with businessmen filling out lottery tickets and old men who at half past nine in the morning sipped sherry and deposited trembling pieces of doughnut between their noses and their chins. Everyone got a shot glass of water, there were the hard-boiled eggs in their small rack, a euro each, the Café Richard sugar tucked into your saucer... then, too, this was a time, 2005, before the smoking ban, when the floor beneath the bar was an enormous clutter of cigarette ends, flaked bread, and torn sugar packets, all of which you were meant, as policy, to drop at your feet. Every half hour or so a small man would come out with a vast broom and sweep the detritus cleanly away, almost archaeologically, like a dream of how life should be: fixable, clearable, there should be fresh starts. Seeing Kristen had reminded me of Alison.

"So how is everything here?" I asked her.

"It's good."

"You're the only other person I know who kept their promise about leaving the country if Bush got reelected," I said.

"It was partly that. I was sick of New York."

"I can't believe we never managed to get together when we were both there."

She shrugged. "Campaign friendships are always the same."

"Don't say that."

"No, it's fantastic to see you! It's great to see you."

"You, too."

I remembered trudging through an early snowfall in Ohio with her and thinking how beautiful she was, on our way to yet another rally. Through the whole six weeks we were together in Columbus we had just been friends, in part because she had been sleeping with the campaign's star, a strategist from D.C. who was rumored to be making fifty grand a month, and of course because I was with Alison.

"So you and Alison . . ."

"It didn't work out."

"Dead and buried?"

I shrugged. "Can you ever be positive?"

She laughed. "Yes," she said, and her voice was emphatic.

I shook my head. "It was jarring how abruptly the campaign ended."

"They always do when you lose, no victory lap. Then some poor asshole has to spend three days breaking down headquarters and sending out the last checks. No more volunteers to lord over, just an empty building full of depressed staffers."

"Yeah, that was me. I stayed. Kerry never showed his face again."

"You stayed? I couldn't face it. I just went home and collapsed."

"Who do you like in 2008?"

"Two years out it's tough to say. I guess Hillary's the presumptive. Edwards will run. He seems like a guy with integrity. What about Mark Warner?"

"From Virginia?"

"Uh-huh. He'll be in there. For me, for us to win, we don't need southern votes as much as we need the West. Like if we can get Colorado, maybe Nevada, Montana."

"That's not many electorals."

"But if he could pick those up and bring Virginia, that would almost cover us losing Ohio again. Of course, Florida would be grand. However we can do it. I just don't want to lose again."

"I don't think we lost it last time."

She sighed. "No, I know, the voting machines." She shook her head. "We should change the subject, before we get too engaged. Really. Tell me about Oxford, distract me."

I noticed she had on mascara and eyeliner and wondered whether it meant anything. "It's fun."

"Are you in looove?" she asked, jokingly.

"I don't know. No. You?"

She nodded. "I think maybe. I have a boyfriend."

"Is it serious?"

"Not yet. I work with him. I'm worried he's back in California, hooking up with everyone he ever went to high school with." She looked at me, suddenly remote, her cup at her cold red lips. "Are you sad you came?"

"Kristen, are you serious?" I took a sip of *café crème*. "Do you remember when I told you that I only wanted to keep one friend from the campaign?"

"I was so nervous when you said you were coming over, you have no idea."

"You shouldn't have been. You're one of my best friends."

"It's shitty being a girl, because you always have to wonder. And we used to have some chemistry."

I smiled. "We did?"

"Oh, fuck off."

We spent that day at her house, both of us in T-shirts and pajama pants, playing video games (she had a PlayStation), recounting stories from the campaign, watching TV, catching up. It was perfect to be with an American person—I didn't need to explain anything, or translate from American English to British English, and all of our stupid references made sense to each other.

After a nap we went out to eat at a café with glass jugs of red wine, still bleary-eyed but in a good mood, and then met up with her friend Amanda at the Café Charbon for drinks and dancing. Amanda hooked up with some French guy.

Eventually Kristen and I went home, and naturally enough, for it was only a studio apartment, fell into bed together. It was just sleeping, though, intertwined, hugging and disentangling and pushing back together, warm and comfortable. It meant the same thing to both of us, I believe, companionship. I felt in a state of vacancy.

"I really do love Cliff," she murmured to me once in the middle of the night, pushing her head under my arm after I came back from the bathroom.

"I know," I said.

When her breath was regular again I got up once more and went to her high windows, opened one, and leaned over the railing, having a cigarette. I could see up the boulevard that led to the river, the greenish Seine I knew so well, which at night runs black and blurred-streetlamp yellow. There's nowhere that life feels more eternal, your dimwit youth more important, than Paris.

Then for some reason my mind turned with a pang to Katie, and as I gazed up at the implacable black of the sky, my body warm from the bed but my face chilled, I thought of the terrible truth we all know, somewhere in our souls: that there has never been a shred of evidence that life goes beyond life. Nobody has sent back word. There is nothing. That does not mean there is nothing. But there is nothing.

There are rarely two kinds of anything, but here are the two kinds of Paris: first, the graveyard, Les Deux Magots, 68, Saint-Sulpice, Montmartre; second, the carnival, Arabs, Brazilian bars in Oberkampf, students lurking in the *shops aux bandes dessinées* behind Greektown. They are meant to be countervailing—every third day *Le Monde* publishes an article about how young people are leaving—but as I saw it each licensed the other to exist.

In the three days I spent in Paris, mostly alone during the daytime to give Kristen space, I visited both. I went to the Louvre and also to BHV, where I bought a flash card for my digital camera, down to Shakespeare and Company, where I once slept a night, over to Bastille, even to the far-flung Butte-aux-Cailles, which is like a French village with a city accidentally sprouted up around it. I sat in the park outside Saint-Julien-le-Pauvre church, gazing up at Notre Dame. I drank a lot of coffee, ate omelettes, spoke French. I sat in cafés and wrote long, improbably stupid poems about Sophie or Alison. I think sleeping in the same bed with Kristen every night made me miss them.

On my last night Kristen and I put on nice clothes and went out to Bofinger, one of the few traditional and grand restaurants in town that hadn't been completely rousted out of obscurity by the

Internet, and had a huge three-tiered fuck-you of clams, mussels, lobster, and crab, and three bottles of cold, sharp white wine, as Hemingway would have said, all followed by cigarettes, dessert, more wine. We sat not far from the 1939 bullet hole in the mirror above a booth.

Afterward we walked to the Caveau des Oubliettes to see some jazz. Our arms were linked, the city busy around us and then quiet, changing block by block. "Do you remember Dylan?" she asked as we crossed onto Ile St. Louis.

"I don't think so," I said.

"He was from the campaign."

"Well, obviously."

"He was from Toledo. He had his car there?"

"Oohhh—yeah, I do. Not on staff."

She shook her head. "No, no, he was an intern. He put in a fuckton of hours, though."

"He used to bring in bagels."

She laughed. "That's right, and like the assholes we were everyone was willing to be his best friend because of it."

I laughed. "What makes you think of him?"

She sighed. "I don't know. Do you think you'll work for someone in 2008?"

She meant one of the campaigns. "It depends," I said. "What about you?"

"That's what I was thinking about. I guess if the opportunity came up I would."

"Who?"

"That's what I mean—I don't think it matters. A Dem, of course, but beyond that..." She waved a hand.

I looked at her doubtfully. "What do you mean?"

She cocked her head. "I don't know, really. I have a theory that whatever you really love, if it's a person or a thing or a job, you'll go back for more, no matter how much bullshit and misery it means. I miss politics. I miss all the hotel rooms and inside jokes and . . . and everything. The Dylans."

"But it's been so disheartening."

"That's what's amazing! All of this horrible fucked-up bullshit hasn't, hasn't dampened my enthusiasm. I mean, it has—but not *really*, not deep down."

"A person or a thing or a job?" I asked.

"Whatever you love."

I got back into Oxford in the early evening of January 9, just a little daylight left. I wanted company. Tom's room was dark; Ella's, too. I learned later that they had gone into London, thinking that I wouldn't be back until the next day—or at least that's what they told me. It's likely that they didn't care. I dumped my bags in my room and checked the MCR, but it was empty, and then I started idly through Fleet's front quad, empty and austere, its white stone cold to the touch, feeling sorry for myself, the aleatory sorrow of passing winter loneliness.

On an impulse I took out my cell phone and texted Jess. She wrote back to me right away.

Hey, it's Will.

So you ARE alive.

Sorry I didn't write back on Facebook, I was abroad. Do you want to hang out?

Nothing else going on?

Would be fun to see you! Watch a movie and order food?

Then there was a long pause, until she wrote:

Too much of a palaver here with roommates. Can I come there?

Sure.

She appeared at my door an hour and a half later, her face decorated with the exaggerated but strangely beautiful makeup of the English working-class twenty-something, her arms bare and cold when she leaned in to give me a kiss on the cheek.

"I can't believe you never wrote me back, to my message," she said. I was always surrounded with BBC accents and always forgot her voice.

"It's been a weird couple of weeks."

She rolled her eyes. "Yeah, okay."

"No, it has. Tom—actually, it's funny, Tom is the one who always tells me to call you because you're so hot—"

"That snot?"

"Yeah. Anyway, his sister—"

"No, it's okay," she said. "Get me inside, I'm freezing. How was your Christmas?"

"Lonely."

"I'm sorry."

I felt a swelling of affection for her, and now I think of what Michael Caine said in *Hannah and Her Sisters,* "I loved her more than I realized." Just perhaps not enough.

Term started in earnest that Monday. Anneliese returned with a tan, and Peter, Giorgio, and Richard resumed their parliamentary wrangling. Anil came back full of plans to dress up for the imminent James Bond bop as James Bond, "but with a twist!" as he told me one day in the kitchen of our house. We were making tea.

"What's the twist?"

"You know what?" He was full of sudden resolve. "I'm going to show you my costume. If you swear yourself to secrecy."

"Why me?" I asked. "I'd have thought you'd show Timmo."

"I know you've been to the 40/40 Club."

I would never achieve anything greater in Anil's eyes. "I have."

"I need your opinion. You see, I'm going to the bop as James Bond—but black."

"It seems like there's the potential for that to be racist."

"No, no, you'll see. Wait here."

I sat in the kitchen and read for fifteen minutes, waiting for his return.

It didn't disappoint. He was dressed in a plain tux, but his body was baroque with accessories: a heavy gold chain, a huge watch, Adidas sneakers, and a flat-brimmed Yankees hat, from beneath which his chubby Indian face beamed.

There was a loaded silence, until I said, "It's the best costume I've ever seen."

He beamed at me. "Game recognizes game!"

If Anil was unchanged, Tom, in his own way, was the same. To me he seemed mostly like himself. As people returned they all wanted to see him with their own eyes, but other than that first MCR meeting, he had behaved as he always did. Perhaps it was Ella—though after their first flush of romance he did retreat from her slightly, even then he couldn't bear to be apart from her for the night.

For her part Ella was ecstatic. Nothing in her speech or her manner showed it—if anything she was more diffident with him, and her *noli me tangere* air of the start of the year seemed to return, like a bulwark against possible hurt—but if you knew her as I did, it was obvious how tremulously and deeply affected she was. I think she had expected them to be a couple right away, but some final new distance in Tom prevented that. Still, as long as she got to see him every day it didn't seem to bother her. She even canceled a trip to a conference in Leeds and had the money, paid for by her scholar-ship, refunded to her.

I remember exactly how she spent it. We were walking down the High Street together one morning, on our way to get lunch to-gether, and she stopped at the window of a boutique.

"Remind me what Tom's favorite color is, Will?"

"I have no clue."

"Try and remember."

"Is it important? I'm freezing."

"Come on, you know. We were playing that drinking game you taught us? Favorites?"

Then I did remember. It was a game from college; whoever started off had to name a favorite, whether it was a color or a kind of beer, and anyone who shared that preference had to drink. The better you knew each other the more esoteric the categories be-came: favorite character on *The Simpsons,* favorite pub in Oxford proper, favorite philosopher. (Any Wiggum, the King's Arms, and Hume were my answers to those.)

"I do remember, that's right. It was yellow, wasn't it?"

"Yellow," she said, and I saw she had known the answer all along. "Will you come into the shop with me?"

"What do you have your eye on?"

"That dress in the window."

"The yellow one? Because of Tom?"

"No! It just reminded me of that game. That's why I thought of it. Because I drank at yellow, too. I love yellow, too."

"Will your boobs fit in there?"

She smacked my arm. "Do you like it?"

"I just don't think of you wearing dresses. There are no tears in it or safety pins or anything."

She bought it. The dress was made by BCBG and cost 140 pounds.

I remember the price clearly; it scared me to see her putting herself at Tom's mercy like that, though I didn't say anything.

Perhaps I should have. I didn't know about Tom—we hadn't been friends long enough for me to judge his precariousness. Recently he had taken to spending hours and hours in his room researching, of all things, his family history. There was something wild-eyed in it. He had found forums on the Internet devoted to genealogy, and he followed every branch, his maternal grandmother's maternal grandmother, as far as it would go. He found that his father's great-grandfather had been a Crane—my middle name—and set out to see if we were cousins (which we were, a hundred times removed, like more or less all white people). I know he wasn't doing his work. The night before, I had gone into his room and seen him swallowing a pill.

"What's that?" I asked.

"Acetaminophen," he said. "My family—you wouldn't believe—" and on he ran.

The pill had come out of a prescription bottle, I saw. What had Ella let herself in for? There was something immovable and titanic hooking him backward. She wasn't likely to pull against it successfully. Love, though: Who can say.

I understood the position well enough myself. Yet I had hope. Sophie and I were still texting every day, even if we hadn't seen each other since I returned, and both of us were looking forward to the James Bond bop that Saturday, our date.

What should I be? she texted me that Friday, and then, not fifteen seconds later, *I'm going to be Moneypenny! I need a new dress!*

HOBNOBS! I wrote back to her and felt a constriction of happiness and nerves in my chest. Part of me dared to wonder if the bop might be the night when she finally . . . what, became mine? Changed? Yielded? I didn't know. It was more realistic to hope in blurry outlines than for anything specific.

Because of the bop I had had to tell St. John Jarvis that I couldn't come to his annual Christmas party, which he held on the twentieth of January. When I wrote to say as much, he pidged back a note inviting me to have coffee or a cocktail that afternoon, so at three o'clock I headed out past the Fleet lawns, crossed the river, and walked through the fields on the other side to his house. It was gray and wet out, and the forecast was for a sharp drop in temperature that evening.

I arrived at his house soaked. He slapped me on the back, shepherded me through from the porch to his living room, and placed me in front of the huge fire burning in the hearth.

"Warm up here," he said. "I'll get you a drink."

The decorations for the party were a marvel. In the living room there was what must have been a fifteen-foot tree, layered thickly with silver balls, fairy lights, ornaments, and Christmas crackers. On all the walls were ornate snowflakes made of green and red crepe paper. Except for two armchairs all the furniture had been cleared out of the room, and a huge sideboard was racked with thirty or forty bottles of liquor. Another sideboard, presumably for food, was still empty.

There is something sorrowful in an old man without children, and I wondered, as I sat alone, who the party was for—whether it was for himself, to surround himself with people and noise. When he came back into the room with two mugs, bearing a triumphant smile, and said, "Irish coffee—hope you like it," I remembered that he was one of those humans who are sufficient unto themselves, a sovereign nation-state.

"Perfect, thank you," I said, and he sat. "I'm sorry to miss this, by the way."

"Oh, it's my favorite holiday. Though I must say I loved Thanksgiving while I was over in your country, carousing with your uncle. There's something deeply satisfying about watching American football on a full stomach, even if you don't understand it. Christ knows I never did."

"Do you do this every year?"

"Mm, a grand tradition, Christmas in January. They say the holiday should in fact be in August, or something like that—I can never remember exactly when. Apparently it's only in December because of old pagan harvest rituals. I wonder what the pope thinks about that. Have you ever read Jessie Weston, or is she dated by now? I suspect she is. Even if you're not fond of Eliot she's well worth looking into, though, she holds up nicely. Although I forget, you're a modernist. I imagine you're devoted to Eliot."

"Less than some. But why the twentieth of January?"

He grinned and took a gulp of the coffee. "Better to celebrate when people have returned. Oxford is such a tidal city, people in and out, and Christmas is a low tide. I'm sure you left, for instance. How was it? Christmas at home?"

"Yep."

"Did you go back feeling like an Oxford man? Or do you wish you were still there?"

"It's funny you ask that—"

"Ah, here we are. What's the dilemma?"

"Oh, I don't know. I was wondering if I should become an academic, actually. Something my—well, my once-upon-a-time father-in-law-to-be said to me, if that's not too convoluted. It made me think that politics might not be right for me in the end."

"What did he say?"

I told him. "I've been enjoying school, too. I didn't think I would love the work this much."

He looked at me appraisingly. "Remind me who your adviser is?"

"Harris."

"Harris, Harris, that's right. You're Orwell. I once met a chap named Jack Common, Orwell's chosen prole. He lived in one room with a wife and about fifty children and wrote terrible novels. Not that I blame him, mind you. Who could work in those circumstances? Can't have been a real name, either. Anyhow, Harris. So you're enjoying Orwell."

"I am," I said, my thoughts on the Swift Prize. "More than I expected I would. I'm thinking of a doctorate." He smiled, eyes shrewd, and I rushed to add, "Though I'm not sure I want to write for an audience of the same twenty scholars my entire life."

He shook his head. "Very foolish, that anxiety. Academics are the canaries in the coal mine. We shift an idea out into the world and it trickles from fifteen readers in a semiotics journal to a hundred listeners at a dinner party to ten thousand readers in a magazine to a million viewers on a television. I've seen it time and again. What were academics interested in the 1970s? Orientalism, in your field, our field. The perception of race and the other. And ever so slowly I watched as that debate flattened out and grew broad, and then, in the 1990s, finally, after a lifetime of waiting for it, I watched as people became, imagine it, 'politically correct.'" He laughed. "What a triumph, to live to see the backlash against that.

"It's not unlike modern art, which is a passion of yours as it is of mine, as I recall. In 1962 to walk into a gallery and see a painting by Barnett Newman, a few lines on a blank canvas..." He was lost in thought for a moment. Then he returned his eyes to me from the floor. "Now? You can buy a pale handed-down imitation of Ad Reinhardt at a hardware store for thirty pounds, comes with a gold frame, and all the throw pillows and rugs have those Rothko smears on them. Abstraction is decoration. These hedge fund managers buying Brice Mardens are buying decorations, DIY store decorations. They're valuable the way the Ralph Lauren logo is valuable. Ideas have always descended from the high culture to the low culture, William. We open these gates and soon enough people walk through them. There's nothing else I believe as fervently as that. Listen."

"What if that's not fast enough for me?"

He laughed. "I was once in that kind of rush," he said.

"And?"

"There's a balance. The key is to find a home outside of the academy, too—write for the papers, go on television, travel to foreign conferences and sleep with foreign women. That's what I've done. There's nothing drearier than a professor who stays at home all day and beavers away at his favorite Jacobin poet. I wrote for *The Observer* for years, you know."

"How did you get that job?"

"When I was in Japan in the sixties, actually. England was such a self-absorbed little islet back then that if you went to Marseille they considered you an explorer. I might as well have been on Jupiter. I called up an acquaintance who worked for the automobile review section of *The Observer*, of all things, and offered to write a series of letters from Tokyo."

"It's too bad everywhere's so close these days."

"Yes," he said. "The death of the great journey. All of the leaps mankind makes now will be informational, I'm afraid. It's a shame. For a thousand years or so we struggled and strove to see the corners of the planet, and now that's done. It's why I have a computer. But tell me something of yourself. Why are you skipping my party tonight?"

"I paid in advance to go to a bop at Exeter."

"How much?"

"Twenty pounds."

"I daresay you could get twenty pounds of drink here—though of course you want to be with your friends. Have you got a girlfriend?"

I was tempted to tell him about Sophie; even now I pictured her in the shower, getting her hair ready, putting on makeup. It wouldn't be long. "No, just a couple of casual things."

"That's another reason to stay in Oxford. There are always new people, new girls. If the work here is satisfying you ought to stay. Washington will remain where it is, but being twenty-five and abroad—that won't. What's crucial is that you must love the material. You do, I hope? I could never get through *Animal Farm,* thought it was drivel, though people say the essays are terribly good."

"I do."

"Then stay."

Again I stayed much longer than I had intended to stay. I loved his company, his friendliness, his oracular lack of reserve. We talked about what to wear at a job interview, how to fool a board of academic questioners, where I should publish my dissertation if I wrote it, whether Orwell's widow was an angel or the devil, what exactly constituted a perfect Irish coffee. He put Guinness in his, and evidently a lot of whiskey, because when I finally staggered out of his house at five thirty. I was drunk. The Swift Prize never came up, but in his unblinking way he had seen it, and in my pidge later that week I would find the application form. There was no note attached.

I called Sophie as I walked back to the Cottages from his house. "Hey!"

"Hey," she said. "I was just getting ready."

"What are you going to wear?"

"Chanel Number—" She laughed and said, "No, it's too silly, I can't say it. I have a dress with sequins all over it. You'll see."

"I bet."

"Are you going to get me drunk?" She seemed buoyant. "I haven't been drunk in forever. I can't believe how madly I worked on that stupid essay. Thank God it's over."

"You're coming by at seven?"

"Yep. Two and a half hours. Shall we go over in a cab with Ella and Tom, or meet them there?"

"Maybe we should let them have some time to themselves," I said hopefully.

"Cool. I'll just come by yours."

We hung up, and I smiled, thinking first of her, then of my conversation with St. John. Perhaps after all I could see myself at Oxford for good, away from America. Even the idea, unacted upon, was an emancipation.

As I came back to the Cottages Anil, Timmo, and Anneliese were leaving for the park—they wanted to test a kite they were building from a kit, whose maiden flight they would call us out to the lawns to witness next Tuesday, when they would with great ceremony crash it straight into a tree—and Tom was away, so the house was empty.

I showered, and when I had finished I stood in front of the mirror for some time, staring at myself. I shaved. Then I went back to my room to put on my dinner jacket. My windows were open, and the wind was whipping the curtains inward. I put loud music on and then walked to Tom's room and stole a beer. (He always seemed to have a disconcerting quantity of them in his little refrigerator, these days, standing in well-ordered platoons along the three shelves, bearing the soldierly ribbons and regalia of beer-festival victory.) Life seemed peculiar, giddy. The imminence of things, how the wind and the beer and the music can seem to hold a future: That was how I felt.

At ten to seven the door rang, and I knew before I buzzed it open that it was Sophie, ten minutes early, and her earliness added to that sensation.

"Wills!" she called as she came up the stairs. "I'm early!"

"I'm naked!" I called out from my room. I could hear her footsteps on the stairs.

"You'd better be!"

I stepped out into the hallway, dressed, and she laughed. She looked radiant. Her hair was pinned up, wisps of it falling down her neck, and she wore a short black sheath and high heels. At her breastbone was a confusion of silver necklaces, which dipped between the tantalizing nearness of the tops of her breasts.

She put an arm around my neck and kissed me on the cheek. "Give me a drink, would you?"

"Beer?"

"No, wine, you cad."

I grinned. "One minute—go sit down."

"I'm changing the music!" she called out behind me as I sprinted into Tom's room, digging through his things, searching for wine.

"Okay!" I said.

Tom had nothing. Lily Allen had just become popular and "Littlest Things" came on. In desperation I cracked Anil's door and saw, to my delight, that he had four bottles in the rack on his desk. They looked perilously expensive, but I didn't care. I took a bottle, fetched two glasses from the kitchen, and went back.

My bed was strewn with clothes, unmade, and my heart quickened when I saw that Sophie had chosen to sit next to my pillow, cross-legged. She was examining my high school yearbook.

"I found wine."

"You look like a baby!" she said, tapping the page she was looking at.

I smiled. "No credit for the wine?"

"Who'd you steal it from?"

"Nobody," I said indignantly.

"Anil," she said.

"No!"

"Hey, have you called a cab yet, to come for seven?"

"Not yet."

"Oh, good. Don't, then. Let's drink this bottle."

"Perfect. Anil has three more, too."

She laughed, and with a heave of courage I set myself right next to her, so that as we both leaned over my yearbook our heads nearly touched. I poured the wine and told her about the people she pointed out. My mind was only half there; it was happening, I could tell. I had a tension in my breath, and a hollow feeling in my solar plexus of the kind I get with any great emotion, happiness or sadness, and I was all nerves, filled with almost painful joy.

As I poured her second glass she closed the yearbook and pivoted so that we were facing each other Indian-style, knees touching. "What was the most romantic night of your life?"

"Honestly?" I asked.

"Of course."

I wasn't honest. "The first night my old girlfriend from college and I hooked up."

She giggled. "Will."

"What?"

She giggled some more. "I think I'm slurvy."

There was what felt like a very long pause, the music confidential. The candles along my desk, which she had evidently lit, flickered and guttered at every draft of wind. "It's cold in here," she said and rubbed her arms.

"Lula's party was kind of romantic," I said.

"Oh, William," she said in some dazed way and smiled sweetly, looking directly into my eyes. She leaned her whole body into mine and kissed me on the lips and then, after a minute, pushed me into a heap on the bed. We kissed more pressingly, not quite tearing each other's clothes off but with our legs and arms knitted and her hair, she had unpinned it, falling into my face, our faces constantly close. We kissed each other's lips and cheeks and necks. I took her shirt off.

"Nice," I said.

She laughed, straddling me. "Will, you muppet. Don't say things like that."

Then she lowered back down over me and we kissed. My dick was as hard as it had ever been—and may ever be, barring some unforeseen and strange pharmacological intervention—and she stroked it through my jeans. I don't know. I was half in shock. I remember her kissing my neck as I looked out the window at the lights on in the dorms. The door opened, and Anil and Timmo came banging up the stairs, laughing and chattering about their kite and the bop, and Sophie and I laughed into each other's mouths at our new secret, saying "Shh!" at the same time.

It's tedious, I'm sure, to hear too much about how beautiful a girl is, but I think of it: her high cheekbones, the long, unruly hair down her back. She looked flushed and happy, and I remember feeling so relieved that what filled her face wasn't guilt or diffidence but just happiness. I'm sure it filled mine, too.

Her thighs were wet, and as I touched her she didn't moan but caught her breath in the back of her throat, then exhaled it in little bursts. She took off my shirt and as I started to put two fingers inside her she bit my chest and pushed back on my hand. She still had one hand on the outside of my jeans and started to rub it harder—painfully, one of the little irritants that make sex so ludicrous and personal.

"Ouch," I said.

"I'm hurting you?" she asked.

"No, no."

We shifted off of each other and she lay at my side, looking at me with a smile in her face.

"I'm so wet," she said. She arched her back.

I kissed her. "Do you want me to go down—can I please—"

"Just, let's have sex," she said. She threw her thin arms around my neck.

At that moment I paused. She could tell. "Sophie," I said. "You know how I feel."

She looked serious, her hair falling down at me from above, and then she smiled. "Are you saying no?"

I rolled my eyes, smiling, too. "No, I'm not."

She laughed and stood up. The song had ended a while before. "We need more music. Something with words. If we're going to do this."

"Okay."

She put on this random mix I sometimes listened to back then. The first song was "Underneath Your Clothes" by Shakira. We laughed. When she got back to the bed the mood was altered—instead of that passionate, back-scratching foreplay, it was smoother and calmer. She lay back on the bed, smiling up at me beatifically. I half-stood above her and she raised her head to wet my dick with her mouth. Then we lay down and as I sank on top she guided me inside her.

"God," she said, a quarter of the way in.

Nobody has ever described sex accurately. I can't either. There's something near-impossible to record about the sensation of your stretches of skin, something internal, the comprehensive accuracy and correctness of the junction, the corresponding interior sensations, all of it. Don't tell us about hot breath, don't tell us about hair in each other's faces, we know all that—but there's nothing else to say either.

After it was done she fell straight to sleep on top of me, which I adored, and I dozed, too, waking up every few minutes to check that it was all still happening: a curse, always to be looking backward and forward from the moment. She was asleep when I said, "Look," and pointed out at the pale black January sky.

She turned her head, and a drowsy smile came onto her face. "Snow," she murmured and pressed her face again into my bare chest, kissing it with her lips.

As she slept I watched the flurries falling onto the evergreen trees outside my window, scatterbrained, windblown, and wild at first, gusting past the curtains into the room and landing suicidally on my floor, then steady and heavy and plodding, accumulating: the two things, love and snow, that make the world look fresh again, angelic. I thought of when we had gone punting and she said she could stay in Oxford forever, that it was like home already.

Soon everything outside was an unbroken white. The heart, my heart, always understands before I do when happiness is possible.

CHAPTER SEVEN

Foucault theorized that as religious faith began to decline, physicians assumed the role that for centuries had belonged to priests. A doctor and a cleric were equally oracular, passing down decrees the common man didn't have the expertise or language to question. Both could claim admission to the penetralia of a body unintelligible to most men. It was never faith that disappeared—it only turned inward rather than upward, and the bearer of its news changed uniforms.

At Oxford we had scouts. With the next two cottages, Tom, Anil, and I shared a windburnt man with a white mustache named Strickland. He would vacuum our rooms and empty our bins, but he had no real interest in the constant service of the antique world, nor any real warmth. Yet he knew everything: how to cheat an extra mug's use out of a tea bag, when we were supposed to run down to Merton and walk around the quad backward, how to slide a fourth into Hall without a reservation. Battels, John Evelyn, loons, mods, prelims, hacks, rustication, bumps, vivas, the Other Place. Most of the day he would sit on the banister reading the *Daily Sport* (a tabloid dedicated almost exclusively to soft pornography) and smoke Woodbines. We treated him with intense respect.

When I slipped out to the bathroom in the hallway, with Sophie still asleep, he was on the banister. On our hall table were two white drinks in handled glasses.

"Take her them," he said.

"What is it?"

"Rum, egg, nutmeg, and cream, hotted up."

"Strick, I can't give her that, it sounds disgusting."

He looked at me levelly, trying to assess the true depths of my ignorance. "It's an Oxford Dairy. Tradition when a young lady stays by. I brung 'em to Lord Threepwood by the dozen."

So I took the drinks to Sophie. She laughed. "We always heard about these in school. What a tart I've become." We drank them in silence—they were stronger than I would have expected—and watched the snow fall outside, as the brilliant hard light of morning slowly suffused the pine trees, shagged with ice.

The night before, after sleeping together, we had roused ourselves into our clothes and gone to the bop with Anil—whose black James Bond costume met with universal censure—and Anneliese, meeting Tom and Ella there. Tom had been dangerously drunk. Sophie had warned me not to kiss her in public, but in the end we had nevertheless siphoned ourselves off behind a column with a bronze bust of an old don and clung to each other, and at eleven we decided the hell with it and flagged a taxi home. We slept interleaved on my narrow bed, the windows still cracked, our heat under my heavy down blanket balanced by the chill of the room.

At eight or just after she had stirred.

"Hey, Will," she murmured. I ran my fingers over one of her breasts and then the rib beneath it. "Mm," she said and stretched like a cat.

"Are you sober now?" I smiled as I asked this, but she detected the seriousness of the question and turned her head away, human on my faithless arm.

"I feel..." There was a break as she searched her feelings, then decided, "Hungover and happy."

We were silent for a minute. I tried not to, but at last I said, "What changed?"

"Oh, Will."

"You can understand why I'm curious."

To my surprise it was something specific that had brought her to me, not impulse. "I found out on Wednesday, my friend Clementine called me—one of Lula's best friends, actually. She's a horrible spiteful girl. She told me that I had to know, that Jack's been sleeping with a girl we all went to school with. Minka, not that it means anything to you. She was a nightmare back then, too."

"Did you like anyone at school?"

She smiled sadly. "She was pretty, though."

"I'm sorry."

She turned over and got up on her elbows. I was still on my back, so she was looking into my face. "Do you know what happened when Clem called me? I was in seventh heaven. I knew I could finish my essay and then come over and be with you."

"Be with me?" I repeated carefully.

"Sleep with you," she said.

"Just that?"

She studied me, her light brown eyes hunting in mine. "I think just that," she said. "I'm sorry."

I looked at her for a long time. I didn't say anything.

"What, Will?"

"Nothing."

"He's apologized."

"And that's it?"

"I'm not going to turn everything upside down. I know him too well by now for that." There was a silence. "People are flawed."

This was a boilerplate evasion, fatalistic, but I thought I perceived a pleasure she took in it. It's hard to describe. It was tied up in her Englishness, in her youth, in her parents. Perhaps it was that in the end she and Jack were the same. Having no home for so long, they had each had made a home of their manners. There was something sent-away and patrician about it: prejudiced, cold, insular, correct. Would she rather have felt loved or secure? Sometimes they're shaded into each other.

"You have lots of choices," I said.

She was silent for a while. "I like you," she said at last, her voice very quiet.

The sun grew brighter in the room, and after a while she sat up and started to gather her clothes, sitting on the edge of the bed. I reached out and touched her arm, and then it took no effort to pull her back to me. We kissed and it all started again.

Everyone in college was a wreck because of the bop, but at sundown word went around the cottages about a moonlight snowball fight on the lawns, graduate students against undergraduate students, with Giorgio and Jem as team captains. (The referee was Anil, deemed appropriately judicious because he liked all the graduates but was irrationally terrified of the bartender.) Sophie and I went out and took turns playing and then going into the bar, where there was hot chocolate. When we got tired of playing we sat in the snow together, my back against a tree, her back against my chest, my arms over her shoulders.

By far our best player was Anneliese, who not once but twice ran across the median and freed our prisoners. Both times she was rewarded with ten pounds of snow in the face, but entered jail holding one hand up in a fist of solidarity to the overwhelming cheers of our team. Because of her we won.

Our faces stinging, we gathered in the MCR for drinks afterward.

"I'm going to miss this next year," Sophie said fondly, gesturing out toward the loud room. We were alone in the kitchen because we had said we'd fetch more wine.

"What do you mean?" I asked.

Now she looked at me. "The AHRC wouldn't give me money to stay."

"Shit. What are you going to do?"

"I don't know. Travel, perhaps. Jack will be somewhere."

"But you love it here."

She smiled faintly. "Yes," she said. "I love it here."

I took her hand. "Shall we slip away?"

She looked at me. "I think I'm going to turn into a pumpkin anytime, now."

"What?"

"I should go back to my room." She gave me a soft kiss on the mouth. "Thank you, though."

"We don't have to stop."

"I told you before." She crossed her arms in front of her chest, bumping her necklace. "I'm sorry, Will."

She was true to her word. For the rest of January and into February I saw her only occasionally, in town or biking past Fleet, her long legs down on her pedals. Her manner at these times was easier than ever, friendly, I thought perhaps even full of love.

My heart sank when I thought of the time we lived in the same city diminishing. We had that night, though, it was mine to keep;

because of that there was some reservoir of hope still inside me. Indeed, every evening when I returned from the library I half-expected to find her waiting in my room.

I never did. Once in Paris I was with a French girl I knew, and I asked her why she had never managed to go back to school, why she had stayed at the investment bank where she worked. She laughed and said, "Anything can happen in life, you know. Especially nothing."

It was unoriginal of him, but Tom started to drink too much: not just on weekends but each afternoon, each evening, on weekdays. Ella tagged after him fairly often, but she had commitments in the lab, and I sometimes dodged over from the Bodleian, but in the end it came to him drinking alone four, perhaps five times a week.

He chose a noble venue for his decline: the King's Arms, Oxford's most famous and visible pub, situated at the end of Broad Street, the town's busiest thoroughfare, a stone's throw from the Bod.

It was a cheerful place with a big room in front and three smaller ones in the back, one of which had a high fireplace in it. There was more light at the KA than in other pubs, with windows along every wall because it was at the corner of two streets. There were oars commemorating ancient Boat Race victories hanging among the rafters, college photographs dotting the walls, and above the bar 1950s advertisements for beer. Its walls were honey-colored, its couches soft and comfortable. All of the fixtures at the bar were brass, which gleamed brilliantly, their light reflected off of the rows of glasses that hung above them. Oxford students will tell you that it's a tourists' pub, but every one of them seems to be there after exams, or on the first day of spring when they put tables outside.

The KA served as a hitching post in town, and gradually people from the MCR other than Ella, Anneliese, and I realized that Tom was always there, always at the same small table stacked with papers and books about genealogy, doing who knows what, tracing out family trees, I suppose, utterly absorbed. I had to have the same stupid conversation with a dozen different people, all concerned about him drinking alone, the empty pint glasses stacked in front of him. They knew about his sister, of course. In a way I'm afraid that at first I didn't mind, even liked, that feeling of being at the center of intrigue, the hushed conversations, rich with false degrees of anxiety to justify their gossiping tone. But I reached the limit of my patience when Giorgio said something.

Giorgio's daemon at Oxford was his electronic organizer, a bulky piece of hardware he managed with an officious little stylus. He caught me in the MCR one day (I was probably hanging around to see if Sophie would come along, like an idiot) and whipped this contraption out.

"Will, Will, good," he said. "I know I meant to speak to you about something... what was it? Hmmm... ah, yes, here it is." He looked up. "Tom. I hear Tom's been spending too much time at the pub."

"What?"

"Drinking too much, Will. Of course, his poor sister died recently."

I frowned at him. "You put that in your PalmPilot?"

"It's not a PalmPilot, actually, it's—"

"Tom's not MCR business, Giorgio."

Here he felt on firmer ground. "I understand your feelings as a friend, Will, but I consider that the welfare of my students here at

Fleet is primary among my responsibilities. I have a duty to make sure each and every one of you is healthy and happy. Now, a few questions." He read from his PalmPilot. "How often does Tom have more than six drinks at one sitting?"

"What?"

"How often during the past year has he failed to do what was normally expected of him because of drinking?"

"What is this?"

"Has his drinking affected his sexual performance?"

I burst out laughing. "Giorgio, this is ridiculous."

"Has he or anyone else been injured because of his drinking? These are medical questions, Will."

The next afternoon—at the King's Arms—I told Tom about the questionnaire. I presented it as a joke to see how he'd react.

"Fucking hell, is that what people are saying?"

"Kind of," I said.

"You used to love drinking."

"I still have that passion, never fear."

He was quiet for a minute. "I guess I could try to cut down." Then he smiled and stood up. "I wish Giorgio would ask Ella about my sexual performance. She would smack him. I'm getting another pint of Young's, do you want one?"

I nodded. "Yeah, why not. Let's grab those seats by the fireplace, though. It's freezing by the window."

"No, let's stay. I like to look out."

In class that early February we read *Pnin*, Nabokov's comedy about a Russian professor in America and his many befuddlements. On the day we came to class to discuss it, our teacher—whose mood we had advanced far enough into the year to judge—looked dangerous, brusque, and bored. Then Larry made the mistake of declaring he thought the book a postmodernist trifle.

There was a long moment of tense silence before she said, "Larry, why would a person choose to write a novel?"

"Ego," he answered immediately.

"Anyone else?"

Money, someone said, and then a third added perhaps just aptitude.

"Then why not write a television show? More money in that. More sex, too."

"It's hard to get a television show made," Helena offered.

"That's a pathetic reason to write a novel."

"A good novel makes you love life more," said Sullivan.

"Don't quote at me. Give me a reason."

"Diegesis," I said.

She shook her head. "Regurgitation from Michaelmas. Wayne Booth." Then it had been one of her favorite subjects: how the novel alone could present interior states, whereas plays and movies had to present the action without authorial comment. "What I want to know is why you're all here—why we care about *Pnin*, all of us other than Larry."

"I care."

"Anyone else?"

There was silence. I'm sure we all had our answers, but our teacher, a wispy, caffeinated woman, was, though usually amiable, in her rare moments of unfriendliness, such as this one, intimidating.

When none of us spoke she did, and what she said troubled me, forced me into thought, and, in the end, altered my plans.

She began by saying that our class was starting out at the end of time. No, she wasn't speaking about belatedness—she meant it seriously. The past century had been an arms race of postmodernism, from Joyce to Borges to *The Interrogation* to *Satantango*. The outright self-eradicating absurdism of Barth and Barthelme, the purposive nonsense of *Tel Quel,* had taken the long saga to its logical extremity. Romance novelists now used the same tricks that had dazzled the avant-garde of the thirties and forties; what had seemed daring in *Hopscotch* was the favored structure of a series of children's books. There might still be incidental curlicues of invention to come, but effectively the possibilities of formal innovation in fiction had been finalized.

For a postmodernist trifle, she said, try David Foster Wallace—a sterile sense of play, at bottom sentimental, but ironized to a degree of coolness. Franzen and McEwan wrote big Victorian triple-deckers, excellently plotted, conservative at heart. The incorporation of minor postmodern tricks made it possible for them to retain character and story, the pleasures that made the novel, while retaining the snob appeal of postmodernism. It was a runaround.

Here we returned to *Pnin.* If you wanted to study postmodernism, technique, the formalities of fiction, it was a fair pursuit, she said. But what came first for her was something older, what the novel could achieve, she felt, that no other form of art could: The novel was where our deepest correspondences called out to each other. It was how we moved each other into recognition of ourselves.

There was a silence in the room.

Take her example, she said, television. Its consumption was passive—there had been neurological studies about that—and then by the time a show reached the air, most shows, it had been so diluted of its intent, by notes, by commerce, by the choices of actors, that it was streamlined and glamorized into dangerous serial purity.

What about music, someone asked, or painting.

She smiled. She loved music, she said, but it's an emotion. A very deep emotion, but one that bears little analysis. The opposite of visual art, in a sense: visual art one could absorb in five seconds, but beyond that it was hard to see it freshly, it gave way to analytical reification. There was no duration to visual art. She loved both, and neither was in competition with the novel—but if they had been, their inarticulacy was their doom, pushing them briefly ahead of fiction, striking quickly and then falling off, the hare and the tortoise. No, it was the novel that offered the most sustained, honest interrogation of the human experience. It was interesting to consider *Pnin*'s formal syntax, but it moved her only as a tool that came to express Pnin's solitude, his helplessness. In the end, for that least academically fashionable reason, too: because it was autobiographical. Nabokov left Russia at the revolution and lived out his life in a country where the train timetables looked wrong, the butterflies were named differently. She looked at Larry gently and said that she would like him to read the book's last pages again, just the final two or three. Then, smiling to soften the intensity of her long monologue, she said not to forget, after all, that Nabokov wrote a novel in footnotes before Wallace was born. Though she had enjoyed the cruise ship essay.

"Christ," muttered Sullivan as we walked out of class.

"Tell me about it."

For the rest of the afternoon I felt a terrible disturbance. What was I studying in Oxford? There was the esoteric syntax of academic writing, virtuosic in its way but always half-a-trick—guilty until proven innocent, as Orwell said all saints should be. The essay I had just turned in used the words "sessile," "chthonic," and "Bakhtinian"—in its first sentence. I took it for granted that many academics loved their language as involuntarily as I loved the plain absorption of reading, but not me. I did like showing off, however. I wondered if that was all I had done in Oxford.

At the start of the year I had hoped in a way that I would fall in love with academic life, and even that morning I think I would probably have guessed that I would stay and finish a doctorate. For weeks I had been carefully filling in my application for the Swift.

Now I thought of what she had said, and of next year. Oxford wouldn't be new to me any longer. Sophie would be gone. The joy of being in love, even unfulfilled love, would be imprinted in inverse upon my days, as they extended farther and farther from the magic of my first arrival in the city. Like a woodblock, the first impression leaving a deep and vivid stain, and each successive year, as the paint faded on the block, fainter, less saturated with color, until I was left without any of the novelty of Oxford and all of its minutiae of mind and spirit, without love, Pninish: blankness.

That evening after class, in a clatter of anxiety and self-doubt, I pulled out my address book and started calling campaign people. There was Chuck Rode in the office of the junior senator from California, Tyler DeGiovanni doing ground operations for a congressional campaign in New Mexico, the prodigy Alfie Steinberg consulting on K Street, there was James Pincus, Jimmy Pink, writing speeches for the mayor of Los Angeles.

I called them all. It wasn't so much that I wanted a job; I wanted to know I could get one, if I felt I needed to.

There weren't any.

It was Tyler in New Mexico who was most honest. "It's a great time to be a Democrat. We're going to slay these midterms, but the one name nobody wants to hear is John Kerry. Believe me, I was in Ohio with you, I know you're capable—but it's going to be tough for you to find a way back in. There's a smell on that campaign."

"Even now?"

"That's why I took this no-hope job. And here we are, about to win! Our opponent is terrified and running these incompetent attack ads—I've gotta send you the videos, remind me about that, like literally twelve of the thirty could be an ad for us—and we're basically margin of error behind in the poll."

"Yeah," I said glumly. "I sent you guys fifty bucks."

"Hey, thanks. Listen, if anything comes up in my campaign, or if I hear about anything, I'll let you know. Have you tried Alison's dad?"

"Not yet."

"I got a Christmas card from that family this year and I was stoked. That's a solid connection, man. Stay on top of it. Really I don't even know why you're calling me."

"Alison and I are on a break."

"Oh. Shit."

I was unhappy. By nature I'm a planner, provident and cautious. I stayed up late, answering the questions of the Swift Prize application, class half forgotten—options, I wanted options. When I woke in the morning I went to my computer to look at the job listings the university posted: banking, consulting, management. These applications were simpler. By ten I had filled out three and felt better. In the next days I filled out another dozen.

Why not sell out? I said as much to Anil ("If I don't have a true vocation, like politics or academics...") in the way people sometimes do as they test out things to say in future conversations on someone whose opinion they don't especially care about. As was only right, given that condescension, Anil's insight took me aback.

"I'm not surprised at all. We're both foreign. I don't think people like us end up here because we know exactly what we want to do with our lives."

"You know what you want."

"Do I?"

"Aren't you going to move back to Mumbai and go into business?"

He smiled ruefully. "That doesn't mean it's what I *want*. I'll end up doing it, but I want to own a record label, as you know."

"If I can't think of anything amazing to do with my life, I should at least live in a nice house."

"Maybe."

There was a pause. "You want to own a record label?"

"Yeah."

"What, an Indian one?"

"I would like to own Def Jam records"—he grinned—"but even an Indian one would be exciting to me, yes."

"Could you afford it?"

"Oh, sure. I even know a couple of people in Mumbai, on the music scene. There I'm considered quite knowledgeable." I noticed he hadn't said anything about gangsters or haters for our whole conversation, which was uncommon. This was serious Anil.

"Rappers?"

"But of course."

"Then why don't you do it?"

He laughed. "I see you haven't met my father."

February was dark and cold; I remember it chiefly for how welcome a pint in the King's Arms became after a day's work in the Bod, and soon enough we were all joining Tom there. It seemed to get dark at about noon. I worked long hours and did good research, met with my adviser, wrote two-thirds of my dissertation, and permitted myself until June to complete the rest, a slow pace. Twice in three weeks I went to St. John Jarvis's house and had coffee with him. I played a great deal of chess with Peter, my redheaded friend, in the MCR.

For the first time I found myself longing for home. It would irritate me that Oxford didn't have decent pizza, or that the movies there were three months old in America. Even the British themselves started to irritate me—the way any nation comes to seem provincial in time, except perhaps more so, because they were from an island. There is a caricature there of the Little Englander, which runs across every line of the inelastic, indissoluble class system: the poor miner who hates the darkies next door, the closed-minded privet-hedge Dursleys, the underlearned, overfed Tory squire who finds the French "beastly" and thinks the poor ought to work harder. Oxford was too international, too cosmopolitan, to permit of many of these types, and yet I began to see that even the most enlightened Englishman had a homeopathic trace of the feeling. How strongly they seemed to believe in the village, the hedgerow, the vicar snoozing over tea! Think of that famous 1930s newspaper headline, FOG IN CHANNEL, CONTINENT CUT OFF. No other people I had met were either as self-loathing or self-idolizing as the English. America, whatever its faults, however panicked its borders, has the luxury of not always contemplating itself. It's too massive and too powerful to worry about its significance.

I came to miss the generosity of America. Every time I walked into one of those sparsely supplied English bars I thought of their overgrown twins in New York, which seemed to have thousands of bottles in them, liquid in every hue of brown and clear, wine reaching clear to the ceiling, that easy profusion, as if none of us would ever die. Probably there was no worse decade in which to come from the United States, and yet I could see its virtues, now, from afar. The American lack of reserve came to seem like an achievement of civility; what the English call manners, or reserve, was blazingly often a cover for simple recalcitrant meanness. No shop would stay open an extra minute to help you. A mocking little laugh when you ordered the wrong book at the Bodleian; should have got it right. The psychopathic national hatred of anyone who did well in public, anyone who made good. The love of valiant failure.

Work, boredom, staleness. It was only a period of a few weeks—weeks without Sophie—that I felt this irritation, this angst. I wished for an American girl of the kind I had grown up falling in love with: the shabby sneakers duct-taped over the laces, the cigarettes, the curly dark hair, the existentialism reader, the rich parents, St. Dymphna's and Muldoon's where they didn't card, the sweet pliability in bed. A longing for the age of sixteen.

Soon enough, thank God, it was spring, and all that ended. One day in mid-March they pushed the clocks back an hour and our lives were suddenly flooded with daylight. People found they were willing to go out at night, now that it was warmer. There were hints of warmth, of summer, of hope, in the wind and the sky. Larkin, who else, said it best:

> The trees are coming into leaf
> Like something almost being said;
> The recent buds relax and spread,
> Their greenness is a kind of grief.
> . . .
> Last year is dead, they seem to say,
> Begin afresh, afresh, afresh.

Afresh, afresh, afresh.

It was a week before the clocks went forward—during the early part of March—that we went on our disastrous trip to London: Tom, Ella, and I.

They were in a strange state. Not many nights passed when he didn't sleep in her room, but they weren't a couple. "It's as much to stave off the cold as anything," Tom would say with an impression of his old, mischievous grin. In the presence of others they never behaved as if they were dating, but around Fleet people neverthe-less assumed that they had become a couple, and treated them that way.

We left for London on a Friday afternoon. A friend of Tom's at King's had told him about a blowout at the King's bar, on the South Bank. Their bar was famous for having the best view of the Thames in London; it was on the seventh floor, and an entire wall of it was a window that showed a panorama of the city, Docklands to West-minster. We were going to crash with his friend.

As a concession to Ella and me, we spent the late afternoon as tourists. We walked through St. Paul's, then crossed the Millen-nium Bridge to the Tate Modern. (What a terribly lightless and despondent museum, alas. Its great hall must be the worst place to look at art that I've ever visited.) Then we found an Italian restau-rant in Soho and had a dinner full of high-spirited toasts with red wine. Tom paid for Ella's part of everything. When we were done eating we went to see his friend.

Tom was fond of calling himself a disowned Harrovian; in his last year at Harrow he had nearly gotten kicked out for public drunk-enness. His closest friend from school, a much-discussed figure named Wilkie, was out on a Portugese fishing boat for fourteen months, spending his wages on the nightlife in port. It was Timmo who told me that being a "deckie" was upper-class, a rough play-ground for those who wished, interstitially, to live hard. Like all the things the aristocratic Brits I knew achieved in that line—hunting, rugby, date rape—it seemed by that time in the year slightly pitiable to me. Jackal had ruined the glamour of his class for me.

At any rate, Alex, Tom's friend at King's (the fifth or sixth best of the big British universities, after Oxbridge, Durham, LSE, Imperial) was another disowned Harrovian; the same incident that had seen Tom nearly expelled had been the end of Alex's tenure there. They were both secretive about it. Some rite of initiation or passage, I would hazard. He was good-looking in a Glastonbury way, with shaggy brown hair and flip-flops.

It was to his spacious, smoke-filled room at King's that we went after eating dinner, and for an hour or so we listened to music and drank mineralish wine. A morose exquisite blonde was playing a PSP in the corner of the room, and after introducing herself as Gemma she fell silent and shortly afterward disappeared from my life forever, much regretted. Later Alex explained that she was his sister, not his girlfriend, and that she was only fifteen. I stand by my assessment of her looks. Prosecute me.

While Tom and Alex engaged in a lot of rapid-fire nostalgia about school, Ella and I talked. "Is Tom going to be boring all night?" she asked me and giggled, visibly happy.

"What's going with you two, anyway?"

"It's good. I think he's been drinking less."

"What about pills?"

She looked at me quizzically. "I don't think so. Why?"

It was ten o'clock by then, and we were going to the party at eleven. At a quarter past ten there was a knock at the door and someone named Percy was outside, a bottle of Bollinger aloft in one hand, grinning.

"It's me," he announced.

Apparently he was another old schoolmate of Tom and Alex's—they reacted as ecstatically as if he had been lost at sea. He was a student at Cambridge now, obdurately laddish. My primary recollection of him is that he wore a paisley waistcoat and torn jeans.

He was pale with garish orange hair. Later Tom told me, with a mix of admiration and revulsion, that he had spent thirteen months in Buenos Aires after university, producing and directing videos of local girls having sex. He sold them on the Internet. Eventually he made about sixty thousand pounds: coals to Newcastle.

"But I thought you couldn't come?" said Tom and Alex almost at the same time.

"I didn't think I could, but I managed to shake Melanie, the slag," said Percy.

That was Lady Melanie Rothmere, I learned when we later met her at the Boat Race. "Well, it's fucking brilliant," said Tom. He had the good grace to look at us expectantly. "You two don't mind if Perse joins up, do you?"

Ella and I both said of course we didn't, the more the merrier, world without end.

"Now listen," said Percy, when everything had settled down. "I'm going to pop this champagne, and we'll neck it, and then who's up for some good-natured druggishness?"

Tom shrugged. "Yeah, sure," he said.

Alex nodded; I said I was okay, and Ella, rather bravely, said she didn't do drugs.

Percy didn't comment on that. "A school reunion in the bathroom for the three of us, then."

They were in there forever. Ella and I chatted and drank Percy's champagne, ignoring the sudden tension, the pressure on the night's expanded surface area; there was a kind of aggression pooled among Alex, Tom, and Percy that hadn't been there before. At eleven fifteen she went to the bathroom door and said, "Boys, don't we have to go?"

"Fleet time," said Tom in a singsongy voice. "Fleet time, Fleet time, Fleet time."

There was laughter inside. Ella looked at me as if to say *what can you do?* and then went behind a freestanding Japanese changing wall and put on her yellow dress, the one she bought with her conference money.

"The yellow dress," I said.

She looked at me lightly, but imploringly, too. "Will, be nice."

"You look great. I feel underdressed."

"Don't I?" She pirouetted.

The guys came out just as she did that and all burst into laughter. "Well, don't let us stop the ballet," said Percy.

"You look like a banana," said Tom and then laughed to undercut the harshness of his words.

"Tom," I said, reproachfully but not enough so as to cause confrontation.

"It's okay," she said. She was blushing. "It's okay. Should we get ready to go?"

She put her overcoat on over her dress, her hem and bare legs protruding from it when she sat next to me.

"Let's have another look at the dress, Ell," said Tom.

"Let's have a shag, Ell," said Percy. "Will, please excuse the four of us."

"No, she's not Lizbeth," said Alex, and the other two went into further fits of laughter.

"Who is that?" asked Ella, an edge to her voice.

"Everyone called her Jizzbreath," said Alex over their laughter. "She was one of the tutor's daughters, a bit older than us, loose as change."

"I'm glad you don't think I'm like her," said Ella, but they were immune to sarcasm.

"Should we go?" I asked.

"Soon enough," said Percy. "I'm feeling wonky."

"Will it be any trouble getting in?" Ella asked Alex.

He was a decent guy, and as best he could he sat up, shaking his head, and said, "No, no, it'll be fine. My friend is working the door. I put down your names. Not Percy's, but we'll slide him in."

"Well, it's no fucking rush," Percy mumbled. "Wait a minute or two."

Tom was grinning through all this but silent. His eyes were closed. I wondered what drugs they had taken. Ella and I shrugged and drank, and for five or ten minutes Alex and Percy made jokes, Tom silent all the while, his eyes still closed. Then he seemed to startle awake and sat up.

"Wills, you know who I quite fucking fancy?" he asked, his voice raspy.

"Ella," I said.

"No, no." He waved a hand. "Your bird, Jess. Jess the townie. Remember her in the silvery black dress at the Turtle, start of the year?"

"I guess," I said.

"Tits?" Percy asked the room, eyes fixed upward at some invisible infinity.

"*Some* tits, not enormous," Tom said slurringly. "And those working-class girls are loose, loose as change."

"Don't be an asshole."

Ella waved a hand. "Will, it's not—leave it."

Tom sat up further and seemed entirely awake for the first time since he had come out of the bathroom, though he was slurring his words. "I'm an asshole?" he said to me.

"Forget it."

"I'm an asshole?" he said again. Then he leaned back. "Yeah, okay. Sometimes I am. But at least I didn't fuck a girl while her fucking boyfriend was in Iraq."

There was a long stop in conversation. "Jesus," said Percy at last. "Heavy."

"He's not even overseas, he's like two hours away at training," I told Percy.

"He'll be going over soon enough to get shot up," said Tom. "Then we'll see how you feel."

"Let's take a breath here, ladies," said Alex. He opened a window and cold air rushed into the room. "Tom, that was some heavy shit."

I felt a wave of nausea. I had drunk too much over the course of the day.

"I'm fine," said Tom. "I'm fine, fine, fine. Let's just go to this party." He stood up and stumbled and then looked around at the rest of us, still sitting. "Will, come on. I'm sorry, mate. Are we cool?"

"Sure," I said.

"Ella?"

"Of course, Tom," she said, as if we would always forgive him. Anything.

We all stood and put on our coats while Ella waited at the door. By eleven thirty we had walked the short distance to the bar.

King's did have an extraordinary view of London. I tend to judge cities by their rivers, and by that standard Paris beats New York and London alike, but the Thames was beautiful, dark, and swift beneath the billion yellow and white lights of the city, its bridges strangely unpersuasive, toylike. We found our way into the party without any trouble, and on the big primary dance floor there were already strobe-lit multitudes, moving in syncopated time.

Tom, Percy, and Alex went straight to the dance floor. Now that

I think it over they must have been on heroin: the modulating energy, the irritability, the mix of focus and dreaminess. Who knows what else Tom had taken. Soon they had integrated themselves into a group of dancing girls, as Ella and I stood at the bar, drinking. Her eyes were fastened to Tom. He was out of it, gliding slowly but surely away from Alex and Percy and their group of girls, not dancing even, really, swaying back and forth. His eyes were closed again.

"Should we get him?" Ella asked.

"He'll pep up. Let's get another drink."

She looked unsure. "Okay."

Her concern was correct. At some point between ordering our next round of drinks and paying for them, Tom disappeared.

For a while we couldn't even be sure that he had gone. We walked around the dance floor looking for him. Alex and Percy had lost track of him, but neither seemed to think he had gone far. Ella called him; we checked the bathroom. At last we asked the guy at the door, Alex's friend, if he had seen Tom leaving, and he had.

The elevator had just gone, so we ran down the stairs. Ella was frantic, out of control herself. We looked up and down the street, but there was no sign of him.

"You go right," I said. "I'll go left, and we'll meet on the other side of the block if one of us doesn't find him first."

She nodded and clattered off, wearing just her high heels and her yellow dress. I started to walk around the corner, but after only an instant I heard her shout my name, and I ran back.

Tom was slumped against the trashcan by the traffic light, with vomit all over his shirt. Ella was leaning over him.

"What should we do?" she asked again. He murmured something. "He's talking at least. He's awake."

"Let's get him home."

She didn't move. She was shivering, so I put my jacket around her shoulders. Still she crouched by him, watching silently, and I saw that there were tears standing in her eyes, about to slip away one by one. The full force of her love for him, its hopelessness, its delusions, its infiniteness, was apparent, and for a split second I was more worried for her than for him.

I noticed she was clutching something. "What's that?" I asked.

She looked down at her hand before she remembered. "His wallet."

"Why do you have it?"

She showed me her other hand, which was full of plastic shards. "He snapped every card he had. His Oxford ID, his Fleet ID, his credit cards, his driver's license. His fucking NHS card. He tore up the cash."

"Anything else?"

"No."

"I wish I knew what he took."

She looked at me. Her mascara was running with her tears. "I don't know, I don't know, I don't know."

We had been almost ignoring Tom, though all our attention was supposed to be on him, but then he started to convulse and bile burst in a bubble from his mouth. Almost simultaneously I saw that there was a ragged line of blood on the side of his neck. I turned his head; there was an open wound there. When he had fallen he had broken open his scalp.

"Fuck," I said. "I'm calling 999."

She knelt down on the ground next to him and took him in her arms, even though it meant blood and spit and vomit on her bare chest, on the top of her dress. She was sobbing. The ambulance was there three minutes later, and eight minutes after that he was in the emergency room.

It was Ella who sat with Tom at the hospital while I went back to King's, found Alex, and retrieved our light bags, it was Ella who watched as they pumped his stomach, and it was Ella who decided to rent a car the next morning and drive back to Oxford to save Tom from the train or the bus. It was Ella who sat in Tom's room, running out occasionally to the kitchen or Sainsbury's, for the drag of the next three days, until he was better.

On the fourth day, he broke things off with her.

For three days he had been passive, until finally his agitation erupted. It happened in his room, and when their voices rose I could hear what they said. (I wish I could pretend that I didn't eavesdrop. It reminds me of a story my grandfather used to tell. He was a journalist for *Life* in the sixties, interviewing Truman Capote at a roadside diner in Kansas. At some point Truman went silent, and my grandfather started to repeat his question. Truman shot him a look, scrawled something on his notepad, and pushed it across the table, *Shut the fuck up, I'm trying to eavesdrop.* The scrap of paper is in a frame in the front hall of my uncle's house.)

"Just leave me alone!" Tom shouted. "I'm an adult!"

"You need someone to take care of you," Ella said.

"I didn't slash my fucking wrists!"

"You might as well have."

"Oh, Jesus, the melodrama."

"Me? What about you?"

"What does that mean?" he asked, his voice softer.

"You know what it means."

"No, what does it mean, Ella? If you're talking about my sister—"

"I'm talking about *you,* and how you wallow."

"Please just go, leave me alone."

There was a silence. "I love you."

"Ella."

Now there was a long silence, a minute or two. At last, she said, "Are you drinking your fluids?"

"There's not much else to do with them."

"Tom."

I heard that symphony-chord sound of his Mac powering on. After that there was another passage of silence, and then Ella left. As she was going I opened my door, but she brushed past me without looking and went down the stairs.

I went into Tom's room. "What is wrong with you?" I asked.

He still had a bandage on his head. "Jesus, not you, too."

Nevertheless, that evening he went over to Ella's house to talk to her again, more gently this time. When I saw her the next afternoon she was puffy-eyed and impassive.

"Well, it's over," she said.

We were standing in the MCR together making coffee. It was a cold day. "What happened?"

"I never know what to believe with these things." She tucked a strand of pink and black hair behind her ear. "He told me...he said that he could have loved me, but for him I'll always remind him of...of this time."

"Anyway, you helped him after Katie died."

She shrugged. "If that's true, I would do it all again. It's not much of a sacrifice."

I could see in her eyes that this was untrue. "Maybe you two will—"

Before I could finish speaking she cut me off, however. "No. Never."

Amid all of this drama, the worst thing of all happened: *Big Brother* turned down Timmo. He was distraught and started speculating about whether they took Brits on *Survivor.*

"It puts my own ordeal into perspective," said Tom. "Thank God he's strong."

Not much later, I had a call from Sophie. It was a Tuesday night in the third week of March, and I was walking home, through Radcliffe Square, from a seminar at Balliol about neutrality in fiction. Its subject was the novelists of the 1930s and 1940s—Henry Green, Evelyn Waugh, Ivy Compton-Burnett—who had chosen to write almost exclusively in dialogue. Was it a reaction to the war—a silence? A reaction to the discursive self-regard of the previous generation, Proust, Conrad, Joyce, Woolf? There was something of Pontius Pilate in the inert disinterest of these writers, refusing to speak in their own voices, but something great, too. Their ambiguities invited the reader's participation, the reader's choices, in a sense even the reader's coauthorship. Still, I thought that Orwell's way took more courage. He took the burden of judgment upon himself. Perhaps as a result he didn't write with such terrible coldness.

It was an hour of conversation that won me another few paragraphs for my thesis. It was times like that when I was gladdest I had come to Oxford.

My phone buzzed in my pocket, and I pulled it out and answered. "Sophie?"

"Hey," she said. "Can I come over there?"

"I'm on my way home now. I won't be back for ten minutes or so."

"Pick up beer, would you?"

"We have some."

"What kind?"

"1664."

"If you pass a shop, get some Guinness." There was a beat after this command, and then, as if she were answering to some deeper reflex of politeness, something I understood so well, like the older magic in Narnia, she added, "If you don't mind, of course."

"No problem. See you in twenty?"

"Thanks."

When I arrived at the Cottages, she was on our steps. There was still some last white light lofted high over the still city, the air colder than ten minutes before.

"Hey," I said.

She stood up and smiled. "Hey."

In my room—which Strick had tidied just that morning, thank God—she went over to my computer and put on *Room on Fire*. Then she took one of the beers and drank half of it without speaking.

"Are you okay?" I said.

"I don't know what I'm going to do when I have to leave Oxford. Who knows where Jack will be. It all seems like a mess. Everyone has someplace to be, except me. I wish they wanted me here."

"You could stay."

She laughed. "I wish."

"Why don't you? Did you apply for the Swift?"

"I told you, they wouldn't give it to someone studying French language. Not academic enough. Maybe if I did literature." She finished the beer and looked at me. "Anyway, I didn't come over to talk. Let's sleep together."

"What?"

She came to the bed, pushed my things onto the floor, and lay down. "You do the work," she said.

So I did: I unbuttoned her jeans, ran my fingers over her hipbones and her thighs, kissed her from her neck to her breasts, brushed her hair away from her face and put my mouth on hers, felt the slight pressure she returned, and then the involuntary rise of her hips against my hand, and after only a little while she had turned me on my back and started to do the work herself.

When it was over she held me tightly. "This was the last time," she said.

"Okay."

"Sorry."

We lay there in silence for a very long time, perhaps half an hour, until, not wholly to my surprise, she started to cry. "What is it?"

"Nothing, nothing."

"Okay. You don't want to talk about it?"

"No." There was a pause. "Are you ready to go again?"

"Not quite."

She rested her fingers in the declivity between my stomach and my right hipbone. "One more time, that will be the last."

"Okay."

I was going back to America for two weeks, the term break. My flight was a late one from Heathrow to Logan, and I spent the day before I left doing laundry in the MCR. Timmo, Anil, and Anneliese hung out with me for most of it, playing table football and watching the entire *Lord of the Rings* trilogy. Nobody seemed to have any work.

I was leaving for the airport at six, and at half past five I walked over to Sophie's house, hoping to say good-bye. We hadn't exchanged fifteen words since we slept together.

Her room was directly at the top of the stairs on the second floor, so that she had less privacy than most of the rooms. When I was near it I realized she was talking to someone.

I hesitated long enough to hear a male voice, cracking with emotion, say, "I just can't believe it."

"Baby," said Sophie, as soft as motherhood.

"One stupid week." With a shock I realized that it was Jack's voice, vacated of its customary command. What were they talking about? "I need the loo."

I was poised on the top step, one foot lifted to its toes, listening, and the door opened too quickly for me to start back down the stairs. The bathroom was just adjacent to Sophie's room, and Jack must have thought he could slip into it without anyone seeing him. He hadn't bothered to wipe his cheeks dry.

"Will?" he said, confused.

"Hey."

His stare hardened. He went into the bathroom and slammed the door. Sophie then came to her door to discover what had happened and saw me.

"Jesus, Will," she said, "what are you doing here?"

"I was seeing if—if Marta was in," I said. Marta was a sixty-year-old Brazilian woman, headmistress of a school in Pernambuco on leave to study education, who spent the majority of her waking hours on the phone, talking to her husband. I can say with incontestable certainty that she didn't know my name. "I'm going stateside for a while." I gestured toward the bathroom. "Is everything okay?"

"Jack's going to Afghanistan next Tuesday."

"Shit."

"No, no, it's good. It's good for his career."

"Oh. Good, then. When did he find out?"

Her face was unreadable, but her eyes flicked to the door, to check if he could hear perhaps. Her arms were folded across her chest. "About a week ago."

I thought of her visit to my room, of course. "Wish him luck for me."

"I will."

"Good-bye."

For the rest of the day and all through my flight home, I thought about Jack. I couldn't stop imagining the ways he might die in the war. There were helicopter crashes, stray bullets, improvised roadside bombs, ground-to-air shoulder launchers, there were plain old car accidents, and of course the fighting, which I understood only somewhere between the abstraction of terror and the over-realism of movies and TV.

Those were black years, during those two wars; every day I brooded over America's politics, and brooded then on top of that because I had removed myself from them, and therefore, in a sense, relinquished my right to object. The fantasia of Oxford, its self-regard, its late nights—how pointless it seemed when I considered the state of the world elsewhere.

The worst part for me was thinking about him and Ella. A month before, we had all been together at the Fleet bar and he and Ella, previously just civil, out of nowhere became intensely absorbed in a conversation about classical music. Both of them listened to it, it turned out, and as Jack picked up on her answers, offering names I didn't know ("Albinoni's cello suites!") his face softened out of itself into something like warmth. After that the two of them could always chat together. They even traded music sometimes, I believe, though I can't remember for sure. I kept thinking about it on the plane.

We landed at around midnight American time. The first thing my eyes lit on was a metal garbage can, and its familiar American shape. It had suffused me all at once with the prestige of my own memories, located in the dull objects of life as much as in people. The garbage and the whole terminal of restaurants it implied and spawned by its existence. I realized I was home. It felt strange. At the exit I saw my mother, and her presence was almost difficult to register, since all of my feelings were already so quick to arise at the slightest pressure, at the garbage can. How was I supposed to handle anything as full of meaning as my mother's cheerful face, her halo of dark hair? I started to cry, which I don't imagine I had done in her presence since I was nine or ten.

"Sweetheart!" she said. "My goodness, what is it?"

"Hey."

"What's wrong?"

"I don't know. Seeing you is hard." It all seemed like too much to handle. "My friend is going to Afghanistan."

"Oh, Will."

I let her hug me. "And I miss Dad, obviously."

CHAPTER EIGHT

I was an unhappy child: intelligent, anxious, solitary. My parents divorced seven violent years into my life, and when in college I read *Tender Is the Night* I noted with special interest that the Divers' son and daughter had "that wistful charm, almost sadness, peculiar to children who have learned early not to cry or laugh with abandon." My father and the stepfather who followed him were angry men. At the footsteps of either I would slip into an empty room if I could and wait. I did my schoolwork perfectly and my chores as well as I could, hoping to escape notice. I read a lot of books.

Until I was twelve or so my life was full of deep terrors. I used to be convinced beyond persuasion, for example, that one day I would be kidnapped. In one of the lunatic misunderstandings of early childhood, I would have guessed then that around ten percent of children were stolen at some stage. Especially at the age of seven or eight I would lie in bed envisioning how it might happen. I never wanted to bother my father—later, my stepfather—so I would remain in bed, paralyzed with fear, clenched all along my body, until my terror reached its highest pitch and I would sprint, sobbing, to my mother. It was a transgression my stepfather in particular hated, but that I could never manage to stop myself from committing. How bizarre that I should have been reprimanded! What was I back then? A little particle of being. Why would it have angered them to see me afraid?

Of course I was happy, too—and bored, devious, gluttonous, curious, normal. I loved baseball. As comfort I had my mother, a particular grandfather, and books. I think probably I was more grown up than most children; I knew from a very young age that my father, who at that time was a drug addict—heroin, I think, but nobody has ever spoken about it with me, though by the time I reached middle school he "only took pills"—was untrustworthy. I loved him.

He died six months before I departed the States for Oxford, a heart defect. It was a month or so afterward that I had submitted a late application to the university. When I left Alison and America I annexed the fact of his death away to one of the least-visited chambers of my heart. I don't think anyone at school knew other than Anneliese, whom I had told in a fit of self-pity one afternoon.

Seeing my mother jerked something primal in my brain, and I thought, *Yes, that's right, the other human I'm half of is gone.*

What was he like? "You always take the side of the dead," Gabriel García Márquez wrote. So I will say that my father was terrifically bright and fun, at home in conversation, though with sometimes a scary avidity in his eyes—a manic one. He had a terrible temper. He had less sense of right or wrong than most people. He was small, shorter than I am. His weight fluctuated. He was seedily handsome.

His childhood was conventional like mine. My grandfather (who outlived his son) had been born into the true New York Episcopalian aristocracy, which existed from around 1850 to 1950. How to describe it? He and his brothers, my father's uncles, grew up in a town house on Fifth Avenue that is now the consulate of Gambia. When the diocese needed a new bishop my great-grandfather sent a succession of men up to Andover to deliver guest sermons, a kind of road test, and selected the one his boys recommended for the job. For two straight years in the thirties the family had a horse finish dead last in the Kentucky Derby. Each Sunday they had a supper in which every dish was white. They had a huge farm in northern New Jersey, which they sold in the fifties, and is now a two-hundred-unit apartment complex. When my great-grandfather died many of the flags of Park Avenue flew at half-mast, north of Fifty-ninth. When the family cat was lost and then found there was a story about it on the front page of the *New York Herald*. What's left of that? Portraits, silver, gold carriage clocks, the family nose, old menus from the Waldorf, some money.

After Yale and Yale Law my grandfather became a partner in a New York law firm and moved his family to Sixty-fifth and Fifth, with a cook and a maid who lived in. My father was a passable, distracted student but a great athlete—baseball and golf. The first hint of change came in college, though in his telling some trauma of youth had been boiling away before then, whatever would lead to his addiction, ultimately. Perhaps. However it came to pass, he started taking drugs. During his sophomore year at Vassar, he dropped out and took the refund on his tuition to move to New York. It was the first of a dozen times that he took money from his father without bothering to tell anyone.

New York: Heroin was his primary addiction from all I can gather, then methadone when I was a child, then heroin again, but he smoked pot, dropped acid, took pills, did coke...He disappeared for the first years of my life (after six months of an attempt at marriage with my mother, inspired solely by her pregnancy) into a blank netherworld of drugs and downtown, music, squalor. My grandfather, who had a deep soft spot for his only son, gave him an allowance, so he never worked. One of my favorite things to do as a child was sit in a big plush armchair at this grandfather's law firm, eating pink rock candy and listening to tales of my father's childhood athletic feats. My grandfather always wore a suit and a hat, and ran rule over dozens of subordinates, but during those afternoons he left behind his grown-up ways and the two of us, seventy-five and eight, escaped into a conversation in which my father was perfect once more, unaged, immortal.

Until I was seven I wasn't permitted to see him. It was when he was on methadone, which is the drug you take when you're getting off heroin, that I could. From my seventh birthday to my twelfth or so he was tolerably healthy, then again from my seventeenth birthday on, when he stopped using drugs again. Around then a manuscript he had begun about the golden age of jazz began to absorb him, and between that, the Dodgers, and a daily trip to the clinic, he just about led a normal life. Normal, well; he was violent, narcissistic, angry, spiteful, a bully, to the people—me and his father—who loved him most. There were moments in between when everyone loved him again. It never lasted.

He was a figure of fascination to me. When I was seven or eight he would lurch back into my life for an occasional Sunday, usually first to the church where we had both been baptized for the ten o'clock service, Christ dissolving on our tongues, then to a lunch, then, the afternoon appearing endless, in an aimless trek between baseball card shops, record stores, movies, and restaurants. (All of his childhood passions were intact, so our interests coincided.) I remember a great deal of advice about alcohol. He drank at lunch and again when we stopped for my ice cream sundae at three thirty. Only hold a champagne glass with your left hand, close to your heart; a rosé is acceptable during a picnic in the South of France between May and August; a Bull Shot, not a Bloody Mary. Wrinkles of the WASP code. It gave me such happiness to be with him.

Then there was a bad Sunday, and for three years afterward we weren't together unsupervised.

It was spring. He picked me up in the morning and we got straight into a cab, which surprised me because in general he didn't have much money, his father covering his few steady expenses directly. The cabdriver double-checked the address with him, surprised, which in retrospect was an ominous sign, and then we made our slow way through upper Manhattan: first past the gleaming pitiless brick buildings of Park Avenue, doormen outside them wearing gold-buttoned coats, like generals in the Crimean War, then toward the shabbier reaches of Yorkville, yellow tenements with zagging black fire escapes, crowded with dead plants and smoking mothers, and finally across the Rubicon of 125th Street.

"Where are we going?"

"To see a friend of mine," he said.

"I have to pee."

"Afterward."

We stopped in a poor neighborhood. I was scared of black people when I was five, I don't think I knew better. (I still often am, I suppose, it's awful but it's true, even writing it makes me realize that, and I feel a horrible compression of guilt.)

My father found the door he was looking for, which belonged to a vacant brownstone. "Wait ten minutes?" he asked the cabdriver.

The cabdriver looked at me and then shook his head. "Sorry."

We stood on the sidewalk. This was the eighties, before corporate money disciplined the city into Orlando, swept Times Square free of needles, and gentrified Harlem. As the taxi pulled away my father looked down at me. "I'll be inside five minutes. Tops."

"I can't go in?"

"It's not for little boys," he said. "Wait right here. You'll be fine,

I've walked around here a million times. People are friendly. When I'm back we'll go to Joe's and get a slice."

I watched him go in and then sat down on the stoop, miserable, feeling waves of sickness. I felt like I wanted to cry. For so long I had heard that my father was unstable, and here it was, the terrible proving moment. (I think now: What was I wearing? Who was that boy? Orwell: "What have you in common with the child of five whose photograph your mother keeps on the mantelpiece? Nothing, except that you happen to be the same person." I imagine my Yankees jacket, my one indispensable piece of clothing then, some blue jeans, my Yankees backpack.) We were supposed to be at the Great Lawn. My glove would have been in my backpack. It's pure treacle, evanescence, stupidity, but I can think so clearly of the glove—the signature of Don Mattingly in it, my favorite player, careful creases where I had left it folded underneath my bed. Self-pity can be gratifying, true, strange. Strange to think it all happened, it was briefly as real as right now. It was the newest event in the world.

After a minute my father came out, and my heart lifted, it was over. I was wrong. "Did your mom give you any money? For emergencies?"

I shook my head. "No."

He looked at me as if I were useless. Then he went back inside. The worst part now was how badly I had to pee. I had had to since I left my apartment and it was getting close to intolerable, and even though the look on his face was running through my head on a loop like a GIF, I almost forgot the situation I was in, where I was. I thought about knocking on the door, but in the end what I did was go into the little alley next to the building and peed, with carnal relief, against the wall.

The alley connected through to another avenue block, and as I zipped up I saw something from my life every day: a New York City bus. I ran down the alley (yes, I must have been wearing the backpack, because I remember it bumping) and got on it without hesitation, submitting myself to the great uncaring safety of New York officialdom. Forty minutes later I was home. What I remember chiefly from the bus ride is thinking that at least we had been alone, that I didn't want to embarrass him. I thought of how I could protect him in the way I told the story. I must have failed, because it was a year before I saw him again.

That was my father. How I miss him! We had the same name, and it occurred to me once that when I write my own name down I'm writing his, too. There's a shiver of religion in that. But no, maybe I only wish there were, and there's not. He's gone. Nothing, not superstition, not even love, will change that.

That week was my mother's fiftieth birthday, and there were two separate parties for her. Aside from that she made me go to yoga twice (the girls were beautiful, I've never been to a yoga class or a rock concert where I didn't fall in love) and every evening we watched a movie.

After eight days in Boston I went down to New York and spent five more on my friend Matt's couch, seeing everyone who still lived in the city—or, everyone. While they were at work during the days I went to my old places, Central Park and the Met. (The Petrus Christus Carthusian; Breughel's mowers; the Lavoisiers; Dendur; the Frank Lloyd Wright room: I check in on those five every time.) Nothing makes a New Yorker feel at home after a long absence like walking through Central Park with coffee, while the tourists on the footpaths argue about where they are and consult massive, wind-flapped maps, stopping in large groups at inconvenient places. Give them a dirty look and an exasperated sigh as you step around them, and you feel with a derisive majesty that you're once again a member of the federation that really possesses Manhattan.

I debated each day whether or not to call Alison. Finally, the day before I left, I did. We agreed to meet under the clock at Grand Central and then have lunch in the mezzanine.

Her brown hair looked thicker than I remembered, longer, too, and she was pale. She was a Thoroughbred: leggy, slim, tall, slightly restless. She had on long brown boots over jeans, a black blazer with the arms pushed up, and big hoop earrings. When she smiled, her teeth, even and brilliantly white, shone, slightly wetted.

I ordered as expensively as possible, which caused Alison to roll her eyes and smile. "You happy now?" she asked.

"Your dad still lets you use his account here, right?"

"Like he'll notice anyway." She smiled. "So how've you been?"

"Not bad. What about you?"

"How's your mom?" she asked.

"Oh, she said hi and sent this." I took a small wrapped box out of my messenger bag. It was a set of Hiroshige notecards. "Open it later."

She smiled. "Thanks. I'll write her."

"So? How about you?"

"Oh, I'm okay."

"Work is good?"

"Yeah." She kind of smiled. "Anyway. Have you hooked up?"

"Not really."

"What does that mean?" she asked.

"I kissed a girl."

"Who, Sophie? Ella?"

They were just names to her, from the start of the year. "No, some random. What about you?"

She hesitated, whether because of prevarication or fear of vulnerability I couldn't tell, and said, "No. Not me."

"Thanks," I said. "You can now. I was being stupid."

She rolled her eyes. "I can't wait to tell people I'm open for business."

"No, I—"

"You're going to be jealous."

"Probably."

"Would you be?" she asked. Her voice was as light as nothing.

"I don't think I'll ever be comfortable imagining you with someone else."

She hesitated, staring into her sparkling water, then said, "I heard you called up Chuck Rode in Washington? He shot me an e-mail afterward, asking if it was true we were dunzo."

"Yeah. There are no jobs. I'm going to sell out instead."

"I can already see you in the McDonald's uniform."

"Hilarious. Oh, look, my glass of Mumm's." When the waiter had set it down and left, I lifted it by the stem with my left hand. "Tell your dad thanks."

It was sunnier when I got back to Oxford. In Fleet's beautiful sunken gardens, leading back to the river, were littered snowdrops and crocuses. At the bar at night the doors were opened out to the patio, letting in a breeze.

"What's up, ugly," said Tom, peering over the banister when he heard the door open. He came down the stairs and took one of my bags. "How was Murrika?"

"Fine."

"Anil's taken to singing in the shower."

"Oh no."

"This morning it was one that went 'Sucka nigga, nigga nigga, I throw the sucka in the front for the ones who front. Sucka nigga, nigga nigga, nigga nigga.' Then he repeated that about sixteen thousand times."

"HATERS ARE GOING TO HATE!" Anil's voice called down the flight of stairs to the second story.

I laughed. "How can you hear him over the shower?"

He looked pretty well. "Will, you've been gone too long. We could hear him because we listened at the door, of course."

I tried Anneliese that night and agreed to meet up with her the next morning for breakfast. Sophie answered a similar text by saying, *Can't hang out for a while, sorry.* Only Ella didn't respond at all, to texts or phone calls. I didn't see her until three days later at Hall. I asked her where she had been.

"Working," she said. "It's been terrible. Sorry about the phone calls."

"That's okay."

She looked at me. "Uh, well, I promised I'd sit with Peter."

That was my reserved chess friend, the one whose brave and futile battle against Giorgio and Richard was a source of admiration to us all. "You did?"

"Actually we've started seeing each other," she said.

"You've—really?" Peter was sweet but so quiet, and Ella with her tattoos and hair and boobs: There couldn't have been two more different people in college. As I absorbed this new information I saw Tom come toward me from the door to Hall and then veer off when he saw Ella. "What about Tom?" I asked.

"What about him?"

"You're fine with that?"

"I'm fine with that," she repeated sarcastically, as if I were being stupid. "Look, I've got to go. Are you sitting with Tom?"

"You can't even sit with him?"

"Oh, no, I'm fine with sitting with him, but I said I'd sit with Peter."

"Can we all sit together?"

"I'm not in the mood."

"Then I'll sit with you guys."

Finally she smiled at me. "Really?"

"Yeah, obviously. I see Tom all the time."

"Thanks," she said.

For a week or so it was awkward to be friends with them, and certainly for a while Ella appeared upset when she saw him, in the subtle ways a friend can see. Gradually they could be in the same room. Tom, to his credit, always tried to include her. I guess her anger subsided. By May she, Tom, and I could all hang out together without any serious tension. Though it didn't mean Ella had moved on.

Giorgio and Richard surpassed themselves that first week back, as they seemed to whenever Tom and I happened into a student government meeting.

We had gone to the MCR looking for a game of table football. Peter, now with Ella by his side, was faithfully recording for posterity every clause and sentence in the accreting record of Giorgio and Richard's official madness. Ella and Tom exchanged nonglances when we came in.

There was obviously an argument going on. Peter, in his quiet way, kept mumbling, "But it's a quarter of the spring budget," and Bert, the third-year who always came to meetings, said, "And only seven people could go! Nobody I know even likes skeet shooting."

"This is about skeet shooting?" I asked.

"Wait," said Tom, "only seven people can go at a time? And are you two on that list?"

"In a supervisory capacity, Tom, yes, we must perforce be there," said Richard.

"But not shooting. Simply supervising. That's a relief, because it means seven people from the MCR can go."

Richard reddened. "After all the energy we've put into this, we would shoot as well... Giorgio has a gun and I..." Here he trailed off in a growing din.

"So there are five open spots?"

"Well," said Giorgio, with the good grace to look discomfited, "Chin and Xi have preregistered."

That caused an uproar. Chin and Xi were two Chinese statistics students who, perhaps because they had grown up in a totalitarian regime, worshipped Giorgio. I actually liked Chin, who played basketball with me sometimes; it was Xi I didn't trust.

"Where was preregistration?" asked Peter.

There was a long pause. "Online," Richard answered at last.

The MCR had the least-visited Web site on the Internet. It required two passwords to access, and nobody knew one, never mind both, except Giorgio's inner circle. After Peter successfully lobbied for the passwords over the course of two long, fraught, heated meetings, he found that the site's only contents were a series of pictures of Giorgio and Richard (and occasionally Chin or Xi) having various expensive-looking picnics, all in a file generously marked MCR PICTURES. Peter had gone back in the record and discovered that these champagne-and-caviar affairs had been charged to the MCR.

So the Web site was a sore point.

"You're not going skeet shooting," said Tom flatly. "Over my dead body."

"Fortunately you have no power in this meeting," said Giorgio.

"I'll go talk to Sir George."

Laughing, Richard said, "Master Ballantine is a close friend to the MCR, Tom. You won't get very far there."

"Well, I don't care," said Tom hotly. "You're not doing it."

Peter stepped in. "We can certainly delay such a major expenditure by passing a vote to revisit a spending item over a thousand pounds at the next meeting."

"Holy fuck, it costs more than a thousand pounds?" I asked.

Giorgio looked angry. The motion passed 15–3. The third vote was Anil's. He wanted to go skeet shooting.

Then Peter, blushing and visibly unhappy, said, "And there is one other thing, in fact . . . I—it's a bit awkward," and as if to prove it he laughed a bit awkwardly. "It appears that someone has been having sex on the dining table in the MCR. Two separate people have reported something of the sort to me, on three different dates . . ."

There was a great deal of chatter at this intelligence.

"I'm only asking whoever it is to stop. Please pass the word. There's no need to bring the master into it. Only I'm tired of coming in every morning to wash the table, just in case."

On several nights in early and mid-April, Tom disappeared. In total it must have been about four separate times. He claimed he was going on a walk, and while that put me in mind of his long winter walk after our last eventful MCR meeting, he seemed more content these days. I didn't think about it much.

One night just before I left for an evening seminar on Jane Austen, he departed as he had on those other occasions, popping his head around the door to say good-bye. I went out shortly after him and spent a few hours discussing *Persuasion*. Sullivan kept trying to introduce Joyce into the conversation, with increasing irritability—modernists are a fractious phylum—but the teacher wasn't interested. I wasn't either; spend a year with people who study them and you never want to hear about Joyce or Woolf again.

After class, mind pleasantly occupied, not ready to go home, I wandered toward Freud's. I suppose I was thinking of Jess. It had been some time since I saw her, and Freud's was the place where she and her friend Elena spent many nights, right past Worcester near the Oxford University Press, because, though it was expensive, they were friends with one of the owners, who had made good from their neighborhood of row houses. It was a big, darkish, eerie place, once an Anglican church, its altar converted into a bar. They served fancy drinks, Mojitos with freshly shaved sugarcane, that kind of thing.

There was a table in front of the DJ's booth where Jess and Elena often sat, and I was pleased to see Jess there, with two dark-haired guys. Elena was absent. One of the guys made a joke and the whole table laughed, and then he put his arm around her.

With a shock, I saw that it was Tom.

After a moment he leaned over and kissed her on the mouth. She pushed him off in the mock-angry way, full of indignation, that I knew so intimately. Then, as she was flicking her ponytail, she caught sight of me.

It had been ages, and I was there that night because of a melancholy, lonely feeling that a brief phone call with Alison, no more than a check-in after our lunch in New York, had raised in me.

It was too late to slink out quietly. She waved me to their table, and I saw that she meant to brazen it out. A second shock to me was the person with her and Tom: Anil.

"Hey, Will!" said Jess. She was wearing a lot of makeup and a shirt that showed off her shoulders. She looked good.

"Hey," I said. "How's it going?"

"It's brilliant! I haven't seen you in eons."

"I thought a friend of mine was supposed to be here, but he isn't."

Tom had stood up, and I think he must have thought that was a shot at him. Which it was. "Hey," he said. "How was your class?"

"Fine," I said.

"Do you want to go get a drink at the bar?"

"I guess."

"What do you guys want?" he asked them. It turned out they both wanted Guava Screwdrivers.

Anil, who had greeted me without surprise, said, "Extra guava!" twice, to be sure, which made me think he didn't know anything awkward was happening.

As soon as we were out of earshot, Tom said, "I'm sorry, mate. I'm so sorry."

"What happened?"

He shook his head. "It's hard to say. I was just trawling around Facebook one day and I came across her profile . . . I don't know, I'd quite fancied her. I messaged to see if she wanted to get a drink. We've been out a few times."

"Those nights you went on your walks?"

"It was wrong of me." There was a pause. "We haven't slept together or anything." Another pause. "And the two of you haven't seen each other in ages."

"It's fine," I said.

With a hint of desperation, he said, "Come on, Will. You must be furious."

"I'm not. I'm really not."

"It just happened."

"To be honest, I'm most surprised that Anil is your wingman."

He smiled. We were at the bar by now. "I know."

"It's funny. She doesn't seem like your type."

"I don't know if she would have been." The drinks came. "Here," he said, "I'm getting these. Come sit at—"

"No, I should go."

"You're mad?"

I shook my head. "No. I'm not mad. I guess it might bother me a little. I don't know." Suddenly I felt cruel. "One thing, though, I hope you know she has chlamydia."

He turned white as snow and said, "What?"

"Just kidding," I said, but I felt vindicated: It proved they had slept together. "Have fun."

As I walked home, the wine wearing off, the night late and the streets abandoned, some self-pitying corner of my mind, or some self-rejecting one, thought that perhaps Jess had been what I needed all along. I thought how tied up she was for me in the beginning of the year, in that first night, and then thought about the way I could make her laugh, the effortless chatter. The hooking up. Even when you don't mean to, if you spend enough time in somebody's bed you know them. How unkind I had been to her! Was I different than Jack at all, in the end? I thought about days in the teashop, her big, athletic brother—I would never meet him now, after having heard so much about him—her basic gentleness. I thought about how at ease I had been with her. Still, there was something hard and unyielding at the back of all this, a barrier beyond which I knew that sort of sentimentality would never take me. It was Sophie.

Guava, I ask you.

For a week Tom was abjectly apologetic. The next day he wrote me a long letter, which I barely read, and for days he kept checking with me, "Are you sure you're not mad? Come on, just tell me." He made sure I observed him going to bed in our house. He liked her, though, and I didn't especially care. For a while they stayed away from Fleet. Then they didn't. Tom was happy.

Sophie, on the other hand, seemed unhappy. When I saw her around college she looked harried and tense, her arms always crossed over her chest. I didn't dare call her or text her. I thought often of her impassive, unreadable mood when we last slept together, and the timing of it, and I thought often, too, of Jack. I wondered whether I had known her at all. Slowly my obsession began to return, and though I did my best to suppress it I would find myself checking to see if her car was outside when I woke up, lingering as I passed her house in case she came out. I wanted so badly to see her, that feeling of illness back again. She was constantly in my thoughts.

Anneliese was Sophie's closest friend at Fleet, and she would listen to me describe this without judgment. We spent long afternoons walking out into the university parks, where she photographed trees that she liked, and we sometimes stopped to watch the varsity cricket matches. I found her monologues about the trees comforting.

"This is a very interesting one," she said to me one day in a serious voice. She adjusted her lens and snapped a photograph. "You can chew its sap, like gum, though it doesn't taste very nice. You can make furniture out of its wood. And look how the leaves grow reddish there along the fringe, where it overhangs the lake! I wonder if they get more light because of the reflection of the sun, and die sooner."

"Let me see the picture," I said.

She showed me. "When the light is very clear like this the branches look beautiful. My f-stop—"

"You should take pictures professionally," I said.

"Oh, no, it's only a hobby." She brought her camera away from her face and looked at me then. "Will?" she said. "Do you want to talk more about Sophie?"

"No, no."

She touched my forearm. "It's all right."

I paused, then said, "Well, how is she?"

"She's worried. She worries about Jack."

"Has she mentioned me?"

"Not recently."

"What is Jack doing?"

"He is at something called a PRT, a Provincial Reconstruction Base. It is in a place called Ghazni. Sophie and I looked it up on the map in the Senior Common Room. His job is to help the local government, but they must also run after the terrorists, he says."

In her clipped German voice, less prone to contraction, it sounded like a news report. "And he's an officer?"

"Yes. But there is no officer's mess, really, and there are only thirty people around him, and he is the youngest lieutenant there, and he hates it. He thinks he is too inexperienced to be there. And he is afraid, also, Sophie says. And an American laughed at him. I think it must be difficult because the Americans don't care about his background, his credentials. I didn't tell Sophie that."

"They talk? Jack and Sophie?"

"He sends an e-mail out once a day to a list of people, telling them he is still alive. Otherwise it's difficult to reach home. So they do not talk, I don't think, or not much, and she can't reach him, and every day at around five in the evening she gets very fretful because perhaps he will not write."

I nodded. "Thanks."

"You know she'll never sleep with you again, as long as he's there."

"She told you about that?"

Anneliese looked up at the wind in the trees. "For a long time she seemed to cry about it every time I saw her. I told her she should be more gentle with herself."

"Oh."

"I wouldn't tell you this, normally, but I want you to know." She glanced at me. "Can you understand?"

We were walking down an avenue of lime trees, and I was silent for a while. We stopped when we reached the end, and sat on a bench. "Was it so wrong?" I asked.

She looked away from me, then took my hand and smiled sorrowfully at me. "Yes, I think. I think it was wrong of both of you."

In 1722, when an aristocratic reprobate named Nicholas Swift was a student at Corpus Christi, his servitor caught him rutting with a woman well over the age of sixty, who worked the kitchens. To forestall their heir's rustication his family established the Swift Prize.

It had grown so rich, three centuries later, that it awarded room, board, and tens of thousands of pounds to twenty students at a time, four new ones every year, without demanding of them any definite responsibilities.

Nearly everyone I knew applied for it—not Tom or Anil, those with direct professional paths ahead of them, but everyone in the humanities—and nobody expected to get it, except, perhaps, me. I had Sinjun on my side.

The person who got it was, in the end, also the person who spoke least often about her work. It was Sophie.

I was at the MCR bar one day when Ella came in and told me the news, irritatingly pleased for our friend.

"They've posted all four names?" I asked.

"Oh, shit," she said with sudden concern. "Did you apply?"

"I did. But it doesn't matter. I don't even want to stay."

"No, and Sophie does."

"Yes," I said quietly. "She does."

I e-mailed her my congratulations and got a reply a few days later. *Thnx, miracles do happen! Not even sure if I'll take it.*

I wondered about St. John. Had I told him her name? I had, I knew I had, and her story too.

When I contemplated four years more of Oxford, the only appeal they had was in other people. For Sophie it would be different; to stay would mean something. She had been pushed out into the world on a little raft when she was eight, alone mostly. Even Jack barely wanted her, the fool. The more I thought about the Swift the more I thought about that word she had used, "miracles," and what it offers us.

My vague plans of selling out took on practical contours now. I prepared my résumé and took it to a depressing building near Summertown, where I met with a pale career counselor who frowned at its untidiness.

"What are you looking for?" he asked.

"Something that makes a lot of money."

"Where?"

"Anywhere in London or Oxford. Preferably Oxford."

During some of the winter months I had occasionally had sex with an undergraduate girl, Melissa. She wasn't especially interested. British girls seemed more experienced than American ones, and less generous, too, and her grumbling criticisms and exhortations (*"There, not there!"* and "You're pinching my skin! You're pinching my skin!") seemed to me to prevent her from achieving whatever state of bliss she expected.

Still, because I was one of the few people known to have been hooking up, in the MCR I was widely suspected to be the Sex Bandit—the nickname everyone was calling the person who had sex on the dining room table. I protested that it was all over long ago—since I'd slept with Sophie, in fact, though I didn't say as much—but people still eyed me charily. Personally I suspected Peter and Ella.

As it fell out, though, we were all wrong. Before a meeting in the third week of April, word spread that someone was going to step forward. Because of this it was unusually crowded. I'm not sure what we were all expecting, but we got it right away. The moment new business was called for Peter's hand shot into the air.

"Yes?" said Richard reluctantly.

"I just wanted to suggest the cancellation of the skeet-shooting vote," he said. "Nobody supported it in the last meeting, and I don't think that you should use your override, Richard."

Giorgio looked furious. "How is this new business?"

"It's not. I just wanted to make that suggestion. Do you agree to it?"

"Of course not," said Richard. "Even the suggestion is ludicrous."

Peter sighed and looked deeply conflicted. "It will eat up such a lot of money."

"The issue is off the table," Giorgio said.

"Unlike the Sex Bandit," said Anil.

"In that case, I do have new business. I know who the Sex Ban— who has been having sex on the dining room table."

There was an intake of breath in the room, and then a long silence.

"Well?" said Tom, rocking on the balls of his feet. "Who was it?"

"I came in at 4:00 A.M. last night after working in the library. About fifteen minutes later, two people came in. I had dozed off, or I would have said something before they started. As it was, I left before they noticed me, but I saw their faces."

Peter paused. "Well, don't keep us in suspense!" said Tom. "Who!?"

"It was Giorgio," said Peter.

Giorgio was bright red, and above the din he said. "This man is a liar."

"I saw it, too," Ella said quietly.

Peter waited until the room was quiet.

"The other person was Richard," he said.

This revelation caused the most profound pandemonium I had ever seen in the MCR. Several people shouted out, others looked on with unspeaking but deep gratification, nearly everyone broke into a conversation at once, and one sensitive soul, Bert, the chemistry DPhil, was so moved by the news that his glass of water slipped from his hand.

When the din finally settled, there was a protracted discussion in which first Giorgio denied Peter's account, then Richard stood up and proudly admitted it, and said, pounding his chest Gallically, "To use the MCR, is it not an appanage of office, ladies and gentlemen! Why should I be ashamed?"

To which Tom said, "You should be ashamed because you wanted to go skeet shooting and spend all of our money and made Peter come in every morning to wash the MCR table, you prat!"

Peter, a more peaceable soul, said, "A standard punishment for public indecency, according to the—erm, the amendment that you wrote, Giorgio, to the MCR Constitution, would be a three-month suspension of MCR membership. With an accompanying abdication of any office held within the MCR government."

Giorgio stood up. "I'm leaving."

"You'll recall I argued it was too harsh at the time," said Peter.

Richard said, "This is homophobia!"

"Please," said Tom.

"Gay or straight," Peter said, "it is inappropriate to have sex in the MCR, or indeed in any college building."

"Yeah," said Ella.

"Yeah," said Tom. Then he looked at me with a grin, because he knew I knew he and Ella had once had sex in the Fleet library. Fortunately Ella's eyes were on Peter.

After a day of hushed consideration Giorgio and Richard agreed to leave office if they did not have to suspend their membership in the MCR. They also came out as a couple, which right away increased their popularity—their mutual loyalty made so much more sense that way. Shortly thereafter Peter, following a very low-key campaign, was elected president. He was suited to the position and filled it admirably, soliciting with special care the opinion of the former president; but every so often I would see Giorgio and Richard huddled in some corner of the dining hall, speaking quietly, occasionally with Xi or some other acolyte, and feel certain that they were planning a coup.

———

I think perhaps it sounds as if I were unhappy in Oxford, especially during this March and April, but I wasn't. The failure is in my telling, because those days were wonderful, altering, rich in their inattention, profuse with chance.

Already I've forgotten to explain how the Bodleian looked under snow, how total the silence of that inner courtyard became, above all how companionable it was for all of us working anonymously together in the bright reading rooms, warm. How we all glanced through the window from time to time at the chill fall of light, how honored and safe it seemed to belong to that loose net of humans inside the Bod, in the days after it snowed, for a moment present in the infinite continuum of Oxford.

Or when spring came I found this pub of my own, the Wheatsheaf. I never took anyone there. The windows were propped open with old books, letting the breeze in, and on the walls were sepia cricket pictures and menus from the nineteenth century. There was a cigarette-smoke-dirtied portrait of Gladstone hanging over the taps. I went there every morning to have coffee and croissants. It was usually mostly empty, so I could have all to myself one of the high-backed booths, upholstered in rich green, that ran along one wall. Copies of the daily papers would be scattered around the room at random, and I would take one and read. The same group of three old men sat at the bar every morning between nine and noon, nursing pints of bitter, and on the first day when they all said hello upon my entrance I felt triumphant: a regular.

Then, and I know it doesn't sound like much, but it was, there were the kebab vans. Anybody from Oxford will know what I mean. Arabic men ran all of them, and they all had their proponents, but Tom, Ella, and I liked one called Hassan's, on Broad Street, to which most of Fleet was devoted. (St. John's liked Houssain's; Christ Church liked Sid's Kitchen.) Anyway, they served everything, open until dawn. The two most popular things they had were kebab pitas, stuffed with dubious-looking meat, lettuce, mayonnaise, and hot sauce, and chips and cheese, which was what I got. I can taste it now. Because Hassan's was so busy the chips were always fresh and damp, newly salted, and it makes my mouth water to think about every random night after the Turtle when I would get a medium-sized foam box full of them, smothered in some generic kind of cheese with ketchup and mayonnaise. All of it melted together into a mess. I can't think of any late-night snack that compares to it— not New Haven pizza, not a hot dog on the street in New York.

A million words started to mean something: *Green Wing*, Arsenal, Parky, Paxman, Jonathan Ross, Cesc Fàbregas, Jodie Marsh, Prime Minister's Questions, Michael Hague, Jordan and Peter, Jemima Kahn, *Akenfield*, the Stig, "put paid to," "bottle," "nous." Or my favorite, "tired and emotional"—a phrase that, applied to politicians, meant drunk.

It was a great mental unburdening to live there. Even when I worried about the future, New York was still a million miles away; the life I had left behind there, Alison, all of the human beings succeeding and failing, the people pushing through medical school and law school or trying to get above the fold at the *Times*, all the people working in politics—it seemed mute and evanescent in the daily e-mails I received from friends back home. What a relief, after so many years of striving! From high school to college, from college to New York, from a job to a better job. Like having a headache so long you forget what it's like to feel well, and then one day, the pain rising, and vanishing, and the world all right again. That was Oxford for me.

That and all of it: the old quads, the mellifluous summer whisper of tree and water, Mob Quad, the fat lazy walk down Broad Street, the chintzy tuck shops and sandwich stands near the bus station, the lawns behind Trinity, the dust of the Ashmolean, the cracked eggs and glitter and white flour scattered outside the Exams School after people were trashed, trips down into the dodge of Cowley, used bookshop, the covered markets, the Bear, all of the city's spires lined up toward the Bodleian...

It's hard without some pain to think of the past, how perishable both it and its certainties are: how once upon a time we belonged to something, to a school, a person, a group of friends; and how we no longer do. In many ways Oxford was a terrible place. Like anyone else who went there I acknowledged the legitimacy of what C. S. Lewis had said, "The real Oxford is a close corporation of jolly, untidy, lazy, good-for-nothing, humorous old men, who have been electing their own successors ever since the world began and who intend to go on with it. They'll squeeze under the Revolution or leap over it somehow when the time comes, don't you worry."

Still, I loved it. C. S. Lewis, whatever his grumbling, never left, and I wonder if perhaps he, too, preferred Matthew Arnold's description, of the city venerable and serene, how its gardens spread themselves under the moonlight, home to forsaken beliefs and impossible loyalties, the city itself a mystery and a charm: whispering, from her towers, the last enchantments of the Middle Ages.

CHAPTER NINE

On the first day of April I saw Sophie outside of Fleet Hall.

"Hey," I said.

"Hi, Will." Her tone was neutral.

"Are you coming into Hall?"

"No, picking up a snack." She held out an apple. "My long essay's due soon. I should run."

"Okay. Maybe later."

"Bye."

I had been thinking about Jack all the time, wondering how his life compared to mine. Was he eating those meals that came in plastic slipcovers, MREs, or was that just the American army? What food did he miss? Did he have access to the Internet? What was the toilet paper like? Was he sunburned? What if he needed ChapStick, did you have to get it requisitioned or was there a shop? If he was craving peanuts, could he get ahold of peanuts? Was it a desert he was in or were there trees and scrub? How many hours of his waking day was there not a gun in his hands? Why was he there? Why did he have to apply to Sandhurst out of public school instead of university? Bad grades? Family tradition? Had he seen anyone die?

Did they let them have iPods? If so, what was he listening to? Music that Ella had given him? Was there a picture of Soph tacked up on his bunk? In his bag? What picture was it? Could she possibly have given him a naked picture of herself, if he cajoled her into it? Was that in her? And how could I feel jealous even now, when it was only an invented question in my mind, what was wrong with me? Did he jack off into a sock thinking about her body every night? About Minka's body? Was there the privacy for that? Did he get the news from England? What did he say to his mother in letters home? Did he read books there? Could he get a copy of *The Times*? Did he think about me?

I could wonder about these things and at the same time I knew that if she had asked I would have walked back to the Cottages and slept with her as many times as she wanted, however she wanted to betray him, whatever she wanted to do with me. It was hopeless love.

Ella was across the quad when I said good-bye to Sophie, and she came right over. "What was that?"

"Nothing much."

She snorted, not unkindly. "It sucks, huh?"

"Are you getting food?"

"Yeah, let's have lunch."

"Has it gotten better for you yet?" I asked as we went up the steps to Hall. "With Tom?"

"Not especially. A little."

"But Peter—"

"Not especially. A little."

Bank after bank returned my application with thanks and a rejection letter. Soon I started to fear seriously that I would leave Oxford without any plan. Should I begin a doctorate? I could afford to pay my own way. I could try to find a job in journalism. Could I write a book, perhaps about working in politics? There would be an election in 2008, and for six months or so political books would be bestsellers again. No, I didn't think I could. So many people I had known mistook themselves for writers because they thought they must be something special; they always had been so far. (Or else such people were photographers, so many of them.) What occurred to me was that maybe I was nothing special at all.

The truth was that I didn't know my own mind. Just as you might move into a house and in the scatterbrained days of unpacking leave a broom in some corner, where it remains until someone uses it and then returns it to that corner, not knowing that it was there by casual chance, until slowly that corner becomes its hallowed place, where you can always find the broom—just as all traditions begin as accidents, how the borders of countries are formed, how we marry, how we make friends and children—so, until Oxford, had I lived, within a sequence of nondecisions, and yet with the same misdirected conviction of intentionality with which humans infuse their errors and felicities alike.

One day I explained my anxiety to my mother. She cut me off. "Oh, go see your cousin's husband in London, Franklin. He'll give you a job."

"He will? What are you talking about?"

"He does investments. He'll like you. He married your cousin Maggie, Lucy's sister."

"There's no way he'd hire me. I'm doing an English degree, and I'm American."

"He married an American. Listen, if I set it up will you meet with him?"

Two weeks later I took the train to London and after a tube ride found myself standing in the lobby of the Gherkin. I felt like an impostor in my suit, the way a teenager dressed up for the first time thinks everyone on the street is staring at him.

I was encouraged when I got to the thirty-seventh floor and discovered that my cousin's husband didn't work at an investment firm—he ran one. The thirty-seventh, thirty-eighth, and fortieth floors housed the offices of Franklin Cross. (I don't know what happened on the thirty-ninth floor—ritual killing and satanic orgies probably, or a gym.)

Our meeting began exactly on time. "How do you do?" he said, leading me into his office himself, a red-cheeked old rugby type. He had a view of the city that ran from the Tower of London to the Houses of Parliament, westward down the Thames. "Pleased to meet you."

"Thanks so much for seeing me."

"Our Maggie has a good eye. You study English, she mentioned? I like that. The best chap I've got has a DPhil in philosophy. A Jew. But he doesn't bother about it, he would sell Spinoza's bones if there was a buyer. He makes a million pounds a year, or thereabouts anyway."

"Should we start our bargaining there, then?"

He smiled. "Good lad. All right, you're meeting with a couple of my senior men. They'll give me their opinion of you, administer a test, look at your records—Maggie said you're some kind of thing in politics, which is good, people skills—and if everything's positive you've got a job. It's a hundred twenty a year, and benefits. The usual sort, gym membership, private health insurance, life insurance, retirement. Raise every six months, ten to twelve percent. Six to eight if the economy tanks. We'll work you to the ground. You'd start in September."

He stood up, and we shook hands. "Thank you. Thanks so much."

"Give those fuckers at Christ Church hell for me, would you? I was in Oriel myself."

That was all I saw of Franklin—a minute, ninety seconds—and then I spent the rest of the day with two men. One was fat and one was thin, and to my astonishment they were called Mr. Black and Mr. White. ("We aren't like those chaps in *Reservoir Dogs,* don't worry," said White in a practiced tone.) They asked me about two hundred questions, most of which were incomprehensible. ("What did the LIBOR open at this morning?" "How many basis points has the Nikkei risen year-to-date?" "What is a safe BRIC exposure for an aggressive fund?")

"How many people could you fit in this room?" White asked.

"Twenty."

"The right answer is, with or without the furniture," said Black, shaking his head.

"With or without the furniture?"

"With."

"Twenty."

Neither of them laughed. "How many golf balls could you fit in this room?" asked White.

"With or without the furniture?" I asked.

I left London certain that I hadn't gotten the job, and so of course two days later I got it. For the fiftieth time I did the math in my head—$190,000 a year, and for what, for qualifications that I didn't have. I couldn't quite believe it. I had some money from a trust that my father's death had dissolved, but my family is wary about capital and I was loath to touch it. Here was real money, to spend. Every night as I fell asleep I repeated the figure in my head, surprised, and imagined the crisply decorated one-bedroom apartment I could get, looking over the Thames, furnished as if I were an adult. I pictured Sophie visiting me there and dropping one of her soft brown leather bags on the kind of modernist chair on which it deserved to be dropped. I did my best to forget how I had gotten the job, through the same well-worn avenues of nepotism that, I harangued people every day by e-mail or at the bar, had ruined the American government, had manufactured the gross inequality of my home country—had given me my whole life, in truth, if I thought about it.

Before too long I knew what the LIBOR was and where the Nikkei was trading. I studied the markets every morning when I woke up and read books about the essentials of the stock market. I canceled my print subscription to *The New York Times,* figuring I could read it for the political stuff online when I had time (no paywall in those days), and replaced it with one to *The Wall Street Journal.*

A few afternoons after I got the job, I ran into Jess in Blackwell's.

Blackwell's is Oxford's primary bookstore. It sits flush against Trinity College and looks as if it belongs to Diagon Alley, two smallish crooked houses of irregular rooms. The stock is an eccentric mixture of popular and academic books, and there's a café with a fireplace and armchairs. I used to go there often simply to read, but when I bumped into Jess I was in search of a copy of *A Clergyman's Daughter,* Orwell's worst novel. (*Coming Up for Air* is pretty good, *Burmese Days* interesting as a document, *Keep the Aspidistra Flying* outright underrated, and of course *1984* and *Animal Farm* have their immortal moments, but otherwise it's best to stick to his essays and memoirs.) Jess was facing a bank of oversized art books, looking through a collection of paintings by Pieter de Hooch. She looked pale, I thought. Her blond hair just touched the pages of the book as she looked down at it.

"Jess, hey," I said, tapping her on the shoulder.

She turned. "Oh, hullo, Will." Her smile was so familiar. "This is a bit awkward."

"No, no. I'm happy for you. I think you're great for him."

"Do you? Do you mean that?"

"I really do. He seems different."

She looked reassured. "I'm so glad you said that. I think he does, too."

She really had changed him. Unlike Ella she had a soft touch, a yielding that was its own variety of strength, and over the past few weeks I had watched Tom come to more closely resemble himself again. He never slept at the Cottages anymore, but I saw him each day, and he seemed more at ease with himself.

It was strange because Tom could be such a snob sometimes, and Jess, working in her teashop... Before they started dating I would have expected him to comment on how she held her fork and knife or her diction, "skive," "cock-up," "bollocks," but he didn't.

I said none of that to her, just, "Really different. And you, are you happy?"

"You have no idea."

I was hurt by the fervor of this. "We had fun, didn't we?"

"Oh, yeah, it was a doddle."

I wanted to hear it. "What?"

"I don't need to tell you the ways you were a shit to me, Will. I never heard from you. You made plans with me and didn't follow through with them, even when I was so excited." She shook her head. "I'm happy now, let's leave it at that."

There was a pause, as I contemplated her own anxieties by the telephone, her own unhappy autumn. "I'm sorry," I said at last. "I was selfish."

"Everything worked out."

"No, I mean it. I'm sorry."

She looked away, perhaps embarrassed by the honesty in my voice. Her eye caught the book she was holding. "Do you think he would like this?"

"That book? Sure."

"But do you really think so? I never know—I feel so nervous about messing it up."

My heart went out to her. "He would like this better," I said and pulled down a similar book about George Stubbs, Katie's favorite painter.

"Oh, thank you," she said, relieved. "Thank you."

There was a beat. "Is Tom weird about it?"

"About us?"

"Yeah."

"No." A foxish smile stole across her lips. "He's funny about it. He just talks about how it's a good thing he's amazing in bed, or it might bother him. I mean, you know."

I laughed. "He must be fun to sleep with."

"Will! What a weird thing to say. Anyhow, you were fun, too."

"I guess a threesome would have been insanely entertaining for you."

She laughed now, a sincere laugh, as I did, too—and suddenly as we stopped laughing a formal feeling came over the moment, a hush; a junction, an ending, in the affairs of two people who might have been something else to each other, but who have after all been something. From then on we would only be friends—truly nothing more. We stood just at an angle to each other, as daily and yet ceremonial as two figures in one of those de Hooch interiors, the people milling around us in Blackwell's unaware that life was happening near them.

"Well, good-bye, Will," she said.

"Good-bye," I said.

She stood on her tiptoes to kiss me on the cheek and gave me a swift hug. Then we parted, and I went up to pay.

I was one of Anil's closest friends at Oxford, less close to him only than perhaps Timmo, Anneliese, and a school friend of his from Mumbai, Shateel, who did economics at Wolfson—and who, I am sad to report, did not find his name's resemblance to "shitheel" as humorous as Tom did—but I don't know how well I can say I knew him until the end of the year. Seven or eight days before the fateful weekend of the Boat Race, I met the limits of my knowledge.

I was at loose ends one afternoon, having finished my work for the day not long before, and I wandered through the quads. Out on the lawns there were three undergraduates in boaters with champagne and a wind-up gramophone, a mockery that was nine-tenths love. The day was flooded through with the bright yellow light of near evening, the delible mercy of a beautiful sky. I decided to go to the teak chairs by the river. These were mostly empty now, the libraries full in their stead as year-end exams grew close. The air smelled of the grass of the lawns.

Only when I was close to the water did I see Anil was sitting on the chairs, staring at the swans on the riverbank. "Hey," I called out.

He was startled by my voice. "Oh, hey!" he said. He stood up quickly. "It's too bad you're just getting here, I have to go."

"Where?"

He paused, twisting the cord of his white iPod headphones around his finger. "Did you know Ella and Peter are dating?"

"I heard something about it."

"Yeah, I was thinking it is good for them. They are both very nice people. Okay. So I'm going."

"See you back at the house."

He took an irresolute step, then stopped.

"Is anything the matter?" I asked.

"No, nothing."

"Is it because Tupac's dead?"

He laughed. "Tupac's alive."

"Oh, right."

Something was off, plainly. He sat down in the chair again. There were tufts of dandelion fluff suspended over the river, lying against the soft wind. I waited him out. "Will you keep a secret?" he asked at last.

"Sure."

I didn't know what to expect. Because he was so irrationally self-assured and so good-natured, it was hard to imagine him suffering. He had always seemed as steady and forward-bound as one of those battleships that needs fifteen miles to stop.

"I'm homesick," he said. Then he laughed. "Have you ever eaten a panipuri?"

"What is that?"

"No, I'm not even really homesick I don't think." He looked into my eyes for the first time. "Will you keep it a secret?"

"Anil, yes, obviously."

He sighed from the bottom of his stomach, and said, "I think I very much like Ella."

"What, our Ella? From the MCR?"

"Who else?"

"When did you—when did you start liking her?"

"A while ago," he said. "She's so nice to me. Not like you and Tom. I know you're my friends, but not *nice* friends."

"I'm sorry you feel that way."

"It's fine. I like you even after the cream cheese."

A week before, Tom had snuck into Anil's bathroom while he was showering, lopped off the top of his deodorant stick, and molded cream cheese over what remained. The yelp of dismay had echoed through the Cottages.

"Tom didn't like you saying the word 'Paki.'"

Anil looked skeptical. "He is far more racist than I am."

"Would you ever talk to Ella?"

He shook his head. "No."

"Why not?"

"In this world there are people who can say things to people like Ella and there are people who cannot say things to people like Ella."

"You never know what she'll say." He merely shook his head, and in truth I understood. "Has it been a while since you've dated anyone?"

"Not since I left India."

"Ella likes you a lot."

He didn't say anything, and for the first time I saw that he was in a state not of mild distress but of real true unhappiness, nearly grief.

I put a hand on his shoulder. "Jem's opening the bar early tonight. Would you like to get a drink?"

"Absolutely." He stood up. "I've been meaning to try gin and juice."

"It's disgusting," I said. Then, because the pause was getting long, I added, "So, do you seriously think Tupac's alive?"

"Will, don't be naive."

"Maybe he'll be at the Boat Race Saturday."

"No, he's in hiding."

I waved a hand. "He's not even that good."

Anil rolled his eyes. "Haters gonna hate."

So, the Boat Race: as marmoreal and anachronistic as Hall at Fleet, as Chatsworth, as the House of Lords, all of England's spruced-up subjugations, and yet, like all of them, vivified by its straight-faced enactment.

It happens every spring and lasts twenty minutes, two long, slim boats from Oxford and Cambridge, lined with eight giants and one pixie, traversing a turn of the Thames. What struck me about it wasn't that people at the two schools cared about it but that *everyone* in England did. Pubs show it, tuck shops set up small TVs on rickety tables, and in all the staid little row houses of towns and cities unvisited by greatness, Mams and Pops put it on for an hour after their Yorkshire pudding. It's part of some dank collective nostalgia that people who have never been to Oxford or Cambridge have for the universities. As if they were national property, like Buckingham Palace, rather than preserves of the rich where people can afford to spend all of their time rowing. Another vanquishing myth of hierarchy handed down to Britain from the Victorians.

Maybe I'm being unkind. The British seemed to me to have a vexed and painful longing for what they call Merry England, Deep England, the country of sheep-scattered fields and wireless radio that never existed. Where everyone boat-raced. The French have it, too, *La France profonde,* a phrase that calls to my mind a boy in a striped shirt running down a Paris alleyway with a baguette under his arm, headed home.

As ever, Orwell got it best, this island quality, this peculiar blind wistfulness, the titanic security of tradition and money, predicated on people being poor—but elsewhere, elsewhere: "There is a cosy fire in the study, and outside the wind is whistling. The ivy clusters thickly round the old grey stones. The King is on his throne and the pound is worth a pound . . . At the outposts of Empire the monocled Englishmen are holding the niggers at bay. Lord Mauleverer has just got another fiver and we are all settling down to a tremendous tea of sausages, sardines, crumpets, potted meat, jam and doughnuts." I suppose it was this vision that I had loved myself, as a teenager reading about Blandings.

We left at sunup on that Saturday, aboard a bus that Fleet had hired. Most people went, even, somewhat to my astonishment, Sophie. She sat with Anneliese. A row back Tom snored away on Anil's shoulder for the whole ride.

At Hammersmith Bridge it was chaos, cockney teenagers selling beer from drag-behind coolers, unlicensed souvenir stands, pubs with their doors flung open in surrender. People in Cambridge pale blue and Oxford dark blue crowded both banks and hung their feet off the bridge.

It was a sunny day, and by eleven o'clock or so, when we arrived, girls were already in their halter tops. We walked along the east side of the river, finding a picnic bench at last to settle at, and just as Anneliese wondered out loud whether anyone really could expect us to start drinking in the morning, Tom caught up with us after lagging behind, his arms full of eight oversized cans of Stella. Soon we had all drunk them except Anil, who was unwell, but even sober was vowing to sabotage Cambridge's boat—possibly by playing a Method Man song with a heavy bass line that he knew, which he claimed would throw the cox off rhythm. How he planned for the music to affect only the Cambridge cox he never made clear.

"We're in for a long day when Anil is making plans about rap music at eleven," Tom said.

Anneliese had overheard. "What is a Method Man?" she whispered urgently.

Anil heard this and, speaking low in his clipped Anglo-Indian accent, as if it were almost too embarrassing to discuss, said, "You don't know about Wu? Rza? Gza? Inspectah Deck?"

"No."

"Ghostface Killah? Cappadonna? Oh, Anneliese!"

Anneliese shook her head apologetically. "I don't think they're very big in Germany."

"Hasselhoff," Tom and I said in unison, imagining that we were tremendously clever for making this well-worn joke.

"Shut up," she said. "I told you clowns a thousand times that nobody really likes him."

"Clowns!" Tom cried. "You got it right! You didn't call us jesters!"

She allowed herself a prim smile. "Yes, my command of English is excellent."

Meanwhile Anil looked agitated, and Sophie, sensing an incipient monologue, said, "What time do the boats come by?"

"Not until three thirty," said Tom. "How I hope one of the boats sinks, you can't imagine."

"Cambridge's boat, you mean," said Timmo.

Tom shrugged. "Preferably. Either would be good. Cambridge sank in 1978."

Sophie acted strangely as the day went on. Her manner was athwart of my intent, which was simply that we should be friends. She often whispered in my ear, or rested her head on my shoulder, or grabbed my hand to draw my notice to something. At last, after we had all moved into a shady spot farther down from the bridge, she said, "Will you go find a souvenir with me, Baker?"

"Sure," I said. "What kind?"

"I don't know, some tatty thing to pin to my bulletin board. Or for my father."

"How about a poster?"

"Hmm...actually I want one of the big foam hands with one finger sticking up."

"An elegant choice."

So we went off together, promising to be back soon. As we walked, we passed dozens of people we knew, saying hello and good-bye without too much ceremony, as if we were in Oxford. Sophie stopped and had a brief word with a guy I had never met, but who from their talk I gathered was one of Jack's friends. About his news, perhaps. We stopped at each of the souvenir stands but couldn't find exactly what she wanted, and kept on walking in the hopes of stumbling upon the right place.

It was after about half an hour, full of genial chatter, that we saw something astonishing: Jack, the Jackal, in a group coming out of a pub.

It was astonishing, that is, to me; I can't imagine what it must have been like for Sophie.

"Jack!" she cried out involuntarily.

He swung around, his eyes heavy-lidded with drink and indifference. When he saw her he raised them slightly but didn't say anything. Then he saw me and laughed.

"This dickhead. Thought you and I had a talk," he said to me, as if that alone meant I should have ceased to exist.

Sophie was rigid with anger. "You're here?"

The smile left Jack's face. "My grandfather died."

The information didn't deflate her indignation. "And you didn't feel like telling me you'd be back?"

"It's only three days," he said. "Dad was a friend of my brigade's commander out in Affgo, so he let me hitch back without kicking up a fuss."

"And you didn't feel like telling me? That you're at the fucking *Boat Race*?" she asked. "You didn't think that maybe you might see me here, you idiot? Or that it might be nice for me to know that you're in fucking *England*? Jesus, Jack! I never get a fucking letter from you, I'm worried sick all the time, and—and—"

He was a dark brown color now, exceedingly handsome. "I can't be with a girl that holds me down," he said.

"You're drunk and showing off." This accusation seemed to make her notice that she was amid people, and she said, "We can talk about this over there."

So they went behind one of the pubs, down an uninhabited alleyway. I couldn't quite make out what they were saying, though her voice rose now and then.

I waited, obviously.

After twenty minutes she came back to me. She was crying. It had grown windy, and her hair was flying around her face.

"Are you okay?"

"Just take me to a bar," she said, "and not one of these crowded ones. And for God's sake don't try to kiss me if I get drunk, for once."

"Of course not. Of course not."

I texted Tom that we were leaving. She and I walked away from the river and found a calm pub, the Boat Race coverage on muted TVs here and there. I ordered us red wine, her preferred drink, and we sat at a table far from everyone else.

"I can't believe how stupid I've been," she said.

"You haven't been stupid at all."

"Of course I have."

"What happened?"

"He's broken up with me." She said this in a normal voice, but tears were rolling from her eyes. I thought I had never seen anyone so hurt. "Why on earth would he do that?"

I loved her to the degree now that I would have put them back together if I could, to lessen her unhappiness. Yet it was strange: Much of me went to Jack, then, and less to Sophie. For one thing I wondered if his grand and brutal diffidence, his almost cruelty, came from being Over There, as I thought of it—fighting. He was in a war, really a war. Not the television war, the thing itself.

"I'm sorry," I said.

"I tried so hard. I wrote him every day and sent him e-mails and pictures. And he never really wrote back much more than a line or two. Not that I needed much to get by. I spoke to his mother on the telephone once a week, and visited his brother at Eton and sent him tuck, which Jack used to do. I tried very hard."

"You were great to him."

"No, I wasn't. I was racked with guilt every day. I missed you," she said. She paused. "I wanted to come see you every night when I went to sleep."

"Me, too."

"No, but it's not like that, I wanted to go see him every night, too, I wanted to hold him, too. Don't make it seem that way. I wanted him to move to Oxford and I'd be in school and we could have one of those houses by St. Giles and—" She broke off, having shared, I saw, too much of a private vision that had become more real to her through unspokenness than it should have. "But I felt so content with you, that weekend. You were so nice to me."

"Jack wasn't?"

"No, but that's okay. That's the kind of thing I can forgive. But not to care—that's different. Imagine him not calling me! Can you believe—" She burst into fresh tears, and two reddened white-haired men at the bar looked at me reprovingly. As if she had remembered how far she was forgetting herself, Sophie turned away and cleared her throat, trying to achieve some restoration of her usual guardedness. Then she gave me a formal look. "I'm glad you're here, Will, but nothing's going to happen."

"I know," I said.

"Good," she said.

"Maybe we should have a cigarette. Not even a secret one."

She laughed and hiccupped and cried at once. "Okay," she said. "Okay."

Eventually we roused ourselves to go back to the race, but it was over. I called Tom, and he said they were all going to the Cheshire Cheese, a pub on Fleet Street. ("Double Fleet time!") However, Sophie said she wanted to go *do* something, not just sit around, and so we went and drifted through the cold of the British Museum, never really looking at anything much. Aztec bowls, Egyptian funeral boats, Turkish tiles: all these civilizations at such a desperate disadvantage to us because we, happy or unhappy, were alive. At some point she started to hold my hand.

We missed the bus back and then had a forlorn pizza near St. Paul's. Still she kept talking about Jack, still her shield was down. When at last it was time for the second bus we walked silently across the dim city, back to pick it up at Marble Arch. On the way there were endless repetitive shops full of clothes and books and jewelry and electronics, the uncaring intricate rented world, and soon the only thing that seemed real to me was her. I thought to myself at one point that perhaps all the gold wreathed around her, the stars and moon and streetlight, her lips slightly parted, her face worn out from crying—thought to myself it might have been no more than my love, which surrounded her wherever she went.

Oxford won, by the way, even though Cambridge was the heavy favorite. Floreat Oxonia. Or Greyfriars, or what you will.

I suppose in the next days I expected Sophie to be around more, but she wasn't. For the last two weeks of April, after the Boat Race, she went to her parents' beach cottage in Dorset to finish her long essay, trundling all the way home first to pick up Chessie, her ancient spaniel, for company. She did text me occasionally—random jokes and complaints—and once we spoke on the phone. I asked about Jack.

"I still get his daily e-mail," she said. "Otherwise nothing. I expect he's with Minka now, the slut. I'm sure she does all sorts of things with him I wouldn't."

"Like what?"

"Oh, three-ways and coming on your face and playing with your bottom and all the stuff boys want to do."

I felt a sense of relief that she hadn't allowed Jackal those violations. "Are you coming back soon?"

"Soon," she promised.

260 | CHARLES FINCH

"What about the Swift?"

"I don't have to tell them for a month. I'll see how the essay goes. Speaking of which, I should get back to work."

"Say hi to Chessie for me."

"I will."

"And make sure you're stocked up on Hobnobs."

She laughed. "See you soon."

"Good-bye."

The next week, as April ended, Tom knocked on my door. It was late at night, past midnight, and I was downloading music illegally and chatting with Ella on AIM about a summer trip we might make to Amsterdam. I told her to wait.

"What's up?"

"Hey." He was holding his phone and biting his lip, his face thick with concentration. "I just got a text. Daisy is in town."

"Are you going to see her?"

"Do you think I should? Will you come?"

"Won't that be awkward?"

"Just come."

At a table at the King's Arms sat a girl with feline eyes and dark, lustrous, Trianon-milkmaid hair. She had big sunglasses propped on her head (it was past midnight, let me repeat) and a handbag large enough to hold an infant. On her face was that constantly re-calibrated baseline sullenness of the pretty English upper-class girl. Her shirt was of some fashion I was too ignorant to appreciate, with a dorsal pleat that ought to have looked absurd but made her shoulders seem especially soft and beautiful.

She ignored Tom. "I'm Daisy." She put out her hand, her bag hanging from her forearm so that I had to reach. "Pleasure to meet you."

I knew who she was, of course. I also knew that she and Tom had spoken only once, for five minutes, after his sister died. "How do you do," I said. "What brings you to town?"

"My firm is consulting here. I'm at the Old Bank." She gestured lazily behind her. "Poky city."

Tom was staring at her. We hadn't sat down yet, and just as I was about to, he burst out, "Will's on his way to meet our friend Ella, actually." He turned to me. "Thanks for walking me, mate."

"Sure," I said.

Daisy wasn't fooled.

On the short walk back to the Cottages, I got a text from Tom. *I owe you one.*

No worries, I wrote back.

I was just about to go to sleep, an hour later, when I heard the door. Anil and his friend Shateel were visiting Hadrian's Wall overnight, with Anneliese—both Anil and Anneliese had a checklist of places to see while they lived in England—so I knew it was Tom. Accompanying his footsteps was the peal of a girl's laughter. It wasn't Jess.

I ran to open my door and steadied it to make it look like I'd left it that way casually, then sat with a book in the armchair that faced the hall.

"Hi, Will," said Daisy. "How was Ella?"

"She's good."

"I look forward to meeting her."

"Daze, grab yourself a beer from the fridge," Tom said and ushered her into his room. "Will, this is that Web site I was telling you about."

"What Web site?" Daisy called from Tom's room.

"Just about football."

"Oh," she said without satisfaction.

He opened Google and typed "THIS IS A FUCKING

DISASTER JESUS CHRIST" into the search bar. A Web site called *Jesus Fucking Christ* popped up.

"Yeah, look around it, there's some pretty cool stuff about Arsenal on there," he said to me. "All right. Daisy and I are off for a walk. We just stopped back here for beers."

They were gone an hour, and when Tom returned he was alone. He came into my room and without saying anything spilled himself into one of the armchairs by my open windows.

"My life is fucking over," he said. "She's here for five weeks."

"You don't have to see her."

"I'm the only person she knows in the entire city."

"That's not your fault."

He sighed and ran his hands through his hair. "It's not so simple."

"Why?"

"You know better than anyone that I never wanted to break up with her."

"But that was a long time ago."

"She's single," he said, not quite irrelevantly. Then, more relevantly, "Fuck."

"Stick with Jess," I said.

"You think so?"

"Yep."

"She looked great."

"Daisy?"

"Daisy, yeah." Then, ruminatively and summarizingly, he said, "Fuck."

That April and May run together in my mind. I spent more time with Anneliese and Ella than with anyone else. Anil suddenly had to study very hard for exams, and Tom, though I knew he had seen Daisy now and then, was still with Jess every night. At some stage Sophie returned, but we only saw her once or twice a week. As I should have realized after she got the Swift, she had all along been working much harder than any of us realized, and like Anil she spent most of her time in the library. After she was back from Dorset I would visit her there most evenings, bringing a cup of coffee, a candy bar, and she would squeeze my hand and thank me and after ten or fifteen sentences of conversation turn back to her work. Slowly and gently I began to let go of my hopes of her. No, that's not accurate: I never let go of my hopes, but I saw that they were slipping away whether I wanted them to or not, and the excuse of her work, of Jack's desertion, softened the pain.

In the second week of May, on a very hot day, the lawns scattered with undergraduates burning themselves imperial red, I received an unexpected phone call. There was a booming American voice on the other end of the line.

"Is that Will Baker?" it asked.

"It is."

"You're a hard man to get ahold of. Dougie Bryson," said the voice. "Maybe you've heard of me?"

"It rings a bell," I said, which was a lie.

"I thought it might. I was on Kerry, too, but in Colorado. I ran the field office out there. It was rough. Hopefully we set 'em up for the next election, at least. We definitely cut some good turf."

"Doug Bryson, sure, of course."

"So listen, any interest in getting back into politics?"

"You know I'm in England, right?"

"I just called you, smart guy."

"Very true. What's going on?" I asked.

"If you want it I have a job for you, actually."

"Wow."

"Well, we're short on time. What it is, I'm running a congressional candidate out of the Ohio Seventeenth, a Democrat named Viskovitz, David Viskovitz. You'd love him. He's a veteran, Panama, and he's owned a contracting business out here for about ten years. The business is clean, which it's reassuring to know. Really weirdly handsome, blond wife, the kids. Actually one of the kids is Down's, too, which—it's not a disadvantage, quality of life aside and all that, not trying to be insensitive. Sweet kid. Anyway, Viskovitz, he's local chamber of commerce, hangs out at the hardware store, concerned parent at school meetings. The whole thing. Sounds like a Republican, doesn't he? That's why we're excited to have him."

"And you're running him."

"We need a comm director. I know you worked senior staff, but the people I was in touch with from Ohio told me you were a decent writer, and if I'm not mistaken you freelanced in the comm shop?"

"Yeah, all the time. It was us who got Polsky."

"Nice. Well, it doesn't pay much, sixteen hundred a month, but there's a car and an apartment, and you get fifty bucks per diem on weekdays, so that's another thousand a month." He paused. "I won't lie, the numbers are trending against us, and right now it's me and a phone bank, and some people from the community who are, look, they're nice folks, but they're not exactly seasoned operatives. The presumptive nominee had to drop out, some shady financing stuff. It's last minute. But even still, it's close, man. We gotta fight, right?"

"Of course. I'm honored. It would just be a big change."

"Two years of votes against Bush. If we can get this guy in office, I don't give a shit if he gets voted out in oh-eight, I don't give a shit if he fucks the prom queen in the ass on Main Street or does meth with Marion Barry, it's two years of votes against Bush. Just a big 'Nay' next to his name on C-SPAN every day. Because fuck those guys." His pitch was done, and he waited for my response. "Will? Did I lose you?"

"No, just thinking." The thing was, now I did remember Doug Bryson's name. He and a small band of field operatives in Colorado had stopped taking the orders of the national campaign in August, not long before the election, a briefly famous *trahison des clercs* that immediately bumped Kerry six points in local polling. In the end it had gotten him promoted, and he had been on TV a few dozen times. He was an interesting contact.

"Well?"

"Can I get back to you?" I asked.

"I can give you a few days to answer and two or three weeks to get out here, but that's it. No more, just because we're trying to get this thing up and running and we're already short on time. Look up my guy, Viskovitz. And take down my number."

I wrote it down. "By the way, have you heard of a guy named Jim Sawyer?" I asked.

"Of course, in New York?"

"He didn't call you, did he?"

"I've never spoken to him in my life. Why?"

"Sometimes he—he's looked out for me once or twice."

"No, no, this is a Kerry thing. I knew some of those Ohio people pretty well. Tucker, Monty, Steiny—"

"Oh, how is Monty?"

"I love that little guy. No idea how he's doing. Anyways, think about it. We'd love to have you on board."

"Cool. Thanks, Doug. I'll be in touch."

"Make it soon, okay?"

I hung up and stared at my phone, feeling a powerful ambivalence. I decided I would put the subject out of my mind for a couple of days. But part of me already knew that I would go.

The next week, three things happened that made me realize that the call was only a taste, after all, that whether it was in two weeks or three months or whenever it was I would actually have to *leave* Oxford. In the morning I turned in my long essay, the final piece of work I had to submit to the faculty; in the afternoon I got a slip under my door confirming that I could keep possession of my room until August 31 and not longer; and just before the business day ended at five o'clock, I got an e-mail from Franklin Cross, telling me my start date was September 3 and I should give them a correspondence address in London at least one week before that, appended with the details of firm-approved housing agents (they would pay), gyms (they would pay), and London Underground passes (they would pay).

I wrote back to acknowledge the e-mail and said nothing about the possibility that I might not take the job. How often I thought of that $190,000, how I spent it in my head! Yet each morning when I woke up it was with campaign thoughts. I had researched Viskovitz and already had a notebook a quarter full of plans for him.

The long essay I submitted, incidentally, was about Orwell and his imbrication of cultural and personal writing, history and autobiography, which I argued prefigured the generic uncertainty of so much late twentieth-century fiction. To this day the essay is considered a minor classic. No, I'm kidding, of course. I doubt anybody ever read it all the way through then, including my supervisor, and certainly nobody has since. I got honors for it, however. So did Anneliese. So did all the Chinese statistics students except one, who was rusticated for plagiarism.

I was there on the day when Sophie turned in her long essay, whose subject was Mauriac and Camus. I proofed it for her. She had promised again and again, to all of us, that when this piece of work was finished she would be free again to spend time with us, and of all people it was Anneliese who decided that we should trash her, to keep her to her word. Trashing was the tradition at Oxford when someone handed in their final piece of work: as they left the Exam Schools in their *subfusc*—black tie for men, white shirts and ribbons for women, academic gowns for both—you pelted them with flour, glitter, and champagne, or, in the case of the university's more laddish contingents, disgusting variations, fish that had been left to rot, ketchup, vinegar, soap, milk.

In the morning Sophie texted me. Somehow she had caught wind of our plans. *Just don't let them throw eggs.*

Well, I can promise you that I *won't throw any eggs. I'm not in charge of Tom.*

So Tom's going to throw eggs!?

I don't know what he's planning.

At ten to three all of us walked through town together, plotting strategy. "We have to throw the water and *then* the flour," said Anneliese. "That way it will stick."

"Good thinking," said Ella.

"Neither of you has any eggs, do you?"

"YES, WE GET IT, NO EGGS!" Ella said. "It's not like she's allergic to eggs!"

Anil was waiting for us on the corner of the High. He had a dozen yellow balloons that said HAPPY BIRTHDAY! in big blue letters. Balloons were a tradition, too.

"You got birthday balloons?" asked Ella.

"You noticed that?" he answered, crestfallen. "I thought they would blend together and look blue and yellow."

"Anil."

We reached the Exam Schools just as Sophie was coming out, and her face lit up. "Guys!" she said. She ran toward us in her black gown, cap under her arm. She looked happier than I had seen her in a long while. "I'm done!"

Instinctively I opened my arms and she flew up and hugged me. "Congratulations!"

Then I felt a firm thwack in the middle of my back.

I turned, and Tom was there with two cartons of eggs. "You don't get off without a pelting."

Then Anneliese, Anil, Ella, Timmo, and Peter, all of them so recently my allies, started to spray Sophie and me with champagne, toss water in our faces, burst open bags of flour over our heads, dust us with handfuls of glitter. Tom roved around the perimeter, throwing eggs.

"Tom, you asshole!" Sophie yelled.

"Eggs are a tradition!" he said. "You'll thank me when you see the pictures!"

"Oh, Christ," she said. "Anneliese's taking pictures, isn't she."

Then there was a whoop and a massive red streak in the air. It was Jem and two of his friends.

"Ketchup?" I said. "Fuck." I wiped it out of my eyes.

"Congrats, Bake," he said. "You dick."

Sophie and I huddled together until everything they had brought was clotted in our hair and grimed into our clothes. "Motherfuckers," she said in her proper accent, smiling.

We were disgusting, but by the rules we had to stop at the King's Arms and sit outside in the heat, the flour and champagne turning into a coat of cement on our skin. Afterward we went off and showered, then reunited at the porters' lodge and went punting together in a large, loud group, returning at eight, sunburned and drunk.

There was a bop that night, the Saturday of Trinity Seventh Week. Masses of undergraduates had finished in the previous days.

"I can't believe I'm here another three years," said Ella as we watched them from the bar. They were all dancing outside on the terrace and the lawns, finding mischief with each other early in the night.

"I'm sure they'd all be jealous. Anyway, I'll be back to visit."

"If I'm going to bops in two years, please shoot me."

"Please shoot me if I'm not."

She looked at me. "Are you going to say anything to Sophie?" she asked.

I shook my head. "Not tonight."

Ella and I did a shot then; Tom showed up with Jess; Anneliese and Sophie were already dancing and laughing together outdoors. Soon enough we started to dance, too. I remember the songs so well: There was "Angels," by Robbie Williams, and we all yelled the chorus together ("Nothing like a bunch of pissed mates screaming 'Angels,'" Jem observed), and there was "Back for Good," obviously.

The bops ended at midnight. (Coming from New York, where that was the time when Alison and I would leave the apartment, that always seemed touchingly provincial.) For the last song the DJ put on something slow, that one by Alphaville, I think. Sophie and I had been dancing in a group together all night, and earlier she had bought me a beer and sat at the bar with me, talking and giggling, but only now did we find each other among all of the nineteen-year-old couples swaying on the lawn and dancing together, just the two of us.

Her skin was warm and soft. I put my arms around her waist.

Neither of us talked, but she rested her head on my shoulder, her face against my neck.

When the song ended neither of us let go. "I might be leaving sooner than I expected," I said in a low voice.

She looked up at me. "For where? For London?"

"No. For the States."

"In how long?"

"A couple of weeks."

"What about your job?"

"There's a different job I might take."

"I was so looking forward to all of us being here this summer," she murmured. She stayed in my arms, though no new song had come on.

My heart started to race. "Could anything happen between us, if I stayed?" I asked.

There was a long pause. "No," she said at last. Then she squeezed me in her arms and stepped back. "I'm sorry. It's not possible. All that is over for me."

"Is it too soon after Jack?"

"It's not that. Please don't ask me again, Will. I don't like to hurt you."

I went home that night in a daze of grief. I woke in the same daze. The trouble was that I believed her. I spent the day heartsick, lying in my bed, immune to distraction, a lump in my throat the whole while. Finally at four o'clock (when it was still just ten in Ohio) I called Doug Bryson and took the job.

"Welcome aboard," he said.

"I have a bunch of ideas. I'll e-mail you. I think there are persuadables in Pine Heights."

"The trailer parks? We're polling fifty-five there."

"I think it could be eighty. He just has to soften up on guns a bit."

I could hear Doug smile. "Get over here as fast as you can."

America was where they kept real life anyhow. I didn't want to go back; in particular I didn't want to miss the chance of seeing her at random every day, and at moments it felt as if that would be enough, my aspirations had so diminished. In more sensible moods I knew the best thing I could do was leave.

Then, a day later, as if to confirm it, America reached out and grabbed me back. I think it was the most surprised I've ever been.

I had been doing laundry in the MCR and played a few games of table football against Giorgio and Anil, Anneliese as my team-mate. The four of us were planning to go to Hall afterward, but I ran back to the Cottages to fetch my windbreaker first, because it was a chilly evening, raining.

There I saw that I had a visitor: standing on my stoop, a slim rolling suitcase at her side, was Alison.

Two days after Alison arrived, a miracle happened. She missed it, unfortunately, because she was having lunch in town with a friend of her father's. It happened when Timmo, Anil, and I were sitting in the MCR together, playing FIFA 05, and Timmo's mobile rang.

"Timmo," he said, his invariable and vexing salutation on the phone, then, "Yes, Timothy Cooper. Why?"

He was silent for long enough that Anil and I started to stare curiously at him. Finally Anil whispered in an urgent tone, "What is it?"

"Thank you," Timmo said to whoever was on the line. "Thank you . . . okay . . . every day . . . yeah . . . I'll wait for the e-mail. Thank you!"

"What the fuck was it?" I asked.

He grinned. "This is huge."

"WHAT?" Anil and I shouted in unison.

"It was *Big Brother.*"

"Holy shit."

"Oh my Lord," said Anil with an awe in his eyes usually re-served for religious and sexual experiences.

It was the happiest day of Timmo's life. We ran around finding everyone we could and telling them the news ("Timmo's going to be on *Big Brother!*" I shouted at Sir George across First Quad, giddy with excitement. "Ah, excellent," he said with a puzzled smile. "Bring him to Hall.") In the MCR it was a bombshell. That night we sat in a group of fifty and watched past seasons of *Big Brother* on DVD while Timmo, in a chair inches from the screen, took assiduous behavioral notes. *The Sun* called him because they wanted to have capsule profiles of the new housemates prepared, and *The Cherwell,* Oxford's student paper, heard the news and interviewed him at length.

His master's course was done, and there were only five days between the call and his departure (he was a replacement for a housemate who had to go into rehab). His idea of doing a PhD was gone, of course. As he packed to leave on his last morning, Tom, Anil, Ella, and I sat in his room.

"What put you over the top?" I asked. "It was the video, obvi-ously. I don't know why I'm asking."

"It was the push-ups!" he said. "There's a gym in the *Big Brother* house."

"A gym," muttered Tom, whose indignation was running high.

"Nobody in the cast they chose would have used it, and they wanted to"—he frowned, trying to quote verbatim—"they wanted to make sure every part of the house was also part of the show."

"What do people from the show do afterward, usually?" asked Ella.

"Aside from astrophysics and peacekeeping missions," Tom said.

"Depends," he said. "Some of them don't do anything. Some do local appearances in pubs and bars and that. Some of them do big stuff, of course. Who could forget Chantelle and Preston?"

The unironic delivery of these last words was too much for Tom, who stood up and began to pace the room.

"What do you want to do?" Ella asked.

"I'd do appearances, I guess," he said. "Five hundred quid and unlimited drinks, sleep with a bird, just for showing up in Rotherham? Yes, please, money for old rope."

Anil was getting agitated. "But Timmo," he said, "certainly you'll be coming back soon? To Oxford?"

He shrugged. "Maybe."

"Please come back," said Anil. "You have friends here."

"Yeah, don't get too famous," said Ella.

"I won't be back if everything goes well."

Anil looked despondent. "Really?"

"Forget about Timmo, Anil," I said. "Ella, start doing push-ups."

Timmo was the second person voted out of the house, as you'll know if you followed *Big Brother*. (Also, may God have mercy on your soul.) Then he was recalled by fan vote and went on to finish third. For a few weeks he was famous, and nowadays he has his own radio program and hosts a *Big Brother* talk show on TV, both with a zany, pattering guy from the previous season of the show named Chicken, who uses Timmo as a straight man. I have to say, Timmo's good at it. Chicken calls Timmo "Professor" because Timmo went to Oxford—and yet, as Chicken points out very often, never says anything smart.

Sometimes I hear from him. He has a stunning girlfriend, a glamour model (as the Brits call them) from Hull. Usually he sends me some video on YouTube that was popular three weeks before. I know he talks to Anil every day. There was even some word of them going out to India together, but I don't know if that happened. I could find out. People drop out of touch more quickly than you expect.

The news was of surpassing significance to Timmo, but in those confused days I have to admit that for me it was only a footnote to my life, because of Alison.

When I saw her on my stoop, I said, stupidly, "Alison?"

"Hey." She was smiling. "Are you surprised?"

"I'm shocked."

"I had some business in London."

"What business could you have had in London?" I asked.

"Terrorism stuff," she said. "There was a conference with the London police and they sent me over."

"Well—great. How long can you stay?"

She shrugged. "I didn't book my flight back until Sunday night."

I hugged her and kissed her, then sat down on the stoop beside her. We were covered from the rain there, looking out at the wet world, the yellow streetlights, the pavement glittering as if diamonds had been flung across it. I could smell her clean familiar saline scent, and I could see the white scar under her collarbone, from a bicycle accident when she was young. Her physical presence reached out and gave me, without warning, a yearning for things to go back to what they had been. In some universe we were still together. I felt the cruelty of living only once.

I grabbed her hand. "You'll have to come out tomorrow night. We're all going to the Turtle."

"The famous Turtle," she said dryly.

"Come on, let's get your stuff upstairs."

"I can get a hotel."

"Don't be ridiculous."

When we were in my armchairs some time later, her presence in that bedroom slightly alien, as if two parallel lines had touched, she said, casually, "You know, I still haven't hooked up with anyone."

"No?"

"What about you?"

"No," I said. "Not especially."

The first night she was there Alison and I watched a movie; I slept on the floor. We caught up about old friends and sat around in our pajamas. There was a closer feeling between us than there had been in a long time, and the more I was with her, I found, the hungrier I was for her company.

The next day I showed her Oxford—the things you saw if you ever went there, the Radcliffe Camera, the Ashmolean, the grand stone stairwell at Christ Church, dipped in the center of each stair by generations of footsteps.

It was a Friday, and as I had told her it was supposed to be a big night. A ragged group of twenty or so Fleet MCR people was meeting up for dinner and dancing, in celebration of so many people finishing. Tom was absent—he texted me that he was with Jess—but over dinner Alison got to meet everyone else. Anil and Timmo (still a day shy of his earth-shattering news) strolled in a few minutes late, Anil in a Raiders hat and with his special gold chains around his neck

He lit up in a smile when I introduced him to Alison, his fancy glasses perched under the brim of his cap. "Will has told us much about you!" he said.

"Anil, why are you dressed like that?" I asked.

"To protest the Turtle's racist policies. My black brothers are being discriminated against."

"Your what?" asked Sophie.

"They won't let you into the Turtle if you're wearing necklaces or baseball hats, Sophia! It's an outrage, really an outrage. On behalf of the black community—"

"Oh dear," said Anneliese.

As things shook out, Sophie and Alison sat next to each other at Pierre Victoire, the French restaurant on Little Clarendon, and with their good breeding, like a shared property line, soon they were best friends. Sophie kept saying things like "You never told me Alison has so much responsibility at her job!" and "You never told me Alison went to Patagonia!"

"I can't believe I didn't mention that."

Alison rolled her eyes. "Isn't he too sarcastic to deal with?"

Sophie smiled. "Yep."

As we walked toward the Turtle Alison and I put our arms around each other, both softened up by a great deal of wine. On every sidewalk were people our age, scattering in the twilight toward small aims, and I thought of youth, how youth is. We went into the dark cellar of the Turtle in a mood of festive exhilaration, ordering Orielgasms and Jägerbombs at random, whether we already had drinks or not.

After a while I noticed Sophie was gone. I looked for her and saw that she had run into some of Jackal's friends. I turned to Alison and said, "Do you want to get drunk?"

"That's why I came to England."

So we had two martinis, mango for her and vodka for me, and then we started dancing. The hours and the drinks passed, which is usually how it happens. Alison and I would occasionally find Anil or Ella and dance with them, Sophie once as well, but mostly we just danced together in between drinks. Then the song of the moment, "Mr. Brightside," came on, and everything seemed to turn up a level, the adrenaline in the room, and it turned into that ecstatic kind of dancing, when you're sweaty and happy, and everyone is screaming in unison. When at some point Alison fell into me, accidentally nudged by someone from behind, I slipped my hand under her dress to feel the crease where her ass hung over her thighs. She tilted her head up toward me and grinned, her dark hair falling messily around her face, then gave me a kiss. Her lips were salty.

"I took a job in Ohio," I called out to her over the music.

"I know."

"What?"

"I wanted you to take it on your own. You can't be a banker, Will."

I realized she was right, and I realized why she had come when she did, that neither the job nor her visit was an accident. I found I didn't care. I looked around and couldn't see anyone I knew. "I missed you," I said.

"I missed you, too. This whole year."

CHAPTER TEN

In the next days we began to blend our lives back together. I booked a ticket to New York, where Alison said I could drop my things at her apartment while I was in Ohio, and then booked a second ticket to take me on to Columbus. I gave Doug Bryson my Social Security number, and he started a routine background check. I told Fleet I would be leaving my room earlier than I had anticipated.

At the same time Tom, too, was making a decision.

I had still only met Daisy once, but over the course of the year he had described their history to me. How they met at a London charity dance when they were both still in school, aged seventeen, an event with, as he recalled it (I think it can't possibly be true) every stripe of crippled and contagious human article staggering around them in a lurid Buñuel waltz, how after school he went off to LSE while she went to its inferior neighbor, King's, how while there she studied the Yves Saint-Laurent catalog, yoga, sexual guides she found online, and, in the margins of time these activities left spare, Spanish. It was sex that kept Tom enamored of her. I know for a fact that he believed he had never dated anybody as good-looking or as out of his league as Daisy. He was underestimating himself; she was a creature of upper-class dreams. She had money but he had real origins, Charles the Second stuff, whereas she was one or two generations removed from the working class. Her parents were the first rich members of her family, possibly her grandparents, but it went no further back. Her background was like Kate Middleton's in that way, I suppose. She was very intelligent; I could tell from the e-mails she sent, from her face. Personally I never could have liked her. We were too different. She cared about things like fashion and food, those ruthless twin commerces mistaken by idiots for culture, and she distinguished herself from other people primarily by what she bought. (Here she was of her class. No spoiled Malibu teen could care more for *things,* cars, clothes, jewelry, than certain members of the British gentry. In every gesture they assert their status, commodifying even their children's names, infant Rollos and Tristans and Leanders.) Tom was changeable; he could be led into or away from his snobbishness. For much of their relationship I think she led him into it.

The reason this is of more than academic interest is that on the day after I took Alison to see the Turtle I had a note from him on my desk, and it was about her.

Bake—

> Daisy finishes working in Oxford today. She says good-bye. I'm driving her to London. I'll be back in a few days, maybe a week, definitely in time for the LMH grad bop. Monitor Anil's music for me—if he thinks he can start blitzing Nelly just because I'm gone he's mistaken.

> Raleigh

I called him. "Hey, Will," he said, picking up. I could hear the highway.

"Are you on your way to London?"

"Yeah."

"So wait, the past couple of nights you've been with—"

"With Daisy, yeah."

You missed meeting Alison. "Did you tell Jess you were going?"

"I talked to her. Listen, I have to run. Daze says hello. See you soon."

I tried to picture them together. I earnestly doubted that Daisy had said hello, or for that matter the good-bye Tom had relayed in his note. I went back into my room from the landing. "Who was it?" asked Alison. She was cross-legged on the floor, sorting through her dirty clothes. We were going over to the MCR to do laundry.

"Tom. It seems like he and Jess might be breaking up."

She frowned. She was partially caught up on the story. "That's too bad."

"Yeah."

"How did they meet?"

"Oh, just around," I said. "She works in a teashop. Which is maybe the problem."

"Not everyone can be happy like us," she said and rolled her eyes, though she was smiling, too.

"Hilarious."

I put Tom out of my mind then, until my phone rang several hours later. It was Jess.

"Hey," I said cautiously. Alison was in the room.

"Hey, Will."

I walked out into the hallway. "How's everything?"

"Fine," she said. "Listen, is Tom next door by any chance? I can't get him on the phone. I wouldn't ask, but I haven't even had a text from him since yesterday."

"No, he's not around."

She paused. "He's with that girl, right?"

I didn't know what to say. "Who?"

"Okay," she said. "Well, thanks for nothing."

"I'm sorry."

I thought she was going to hang up, but she didn't. "Will?"

"Yes?"

"When you saw me naked did you ever think I looked fat?"

"Oh my God, Jess, no. Don't be a psycho."

"You promise?"

"Yes. God."

She was quiet for a minute. "Really, I just hope he's happy. I know it sounds stupid."

"I think you've made him happy. Almost as happy as he was before Katie died."

"Do you think so?"

"You shouldn't jump to any conclusions about them, either. I don't think they've hooked up. And I can see why he would find her comforting. For the same reason. Just, she knew his sister, she's from before."

"Is she pretty?"

"No," I lied, loyal in a way to both Tom and Jess.

"That's good."

"He loves you."

"He said that?"

"He hasn't said it to you? I can tell it's how he feels."

"He said it once—once when we were hooking up."

I could hear her happiness as she considered the memory of it. "Let's keep this family-friendly, okay?"

"Oh, grow up."

On the night before Alison had to leave, a day or two after Tom and Daisy went to London, she and I began to pack my room.

"It's weird to be somewhere that you live and I don't," she said, boxing up books. "Everywhere since I lived on Lynwood, senior year, you've lived, too. Basically. Even when you had your own place you never slept there."

"I did too."

"Yeah, like once a month."

I paused and then said, "It's harder to sleep alone."

She looked out through the window and shook her head, as if there were too much to say. It was one of those late summer evenings when it all seems heartbreaking, the world, when the soft light, the trees, and the warmth of the air still your restlessness.

"Are you glad you're coming home?" she asked.

"I guess probably I am." I kissed her cheek. "I am."

"Let's sleep together then."

I smiled. We hadn't done that yet for some reason. "Okay."

She went to my bed, and I went to the door and closed it. Instead of lying on the bed, though, she pulled off my sheets and my pillows, bringing them over near the open windows. There she laid them out. She slipped off her shirt and then lay down between the sheets. When I came over she reached up for my hand, and as I knelt she put it to her cheek.

Then something happened to me; nearby, on the pile of books she had been packing, was a dark blue pennant, triangular and small, only about the size of my hand. Though it was upside down I knew that on the other side it said BOAT RACE 2006 in white letters and had the two seals of Oxford and Cambridge underneath.

The difficulty of life for me is in its individuation: how every stray minute of the day passes at the same pace as a minute during the last ice age, in the same space-time, or the minute you were born. One day on this earth it was thirty million years ago and the next a person as real as you was dying in Theresienstadt and the next you were sitting in a restaurant in New Haven laughing with your new girlfriend. I have so much trouble with those gaps. Where it all goes.

I looked at Alison and then back at the pennant, stricken. I loved her very much, but I had been wrong.

"Is everything okay?" Alison asked.

I knew then that I was going to stay in Oxford for the summer. The only thing I didn't know was how to tell her.

"Will? What is it?" she asked.

"I don't know."

"What is it?" she asked again.

I took my hands away from her. "I'm sorry," I said. "I think—"

She looked at me sharply. "No, no, Will."

I don't need to describe the fight we had. It lasted for many hours and combined ten of the fights we should have had when I first broke up with her. She cried throughout it, and several times I nearly gave in. What was cruel was that during that fight I loved her more than I had in years. I think she could sense that, too; it deepened the mystery of the whole circumstance to her.

It was dark by the time we stopped arguing, a white panel of moonlight lying upon the floor. There were tears on her face. I told her again that I was sorry. Suddenly at the hundredth repetition of this apology her demeanor disintegrated into acceptance.

"Jesus," she said. "I was so stupid to come here."

"No," I said. "You're not stupid at all. I love you, you know."

"I know that, you idiot."

She looked up at me, and I became aware of how close our bodies were, our mouths, too. We started to kiss, and before long our faces were wet with her tears. She slipped my T-shirt off over my shoulders and took her pants off, then ran her hands lightly down my arms, kissing my neck, standing on tiptoes to reach up to me.

The makeshift bed lay half-destroyed at our feet. She slid down my body and started to give me head, and then pulled me down so that we were both lying down together. I went down on her, tugging aside her black thong, and she took my hair in her hand, arched her back, and whimpered, pressing up against my mouth. "Let's have sex," she said after a minute or two. "Come on, stop that, fuck me. I don't want to come yet."

When you've had sex with someone a thousand times and it seems new again, it's somehow better even than when it *was* new; there's the same sense of exploration but not of anxiety. I remember observing her, her skin, her breasts, her hair. All of it had been mine for so long, but now it seemed initial again, with the sense of exaltation that you attach to another person when you sleep with them for the first time.

After we came we lay together for a long time, at first saying the inconsequential, happy things you say after sex. Then we were quiet. Her eyes became flat and unreadable, but she didn't stop lying with me. The neglected punts clicked against each other on the river, a familiar sound, as the water they bobbed on sparkled dimly, distantly.

Her breath evened out and she fell asleep there, in my arms. I imagined seeing her at some random party thrown by a common friend in ten years, twenty years, not talking for long. She would have a husband and children I might never meet. The wide arcs of our lives, now estranged.

Exhilaration, happiness, desperation, dejection, and love— especially love, of Sophie; Jess; Alison; Tom; Ella; Oxford; Anil; Anneliese; myself; my father; an adult complexity of loves—swirled into me. Her head lay on my chest, her naked breasts along my naked ribs. *Good-bye,* I thought and gazed up at the very end of the daylight outside, the final midnight paleness at the edge of dark, until I fell asleep, too.

I took her to the train station the next morning, though I had asked her to stay as long as she wanted.

"You'll call Doug Bryson?" was the last thing she said to me on the platform.

"I'll call him."

"You should keep him on your side, even though you're fucking him over. He's going places."

"I know."

"My dad's going to flip out. He really pulled some strings."

"Sorry."

"No, you didn't ask for it. I'm just surprised you can live with not knowing what's next. It's not like you." She gave me a quick hug. "Bye, Will. I'll miss you."

"I love you."

"Okay."

"Will you call me when you get in?" I asked.

She laughed. I remember thinking that was stylish of her somehow. I don't think anyone, even my mother, had ever understood the unhappiness of my childhood as Alison did, and how that unhappiness had ramified forward into my adult behavior. The generosity of her forgiveness of my flaws was mine to keep, even after we had separated. I realized when she laughed that I wanted to know her my whole life. "Okay," she said.

"I love you," I said again, and she smiled.

I saw her onto the train, then stood and, though I couldn't see her from behind the ticket barrier, waved in the direction of the car she was sitting in. I stood there waving until the train strayed away and I knew there was no chance that she could see me anymore, if she ever had, and then I turned back and went home.

The next week for me was lonely. Tom was still in London, Anil and Anneliese were both working against deadlines, and Ella and Peter had gone on vacation together, a cheap bed-and-breakfast in the Cotswolds. I hadn't tried getting in touch with Sophie. I worried that I had made a mistake.

Occasionally, though, if you make a gesture in neither hope nor despair, the world will send one back. Five days after Alison left for America, my phone buzzed in my pocket with a text from Sophie.

Is Alison still here?

She left a couple days ago.

There was a break of an hour or so. I kept glancing toward my phone over and over until at last she wrote again. Her text thrilled me.

I didn't like watching the two of you together.

Not sure what to say to that.

I'm sorry. It's stupid. What are you doing today?

Nothing. You?

Again time passed. I didn't want to be the one to write her again. Just when I was going to anyway, she sent another text.

Do you want to walk into town?

Okay.

I pulled on some jeans and brushed my teeth, then walked three doors over to her house. She was sitting on the steps, hair back in a ponytail, a purple T-shirt and jeans on, drinking from an oversized plastic cup of iced tea.

"Do you want a sip?" she asked through the ice in her mouth and held the cup out.

"Sure." I took it from her. "Where do you want to go?"

"Will's choice."

I tried to think of something that would take a long time. "Why don't we walk down to Christ Church meadow and look at the cows? We could do the big loop."

She smiled. "What a city boy."

"Well, what do you want to do?"

"No, no, I'll go look at some cows." She stood up. "Should I grab my camera?"

"Shut up."

She laughed. "Come on, let's go."

We walked slowly, her slender hands gesturing as she spoke. Our talk was what people talk about everywhere except in art: the people they know, gossip, old jokes. We theorized about Tom and Ella. We imagined Timmo's daily life in the *Big Brother* house, where he was going to be sequestered the next day.

When we got to the cows we sat down on a bench. Christ Church and Merton were lined behind us, and a wild field in front of us.

"Was it weird having her here?" Sophie asked about Alison.

"It was."

"Why?"

I looked away. "When I got here in the fall she was my life."

"Not if you left New York."

"No, I guess you're right."

"Did that sound mean?"

"No," I said.

"Are you still going to America next week?"

I shook my head. "No."

"I knew it."

"Did Anneliese tell you?"

"No, but I knew."

"You're being weird."

"I'm not! Why, tell me why aren't you going?"

"It wasn't any single thing. It won't kill me not to work this cycle in politics, since it's not presidential, and I'm curious about the job in London. It felt too fast to go."

"I've been thinking, and it's like you and Alison, it's weird, about what I was holding on to with Jack. Just a feeling that it was the right thing for me."

"Sometimes things don't work out," I said. "It doesn't always have to be big and meaningful."

"I still get his emails every day."

"Do you miss him?"

"I miss the danger a little bit."

"The danger?"

"Not of him being there, not that at all, just of him."

I felt for a moment as if I had never understood her at all. I said, "So?"

It was a question that could have led anywhere. There were very few times that year when Sophie spoke to me directly about her feelings, but now she put a hand on my hand, along the bench, looking in my eyes, and said, without elaboration, "I woke up this morning and I thought, *I'm ready*."

"What do you mean?"

She seemed in charge. "I know it's been a long time."

"What do you want to do?"

She scooted over so we were close and then put her arms around my neck and her face into my hair, leaning into me with her whole body. She kissed my cheek. "I don't care," she said.

From that afternoon forward, Sophie and I were together. I can't remember if the two of us got dinner or if we returned to Fleet for Hall, but I know we spent the evening in the MCR, watching a movie with Anil and Peter. In retrospect that seems strange, but it made me happier than if we had just returned to my room.

The ten weeks that followed passed like ten minutes, and the days of that period seem identical as I recall them. We became inseparable quickly, and soon she had an encampment in the corner of my room (which was about four feet wider across than hers, and which, because Strickland expropriated the best furniture for the houses he looked after, was more comfortable). She kept her books and papers there, as well as a lap desk; at this time she was working hard in preparation for the start of her DPhil. She had accepted the money from the Swift Prize already. When we woke up in the morning she would go straight to her corner and begin to work. I rose more slowly, but after showering I would walk to Holywell Street, not far, and go to the dark green tuck shop opposite New College. There I would get us coffee and croissants, her coffee iced, mine hot and with milk. If I felt especially hungry I might get a sandwich for midmorning, too, usually the cheddar ploughman's, and a packet of crisps. Back in the room we listened to music at a low volume as she annotated the margins of *Le grand meaulnes* or *L'immoraliste*, and I either read or worked on a halting campaign memoir I had started. I can't even remember if I still have a copy of it, though it must be lurking like a ghost in my computer.

By lunch she would need a break, and we'd either eat at Hall with whoever happened to be there—we had a permanent station under the tall oil of Inigo Jones near the south windows—or at a restaurant in town. Then she and I would separate. She liked to sleep after lunch, and I would walk down to Iffley and swim in the university pool. The walk was just long enough that I would have digested whatever I ate by the time I got there and changed. Sometimes in the afternoons I would go to a museum or a movie while she was at the library, doing the archival parts of her work, and often I would begin at three or four or five to panic that I would never see her again. As a result, though we usually planned to meet up for the evening at seven, I would often arrive at her door at a quarter to the hour or even earlier, I imagine looking anxious. Whatever time it was, she would smile when I arrived and kiss me, and often we would sleep together for the second time of the day. I don't think we had many arguments. When she was upset she became implacable instead of angry, and I was in love.

Our evenings during that June and July were more sluggish than they had been during term. Each evening a large group of people from Fleet, often with additions from outside of the college, gathered on the lawns. It was generally Anil who organized us. We would sit in a slack ring of chairs with gin and beer in the center, most people as they got drunk gradually shifting down into the grass, on their backs or up on their forearms. The sun didn't fall until eleven. We had stopped punting for some reason, though it was the nicest weather to do it in. Occasionally after it was at last dark we would go into the city, but usually we would just retreat back to the Fleet bar for another drink, or if it was a weekend we might invite the people in our phones to come to our MCR, where we could stay up late. At whatever hour we went home, Sophie and I went together.

I wonder if I got to know her better in this time. I thought I would at first, but then, we had spent so much time together in the fall. I know that her power over me was very great. For instance, the political issue she cared most about—perhaps as a result of having grown up in the country—was the environment, and while I thought I had been conscientious about recycling and reusing she changed my habits quickly and completely. She was far more dogged than I was. She would take ten minutes to isolate the one bit of plastic from a parcel so that she could recycle it. She only ever put high-test gasoline in her car, and she drove it nearly down to empty before she would refill the tank, because it was meant to be more fuel-efficient. Soon enough I was lecturing people about these small matters and, as she did, forwarding them pirated downloads of *An Inconvenient Truth*. (It wasn't that we didn't want to buy it but that we didn't want to add another plastic box to the world's circulation of them. Anyhow, around then YouTube was invented, and most of the significant clips from the movie popped up on it before long.) As for the reverse—I don't think I ever had such an influence on her, but there was a pleasure in seeing at her least guarded someone who had been such an enigma to me.

It didn't seem like life. It seems very bright, lots of sunlight, in my memory—England is farther north than people realize, not too distant from the all-day sun of summer in Scandinavia. Our lively school-year friendships seemed to grow deeper and easier. It may be an unfair trick to describe this time in so few words, but it passed that way, wordlessly somehow, such that even now I annex it to the least intelligible and least articulate part of my memory.

I went that whole summer without seeing St. John Jarvis. In fact, I hadn't seen him since March, or perhaps even February. In the first week of August, however, I noticed an article he had written for *The Guardian* and sent him a note complimenting it. He shot one straight back inviting me for coffee, and so on a wet day, with the sky gray and the radiantly green grass on the lawns combed down by the wind, I walked the half mile over the bridge and to his brown house among the fields.

He gave me a hearty thump on the back when I arrived and put me in an armchair, but he was a different man than he had been the fall before. Then he had looked more than a decade younger than seventy-seven, but now he belonged to his years. His voice was tremulous, and though his brain was still sharp, it was clear that his body was in trouble, one of those unpunctual lurches toward infirmity with which old age seems to surprise people, taking away the even comfort of decline.

"I'm sorry it's been so long," I said.

"Oh, life gets in the way of these things. Will you have a sandwich? The maid is making them."

"Thanks."

"Take a persimmon from the bowl, there, while we're waiting."

We talked over his article for a long while, which was a polemic about the boundaries between journalism and magical realism. This was when Jayson Blair and Stephen Glass were fresh in people's minds. Jarvis condemned those two but argued that the backlash against them was too puritanical and sweeping, that while the perfect truth was something admirable in print journalism, in long-form journalism—journalism as literature—authors deserved leeway. The article, which was called "Permission" and played at length on that word, cited *The Sebastopol Sketches*, García Márquez's memoirs, and Ryszard Kapuściński; it had drawn a tremendous reaction. There was some of his old effervescence in his voice when he spoke about his adversaries.

"That Miles—what's his name, Frederick Miles?—from *The Telegraph*. What a fellow he is. Wouldn't know a work of literary art if it sodomized him."

"Were they pleased at *The Guardian*?"

"Oh, delighted."

Larissa, his maid, came in with the coffee and sandwiches, and when she spilled a stream of coffee into his saucer he chastised her with the fractiousness of a rest-home inmate, turning back into an old man.

"Goddammit," he said. "Excuse me, Will."

"It's all right," I said. "Not at all."

He took out a tremendous handkerchief when she was gone and blew his nose, and when he began to fold the handkerchief in his lap I noticed a long string of snot was hanging from his nose. It trembled and caught against his lip when he spoke.

"Go on," he said. "You want to ask about the Swift."

I smiled. "No, it's okay."

"You didn't really want it."

"I did," I said.

He looked at me with surprise. "Did you, then?"

I had come to his house with a sense of advantage, but now, as he waited for me to elaborate, I realized that it would be cruel to play it, and deceptive. I wanted the Swift Prize now, because of Sophie. Did I want it for itself? "Oh, I don't know."

He smiled. "If you think badly of me at some time in the future, for it, just stop and try to remember what money can do for people. When the right person receives it."

"You're right."

"There's some little fellow out there, call him Clive, who got the prize ahead of you. And where for you it would have been simply another achievement, for him it is a whole life to lead, a refuge. Though, Clive, listen to me, it was three women this year, I believe. Can't remember their names. Some little Clarissa. Some little Sophie."

He had turned his eyes from me as he said this to cough again, and I waited for him to finish. "I understand," I said.

He cleared his throat one last time. "Do you know what your uncle used to tell students, his advice to them?"

"What?"

"He'd say, 'Be happy.' Drove them mad."

"Why?"

He shrugged. "They wanted to hear 'Go work at Barclay's' or 'Join the Peace Corps.' They didn't want to hear the truth. But he was right enough."

"In fairness, it's not much good as advice," I said.

"Get to my age and see if you think that's still true."

I stayed a shorter time than I once would have. As he stood up to say good-bye, he must have realized there was something on his nose, and then, thank God, wiped it away. We shook hands in his doorway, and he exhorted me to return to politics—something we had discussed at length that fall—and not go into finance. "A game for fools," he called it. We shook hands and I walked slowly back to Fleet.

That was the last time I saw him. I didn't return to his house that summer, and in December he died. I went to the funeral and also wrote my condolences to the three nephews the obituary listed as his heirs, though they never replied. As I looked back it became clear to me that his decline had been due not to age but to illness. His obituary in *The Guardian,* which was surpassingly rich—I didn't know he had consulted with the clandestine services in Britain, for example—confirmed that impression, giving the cause of death as pituitary cancer. It also mentioned, in the last paragraph, that only three weeks before his death he had published a lengthy critique of the journalists who had questioned "Permission." I went online and found it, a cogent piece, spiteful in the right ways. As I read it I felt a tremendous affection and respect for him and a sense of real loss—those early autumn days he had been such a lifeline—and wondered, as we do about the dead, who he had actually been.

At the start of June all the undergraduates had finished and left for the summer, except for a few third-years like Jem who stayed on in Oxford. Some of them were joining the MCR—starting master's courses, I mean—but in his case it was to keep playing with his band. We missed the undergraduates, with whom we had amassed a great number of half-friendships and affairs, games of pool, hellos on the paths of Fleet, but nearly all the graduate students remained in town, and the college felt pleasantly deserted, as if we were Pevensies hiding out during the war.

In mid-August we got to see them all in one place again, because Lula had another party in London.

Sophie and I went down to the city early, happy to be together. We walked through museums and parks—the John Soane, the National Portrait Gallery, Green Park—and when we were tired we found a café and read our books over coffee or, as the shadows lengthened, red wine on ice with sparkling lemonade. It was Sophie's favorite drink. I remember what we were reading: I had Norman Rush, she had something of Simenon, one of the *romans durs*. We ate dinner at Rules, upon her insistence, drinking Black Velvet. She paid, which made me smile.

At nine we went to Lula's house, which was raucous with noise. She was standing by the door again, bright-eyed with her hard flapper prettiness, her lips bright red.

"SOPHIA!" she screamed and threw her arms around Sophie's neck.

"Hello, love."

"How have you been? I can't believe I didn't see you for all Trinity, what a fool I feel."

"Do you remember Will?"

"Don't talk slush, of course I remember him, hello, Will! Now, do you know the theme of the party?"

"It's another Facebook one, right?" asked Sophie.

"After a fashion—it's a good-bye to Facebook party."

"You're leaving Facebook?"

"I'm trying—to get into the party you have to sign in and drop me as a friend." She waved a hand. "It's gotten boring. My *mum* is on it, for God's sake."

"But aren't you one of the top vampires in Oxford?" I asked.

She laughed. "I've accomplished a great deal, it's true. Here, sign on, Will. Otherwise, a shot of this awful tequila."

"Has Tom Raleigh dropped you yet?" I asked as I typed in my password.

"Yep. I don't think I'd even met him!"

"Well, that was the point when you became friends," I said.

"True enough."

"Done," I said, after I typed for a moment in silence. "We're no longer friends."

She gave me a vexed frown and shook her fist, then grinned. "Okay! Have a lovely time! Go sit by the pool! You brought trunks, didn't you? Oh, Soph, are you on Facebook?"

"But since we *are* friends, can't we stay friends online?" said Sophie.

"Everyone has to go."

"Oh, all right."

People were congregated by the pool in the back garden, playing a version of Sharks and Minnows; it might have been New Jersey, the suburbs. There was a stereo and a bar full of indifferently organized liquor, which people slopped into their cups with whatever mixer they could find.

"I don't see Tom," I said to Sophie. "Should we go find him?"

She agreed, but on the way through the house we ran into two girls with whom she and Lula had been at school. Their names were Plum and Laura, and they both screamed and jumped up and down. I was just barely introduced to them when they dragged Sophie upstairs to Lula's room, where another of their friends was apparently getting dressed—I had somehow forgotten that Sophie went to the first party because she knew more people there than I did—and with a quick kiss on the cheek she said, "I'll only be a minute."

Not much later Tom texted me, and I found him in the kitchen, speaking to a few of his friends. "Where's Daisy?" I asked after we had greeted each other.

"She's late."

It had been a difficult summer for Tom. We had seen more of him recently—at the start of June he rarely spent more than three nights a week in Oxford, and now he was up all the time usually—but since he had disappeared with Daisy to London in the first place I think he and Jess had only seen each other once or twice, unhappily. He had never quite broken it off with her. In early July Fleet had unveiled a bench in Katie's memory in Anna's Quad, with some small ceremony, and for that Jess had showed up unannounced. It was left to me to look after her. She stayed for the whole time, despite Tom's cold politeness.

Yet he never expressed any sense of happiness about being with Daisy. She worried him. All summer he had been checking his phone to see if he'd missed a call from her. That night at Lula's she never showed up. Tom got terribly drunk. We played beer pong for about two hours, and though we kept winning (as the only American present I had an advantage) he had some side drink that must have been strong.

At eleven or so, pretty drunk myself, I went to look for Sophie among the enormous upper floors of Lula's house. I almost passed right by the room she was in. The door was cracked, and I could see Sophie and her friend Plum, their backs to me. I stood and gazed at them in their sliver of light. I could hear them speaking.

"Of course I miss him sometimes," Sophie said. "All the time, actually."

"I remember when Peregrine and I were together, I mean, Soph, you and Jackal were an *in*stitution, d'you know? We looked up to you."

"It's hard having him over there."

"And your new chap is American?" asked Plum doubtfully.

"He's sweet."

"Is he—oh, my phone."

She shifted and, fearing that they would leave the room, I bolted, my face hot.

I went down a different staircase, took a wrong turn, and ended up in the kitchen, where I found Lula, sitting in her bikini and having a cigarette. There was music playing from a small stereo on the island.

She smiled and pushed her hair out of her eyes. "Hello, Will."

"What are you listening to?" I asked.

"Hall & Oates Greatest Hits."

"That's a whole CD?"

She laughed, then in a lugubrious voice said, "You should be nice. I have no more friends."

"You drove them away."

"D'you want a cigarette?"

I took one and sat down next to her. "Thanks."

"I love Sophie," she said.

"She's great."

She looked at me and smiled. "Watch out with her."

"What do you mean?"

"I'm not sure. She's a tricky one."

"Oh."

"I remember at school half a dozen girls thought they were her best friend. Then at graduation five of them found out they weren't. Each of us at our school had to choose someone to present us with our diploma, you see, and she chose Minka instead of Annabeth or Iris. Or Plum, who's here, who loved her. There was a dreadful row." She fell quiet and at the same moment the track changed, so that it was silent in the dim kitchen. "Can I kiss you again?" she asked.

"You remember that?"

"Go on. The boy I like never came up. It will make me feel nice."

As we kissed she put a hand on my bare leg and kept it there, gripping me. When she was done she leaned in and kissed my cheek, my ear, the fringe of my hair, all in close succession, and then she stood up and walked away.

I went back upstairs to look for Sophie. She had left the room where she had been speaking to Plum, but just as I was going to go downstairs I saw her emerge from a different hallway.

"Will!" she said. She kissed me. "How are you? You smell like cherry lip gloss."

"It's Tom's cherry ChapStick."

"You shouldn't share with him. God knows what Daisy has."

"Okay."

"Kiss me again."

One evening, just past the twentieth of August, only three weeks until my job started, Anil, Ella, Peter, and I were by the river drinking beer. Bud Light had been on sale at the off-license, and Ella bought it out of expatriate nostalgia. Sophie was out to dinner with a friend, Tom was in London. It was warm but not too warm. A conference of middle-aged workers had taken over the bar; like every other college, Fleet rented out its rooms in the summer, after classes had finished, and the companies who came usually asked for the bar to be opened. Jem and I were technically both on the payroll that night, but he had just done that as a favor to me because conferences paid the bar staff double. There wasn't enough business to require both of us.

The summer had been kind to Ella and Peter; they were going to move in together that fall, as they both continued their doctorates. They looked happy now, holding hands.

At about nine thirty, we saw Anneliese striding out to us from the back door of the bar. I hadn't seen her in a few days, for some reason. Of all our friends it was she who had been happiest for me and Sophie.

"Hey!" she said. "I was searching for you!"

"What is it?" asked Ella.

"I have a job!"

"You do?" I asked.

"What about your PhD?" Ella asked.

"I know," she answered, looking guilty. "I just talked with my adviser about quitting this afternoon. He was upset with me, very upset."

"But what's the job?" I asked.

"I get to take pictures."

"For who?" Ella asked.

"For *Die Zeit*."

"Anneliese!" I said. "That's incredible!"

"What—how did you get that job?" asked Ella.

"I got tired of the Crusades. I submitted a portfolio to a couple of German and English newspapers." She laughed. "Probably not as tired as the Crusaders, I suppose."

"But Anneliese, I'll be all alone next year!" said Ella.

"Cheers," said Peter, and everyone laughed.

Anneliese, sitting down, said, "No, but guess where I'll be?"

"Where?"

"London! I'll be based here, taking pictures all over England."

"Oh!" said Ella. "That's much better than Berlin! For me, I mean."

Anneliese laughed. "I know. Will, you and I can take the train up together on weekends to visit."

I grinned at her. "Here, take a beer. We need to toast you."

"Fine, but let's wait until we can have wine," Anneliese said, sitting down. "Beer is okay once in a while, but I'm sick of it."

"You're German," said Anil.

"Well, I can't go around apologizing for that all my life," she said crossly. "I want some nice white wine."

For a while we talked about the new job. She was to begin right away. She talked about buying a medium-format camera possibly, certainly another lens.

"But who *will* be here next year?" I asked Ella eventually.

She thought about it for a second. "Anil. He has a two-year course. Richard and Giorgio."

"Oh dear," said Anil.

She laughed. "Peter, thank God. Tom and Anneliese will be in London. Sophie will be here."

Just then Jem appeared at the door of the bar and started walking back out to us with a big glass pitcher.

"Christ," he said when he came up to us. "These old women will be the death of me. Fleet hired out the conference rooms to the interior decoration society of Oxfordshire and they're all in the bar now, acting as if they're twenty and not sixty. Here, I brought you a jug of G&Ts."

"Thanks," we all said.

He laughed wickedly. "Charged them to the credit card these muppets left. Bake, the other half get out in twenty minutes and they're all coming down."

"You want me to work?"

"Thanks." He sighed. "Once more unto the breach, dear fuckers."

"Jem, what are you doing next year?" Anneliese asked.

Ella interrupted his answer. "Anneliese just got a job at *Die Zeit*, taking pictures."

"The Hamburg paper? Shit, well done," he said. Jem was surprisingly informed. "I'm playing in a band. I'll bartend somewhere."

"*A* band?" I asked. "Not *the* band?"

He shook his head. "We broke up yesterday."

"Shit."

"It was bound to happen. Anyway, Eli and I are talking about a duo kind of thing, maybe more folky, open tunings, like 'Buckets of Rain' only electric."

"I love that song," said Anneliese.

"Yeah, Eli's dad is a session musician, and he can get our tape out to some execs. He said he could definitely find us gigs as well, bars. He plays at this jazz club every weekend. There's even a chance he could find us some cheap studio time, because he knows everyone."

"Remember us when you're famous," Ella said. "You, too, Anneliese."

He shrugged. "Maybe, maybe not. Bake, come help me as soon as you finish your drink."

That day and nearly every other in August someone went punting; we had taken it up again. There was an unwritten rule that anybody could tag along, even if they weren't your closest friends or you weren't theirs. Once I went with Giorgio and Richard—widely held to have mellowed since their deposition from power, though I didn't see it—and their two Chinese acolytes, the statistics students.

On the afternoon I'm thinking of Ella and I went punting alone, going very slowly because neither of us could be bothered to put in much effort. It was nice to spend time together—I had seen relatively little of her, an evening here and there, perhaps lunch. While her lab was on its summer break she had taken a miserable job at an Indian restaurant called Kolkata, where she was the only non-Indian server. On the first night she had dropped an entire tray of food on a customer, who stormed out of the restaurant, which by tradition meant the waitstaff—as a method of pooling risk—had to chip in to pay his bill. Since then none of them talked to her, and they huddled in a corner when business was slow, staring at her and muttering in Hindi. Anil had gone in to vouch for her, but it turned out he was from the wrong part of India.

When we pulled the punt up along a clearing and got out to sit on the bank, our feet dangling over the water, she lit a joint—a new habit, born that spring of the stress of her days in the lab and the prospect of two more years of them—and said, "Peter has been talking about marriage."

"Already?"

"I know, it's quick. Though it's not as if he proposed."

"What do you think?"

"I don't know if I could live in England more than another couple of years, and I can't see him leaving. Maybe he would."

"I don't find myself missing America much."

"I do. Just *Pulp Fiction* stuff, like the kinds of cereal you can get at home. How original, right?"

"Are you over Tom?"

She smiled. "That's direct."

"I'm sorry."

She was playing with her hair, braiding pink and black strands of it together, but looked up now. "I don't think about him."

"That seems impossible."

"I'm not like you. It doesn't all have to be something." She was silent for a moment, then said, "I remember this one day, after he and I started hooking up, when we were out at a pub and he almost had a nervous breakdown. He was just freaking out."

"How?"

"He kept saying, 'I can't be around these people, I can't be around these people, take me home.' And this was like three months after Katie died, not to sound unkind, but ... anyway, I remember thinking to myself, first off, Ella, this is not a person you can count on, and second of all, even knowing that, that I didn't care. Because I can count on myself. I know who I am. As long as I'm alive I'll work hard, and I'll be in charge of my shit, and I'll make money, and I'll make sure my kids do their homework. That's me. And I have enough margin that I could have had someone in my life who isn't that way, like who eats up a little bit of my stability. But the thing is," and she laughed, "Peter is like that, too. Like he might as well be Korean. President of the stupid MCR, right?"

"Do you love him as much as Tom, then?"

She puzzled over this and then answered. "More and less at the same time."

There was a pause. "Can I ask you something?" I said.

"Okay."

"When you're a mom are you going to wear all this stuff? The safety pins, and coloring your hair?"

She smiled. "No, probably not."

"Just curious."

"You know why I do it? Because fuck them. I like it."

I laughed and put my arm around her shoulder, squeezing. "I love you," I said.

"You, too."

We talked for another few minutes, not so directly now, and then shoved off in the punt, soft light striking against the tree-sheltered river. When we were nearly all the way back to Fleet my phone buzzed. It was Sophie.

I need you to come back.

On my way. What is it?

You're still punting?

Ten minutes away.

I took the pole then and started to push us more quickly down-river. When we came into view of the lawns I saw that she was standing there, arms crossed, face dense with unhappiness, the wind troubling her hair. I feared that something terrible had happened.

"Are you okay?" I called out. I let Ella lock the punt to the shore and jumped out.

"It's Chessie," she said. "She's gotten sicker. They want to put her down, straight away."

"Oh, no."

"No, I convinced them to wait. Will you come with me?"

"Of course."

We left half an hour later in her car. I drove, even though I still wasn't accustomed to the left side of the road. It took nearly three hours to get there—we ran into traffic near Birmingham—with Sophie silent most of the way. It was dusk when we arrived in her small village.

"Which way?" I asked.

"Left," she said and then changed her mind. "No, let's go straight to the vet's. Turn right. My parents left her there, the bastards."

The stainless steel and fluoresced white tile of the vet's office looked, somehow even more than in a hospital for humans, like a well-organized mind's idea of death. A receptionist led us back into the holding room, and through a large window we saw the dog, a beautiful white-and-brown animal with an intelligent face, before she saw us. She was lying on her side, breathing very raggedly. Her shanks looked thin. You could tell she was ill. She didn't pay any attention to the vet's assistant who was in the room with her.

When Sophie came into the room, though, some dim sensation of smell or sight must have told the dog that its friend was here. Her tail thumped once and then twice against the gurney and she lifted her head, her tongue lolling out, and snorted with happiness, then struggled—a losing battle—to rise up to her haunches.

It is absurd to care too much about a dog's death and inhuman not to care—that is the world. The anguish in Sophie's face was terrible and real. She went and cradled Chessie's head in her arms, soothing her down and down until she was resting still again. Occasionally the dog's tail would beat in happiness, and when it did I felt a lump in my throat. As for Sophie, she was so silent and impassive that I knew her to be inconsolable, beyond the range of any speech to help her. I thought about Hitler poisoning his dog to make sure his cyanide caplets worked and hated him for it, the trust of the dog taking the pill with a bit of steak. The torturer's horse scratching its innocent behind against a tree. This was followed by a hiss of revulsion at myself for the emotion: Who cares about Hitler's dog; what an absurdity.

The vet came in and introduced herself, a hardy Yorkshire woman of fifty or thereabouts with a monkey face. "You're her owner?" she asked. Her voice was sympathetic but professional.

"I am," said Sophie.

"There's only so much we can do for the pain at this stage."

"How much longer if we—if we kept her like this?"

"She's a very old dog. Maybe two weeks or so. But they would be painful weeks."

Sophie wiped the tears away from her face with the heel of her hand. "I don't care," she said. "Let's keep her alive. Let's do it."

I stayed silent, but the vet said, "It would only be unkind."

Chessie's tail thumped, and Sophie covered the dog's face in kisses. She was quiet for a few minutes, long minutes. "Okay," she said at last.

"You can give her a last treat, if you like, take your time," said the vet. I honored her for her patience; the rest of the practice was shut up for the night.

"Will, go get some peanut butter, would you? There's a shop two doors down to the left."

I went and returned; Sophie scooped some of the peanut butter out with her fingers, and Chessie licked at it once or twice, but it seemed to me it was more to please Sophie than out of any real desire to eat. Finally the vet interceded.

"I'm going to give her the shot now."

"What will you do with her body?" asked Sophie.

"We can give you the ashes, if you like. It takes a day or two."

"Yes, I want them."

"Do you want me to leave?" I asked.

To my surprise, she nodded. "Yes, please."

As I left I watched Sophie envelop the dog in her arms more carefully and wholly, as if she could lift her clear away from death. I went into the lobby and waited twenty minutes. After that Sophie emerged, her face dull. She didn't want to see her parents, so despite the lateness of the hour we began the drive back to Oxford.

When we were twenty or thirty miles from home it began to rain, the red lights in front of us and the white lights coming toward us stained together, the trees along the side of the road no longer individual, a cliff of green-black. Sophie hadn't spoken much during the trip, and when I asked about Chessie she had shaken her head. Then she said something that took me aback entirely.

"I've been e-mailing with Jack."

That saying "My blood ran cold"—it's true, it feels as if your blood loses its heat in your veins for a second. "What?"

"I didn't get his daily e-mail for three days. I worried. I called his mother."

"And, so?"

"He's fine."

"Oh, great," I said, without regretting the sarcasm.

"They lost power at his base. Then he had a satellite phone but he couldn't get through on it, to home, I mean, and so he had to wait until the power came back. He started up with the daily e-mail again."

"What have you been e-mailing him?"

She started to cry. "Only asking how he is."

"Why did you even ask me to come up to the vet's with you?" I asked. My voice was more detached than I felt. "Why didn't you ask Jack?"

"He's not here."

"That's the only reason."

"No, of course not."

"Will you stop e-mailing with him?" I asked.

She was silent.

"Sophie?"

"I don't know," she said.

My skin started to prickle. There was a gas station on the side of the road, with a bright hopeful sign lofted above it in the black of the sky. I pulled in.

"Are you breaking up with me?"

"No," she said, "of course not."

I turned the car off, and with the engine sound gone it seemed too quiet. Now that I started to think of it we had seen less of each other in the past few days. She had a job doing research for her adviser, tedious hours combing through records, and she had been too tired, she said, to do much at the end of the day, though we had still been sleeping in her room, still smiling when we saw each other. Had something been different?

"I don't deserve this," I said.

"Lula told me you two kissed," she said and for the first time in a while looked straight at me.

I heard the words and felt a sense of injustice. How could I possibly explain to her how entitled I felt to those kisses, and how badly they had done the job I set them out to do? I couldn't say any of it. Nor could I explain that it was different if I wrote to Alison, even though I knew in my heart it wasn't. "She did?"

"Did you?"

"This has been the best summer of my life," I said, more to myself than to her.

"Did you?"

Finally I nodded.

"Well," she said.

I threw up my hands. "It's not like what you think, though. I was drunk and I was, I was mad at you. I overheard you telling Plum you missed Jack."

"You eavesdropped?"

"Not on purpose." Then I paused. "No, that's a lie. Half on purpose."

"Then you deserved to hear whatever you heard."

"I know," I said. We looked at each other unhappily. "Does Jack want you back?"

She nodded. "Yes."

"What did you say?"

"I told him no, of course."

My heart lifted slightly. "Good."

"He said that he couldn't promise he would never cheat, but that he would try, and if he did he would tell me, and it wouldn't be with anyone I knew..." She said this as if she knew the madness of it, in a dismissive voice, but to my shock I discerned that beneath her attitude she saw some glimmer of reason in the offer, she didn't altogether mind it. My deferred conviction of his cruelty returned and deepened. Then I thought, *She's his Alison.*

"Will you stop?"

"I'll stop," she said.

"Do you promise?"

"Yes, I promise. Will you kiss anyone?"

"Never again if you don't want me to. Except you."

She looked at the wet windshield, at the thicket of trees off to the side of the road. "I'm tired."

I turned on the car. "We should go home, I guess."

"Let's do. It would be nice to fall asleep together." She leaned her head on my shoulder as we drove. "I'm sorry," she said. "It's been a day."

Slowly we started to say warm words to each other again, but none of them seemed to count.

I probably haven't conveyed the contentment we had felt that summer. From the outside that night in the car might have seemed like merely another reversal in the now somewhat wilted drama of our relationship, but that would be wrong. Almost as if in compensation for those reversals, the summer had been impenetrably calm. Immediately we had become comfortable living together, she just as comfortable as I. For a very long stretch of time, until Lula's party I guess, it didn't even cross my mind that we wouldn't be married, and we talked about distant plans, about returning to Fleet for reunions together in five or ten years, about long trips we would take, about the places she wanted me to show her in America. There was none of that teleological weight some summer relationships bear, like the pages thinning toward the end of a book; there was no skittishness in her attitude toward me. She was as stable as Alison had ever been. I wasn't sure if it meant me living in England for the rest of my life, or if she might be willing to move to my country, but I didn't especially care. She didn't either. At Lula's party I was touched again by that fear I had once felt of losing her, that obsessive feeling, but almost immediately I had accepted and forgotten what she said. It was only natural that she worried about Jack.

Now something changed. There was no diminution in Sophie's affection toward me in the next weeks, as August ended, but our conversations cast a shorter shadow. When we spoke about the future it was in less expansive terms. Perhaps I was in the wrong—I worried that she was writing to Jack, and it might have affected the mood of our companionship.

Others were luckier.

One morning a few days shy of September Sophie left my room to go to the library, to do research, giving me a kiss as she left. I went to the bathroom, and when I came out I saw that standing with Tom in his doorway was Jess.

"Hey," I said.

"Hey, Will," she said, then to Tom, "Okay, I should go." She put her arm around his waist and squeezed him.

"Bye."

He walked her out, and when she was gone he came back to my room. "Beer?"

"It's like ten."

He went and got a beer from his refrigerator, a bottle of water for me, and we sat down in my two armchairs by the window. "That's back on, Jess," he said. "I broke it off with Daisy."

"When did that happen?"

"Last week." His face took on an embarrassed defiance. "I missed her."

"And she was happy to come back?"

He smiled. "Do you know why I love her? When I called her she just came back. And not like a doormat, or like she was waiting for me to call. She told me she'd been seeing someone else, even. But she didn't see the point in shouting at me or in pretending she didn't want to be together."

I nodded. "Do you remember what your sister said about Daisy when we had lunch?"

Caution stole over his face. "What?"

"Oh, nothing."

"No, what?"

"Well—she said that you felt the need to date girls like Daisy, but if she had her choice she would see you with someone different. I can't remember how she put it exactly. Someone like Jess, I think."

He looked out at the clear sky. "Funny, I didn't remember that. I always think I've remembered it all and then someone reminds me of a part I forgot."

"She knew you best."

"I woke up this morning, and I thought, it popped into my head randomly, *I'm going to marry this person.*"

"Wow," I said.

"You sound skeptical."

"No, no, not at all."

I was, though; and I was wrong.

A few days before I was meant to move out of my room and to London, Sophie came over. Her face was tired. We hooked up, and afterward we lay together for a while, silent.

"Jack comes back on leave next week," she said at length.

"How do you know?"

"He e-mailed me. He e-mails me every day."

"Do you write back?"

"No. I promised you."

"Are you going to see him?"

"I don't know."

"Please don't."

She sat up on the side of the bed, still frankly naked, her beautiful hair falling down around her shoulders. Her high pink coloring and the faint freckles around her nose made her look as if she had just come back from a trip to a cold place, or maybe been sunburned badly once, long before.

"I do love you, Will," she said.

"I love you."

She put a hand on my face and looked straight into my eyes. "I think I need to give him another chance."

This was what she had come to say to me, I saw. "I love you."

"And I—"

"No, no, I love you."

Those words: They had never not been enough to say before, in any of my previous relationships. I looked at her face and saw a blankness that chilled me. At this time I was reading Proust and becoming obsessed with certain sentences he had written, to the point that I would read them when I woke up and before I went to bed, puzzle over them throughout the day, sentences that seemed to me to describe not just life but how we conceive of life. "To have a kind heart was everything" was one of these sentences, and as I looked at her I wondered if she had a kind heart. I thought perhaps that she didn't. Then I realized that Alison could have said the same of me, even as I tried to be kind to her, and that now I was the one who loved without reserve, not Sophie. It didn't mean that she didn't love me.

"Please just wait until his next leave," I said.

"Oh, Will," she said pityingly and lay down next to me, holding me tight.

It would be hard to portray the crashing, ruinous unhappiness I felt from that hour forward. In the next days we spent more time together than we had even at our happiest in June and July, and slept with each other over and over, having sex until we were ragged with exhaustion. She drove that even more than I did, and I wondered what she was storing up. I called her cold, called her hateful, and she merely acquiesced to those judgments. All of these hours I could describe in their minute particulars, what we ate and what we drank; how kind Tom and Anneliese were from afar, and then after Sophie left up close; how she left, to go visit Jack, with pained apologies.

Instead what I think of is a different memory completely. It's from one of those first beautiful, breezy days at Oxford, just after I arrived that fall. I was at an MCR new students' picnic. Sophie was speaking to someone—it was the day after I first met her—and when she saw me looking at her she rolled her eyes imperceptibly and grinned over the person's shoulder.

It felt so intimate somehow. She had chosen me. Then what happened next: She made her excuses to whomever she was speaking with and started to walk toward me across the lawn, her tan arms at her sides, her high pink cheeks, her wonderful corona of copper-auburn hair, her white smile. I think it was in that moment, when she started coming toward me, when the world was full of time for us, that I gave over to her mercy my entire future and all its happiness.

Larkin wrote a poem about the maiden name of a woman he loved:

Now it's a phrase applicable to no one,
Lying just where you left it, scattered through
Old lists, old programmes, a school prize or two
Packets of letters tied with tartan ribbon—
Then is it scentless, weightless, strengthless, wholly
Untruthful? Try whispering it slowly.
No, it means you. Or, since you're past and gone,

It means what we feel now about you then:
How beautiful you were, and near, and young,
So vivid, you might still be there among
Those first few days...

On my last morning in Oxford, all of my stuff bundled into a moving van, the job in London lying ninety miles south, she came back to the city and saw me, an hour or so before everyone gathered around to say good-bye. We stood along the street before the Cottages, the indifferent white stone of Fleet high off to our right, and she gave me a long and tight hug.

"I'll always love you, you know," she said.

I didn't say it back because I feared it would be true. I didn't ask her to change her mind either, as I had for the last few days. I felt numb. She looked prepared to discuss it, but also decided; so I didn't say anything, and I saw myself far in the future—a future that for her would contain a whole life, that I didn't get to see for myself— feeling as I had felt about her at that dumb picnic on the lawns: *how beautiful she was, and near, and young.*

We said our last, meaningless words and hugged again—even kissed for a few minutes—and then like that she left.

Here is something everyone starts saying to each other when they turn twenty-six or twenty-seven, near the end of parties, the complacent grandeur of melancholy in their voices, and it's true: When you're finally a grown-up, one of the things you find out is that there are no grown-ups.

For a month I burrowed like a mole into the investment firm, only seeing occasional glimpses of my friends—Anneliese was taking pictures, Tom lived two streets down and came over to mine for beers late most nights, still in his Freshfields suit and tie, Anil visited on weekends—and learning how to be a banker. I loathed it. The exhaustion of the work was annealing, however, after the self-indulgence of Oxford. Punting seemed like an impossible vanity after I had spent eighteen hours staring at a spreadsheet and adding numbers on it, trying to decipher whether the books of a pharmaceutical holding company in China were too pristine.

One morning Franklin, my cousin's husband, didn't show up at the office, and four days later the firm quietly shuttered its doors. There was no great drama about it, no Ponzi scheme. They just ran out of money. It was late 2006—he was one of the first to go under, though of course far from the last. Franklin himself still had the three houses and the helicopter, as I heard it. I got a month's pay, though I had barely been there a month.

The next several weeks I spent at loose ends in London, until finally I knew that it was time, and I packed my things for a second time to take a plane back home.

The last person I saw from Oxford was Anil. His friend Shateel was taking over my lease, and Anil had come down as a favor to him to get the keys from me, because Shateel was in Edinburgh for a conference. When he arrived I was already packed, still an hour or so before I had to leave, and he suggested we get breakfast. He was in terrific spirits then because he had a new Welsh girlfriend, Pippa, from St. Hilda's (Tom called her the Hildabeast, though she was petite and pretty), and he was full of plans to stay in England past the end of his course, to be with her.

In the café we sat at a table by the window. Anil picked up the menu sitting on the table and lifted his glasses with a small frown, peering at it with his accustomed rabbinical focus, which at restaurants always led to decades of vacillation. I felt a huge affection for him. I stood up.

"If she comes by get me the full English and a decaf, okay?" I asked.

He nodded without looking up, brow furrowed, and I went to find the bathroom.

It wasn't immediately clear where the bathroom might be. I took a short hallway leading back away from the street, but it must have been the wrong way, because at the end of it I reached only a small room.

This room looked different than the other parts of the restaurant. There was a Persian carpet in it, and from the floor to the ceiling, in a ring around the whole room, were bookshelves lined full with books. Just off-center there was a single table, and sitting at it was an extremely skinny little boy with blond hair. He had a plate with toast and jam on it, one or maybe two bites gone, and a mug of something steaming, hot chocolate I would guess. There was a stack of books on the table. He was reading something bound in blue cloth, I couldn't see what. He was ten or eleven.

I lifted my hand to waist height and said, "Sorry!" and simultaneously he said, "Oh, sorry!" We laughed. I wondered if he was the son of the owner. He looked a bit like me. I glanced around the room at the bookshelves for another beat while he stared up at me expectantly. After a moment I looked back at him and smiled and said, "Sorry again," and then waved good-bye.

EPILOGUE

I know that as an American September 11th was supposed to have a deep effect on me, and it did, but for whatever reason the images that haunt me from the decade of the 2000s are not of that event but of what happened in New Orleans that August, during Hurricane Katrina. Maybe because the World Trade Center going down was so outlandish, whereas Katrina was all grit and reality and terrible decisions. Still in Oxford as it happened, I searched online for snippets of news, streaming video, op-eds; and I had dreams at night about the flooded streets, the ruined houses, the floating cars, and the stranded people. I felt lacerating anger at the officials on the scene. When President Bush stood in the yard of a senator's fallen country house and vowed to rebuild it, as if that were a priority, I wanted to explode out of my skin. Anyway, it was Katrina—that was why, after returning to New York in the middle of October, I went back into politics.

The job I found was good; being in Congress itself, rather than on the trail, cleansed me of the leftover bitterness from 2004. There was still work to be done. I was staffed in a senator's office, as a deputy in the communications department, writing the less important speeches, updating the blog, occasionally talking strategy.

Living in Washington I missed the week when Anil visited New York with his family, and nobody else came stateside. Tom, Ella, James, Peter, Anneliese, Anil, Timmo, and I kept up a ragged e-mail chain, no e-mails for a few days and then forty in an hour. So did a few people in my class, led by Sullivan, and I discovered that I missed the arcane metalanguage of academic study, looked forward to reading some old classmate's Marxist interrogation of Eliot, offered in a rush when they needed last-minute advice for a tutorial.

Even technology has not removed attrition from life—there were faces I had seen every day at Fleet that I understood, with moving new clarity as time passed, I would likely never see again in this mortal life, because they were in Adelaide or Istanbul, because we had never been that close to start with, humans like me, out there on the great earth, people who had briefly been my friends.

Still, on Facebook I could track people's lives. Lula had joined up again and according to her profile was doing charity work in London. Jem's trio—they had added a bassist—played London four nights a week, and I received invitations to all their shows in my messages folder. I looked for Anneliese's photos on *Die Zeit*'s Web site first thing every morning when I sat down at my computer, and she had invited me to come back to Germany with her in the spring. Fleet's master, old Ballantine, died of liver failure. They brought in a woman, Dame Jessica Mote, to take his place.

In spite of these lingering connections it fell away, as I had known it would.

I had friends in D.C. and became absorbed in my work; I took weekend trips up to New York to see people there; I met a cute girl I didn't like very much, and we started to date. She worked two doors down from me for her mother, who was a congresswoman, and for that reason my choice of her unsettled me, so that I didn't want to look at it too closely. Still, in Washington there were bills to pass, campaigns I had my eye on, opponents who absorbed me. There were big buildings, but people weren't just fucking around in them—and I mean that in the nicest way possible—as they did in Oxford.

It certainly seemed different. If you look for endings you can always find one, but truly I felt as if I had used up the last of my youth, if youth is that finite stage of life when it all feels expeditionary, inexact.

Except: One day in April Tom e-mailed the group from his office (he was getting along well at the firm, while Jess, in London now with him, was working at Harrod's) and suggested a minireunion, and almost everyone said they could make it. I booked my ticket and took my vacation days, and in June, nine months after leaving Oxford, I landed again at Heathrow, again met a surly customs agent, again walked under the weight of my bags to Fleet, looking up at its shining high tower before I went in. The porters remembered me, and in fact when I went to see them Jerry, the porter who had given me and Tom our tour, was leading three girls through the front gate. "The oldest gargoyles and grotesques in Oxford," I heard him say, which made me grin.

We were spread out among two rooms, Liese in with Ella and Peter while Tom and I slept on borrowed mattresses in an empty room in Anil's new cottage. The core of our group was together again except Sophie, who was in London.

I don't need to describe what we did, really. We went and danced at the Turtle; we had drinks at the King's Arms, the Bear, and the Turf; we went to Hall and to the Fleet bar; we walked across Christ Church Meadow; we punted up to the Victoria; we played table football. It was like being back again and not like that at all, because so much of being at Oxford is the stretch of days behind and before you, the feeling of shelter inside that great mammoth body, the security of it. I was very happy. I loved these friends dearly, I'd half-forgotten. It was so easy for all of us to fall back into that blur of verging, canceling pink light each evening, with white wine and cigarettes out on the grass, beneath the high sway of the trees, the quiet river nearby, laughter ringing from all the small congregations out on the brilliant green lawns, and surrounding us the high sun-struck golden-stone walls of Fleet and Oxford: the beauty and camaraderie of it lifting us into a different consciousness of ourselves, a new kind of love, and seeming to speak to other verities than the ones I'd always known. Home again, so far from home.

I was leaving on a Tuesday, and on Sunday night Anneliese, Timmo, and Tom had to return to London, because all three were working in the morning. The Oxford contingent of Ella and Peter (and indeed Pippa) had to work again, too, though they agreed to meet up the next evening, and so I was left with Anil. I felt a mixture of melancholy and merriment in his company. I thought about calling Sophie, just for the hell of it, but I didn't. He and I wandered around the Ashmolean and took pictures of Balliol and Merton.

Then Soph texted me. *Are you still in the country, I hope?* she said. *I'm actually going to be back in Oxford in an hour or two.*

Yep, till tomorrow. At Pitt Rivers with Anil.

Lunch?

Sure.

I have my car, pick you up at like two?

Okay.

So the last time I saw Sophie it was the two of us—and Anil. We drove to a village outside of town called Woodstock and walked around, looking for a pub.

After some initial awkwardness it was perfect again, just as it had been in the fall when she and I were best friends. Everything either of us said we laughed at, and we talked about things that had happened when we were both in Oxford without self-consciousness. It was perfect to have Anil there, in fact, now that I think of it. The whole thing took about two hours. I realized that I still wasn't past her, and in realizing it much of the pain ended. In Washington there had been so many desolate-hearted Saturday nights when I couldn't face the bars, or times when I stopped in my tracks and thought of her. It didn't matter anymore.

She drove us back to Oxford, but just before we left the restaurant Anil went to the bathroom.

"You look good," she said when we were alone.

"You look great."

"Do you like Washington?"

"I miss Oxford sometimes, but yeah."

"I miss Oxford, too, and I live here." She smiled. There was a pause. "I wish it hadn't ended the way it did."

"It's okay," I said.

She took my hand under the table. "You mean the world to me, you know. All those times mean the world to me. I think about them all the time."

"Me, too."

"Someday we'll all get back together and hang out again, anyway."

I shook my head. "For a day or two, maybe."

"We'll have a reunion. When we're all forty and you're gray-haired and I have wrinkles." She laughed.

I thought of the line in *Cyrano de Bergerac* when Cyrano asks Roxanne to spare just a few of the tears she's shedding for her lover for him, Cyrano, and I felt that wish; to be in just a corner of her heart, wherever life took her, whether I saw her again or not.

She didn't let go of my hand again until we left the restaurant, and when she dropped us off in Oxford and Anil was stepping out of the car, she surprised me: She gave me a quick kiss on the lips, a quick run of her tongue along mine. Then she looked me in the eyes.

"Good-bye."

"Bye," I said.

That afternoon was gray, the sky shifting among the clouds. Anil put me on the bus to Heathrow, waving cheerfully and promising to visit Washington, and as we pulled out past Christ Church, and went on past Magdalen and out of the center of Oxford, a soft rain started to tap on the windows. I looked out at those beautiful fields along the side of the road England has, at the baffled yellow-gray light, and thought, *I miss it.* I thought, too, about time. How fleet it is, and how certain, and like death how indifferent to our commentary upon it. Once not long before we had been boys and girls, and soon we would be middle-aged, thickening with rueful pleasure toward the thinness of old age. Would we all see each other, as she said?

I wished suddenly that I could have it all back for good, with Tom shouting at me from his room, or Sophie and Anneliese coming up the stairs to talk about the bop that night, or Anil listening to bad music. I thought that no matter how it had ended, still I wouldn't change any of it.

Honestly, this world. It's the strangest thing.

Timothy Greenfield-Sanders

Charles Finch is a graduate of Yale and Oxford. He has written extensively about books for *Slate*, *The New York Times*, and the *Chicago Tribune*. His most recent novel is *The Laws of Murder*.

Don't miss any books from the
CHARLES LENOX MYSTERIES series

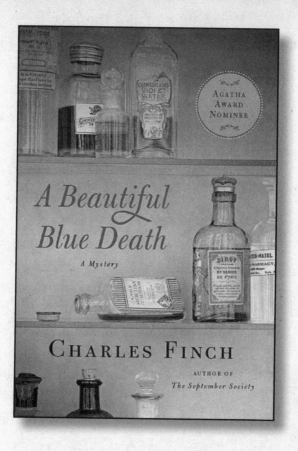

MINOTAUR
BOOKS

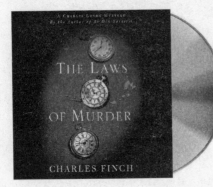